Joss Wood loves books and traveling—especially to the wild places of southern Africa. She has the domestic skills of a potted plant and drinks far too much coffee.

Joss has written for Harlequin KISS, Harlequin Presents and, most recently, the Mills & Boon Desire line. After a career in business, she now writes full-time. Joss is a member of the Romance Writers of America and Romance Writers of South Africa.

USA TODAY bestselling author **Catherine Mann** has won numerous awards for her novels, including both a prestigious RITA® Award and an *RT Book Reviews* Reviewers' Choice Award. After years of moving around the country bringing up four children, Catherine has settled in her home state of South Carolina, where she's active in animal rescue. For more information, visit her website, www.catherinemann.com.

Also by Joss Wood

Also by Catherine Mann

Discover more at millsandboon.co.uk

ONE NIGHT TO FOREVER

JOSS WOOD

THE TWIN BIRTHRIGHT

CATHERINE MANN

MILLS & BOON

First Published in Great Britain 2018
by Mills & Boon, an imprint of HarperCollinsPublishers,
1 London Bridge Street, London, SE1 9GF

One Night to Forever © 2018 Joss Wood
The Twin Birthright © 2018 Catherine Mann

ISBN: 978-0-263-93603-2

51-0518

MIX
Paper from
responsible sources
FSC™ C007454

Printed and bound in Spain
by CPI, Barcelona

ONE NIGHT
TO FOREVER

JOSS WOOD

To Rebecca Crowley: book sister,
fellow writer and sounding board.
I'm going to miss you and your wicked SOH!
Remember: when in doubt, drink wine.

One

Lachlyn Latimore walked into the hallway of what was perhaps the most famous brownstone in Manhattan, possibly the world. Known to New Yorkers as The Den, it was five stories of weathered brick, owned and lived in by multiple generations of the Ballantyne family.

The family she was apparently linked to by DNA.

Lachlyn politely thanked Linc Ballantyne when he took her vintage coat and draped it over the back of a chaise longue chair to the right of the wood and stained glass front door. Lachlyn hoped that he didn't notice the coat's frayed pocket or missing button.

Lachlyn folded her arms across her plain white long-sleeved top and resisted the urge to wipe her damp hands on her black skinny jeans. As the newly discovered, illegitimate daughter of Connor Ballantyne, who'd been jeweler to the world's richest and most powerful people and a Manhattan legend, she had a right to feel intimidated. Connor might have passed years ago but his children were as influential and celebrated as their late father.

Lachlyn darted a glance at the portrait of Connor situated on the wall directly opposite the grand staircase. She'd inherited Connor's blue eyes, bright blond hair, that straight, fine nose. She had her mom's tiny build and wide, full mouth but the rest of her was, dammit, pure Ballantyne.

"Thanks for coming over, Lachlyn. Let's go down to the family room," Linc suggested and gestured her to follow him, but before they could move, the doorbell rang.

Linc sent her an apologetic look. "Sorry, that's my son's babysitter." Retracing his steps, he placed his hand on the carved newel post and called up the stairs. "Shaw? Reame is here."

Linc flipped open the lock to the front door and Lachlyn watched a very tall man step into the hallway to immediately dominate the space. Now, that was a hell of a babysitter, Lachlyn thought. While Linc and the sexy stranger did that half handshake, half hug men did, Lachlyn made a bullet list of the sexy stranger's attributes: caramel-colored hair, tanned olive skin, golden scruff on his jaw. Wide shoulders, narrow hips and a fairly spectacular ass...

She wasn't one to normally notice men's butts, so this was new. His eyes—a clear, light green—touched her face and she felt like she was all woman, utterly desirable. Lachlyn searched for air, found none and decided breathing didn't matter if she had him to look at. She felt alive, sexy, in tune and in touch with every spark of femininity she possessed. He oozed confidence and capability and God, he made her feel alive.

So this was that thing they called sexual attraction. Hot, pulsing, making her ache with a need to touch and be touched. He looked like a modern-day Sir Galahad, the original white knight: strong, capable, decisive and sexy enough to turn medieval and modern-day female heads.

He wasn't her type, though. In order to have a type, you had to be interested in dating, men and relationships.

Hearing a yell from above their heads, Lachlyn dragged her eyes from his muscled thighs—what were her eyes doing down there?—and looked up to watch a young boy dash down the stairs. From five steps up, the child threw himself into the air and Lachlyn released a terrified gasp, convinced that his small body would make contact with the floor. She stumbled forward but before she could make any progress, the tall man caught the child and tucked him under his arm like a football.

Lachlyn placed her hand on her heart and closed her eyes. Holy crap, she'd thought the kid was going to end up splattered all over the wooden floor.

"You've got to stop doing that, Shaw," Linc stated, not looking or sounding worried. In fact, of the three of them, she seemed to be the only one who was remotely concerned about blood, broken bones or stitches.

Linc gestured to Lachlyn. "Reame, meet Lachlyn Latimore. Lachlyn, Reame Jepsen is my oldest friend. And he's holding my son, Shaw."

The man dropped Shaw to his feet and their eyes collided. Whoosh—there went the air in the room. Again.

"Ms. Latimore."

His voice was deep and held just a hint of gravel, a touch of rasp. Lachlyn wanted to know what his words felt like as they hit her bare skin… He held out a hand and she could easily imagine it gliding over her hip, cupping her breast. Lachlyn felt lava flow into her cheeks and ignored his broad, masculine hand. She didn't trust herself to touch him. She wasn't going to risk spontaneously combusting and setting Linc's hallway alight.

"Hi," she muttered, looking down at her shoes.

"Hi back." Yeah, she heard the amusement in his words. Lachlyn forced her eyes up and…yep, she caught his quick smirk. Reame Jepsen liked the effect he had on women and wasn't even a tiny bit surprised by her ridiculous reaction. Usually that smirk would be a total turn-off but instead of being repulsed, she found his self-confidence attractive. Even alluring.

Oh, man. Not good. In fact, very, very bad.

"Unca Reame!"

Reame's eyes left her face—thank God, she felt pinned to the floor—to look down at Shaw, who was hanging on to his bulging-with-muscles arm. *Oh, stop it, Lachlyn!* Shaw monkey-climbed up the side of Reame's body, eventually settling on Reame's hip. Lachlyn watched as Shaw lifted his top lip to show Reame a bloody gap in his mouth.

"I losth my tooth," Shaw lisped.

"I see that," Reame replied. "You look gross."

Shaw grinned before scowling. "The tooth fairy forgot to come."

Standing behind Shaw, Linc grimaced and rolled his eyes. Lachlyn might not know a lot about kids but it was obvious that someone forgot to leave cash under Shaw's pillow. "Bummer. The tooth fairy who services this area must be a bit of a slacker," Reame said, managing to keep his face straight.

"Mom said it's because I didn't pick up my toys and that the tooth fairy is probably a girl and girl fairies don't like messy rooms," Shaw said, looking disgusted.

"Maybe that's it."

There was nothing sexier than watching a handsome

man interacting with a cute kid, Lachlyn decided. They could easily be part of a TV commercial and would sell the advertised product by the caseload.

"Try again tonight, bud," Reame suggested and Lachlyn's lips quirked at the *don't you dare forget* look he sent Linc.

"Can we go already?" Shaw whined, tugging on Reame's arm.

Reame nodded and Lachlyn saw the smile he directed at the young boy. It was open and affectionate and ten times more powerful than his earlier smirk. It was obvious that he enjoyed Linc's son and Linc seemed fully comfortable in handing Shaw into his care. Since everyone in the city knew that Linc was a devoted and protective father, he had to have complete faith that Reame would keep Shaw safe. That was, Lachlyn realized, a hell of an endorsement. Jepsen might look like a sports model but Linc trusted him with his son so that meant he had to have some skills.

Lachlyn listened as Linc and his friend confirmed arrangements for dropping Shaw off and within thirty seconds, the gorgeous man and the gregarious boy were gone and she was alone with Linc.

She wanted to know who Reame was and how he fit into Linc's life. So, strangely for her, she asked.

"I've known him all my life. We lived in the same neighborhood as young kids," Linc replied. "My mom got the job as Connor's housekeeper and we moved into this house but, despite living totally different lives on opposite sides of the city, Reame and I remained friends."

She shouldn't ask anything more, but no man had ever affected her the way Reame had and, well, she was curious. "Does he work for you, at Ballantyne International?"

"God, no, we'd kill each other." Linc shook his head,

seemingly at ease with her questions. "Reame owns a security consulting company. He was in the military, in one of those hush-hush units that did hush-hush things. He has a hell of a military record, including some hefty commendations for bravery. For a couple of years, I didn't see or hear from him for months at a time. That's the life these Special Forces guys lived. Then…" Linc hesitated and Lachlyn gave him a sharp look. He wasn't going to stop talking now, was he?

"Then?" Lachlyn prompted, accompanying the question with a mental slap.

"He had a crisis in his family and he needed to come home. His mom and sisters needed him. He left the military and started work as Connor's bodyguard. He's a natural entrepreneur, so after picking up more clients, he started employing his military friends as bodyguards and his security business was born. Add in cheating spouse investigations and cyber security for corporations, and Jepsen & Associates is one of the biggest security companies in the city," Linc said, sounding proud.

Beauty, brawn and brains. It was a good thing that she'd never see him again; the man was trouble.

Big, beautiful trouble.

Walking away from The Den, Reame slowed his steps so that Shaw didn't have to jog to keep up with him. "So, want to tell me why you sent me an SOS message? I thought we agreed that you can only use that message for emergencies."

Reame hadn't been worried when he received the "help me" picture-message sent from Tate's phone two hours earlier since he'd been on a call with Linc at the time and knew that everything was fine at The Den.

"It was an emergency. Spike wanted you to take me to the batting cages."

Yeah, right. "An emergency is when someone is hurt, or there's a fire or there's blood. Not a message about baseball from a bearded dragon, Shaw," Reame told his godson. "Does Tate know that you used her phone?"

Tate was Linc's fiancée and the reason his best mate now walked around with a dopey, having-great-sex look on his face. Actually, all the Ballantyne men had lucked out with their women. It was strange to see his childhood friends settled down. It wasn't that long ago that they were all running around Manhattan, enjoying their status as the island's most eligible bachelors. But recently, each of them had fallen and fallen hard. Reame, a die-hard bachelor and commitment-phobe, had laughed his ass off.

He liked Piper, Cady and Tate and respected his friends' choices. But settling down wasn't something he was interested in. The thought of placing himself in that situation caused his throat to close and his stomach to cramp.

Marriage, the emotional equivalent of antifreeze...

Pulling his attention back to Shaw, Reame realized that he had yet to answer his question. "Well?"

"Kind of."

That meant no. Before Reame could chastise him, Shaw turned those big blue eyes on him. "It was a 'mergency, Uncle Ree. I would've had to go to Auntie Piper's house 'cause dad wanted to talk to that lady. And I'd have to play with the babies," Shaw complained. "Since you were only working, I thought we could hang out."

Only working... If that's what he could call running a multimillion-dollar international security business. "I needed you to save me from playing with the babies," Shaw stated dramatically.

Master manipulator, Reame thought, but, damn, he was cute. Reame sighed and shook his head. He'd survived brutal training, fought in intense battles both in war and in the boardroom, but he was putty in Shaw's hands. The reality was that if Shaw—or any of the Ballantynes—called he'd drop everything. They were family. It was what they did.

"That lady was pretty," Shaw said, cleverly changing the subject.

Pretty? No. She was heart-stoppingly, spine-tinglingly beautiful and he hadn't had such a primitive reaction to a woman in, well, years. Possibly not ever.

Reame looked down into the mischievous face of his godson and lifted his eyebrows. "Aren't you a little young to be noticing pretty girls?" he asked.

Shaw wrinkled his nose, bunching his freckles together. God, he loved this kid. "She's my Grandpa Connor's real daughter. But she wasn't 'dopted by him, like Dad was."

"So I heard, bud."

When the Ballantynes first heard of Lachlyn's possible connection to their family—thanks to her brother, Tyce Latimore—Reame had immediately ordered his best investigator to dig into her life. On paper, she seemed like nothing special. She lived alone, worked at the New York Public Library, seemed to keep to herself. Nothing about her raised any flags but looking at the photo in the file, his stomach had flipped. Back then, for some reason, and although he'd yet to meet her, she'd bothered him. Despite not knowing anything about her except that she was Connor's daughter, she'd made him feel queasy, unsettled.

The same instinct that had saved his ass on many hot situations as a Special Forces operative had screamed that Lachlyn Latimore would have some impact on his life.

Meeting her hadn't done anything to quiet the raging bats-on-speed in his stomach, Reame thought, keeping a light hand on Shaw's shoulder as they walked to a baseball center a few blocks away from The Den. The photos in Lachlyn's file hadn't done her justice. Her eyes and face were Connor's but her eyes were a deeper blue, almost violet, her face finer, her cheekbones more pronounced, and her mouth looked like it was made to be kissed. She was tiny, she barely reached his shoulder, but curvy and strung tighter than a steel guitar.

It had taken every ounce of his willpower to wrench his eyes off her exquisite face in order to catch Shaw's midair flight. Reame shuddered, thinking that if he'd taken a second longer to react, Shaw would have hit the deck at lightning speed. The kid really had to stop thinking he was a superhero. Or Reame had to keep his concentration around pretty women.

Not something he generally had a problem with.

Women liked him and he liked women, when he had time for them. He usually didn't; running and growing a business took all his energy and what little free time he did have that wasn't spent at work or with his friends—particularly the Ballantynes—was taken up by his demanding sisters and slightly neurotic mother.

But his *me-time* was finally here. His business was established enough and his staff competent enough for him to step back a fraction, freeing up some precious spare time. His family was also, for all intents and purposes, off his hands. For ten years, since his father had decided to go AWOL after twenty-five years of marriage, he wasn't his mother's and sisters' sounding board, their bank manager, the payer of bills. His youngest sister was starting a new job next week and that meant, thank God, he was free of being responsible for her.

In two weeks his mom would take a three-month cruise with his aunt and he would be free of what his mom called her "little problems." Since Reame was the only one of her children close by, she tended to call him. A lot. She also wasn't averse to guilting him into visiting, and when that didn't work, she made up little stories about her health or problems with her house to bring him running.

Those two weeks and freedom couldn't come soon enough. He was going to party hard and date wild women, women who knew the score, who wanted nothing more than a good time. He was going to sow all the wild oats he'd been storing up over the past ten years and he was going to sow them hard and sow them well.

The thought that he might be wanting wild because he was avoiding love and commitment jumped into his head. He was self-aware enough to realize that his quest for me-time went deeper than a simple desire to walk on the wild side. He prided himself on being responsible and part of that responsibility was not subjecting any woman to the chance that he might, like his dad, fail at a relationship, at being what a woman wanted, or needed. He'd never failed in his life and he didn't intend to start now.

Deeper reasons or not, he damn well deserved to live life hard and fast, responsible only for himself. His motivations could wait until he worked this restlessness out of his system.

Approaching the baseball center, Reame decided that he could start tonight, if he was so inclined. After he dropped Shaw off with Tate, he could go out, do something. Reame shook his head, thinking that he didn't feel like hitting a bar and spinning a line. He'd joined a dating app a few months back and maybe it was time he actually put it to its full use. New York was a big city and, in the little free time he had, he trawled through the photos, swiping right when he found someone he found attractive. He'd had a couple of quick conversations with a few women but hadn't made any firm plans with anyone to meet in real life.

That brown-eyed blonde was hot and there was that psychologist who intrigued him more than most. He tried to remember what she looked like but Lachlyn Latimore's face jumped onto the big screen of his mind.

Dating Linc's new sister wasn't an option for a hundred and ten reasons. *Not constructive thinking, dude, not constructive at all.* Frustrated with himself, Reame decided to work and, as per usual, he promised himself that in the morning he'd make it a priority to find himself a date.

Reame pulled open the door to the baseball center and looked down when Shaw tugged his coat. "You really aren't listening to me, Unca Reame."

Reame winced. He hadn't heard a word Shaw had said. "Sorry, bud, what's up?"

Shaw reached inside his jacket and Reame saw a scaly tail, tiny feet and the pissed-off face of Spike, Shaw's bearded dragon. "Spike's going to want pizza when we're done. Batting makes him hungry."

Yeah, food wasn't what he was hungry for. But if Lachlyn Ballantyne offered to eat pizza with him, preferably naked, he was sure he could force down a slice or two.

Two

Back at The Den, which was situated a block or so from Central Park, Lachlyn was being guided by Linc down the hall to a set of stairs leading to a great room on the ground floor. A small picture on the wall to her left caught her eye and she sucked in a quick gasp. That couldn't possibly be a Picasso, could it? They walked past a nineteenth-century drop-leaf table, every inch of its highly polished surface covered with heavy silver frames containing photos of the current members of the Ballantyne family. Lachlyn hauled in a breath, trying to get some air to her too-tight lungs.

Up until her fifteenth birthday, being a normal girl—being part of a normal American family—had been her deepest desire, the one thing she wished for above all else. Living with an emotionally checked-out mother and an older brother who'd been forced to work to help supplement their mom's meager income, she'd grown up mostly alone. Lachlyn had comforted herself by imagining another life, cutting out pictures of wholesome, happy families from magazines and carefully pasting them into scrapbooks. She'd covered the walls of her shoebox bedroom, naming her pretend brothers and sisters and weaving fantasies about midnight snack parties, days at the beach, family arguments and Sunday lunches.

She'd made scrapbooks filled with smart and witty friends, fantasy boyfriends and carefully cut out pictures of men who looked like they'd gallop into her life and rescue her.

Then, one summer's night, her illusions about family, about the bonds that tied people together, had been shattered. Lachlyn's crash with reality had been brutal—she'd ripped the pictures from her wall, shredded her scrapbooks. What was the point, she'd decided, of living in a dream world? Lachlyn had finally accepted that she was alone, that she couldn't, and wouldn't, expect anyone—not family, not a friend, not a lover—to run to her rescue, to be there to support her when her world fell apart. She was the only person she could rely on, *would* rely on. She'd decided, then and there, not to ask, or expect, anything from anyone ever again.

She'd been young but she'd made the right choice and she still lived her life around that decision. Few friends, no boyfriends, some contact with her brother. But damn, those photos made her feel just the teeniest bit envious.

"Are you okay, Lachlyn?" Linc asked. "You look a little pale."

She wasn't used to fancy houses containing amazing artwork, she'd just met the first man who'd ever managed to set her skin on fire and she had no idea of the agenda of this upcoming meeting with the Ballantynes. Was it any surprise that she felt a little, well, stressed?

Lachlyn stopped and half turned to look at him. She wanted to say something smart or charming but she saw sympathy in his eyes. She wanted to tell him that she was feeling overwhelmed, by who the Ballantynes were and the fact that there were so many of them. But it had been a long time since Lachlyn had confided in anyone about how she was feeling. "I'm fine."

Linc's gentle smile suggested that he didn't believe her and Lachlyn realized how very good-looking he was. Actually, all the siblings looked like they could grace magazine covers and, if she wasn't mistaken, they all had at one time or the other. Sexy, educated, talented and successful, the Ballantynes were the American dream personified. Yet Lachlyn, the only person who carried Connor Ballantyne's direct DNA, was anything but.

"I understand that this is a lot to deal with, Lachlyn," Linc said, his deep voice reassuring. "For that reason, it's just us tonight, the siblings. You, me, Jaeger, Beck and Sage."

Four against one…

One meeting, a discussion, and she would be done with them, Lachlyn thought, walking into a great room that rolled from a gourmet kitchen into a dining area and then a messy, lived-in space filled with comfortable furniture, books and toys.

Jaeger and Beck stood up and both shook her hand. Sage sent her a hesitant smile from the corner of the huge couch, her feet tucked under her bottom. Her face looked drawn and she had purple stripes under her eyes. Man trouble, Lachlyn decided. And the man causing the trouble was her brother Tyce.

Cue another awkward moment, but she couldn't ignore Sage's pain so she stopped next to Sage, bent down and touched her arm with the very tips of her fingers. "Is everything okay? The baby?"

Sage nodded and Lachlyn noticed that Sage's eyes were red-rimmed and bloodshot. "The baby is fine but your brother is driving me mad," Sage told her, trying to sound jaunty but failing miserably.

Lachlyn wanted to tell Sage that Tyce was a product of their past, of a family that had no idea how to do family. Or relationships.

"I'm sorry, Sage," Lachlyn murmured, feeling obligated to apologize. Latimores sucked at relationships in general; she needed her solitude and Tyce had his own hang-ups. She and Tyce were masters of the art of self-protection.

Jaeger waited for her to sit before handing her a glass of red wine and then resumed his seat between Sage and Beck on the big sofa. Linc sat down on the ottoman between her and Sage and took a long pull from the bottle of beer Jaeger had offered him. "So, let's get to the heart of the matter of why you're here," Linc said.

Lachlyn placed her wine on the coffee table and clasped her hands together. Linc was going to offer her a payoff, a lump sum of money to go away, to fade into anonymity. They would buy back the Ballantyne International shares Tyce had bought for her and they would squash the reports surfacing in the press about her parentage and connection to the family.

All would go back to being normal. She couldn't wait. People exhausted her.

"We had a discussion about you, about your arrival in our life and what that meant to us," Linc said, his eyes not leaving her face. "The past year has been one of phenomenal change...six months ago we were all single. Now we have life partners."

Jaeger flashed his pirate's grin. "A hell of a lot of babies on the way. Piper, Cady, Sage…"

"Some by blood, all by love," Beck murmured. He raised an inquiring eyebrow at Linc, who instantly shook his head.

"We have a five-year-old bandit and an eighteen-month-old bandit-in-training," Linc retorted, answering the unspoken question. "We've got all we can handle at the moment."

Lachlyn shook her head, trying to keep up with their banter. She hoped pregnancy wasn't contagious. Oh, wait, you had to have sex to get pregnant. Just then the image of a pair of grape-green eyes in a tanned face appeared in her mind. Yeah, that wasn't going to happen…ever.

"It would be a manageable three but Jaeger had to be his usual obnoxious self and one up the rest of us by impregnating Piper with twin boys," Beck muttered, hooking his thick arm around Jaeger's neck and pulling it tight.

While Lachlyn enjoyed Jaeger and Beck's banter, she just wished Linc would get on with his little speech. There was more to come and Lachlyn preferred quick and nasty to kind and drawn out.

"Let's get back to why we are here," Sage suggested and Lachlyn smiled her appreciation. She'd listen, finish her wine, refuse their payoff and leave…

Linc pushed his hand through his hair. "When Tyce told us that you were Connor's daughter we were shocked, Lachlyn. Connor, as you know, died a few years ago but he suffered from Alzheimer's so even if he was alive, we couldn't ask him. But DNA doesn't lie and you *are* part of this family."

Wait, that didn't sound like a brush-off…

Linc continued. "If Connor knew about you, you would've been raised by him, of that we have no doubt.

Connor was anti-marriage and commitment but he was not anti-responsibility and he adored us, kids who weren't his kids. He would've loved you."

Lachlyn wanted to ask Linc to back up, to repeat what she thought she'd heard. They considered her to be a part of this family, a Ballantyne? They wanted her to stay in the fold? *What?* She wasn't part of this family, she didn't want to be!

"And, as Connor's child, we believe it's only fair that you receive a portion of his estate."

They weren't offering to pay her off but were offering her more. Lachlyn pushed the words up her tight throat and through her bloodless lips. "A portion?"

Linc leaned forward, his forearms on his thighs and his beer bottle dangling from his fingers. "As siblings, we own many joint assets and we want to share ownership of those assets with you."

"Assets?"

Linc nodded to a file on the coffee table. "Shares, art, property, gemstones. They are all listed in there. We've also agreed to each pay you a fixed amount from our personal bank accounts to reduce the cash disparity between us."

"Uh…how much?" Lachlyn asked, her thoughts reeling.

Linc's eyes cooled and Lachlyn knew that he was disappointed by her response. It did sound grasping and gold-digger-ish but she needed to know the amount of money they were talking about, how serious they were. Ten, twenty thousand?

"We thought we'd start with ten million each but that could be negotiated."

Ten? Million? Forty million in total? Whoa…!

Lachlyn placed her head between her knees as the air

in the room disappeared. She'd been expecting a brush-off, a couple of thousand to go away, and they were offering her tens of millions. Most frightening of all, they were asking her to stay. They wanted her to be a Ballantyne…

No, that wasn't possible. She didn't do people, relationships, family…

Lachlyn felt Sage perch on the arm of her chair, a small hand landing on her curved back. "Honey, are you okay?"

Lachlyn shook her head. "No," she muttered.

"You'll get used to the idea," Sage said, her hand rubbing the length of her spine. "After a while you realize that it's just money, just another tool."

Lachlyn's eyes widened and she held herself still. Oh, God, they thought that she was freaking about the money? Yeah, it was king's ransom but…so what? No, they had it all wrong. It wasn't the financial side that scared her, it was their offer to include her as a part of a family, their family. She was a loner, someone who was comfortable on her own, who liked living her life solo. She didn't do family…hell, she barely did friends!

But God, forty million dollars. How did one just dismiss that much money? Lachlyn looked inside herself and realized that she could, easily. She didn't need wealth, she needed emotional security, and keeping her distance from people, family and men, gave her what she needed.

It was a hell of a generous offer and she couldn't just toss it back in their faces. Lachlyn started to speak but Beck held up his hand.

"As you might be aware, the press has cottoned on to your connection to us and we're predicting a lot of media attention," Beck said, looking grave. "And when I say a lot, I mean a firestorm."

Damn, just what she needed. Four sets of eyes rested on her face and Lachlyn knew that they were waiting for a reply to their offer, some sort of indication of what she was thinking. All she knew for sure was that it was all a little too much and far too soon. She didn't know them and they sure as hell didn't know her. They all needed time before some massive decisions were made that could, and would, have huge ramifications.

Lachlyn lifted her head and sat up straight. She looked each of the Ballantyne men in the eye before sending Sage the same determined look. She took a sip of her wine and stood up, begging her knees to lock. "I very much appreciate the offer but I'd like to suggest that we not make any major decisions, especially financial ones, yet."

Linc exchanged a long look with his siblings and Lachlyn sensed that she'd somehow passed a test, that their approval of her was climbing.

"I came here," Lachlyn said, sounding hesitant, "thinking that I would have a drink and then go back to my life, my very normal, solitary life. However, hearing about the impending press attention changes that. I can't ignore the impact this will have and I can't just walk away. Nor can I accept your very generous offer."

"Do you think that there's a chance that you might be able to one day?" Sage asked.

"I don't know," Lachlyn said, standing up. "I need to think. And I need to go."

Too much information, too many people. She had to leave, get out, find a quiet spot where she could make sense of this crazy turn her life had taken. Lachlyn, needing air and needing to get away, snatched up her bag and ran.

The news that Lachlyn Latimore was Connor Ballantyne's daughter had not generated the firestorm of attention Beck had predicted. It was far worse than that, Lachlyn decided. She could only describe the constant media presence as the love child of a swarm of locusts and the apocalypse. Because every word she uttered was dissected and every step she took was monitored, Lachlyn agreed to take a two-week vacation from her job as an archivist at the New York Public Library, hoping that the furor would soon subside. She also, reluctantly, agreed to move into The Den because journalists and photographers blocked both entrances to her apartment in Woodside.

To a woman who craved solitude and privacy, Lachlyn felt like she was under siege and that there was no end in sight. She was, mentally and physically, about to jump out of her skin.

It was Cady, Beck's wife and Ballantyne's PR guru who finally persuaded her that it wasn't in her interest to hide from the press—the sooner she gave them the access they wanted, the quicker the attention would die down and life would return to normal. Well, a new type of normal. Cady suggested a photo shoot, interviews with Ballantyne-friendly journalists, and a live spot on morning TV watched by—eeek!—millions, along with other magazine and print interviews.

Lachlyn said no to everything and prayed that some celebrity would do something truly shocking to draw attention away from her. Sage provided some distraction by accepting Tyce's proposal and their engagement was an excellent excuse for a ball. It was also the perfect vehicle, Cady decided, for the Ballantynes to introduce Lachlyn to their friends and business associates. And that was the only reason Lachlyn was standing in the fantastic ballroom of the iconic Forrester Hotel, dressed in an on-loan-from-Sage designer cocktail dress that cost more than she earned a year, making small talk with people who were sometimes sweet, sometimes rude, and always curious.

It was a shark tank, Lachlyn thought, taking a tiny sip of her now flat champagne. And she was the minnow trying not to be a snack.

"Are you okay?"

Lachlyn felt fingers on her elbow and turned around to see Sage. Sage glowed from the inside out, her blue eyes luminous with happiness. Her brother's declaration of love had done that, Lachlyn thought, proud of her sibling. Tyce had taken a chance on love and looked as happy as Sage did.

Brave Tyce.

Sage's inquiring eyebrow reminded her that she'd been asked a question. "I'm fine, thanks."

"Are you thoroughly sick of everyone asking the same questions?" Sage tilted her head to the side, her bright blue eyes frank.

Lachlyn pulled a face and nodded her agreement. Sage took her half-empty glass from her hand, half turned and nodded to a large ornamental lemon tree in the corner. "You look like you need a break."

"I really do," Lachlyn agreed. She was thoroughly peopled out.

"Behind that lemon tree is a small spiral staircase. It leads up to a small, secluded balcony with a great view of the ballroom. It's not big enough for any illicit shenanigans so nobody goes up there, but it's a great place to hang out for a little while and get your breath back."

Lachlyn looked up and she could see a tiny Juliet balcony, partially obscured by a wrought-iron trellis. Yes, that was exactly where she needed to be, for an hour or three. For the rest of the night if she got really, really lucky. Then Lachlyn remembered that she was one of the reasons for the ball and frowned. "Are you sure it will be okay?"

"Just go, Lachlyn, because Old Mrs. Preston is heading in your direction and she's wearing her 'I'll harangue the truth out of her' expression. I'll head her off while you make your escape."

Lachlyn flashed her a quick smile. "Thanks, Sage."

"Sure." Sage returned the smile and moved to intercept the super-thin, super-Botoxed specimen heading in her direction. Lachlyn skirted two men in tuxedos who looked like they wanted to talk to her, ignored the call for her attention and headed for the waiter standing near the hidden staircase. She picked up a fresh glass of champagne and ducked up the spiral staircase, holding her floor-length chiffon dress off the stairs. She stepped onto the small balcony and rested her back against the wall. A little peace, finally.

Needing to mentally escape, her thoughts drifted to the collection she was in the process of archiving for the New York Public Library. The grandson of a noted French art collector and critic had recently bequeathed his grandfather's entire collection of diaries, letters, art and mementoes detailing the Parisian art world of the 1920s. It was a fascinating look back into the glamorous era between the two World Wars and the project of a lifetime.

She couldn't wait for her two weeks' vacation to be over so that she could get back to work, to her quiet, empty-of-people apartment. Hearing shouts of laughter, Lachlyn looked through the trellis onto the ballroom below. She took in the exquisite gowns and breathtaking jewelry, carefully made-up faces and sophisticated conversation. A jazz band played in the corner and a few couples were on the dance floor, swaying to the 1940s ballad.

Lachlyn's eyes drifted over faces, easily finding her

brother Tyce, his arms wrapped around Sage's baby bump. Tyce couldn't understand her need to hold the Ballantynes—and the world—at an arm's length. However, their agreement that she deal with the Ballantynes on her own terms was holding. Just.

Tyce didn't realize that Lachlyn was perfectly fine on her own, that he needed this amazing family, a great love affair, more than she did. She hadn't told him, or anybody, what happened that summer so long ago...

She didn't need to try hard to remember the sour smell of his breath on her face, the taste of his slimy tongue, the feel of his rough hands inside her shirt, between her legs. She'd yelled and screamed but her mom—thanks to depression, sleeping pills or, most likely, disinterest—hadn't lifted her head to help her. Before the assault had turned from horrible to devastating, Lachlyn's elbow had connected with her assailant's nose. She'd followed that up with a knee to his scrotum and he'd scuttled off. She'd sat on the floor of her bedroom, weeping and alone. As a result, asking for any type of support or help, emotional or physical, transported her back to feeling like a helpless little girl, and that was something she never wanted to be seen as. Yeah, it also stopped her from making friends, from having normal relationships with normal men, but that was a small price to pay.

Sometimes, in the early, honest hours of the morning, she suspected that she still might be that girl who didn't want to do it on her own, who might want a man, a family...that she might want to, sometimes, *lean*. What stopped her from exploring that terrifying scenario was remembering the past, the experience of looking for support—asking for help—and finding no one there.

No, she was better off alone.

Lachlyn felt the change in atmosphere and she stepped

up to the trellis, trying to find the source of the disturbance. Yep, and there he was, the *alpha-est* of alphas. Lachlyn took a sip of her cool champagne, enjoying the way it replaced the moisture in her mouth. She'd only met Reame Jepsen twice, the first time at The Den and she'd had another brief encounter with him at the art gallery when Tyce proposed to Sage. But despite not spending more than ten minutes in total with the blasted man, she was irritated that he was the star of some of her very sexy dreams.

Like most alpha males, Reame was big, six foot three, six four? Lachlyn's fingers curled around the trellis as she watched him move across the ballroom. Greeting someone she knew was important, Reame gripped the other man's hand, flashing a practiced smile. Mr. Important dipped his head, a clear indication that he was submitting to the alpha male. Reame stepped into the group Mr. Important was standing with, and all four men, two CEOs of Fortune 500 companies, an investment banker and a world renowned economist, took a tiny step back. Reame Jepsen dominated the space, claiming it as his own. He was the super-alpha in a room of men who were accustomed to calling the shots and taking charge.

Lachlyn released a long sigh. Reame Jepsen bothered her.

No, he bothered the hell out of her.

And here came the moths to the flame, Lachlyn thought, amused. A tall, thin blonde spun around from the next group, squealed and all but threw herself into Reame's arms. Cheeks were kissed before the blonde was elbowed out of the way by a redhead, then a brunette. She supposed it was business as usual for Reame. With his caramel-colored hair, olive skin, masculine face and light eyes, he made female eyes water, ovaries quiver and brains start to churn. Linc's best friend, or so she'd heard, was the most eligible bachelor since Connor Ballantyne, and that list had included, up until very recently, her very hot and rich brothers.

He was a catch, a prize, a goal.

Lachlyn wasn't a game-playing girl.

She was about to turn away, about to pull her eyes off his angles-and-planes face when his head shot up and their eyes clashed and held. He lifted the glass of whiskey to his lips, his light eyes not leaving her face, ignoring the woman hanging off his arm. Lachlyn stared down at him as the air between them fizzled and crackled.

She wanted him.

She was pulsing with lust, attraction, desire, need. Hot, spiky lust. Her womb was as tight as a drum and her lungs had lost their ability to breathe. Lachlyn felt the hair on the back of her neck prickle, goose bumps lifting the skin on her arms. The thought of that sexy mouth on hers, what it would feel like, how he would taste—whiskey, mint, man—drowned out rational thought. The fantasy of her dress up to her waist, his hands on the back of her thighs, her back against the wall as he slid into her was as strong as a memory from yesterday, as powerful as reality.

She understood why. He was the biggest, most powerful, highest-ranking man in the room and millions of years of biology had programmed her, and every other woman there, to want to mate with all that strength and power. Mating with him would ensure her offspring would be given the strongest chance of survival, the best genes. Her attraction to him was pure animal instinct and nothing to cause her any concern.

But Lachlyn didn't date alpha males. Hell, she didn't date at all. It would be easy to chalk it up to what hap-

pened to her so long ago, but Lachlyn refused to give
that rapist-in-training that much control over her sex life.

Sex wasn't the problem, that much she knew. No,
thanks to her mom's disinterest, her lack of response,
her fears had taken on a different form. Lachlyn refused
to ask for anything, to give up even a small measure of
her independence, to make space in her life for a man,
to allow herself to ask for anything, even his company.

Men liked to feel needed and Lachlyn refused to need
anyone ever again. Stalemate.

Lachlyn shook her dark thoughts away, refocusing on
The Alpha Male's face. She could appreciate him for what
he was, a fine specimen, and her response to him was
normal, natural even. Looking at him was like looking
at a Botticelli painting or a Rodin sculpture…she could
admire him, appreciate his masculine beauty, but unlike
art, there was a personality behind it, quite a forceful one
if she read him right. He was tough and strong—someone people relied on. He would expect his woman, his
mate, to allow him to protect her, to shelter her, to slay
her dragons.

Lachlyn had expected the person who should love her
the most to help her slay a dragon once and she'd been left
to do it herself. Luckily, she'd won the battle, but she'd
never put herself in the position of allowing anyone to
disappoint her again.

Three

No.

Hell to the no!

Reame took a hefty sip of his whiskey, disengaged himself from the female octopus hanging off him and wished he could be rid of the panic crawling up his throat as easily. Pushing a hand through his short hair, he looked around and saw Linc across the room. Linc caught his eyes and lifted one sandy eyebrow in a silent but demanding *What the hell is wrong with you?*

Reame was pretty sure that Linc did not want to hear that he had just had the hottest video of the newbie Ballantyne playing in his head, her head tipped back, her tangerine-colored evening dress—sporting a low dipping neckline hinting at great breasts and a thigh split that made for easy access—up around her waist and the soft material flowing over his black suit as he stood between her legs, his mouth on hers, his...

Yeah, don't go there, Jepsen, unless you want to embarrass yourself.

He was damn sure that Linc didn't want to know any of that.

Reame ordered another whiskey from a passing waiter and glanced up to the Juliet balcony, spotting the swish of the orange dress, the flash of a pale neck. He frowned, noticing that the new Ballantyne had cut her hair, that her waist-length, platinum-blond hank of hair was gone. Dammit, he'd had fantasies about winding that hair a couple of times around his fist as he slid into her, those long strands sliding over his stomach, over his…

Reame aimed a mental roundhouse kick at his temple. Lachlyn was not a wild woman and she was not anyone he could tangle with. She was his oldest friend's new sister and you didn't fool around with your best bud's baby sister. Lachlyn was also Connor's daughter and he owed Connor so much— without him he wouldn't have his business. And he definitely didn't mess around with women with eyes that were a curious combination of lapis lazuli, vulnerability and sky-high intelligence.

Lachlyn Latimore was Trouble with a capital *T* and if he was as smart as they said he was, he'd stay far, far away from her. She wasn't what he wanted, wasn't the here now, gone tomorrow woman he was looking for.

"Stop scowling," Linc said. "You're scaring my guests."

"Wasn't."

Reame cursed silently as Linc gestured for Lachlyn to join them. Reame saw her send a quick look toward the exit, as if she were judging how quickly she could escape. Her shoulders slumped as she started to make her way toward them through the crowd, and Reame couldn't decide whether to feel insulted or to sympathize.

Linc picked up Reame's whiskey off a tray and appropriated the drink as his own. Reame tossed him a hot insult and considered wrestling the glass out of his hand. Deciding to be an adult, he jammed his hands into the pockets of his suit pants and ordered another drink. Hopefully, it would arrive soon.

"Why the frown?" Linc asked.

Reame shrugged, deliberately not meeting Linc's gaze. "You know how much I loathe these society events. I'd rather be in a firefight than here."

Linc smiled. "I know and I appreciate your sacrifice."

Reame narrowed his eyes at Linc's gentle sarcasm. Turning his back to his approaching fantasy-come-to-life, he spread his legs wide and folded his arms across his chest. He studied Linc and saw the worry in his eyes, the tense muscle in his jaw. "What do you need, bro?"

Before he could reply, Lachlyn stepped up to Linc's side and sent Reame a cool look. "Hello, Reame."

"Lachlyn," Reame replied with equal ice. Look at them, he thought, pretending that they hadn't just imagined each other naked and writhing five minutes earlier. "You look nice."

If nice meant sensationally and spectacularly sexy.

Those blues darkened to violet as a blush crossed her cheeks. "Thank you."

"Linc was just about to ask me something..." Reame turned back to Linc who tossed back the rest of his whiskey and then rolled the glass between the palms of his hands. Keeping his voice low so that he wasn't overheard, Linc answered his question. "The reaction to the news that Lachlyn is a Ballantyne and that we have accepted her into the fold has been bigger and more intense than any of us, including Cady, expected. Lachlyn has moved into The Den, Reame, and for the last few days the press have camped on the sidewalk. None of us can get in and out of the house without being harassed. Lachlyn tried to go out yesterday and they nearly ripped her apart. She ran into the house looking like the hounds of hell were on her tail."

"I think that's a bit of an exaggeration," Lachlyn interjected.

"Shh." Reame hushed her, wanting Linc to continue. Before he could, Linc was distracted by an old lady with diamonds the size of quail eggs and wrinkles as deep as the Mariana Trench.

Linc turned his attention to the Grand dame and Lachlyn took the opportunity to launch her small elbow into his side. "Don't you shush me!" she hissed.

"I wanted to hear what Linc was saying and you were interrupting him," Reame replied, willing her eyes to flash violet again. "Maybe kissing you to shut you up would've worked better. Far more enjoyable…"

Yep, violet, with sparks of silver. "Are you drunk?"

Drunk on… *Do not even complete that thought, Jepsen.* What the hell is wrong with you? Reame's thumb found the pulse point on her inside wrist and, yep, there it was, her heart beating as fast as a hummingbird's wing. His wasn't far behind. He glanced at Linc, made sure he wasn't listening before speaking. "I know that you were imagining us naked."

Reame just managed to stop himself from lifting her hand to kiss the delicate skin under his fingers.

Lachlyn jerked her hand away. "Your illusions are insulting and annoying. And I need a drink."

He could relate. "Bring me one? A double whiskey on the rocks?" Reame asked, his tone teasing. He wasn't surprised when she rolled her eyes and flounced away from him, her compact and curvy body radiating annoyance.

Reame sighed. Not the way to make friends with the new Ballantyne...

But, dammit, even before he'd met her, she'd *bothered* him. Bother was now too small a word to use to describe how she made him feel...

And why—when there were at least thirty women here whom he could hit on, if he excluded the married ones and he so did—was he wanting to get up close, very close and very naked, with *her*? With his best friend's new sister?

Screwed, he decided. If he didn't get a grip he would be so screwed.

Reame lifted his eyebrows when Linc turned back to him having given the Lady of the Big Diamonds sufficient attention. "You were saying..."

Linc pushed a hand through his blond hair. "Someone dug up Lachlyn's phone number and her phone has been ringing off the hook. She's being harassed on social media and it doesn't look to be dying down anytime soon."

Reame nodded his understanding. "I'll get my cyber guy to bury her social security number, to take her off the Net as much as possible. He'll change her address to your box number and get her a new phone number under one of my companies. We'll put firewalls around her social media accounts. You know the drill."

Linc should. He and his guys had done the same thing for Connor and all the Ballantynes after him. High-profile families attracted criminals and nutcases, and sometimes the nutcases were criminals, too.

Reame waited, knowing that there was more. Linc scratched his chin, his eyes flat with worry. "Tate has to film in the Rockies this coming week and I was planning on joining her there with the kids."

Somehow, Linc and Tate managed to combine his hectic and pressurized job as Ballantyne CEO with Tate's job as a travel presenter without neglecting Shaw or Ellie, their adopted daughter.

"I don't want to leave Lachlyn in The Den by herself but she adamantly refuses to move in with Sage and Tyce or with Jaeger or Beck."

Since she'd be the third wheel wherever she went—all the Ballantynes were still in the cooing and billing stage of their relationship—Reame didn't blame her.

"What's her apartment like?" Reame asked.

"Small, I imagine," Linc said.

"Would it be feasible for one of my female personal protection people to move in with her?" Reame asked.

"I don't think so but what do I know? Lachlyn doesn't talk!"

Reame knew that Lachlyn still hadn't accepted their offer to become a full Ballantyne partner but in the eyes of the world she was assumed to be a very wealthy woman. As such, she was a target. Linc was right, she needed a bodyguard and to live in a place with excellent security.

And security was his business. "How does she feel about having security?"

Linc pulled a face. "She thinks I'm overreacting. She has this idea that she'll be able to go back to work next week, that the furor will have died down by then. She's dreaming if she thinks a haircut will make her look less recognizable." Linc lifted his chin in Lachlyn's direction and Reame finally, finally had an excuse to look at her again.

As he'd noticed earlier, her hair was now short and choppy. Her bangs twisted away from her face, revealing high cheekbones, those incredible sin-with-me-eyes, her made-to-be-kissed (but not by him) lips. Despite her two-inch heels, she still only reached his shoulder, and without her stilts she barely scraped five-two. Her body, despite her being a fairy, was all woman. Full and perky breasts, a waist he could span with his hands, long legs and round hips.

And a truly excellent ass.

"She needs protection, Ree."

Reame groaned, wondering whom he had to kill to get another drink. He ignored the action in his pants and focused on business, on what Linc was asking him to do. He swallowed his sigh. If it was anyone else but Linc making the request, he'd decline the business. He didn't have enough staff to meet the demand for personal protection officers as it was. Liam, his head of operations, was going to kill him. And Liam, being ex-military, as well, actually could follow up on his threat.

But this was Linc asking… "Let me call around tomorrow and have a chat with her, and you. What time are you leaving?"

"Midmorning," Linc replied, briefly grasping Reame's bicep in a show of his appreciation. "Thanks, bud. Will you please charge me or the firm? God knows we can afford it."

Reame shook his head and, as he always did, ignored Linc's request. After he left the military, Connor gave him his first job, had recommended him to his rich friends and clients and he'd lent him the capital to start up his security business. Together with Linc, Connor had been his biggest supporter and his best advertiser, and it was because of their support and loyalty that his company was now regarded to be the best in the city. His business had put his three sisters through college, paid for the fancy apartment he lived in, the repairs on his mom's house. It employed many of his ex-army buddies and sent ridiculous amounts of money into his personal bank account.

For as long as he owned Jepsen & Associates, he would swallow any costs the Ballantynes' personal security needs generated.

He owed Linc, his brothers and Connor a debt he couldn't repay but he'd sure as hell try. Because, unlike his father, he believed in loyalty and responsibility.

He looked at life straight on, readily accepting that it was a series of waves and troughs, shallow waters and depths. All one could do was just keep swimming.

Reame looked across the room at Lachlyn and studied her exquisite profile, the horrible thought occurring to him that she might be the one woman who could make him drown.

The next morning, Lachlyn glanced down at the screen of her phone, thinking it was another call from a super-pushy reporter, but instead she saw the familiar number of her supervisor at the New York Public Library. Annie was not only her direct boss but the closest person she had to an older sister and best friend.

"Hey, hun, how are you holding up?" Annie asked as Lachlyn placed her flat palm against the cool window of the small upstairs living room of The Den.

"Fair to horrible," Lachlyn said, pulling the drape aside to look down at the sidewalk. The crowd standing behind the wrought-iron fence was talking amongst themselves, although many cameras were pointed toward the front door. Somebody caught her movement and, almost immediately, a dozen cameras lifted in her direction. Lachlyn abruptly stepped back and ignored the muted roars for a comment, a photo opportunity, an interview. Rubbing her forehead, she slid down the wall until an expensive Persian carpet was all that separated her denim-covered butt from the rich wooden floors. "I can't wait to come back to work next week."

There was a long pause and Lachlyn's stomach jumped. Annie was usually incredibly voluble and she didn't do silence. "That's not going to happen anytime soon, Lach."

Lachlyn felt her headache intensify. "What do you mean?"

"There's too much attention around you, on you. The phones have been ringing off the hook, people asking anyone and everyone for information on you. It's mayhem, Lach, and you aren't even here."

The monster chomping its way through her stomach took another huge bite. "What exactly are you saying, Annie?"

"My supervisor is suggesting that you take all of your vacation time. It adds up to about two months." Annie said in a tone that suggested she'd been practicing how to break the news.

"I don't have a job anymore?" Lachlyn whispered, terrified that what she was hearing was her new reality.

"You don't have a job for the next few months. After that, we'll see," Annie said, trying to sound jaunty. "Since, according to the press, money is no longer an object, you could tour the great libraries of the world, visit the museums you always talk about going to, see the amazing art you look at in books," Annie said, her voice turning persuasive. "This is an opportunity, Lach, not a punishment."

But Annie didn't understand that, while she didn't mind being alone, she hated not being busy, not having a purpose. Having nothing to do reminded her of her

childhood, of long days and nights without company or
conversation, with only an old television set for enter-
tainment. Her mother would come home from work, pop
some sleeping tabs she bought from the guy on the corner and pass out for the next fourteen or sixteen hours.
Tyce was always out, selling his art in the park so that
they could pay one of the many bills her mom couldn't
cover. The local library had been her favorite place to
hang out and books her constant and unfailing friends.
These days she spent most of her time alone but her work
kept her busy.

"Lachlyn? Lachlyn?"

Lachlyn forced herself to blink, concentrating on the
cool floor beneath her hand, allowing the noise from the
photographers to drift up to her. Then she saw that the
display screen on her phone still showed that she was
connected to Annie.

"I've got to go, Annie."

"Look," Annie said, "if your situation changes I can
have another talk with Martin." But Lachlyn heard her
underlying frustration, her *Why would you want to spend
your days digging through old papers when you could
be shopping and seeing the world, playing the role of the
Park Avenue Princess?*

Nobody realized that accepting the money was the
easy part. It was just a couple more zeroes—okay, a lot
more zeroes—in her bank account. She could take it or
leave it, spend it or give it away. It was the people involved that made this difficult, the fact that this wasn't
just a matter of moving cash around. The family dynamic
of who and what the Ballantynes were and stood for
made this situation complicated. A cold hand squeezed
her lungs together and she deliberately slowed her breathing down and released her grip on her phone, shaking her

hand to put blood back into her fingers. A few months earlier, when Tyce had told her that he was making plans for her to meet her biological family she'd thought that she'd meet the Ballantynes, have a meal with them and that they'd all go back to their very different lives.

She never expected to be offered a fat bank account, a limitless credit card, to be moved into The Den and to be hounded by the press. The possibility of being accepted as part of the family never crossed her mind. She was touched by their actions, amazed at their generosity but underneath it all, she was running scared, bone-deep terrified. Beneath the fame and money, the Ballantynes were people, and people meant relationships.

She didn't do relationships... How could she make them see that?

"Lachlyn?"

Lachlyn heard Reame's low, deep voice and scrambled to her feet. She ducked her head and dashed her fingers against her cheeks, annoyed when she wiped away moisture. The last thing she needed was Reame to see her tears.

Lachlyn looked at the now empty doorway, looking for Linc. His presence would, hopefully, stop her from making an ass of herself with his best friend.

"Hi." Lachlyn placed her shaking hands into the back pockets of her jeans and felt a hole in the corner of one of the pockets. She was wearing ragged jeans, a long-sleeve white T-shirt and banged-up sneakers, while Reame looked fantastic in his dark jeans, pale blue shirt and cream jacket. The royal blue pocket square was a nice touch. He pulled designer shades off the top of his head and tapped the glasses against his empty palm.

Reame managed a tight smile and his eyes skittered off

hers. Huh. "Where's Linc?" she asked, darting a hopeful look at the door he'd closed behind him.

"Shaw."

Reame didn't have to say any more; in the few days that she'd spent in The Den, there had been a few "Shaw" moments.

"Ah, enough said," Lachlyn said, rocking on her heels.

Reame walked over to the window and, standing to the side, pulled back the drape so that he could see out without being photographed. "The crowd looks bigger than it was twenty minutes ago."

"I just wish they would go away," Lachlyn muttered. "I don't understand why they are so interested in me."

"You're young, pretty and you've just won the family jackpot. You are news," Reame said in a flat voice, his back still to her. "You're a modern-day fairy tale playing out in front of their eyes."

Reame turned around and gestured to the comfortable couch. "Take a seat. It's a lot more comfortable than the floor."

Since he noticed she'd been sitting on the cold floor, Lachlyn knew that there was no chance that he'd missed her red-rimmed eyes and her wobbly lip. Reame Jepsen, Lachlyn suspected, didn't miss a damn thing.

Pride had her forcing her shoulders back, lifting her chin as she made her way to the couch and perched on the edge of the cushion.

Reame sat opposite her and leaned forward, his forearms resting on his legs, his hands dangling between his strong thighs. This morning, his eyes were a cool, light peppermint and, as always, invasive. She felt like he could see into her soul, read her thoughts. Lachlyn felt exposed and uncomfortable. God, she hoped that this conversation wouldn't take long.

"Let's talk security, specifically your security," Reame said, his eyes cool and tone brusque.

Lachlyn forced herself to maintain eye contact and responded with a nod.

"Linc is concerned about you being on your own."

"He doesn't need to be. I'm used to being on my own."

"If you were the ordinary woman you were a month ago, I'd agree."

"But you're not Lachlyn Latimore anymore, you're now a Ballantyne—at least in the eyes of the press—and that changes the picture," Reame continued, the warm waves of his voice rolling over her skin. "You're the newest member of a very prominent, very interesting family. The residents of this city have grown up with the Ballantynes. They remember when Connor took in three orphans. They cheered when Connor adopted Linc alongside Jaeger, Beck and Sage. They mourned Connor's death. The interest in the Ballantynes has never wavered and the fact that you are Connor's daughter is big news. The Ballantynes pulling you into the family and sharing Connor's wealth with you is *huge* news."

"I'm not taking the money," Lachlyn blurted out. For some reason she couldn't articulate, it was important that he understand that she wasn't a gold digger and that she had little interest in the Ballantyne fortune.

"You're not?"

Lachlyn squeezed her hands between her thighs. "No."

Lachlyn thought she caught a flash of surprise on his face but a second later his expression turned inscrutable. Linc lifted a big shoulder in a *don't care* shrug. "That's between you and them. I'm just here to talk about keeping you safe."

Nothing in his body language, voice or eyes suggested that they'd shared a hot look across a crowded ballroom and that electricity had sizzled and sparked between them. He was all business, only business.

Good. Then why did she feel a tiny bit disappointed?

Linc sat up straight, leaned back and placed his ankle on his opposite knee. He tapped his finger on his thigh. "Linc also wants me to give you a PPO—"

That didn't sound very nice. "A what?"

"A personal protection officer, a bodyguard," he explained, sounding impatient. "You need a shield between you and the press. And any crazies."

"Crazies?"

"There are eight million people in this city, most of whom have heard or read about you. More than a few are delusional and a handful might think of you as their new best friend, as a potential lover or something more sinister. Until the attention dies down, it's wise to take precautions."

Lachlyn tried to assimilate the barrage of information, to make sense of what he was saying. It didn't help that every time she looked at him, she wondered what his lips would feel like on hers, whether his hands would be rough or smooth against her bare skin. God, she'd never looked at a man and felt her saliva dry up, her heart bang against her chest.

What was it about him that yanked her libido out of its coma?

Let's think about that… Did it have anything to do with the fact that he was the sexiest man she'd met? Ever?

Frustrated with herself, frustrated in general, Lachlyn refocused. What were they discussing? Right, bodyguards.

Reame played with the laces on his trendy shoes. "So in order to give you the best protection, I need some information about you. Let's start with the easy stuff, your job. You're a librarian?"

Lachlyn shook her head. "I work as an archivist at the NYPL."

A small smile touched Reame's mouth and a butterfly in her stomach took flight, followed by another ten. "I love that building."

The Beaux Arts building was her favorite place in the world. "I do, too."

Reame kept his eyes locked on hers, penetrating and steady. "And do you like your work?"

"I love it. Libraries, books…documents make me hot."

Reame's eyes heated and turned speculative and Lachlyn cursed her choice of words. She'd opened the door and flat-out desire walked in and plonked itself between them, its smile mocking. "Uh… I…" Lachlyn stuttered.

Reame looked away from her and Lachlyn saw his chest rise and fall as he took a big breath. His expression was so inscrutable that she couldn't tell if he was feeling the attraction too or whether he was just making an attempt to hide his irritation. So far, she'd seen nothing of the heat she'd seen in his eyes last night…maybe she'd just projected her attraction onto him. Because she was an emotional hermit, she was inexperienced with men so it was entirely possible.

"Let's talk about your living arrangements. You live in Woodside?" Reame asked, smoothly changing the subject and ignoring her flaming face. God, she had all the poise and grace of a walrus.

Lachlyn thought about her bright, cheerful space packed full of books and sighed. "I live in a small apartment above a bakery."

"And that's where you would like to be?" Reame asked.

Lachlyn darted him a hopeful look. "Oh, God, yes! But Linc seems to think that's not a good idea, that it's too small and too far away."

Reame didn't look too concerned. "I'm in the business of making life easier for my clients, not my staff. My paramount concern is your safety." In that statement Lachlyn saw the hard businessman, the tough commanding officer. She had no doubt that when Reame said hop, his people asked how far they should jump.

"If your apartment is a safe place for you to stay, then you can. If it's not, we go to plan B."

"Which is?"

"No idea. Yet." Reame said. "You will have two PPOs assigned to you. One will take the night shift and will drive you to work in the morning. I'm presuming that you aren't in the public eye at work?"

Lachlyn shook her head. "The public doesn't have access to my work area but that's not going to be an issue." Lachlyn rubbed her forehead with the tips of her fingers and shook her head. "I don't currently have a job."

Reame frowned. "They fired you?"

"No, I have a lot of vacation time, nearly two months accumulated, which I'm being ordered to take. They believe that my presence at work will be too disruptive."

"I can't disagree with that," Reame admitted. "So how are you going to fill your time?"

"I have no idea," Lachlyn said wearily. The realization was terrifying.

Lachlyn heard the discreet beep of a cell phone. Reame pulled his phone from the inside pocket of his jacket and scowled down at the screen. "I need to get back to work. The Den is one of the safest houses in the city so you will stay here for now. Later this afternoon I'll bring your PPOs around to meet you. They will escort you back to your place and take over your protection."

Reame hit the buttons on his phone and held the device to his ear. Standing up, he jammed his free hand into the front pocket of his jeans and rocked on his heels. "Cora? Reame."

Lachlyn heard the muted squawk of a female voice and thought about moving across the room to give him some privacy. Then again, he was already standing; if he wanted to move away, he could.

"Yeah, sorry, I've wasted a load of time this morning. Tell them that I will be there in twenty," Reame stated. "I need Liam to pull the folders of anyone who is available for a protection gig starting this afternoon."

Lachlyn narrowed her eyes at his wasted time comment.

"Yeah, open a file, Lachlyn Latimore... Yeah, same deal as usual."

This time the squawk was louder and Lachlyn heard the words *pro bono* and *charity*. She rocketed to her feet and held up her hands in a "just stop!" gesture. She'd been at the receiving end of too much charity in her life—clothes, food, education—and she was damned if she'd take it from Reame Jepsen. Receiving something for nothing was the equivalent of asking for help and she didn't need any, especially not from him.

"No! Not pro bono and not charity," she firmly stated, interrupting the conversation. She met Reame's light eyes and forced herself not to back down at his scowling face. He dropped his phone and held it against his thigh.

"This conversation has nothing to do with you."

"The hell it doesn't," Lachlyn retorted.

Biting the edge of her thumb, she rocked on her heels. "Look, just forget the protection, I'll be fine."

"The hell you will. There are factors to this that you don't understand. Linc and I have an understanding…"

"And I'm telling you that if I can't pay, then this doesn't happen. I'll take my chances," Lachlyn told him, her scowl rivaling his.

She'd never stared down a big, burly former Special Forces soldier before and Lachlyn thought that she'd won the battle when he lifted his phone to his ear again. But Reame didn't look away. His determined expression didn't change. "Cora, two people, their folders on my desk when I get back. Open the file…pro bono."

Lachlyn narrowed her eyes at him as he disconnected the call and before she could blast him, he spoke. "My business, my rules. You don't get to comment on it."

Lachlyn pointed to herself. "My body, my protection, I pay for it."

Reame groaned. "Oh, God, you are going to be one of the pain in the ass clients aren't you?"

"Damn right I am," Lachlyn retorted, noticing his gaze jumping from her eyes to her mouth and back up again. That damn buzz passed from him to her and ignited the flames low in her belly, sending heat to her most feminine parts, the parts that craved him and his touch.

"When I get back to the office, you will officially become a client," Reame said in a husky voice. "But you're not my client… Yet."

His words made no sense but she did notice that he was looking at her like she was a novel he'd been waiting months to read, like the latest creation by his favorite artist. Like she was a world he couldn't wait to explore. Oh, God, he looked like he wanted to kiss her.

Reame's hands shot out and gripped her hips. He yanked her closer and her stomach slammed into his body. She felt his heat and, wow, something that was long and hard and…

"I never put my hands on a client." Reame lifted his wrist and looked at his watch. "But I have some time…"

Her head whirling, Lachlyn blinked as he locked his arms around her waist, his mouth falling toward hers. Lachlyn sucked in some air—she figured she was going to need it—and felt his knees bend as he easily lifted her so that her mouth aligned with his and then… *God and heaven.*

Teeth scraped and lips soothed, tongues swirled and whirled and heat, lazy heat, spread through her limbs and slid into her veins. Reame was kissing her and time and space shifted. It felt natural for her legs to wind around his waist, to lock her arms around his neck and take what she'd been fantasizing about. Kissing Reame was better than she imagined—she was finally feeling all those fuzzy feels romance books described. For the first time ever, she felt dizzy, the butterflies in her stomach were doing complicated aerial displays and electricity river-danced on her skin.

It felt perfect. It felt right.

Reame jerked his mouth off hers and their eyes connected, his eyes now darker, intense, blazing with hot, green fire. He cursed once before diving in again. This time he didn't hesitate, didn't mess around… This was serious kissing, kissing on steroids. This was the kiss you gave a woman when you knew you could never do it again.

For the first time she could remember, her brain switched off and allowed her to live in the moment, free to taste and explore, to experience. Lachlyn pressed herself closer, she'd climb inside him if she could, and pushed her fingers into his soft hair, her other hand exploring his stubble-covered masculine jaw, his strong neck. She groaned into his mouth when his hand ducked under the hem of her loose shirt, skated beneath the band of her jeans and under the thin cord of her thong. She wanted more, his mouth on other places, his fingers dancing over all the neglected places on her body.

She wanted him… She never wanted anybody. And never this much.

"Holy crap—"

Reame stiffened in her arms and Lachlyn yanked her mouth off Reame's and looked over his shoulder to the now open door to where Linc stood, half in and half out of the room. Lachlyn slid down Reame's hard body. She pushed her bangs off her forehead and released a deep breath, grateful that Reame's big body shielded her from Linc.

Lachlyn touched her swollen lips and glanced down at her chest, where her hard nipples pushed against the fabric of her lacy bra and thin T-shirt. She couldn't possibly look more turned on if she tried. It was a very strange and confusing sensation.

"Oh, this is just perfect," Linc said. Lachlyn couldn't look at him but he sounded thoroughly amused. "Want me to go away and come back in fifteen?"

Reame looked at her and, along with desire, she thought she saw regret in his eyes. He slowly shook his head. "No, we're done."

Lachlyn met his eyes and nodded her agreement. Yes, they were done. They had to be.

Four

Back in his office, Reame tossed his jacket over the back of his visitor's chair and threw his phone across his desk where it bounced off a photo of his mom and three sisters. He gripped the back of the chair and closed his eyes, the image of Linc's amused and speculative face bouncing around his brain. He knew that Linc had taken two plus two and reached seventy-eight million...

He knew exactly what Linc was remembering. When he left the military, Sage was in her early twenties and Connor, bless his soul, had decided to play matchmaker. Before Alzheimer's had ravaged his mind, he'd made a concerted effort to throw him and Sage together, dropping broad hints that he'd love to have Reame as a son-in-law.

There was only one problem with Connor's little fantasy: even with a gallon of gas and a flame thrower, he and Sage couldn't generate a spark.

Unlike the raging lightning storm that happened when he kissed Lachlyn. And Linc had seen it…

Reame resisted the urge to reach for his phone to dial Linc, to insist that it was only a kiss, that it didn't mean anything. That Linc should cool his jets, this wasn't going anywhere, ever. It had been a moment in time, an aberration, a curiosity. That there wasn't a chance in hell that he'd ever get involved with or marry a member of the Ballantyne family. He didn't want to marry anyone, he wanted to have a good time, to sow those wild oats that being the family breadwinner and his military career denied him. He wanted to have wild sex with wild women…

He'd recently watched his best friends—Linc and Jaeger and Beck—fall in love and assume a heavy mantle of responsibility and accountability. While he'd had a few affairs, he'd never experienced anything close to the passionate and intense situations his friends were in. Seeing them fall had just strengthened his resolve to have some fun. Relationships, anything from dating to marriage, required a degree of responsibility, and he'd been responsible enough for ten lifetimes. And there was the emotional component to consider. He'd witnessed his mom's devastation when his dad walked out on her after twenty-five years together. Who in their right mind wanted to risk that happening to them?

And worse, what if he met and married someone and then, like his dad, realized that he'd made an awful mistake? Marriage to anyone was a huge leap and marrying into the Ballantyne family was the biggest leap of all. He had a lifetime of memories tied up with them, he owed them so much and they were as much his family as his blood relatives were. If he married and messed up, it would be bad. If he married a Ballantyne and messed up, the consequences would be tragic. He'd lose his best friends, his valuable clients and a huge, wonderful part of his life. Failing at marriage was a risk he wasn't prepared to take...

But hell, that kiss had been hotter and wilder than any he could remember in recent memory.

Crap. Hell. Dammit.

"Reame?"

Reame whipped around and glared at his PA. "What?"

Cora fisted a hand on one ample hip and her scowl suggested that he tone down the attitude. Knowing that his life would be a lot more difficult without the super-efficient Cora in it, he reined in his temper. "Sorry, it's been a long morning and it's not even ten thirty yet."

Cora just lifted one eyebrow and stepped up to him, handing him a stack of folders. She tapped her bottom lip. "Nice shade of lip gloss you're wearing, boss."

Reame cursed and rubbed the back of his hand across his lips. Yeah, Cora on his case was exactly what he didn't need. "Do not say one damn word."

Cora folded her arms and looked up at the ceiling. "She's a client and I thought that we didn't smooch, or do anything else with, our clients. I thought that was an unbreakable rule," she teased, a smile on her lips.

God. "Let's try something new," Reame suggested. "Let's pretend that I am the boss, that you respect me and that I pay your salary at the end of the month."

Cora rolled her eyes. "Okay, so those are the folders of the men who are available to work with Lachlyn Latimore."

Reame, his head pounding, walked around his desk and dropped into his leather chair. He flipped open the first file, saw who it was and tossed it to one side. "Too inexperienced."

He quickly ran through the other folders, finding fault

with each of the six candidates, conscious of Cora perching on the arm of his visitor's chair. He was looking over
the second to last folder when a rap on his door frame
had him looking up to see Daniel, one of his newest and
best hires, standing in the doorway. He was also supposed to be providing security to a visiting Arab sheikh.

"Boss, I just got in and Liam said to tell you that I'm
available to work tonight."

Reame frowned. "Where's the sheikh?"

"On his way back to Saudi a week early. He had a
family emergency." Daniel opened his hands. "I'm free."

Nearly nine years younger than him, Daniel was
twenty-six, and handsome and cocky. And he was also,
damn him, charming. He was the perfect type of guy to
guard Lachlyn, easygoing but professional. Best of all,
he seemed to have a sixth sense about people and could
spot trouble before it even happened.

Reame opened his mouth to tell him about his new
gig and the words clogged up in his throat. He couldn't
get them out.

"Boss?" Daniel frowned, stepping into the room. "Are
you okay?"

Cora, the witch, just smiled and waved Daniel back.
"He's fine. He's just having a Damascus moment."

Daniel looked puzzled. "What does that mean?"

Cora tilted her head, her eyes on Reame's face. "Oh,
just that the boss man is realizing exactly how personal
this new gig is."

Reame felt irritation burn the back of his throat. He
dismissed Daniel and told him to shut the door. When
he was alone, he nailed Cora with a don't-mess-with-me
look. "What the hell does that mean?" he demanded.

Cora didn't look even a little bit intimidated. "It means

that you are not going to allow anyone to protect Lachlyn Latimore-Ballantyne but yourself."

"The hell I'm not." Reame slammed his hand on the pile of folders. "I just need half a chance to decide who will fit her best." Reaching for the handset of his desk phone, he jabbed the extension number and waited for Liam to answer. He and Liam had served together in the sandpits of the world and he was his second in charge at Jepsen Securities. After Linc, he was the man Reame trusted most.

"Daniel says that you are having some sort of moment. What the hell does that mean?"

Didn't anyone bother with a hello anymore?

Reame opened his mouth to curse him, realized that Cora was still standing there and sighed. "I need two female PPOs this afternoon for the next few weeks."

"Yeah…no," Liam replied, amused. "Have you lost your mind?"

"Possibly," Reame admitted.

"Firstly, we do not have enough woman PPOs to handle the amount of jobs we do have, and as fast as we are hiring them, the more clients we have for them. Are you asking me to pull two agents from the field for a pro bono gig?"

When Liam put it like that…

"I could, maybe, reassign Fiona, in two weeks or so," Liam said.

Yeah, too little too late. Reame banged his handset down and drummed his fingers on the surface of his desk. He picked up a file and flipped it open again. He was being ridiculous. He'd made this decision a thousand times before for hundreds of clients. Take one client, assign an agent…

Cora snorted, her expression challenging. "You can't do it, can you?"

Reame tried, again, to verbalize a name who would act as Lachlyn's PPO. Yet again, the words refused to come. Nobody, he finally admitted, was guarding Lachlyn but himself. He could rationalize his decision. She was a Ballantyne, Linc's brand-new sister. He only had his business because of Connor, so he owed it to him to give Lachlyn his undivided attention.

He was also exceptionally good at BS-ing himself.

"Shall I tell Daniel he's got the job?" Cora asked, her tone sweet but her eyes dancing with mischief. There was no way a cocky, charming stud ten years younger than him was going to spend hours alone with Lachlyn.

Cora laughed. "I thought so."

"I hate you so much right now," Reame muttered before banging his forehead on his desk.

Cora's hand patted his shoulder. "Being right never gets old. You want some coffee?"

"Yes. And I need a brain transplant. And a new PA, if you could manage that," Reame added sarcastically.

"Well, one out of three ain't bad."

Back at The Den, Lachlyn sat on one of the leather sofas in the great room and stared out of the floor-to-ceiling windows onto the postage stamp garden beyond the glass. Still feeling a little dazed, she lifted her fingertips to her lips and swore that she could taste Reame. His smell, a dizzying combination of laundry detergent, alpha male and soap, still lingered in her nose.

Lachlyn rested her elbows on her knees and cupped her face in her hands. So, wow. Wow, wow, *wow*.

In her effort to reclaim her sexuality, Lachlyn had, when she was younger, kissed a few men, had indulged in some heavy petting and had been taken over the edge once or twice. Those early dates had been hard work;

fear had been her chaperone every time. Surprisingly, it hadn't been the physicality of the dates that had scared her. Lachlyn found that if she liked the guys enough, she could enjoy a man's touch and she was fine with physical intimacy.

No, what made her chest tighten and her throat close was the emotional component. Somehow, despite her intentions to keep things casual, she always managed to date men who wanted *more*. All of them, within a short space of time, started talking about taking their relationship to the next level, sleeping over, moving in, making a deeper connection. Even the dreaded L word had been uttered—causing her to run as hard and fast as she could, leaving them confused and hurt.

Over the past few years, she hadn't met many men who could compete with a cup of tea and a great book, so she hadn't dated much. There had been a couple of dinners with a historian at NYU and an artist she met through Tyce. She'd controlled the pace of the relationships. Coffee meant a light kiss, dinner, a longer kiss. More dinners, maybe some heavy petting. Both men had wanted more—sex and a deeper connection—so she'd let them down gently.

Kissing Reame hadn't involved any thought. She'd just dived headfirst into that whirlpool. She'd wanted so she took. His mouth had made her skin tingle and her mind swim. She'd felt dazed and drunk…hell, she still did. She still wanted more. More kisses, more skin, him completing her, making her whole. Kissing Reame had been wonderful, exciting, dizzying…

A wonderful, exciting, dizzying *mistake*.

Lachlyn stood and walked over to the door, placing her hand on the cold glass. Her libido couldn't have chosen a more inconvenient time to wake up and shake its tail.

Oh, a part of her reveled in the fact that she could feel so much passion, that she was capable of more than anemic kisses and fumbling caresses. But she was neck-deep in a situation that was rapidly spinning out of control. She was dealing with the Ballantynes, was suddenly a mini-celebrity and had to make decisions that involved millions and millions of dollars.

At this crucial time in her life, at this watershed moment, she could not afford to go off tangent and explore this wonderful new world of carnal pleasure. She had bigger worries...

She had to manage the Ballantynes' expectations of her and somehow make them realize, without explaining why, that someday soon she'd be bowing out and that she wouldn't be much more than an occasional extra body at family events she was expected to attend as Tyce's sister and his baby's aunt. She couldn't explain that she was used to being on her own, that it was far easier to stand alone and that she would never need, want or ask for anything from them.

Those were her big worries, but she had others. How was she going to fill the hours in the day without a job to go to? How was she going to cope with having a bodyguard in her face 24/7? She liked her privacy and her solitude. She didn't have a spare room and living with a stranger was shaping up to be a nightmare.

And the world thought she was living a fairy tale. Ha!

On the bright side, at least Reame wouldn't be around so she had a shot at thinking clearly and acting like an adult.

That shot was blown out of the water when Reame stepped into the hallway of The Den an hour later than he said he'd be. Lachlyn started to peek outside the front door of the famous brownstone, remembered why that wasn't a good idea and jerked her head back.

"Stand away from the door, Lachlyn," Reame said, his tone curt.

Reame closed the door with more force than necessary and pushed his jacket back to place his hands on his narrow hips. Lachlyn wondered if he had those defined hip muscles that made women swallow their tongues.

This! This was why she shouldn't be anywhere near him! "Where are my bodyguards?" she asked, finally remembering why he was back. Why was she asking about the one thing she didn't want and couldn't afford?

Reame shoved his hand through his caramel-colored hair and jerked his head at the door. "I'm it," he said, looking miserable.

Lachlyn frowned. "You're what?"

"Your security detail," Reame said, his jaw tight. "Are you ready to go?"

Frowning, Lachlyn stepped back, her hands raised. "Whoa, slow down there. What does that mean?"

"For the foreseeable future, I'm going to be the one on your six."

"On your six? What does that mean?"

Reame picked up a small bronze statue off the polished drop leaf table, tracing the delicate curves of the ballerina with his big hands. Lachlyn could almost imagine his hands on her back, stroking, kneading, exploring. She wanted that, she wanted him, but he wasn't a good idea. Hadn't she decided that a little earlier? Ten minutes with him and she was being led into temptation again.

"It means that I've got your back," Reame replied and she had to work hard to keep up with the conversation. "Whether you like it or not, I'm going to be close by."

She didn't like it, not in any shape or form. But why,

if she was so opposed to the idea, did she feel a flicker of excitement at the thought of spending more time with this man?

"You can't look after me day and night," Lachlyn told him, using her hell-no voice.

"You'd think that but apparently, because I am a moron of magnificent proportions, that's what's going to happen," Reame retorted, picking up her heavy suitcase and holding it as if it were a handbag. "Look, I'm still trying to juggle some staff around to find someone who would be a suitable PPO for you. I just need a little time," Reame stated in a flat voice. "I thought that I would drive you to Woodside and check out your apartment. Once I do that, I can make better decisions about your security."

Lachlyn wrinkled her nose. "So, I might not be able to stay there tonight?" Her bed, her pillow, her things... All she wanted to do was be in a space that was hers, where she felt comfortable. But something bizarre was happening between them and there was too much heat. Her apartment was small and they'd bump into each other and boom! They'd set the place on fire.

"I'd just like to state, for the record, that you being my bodyguard is not going to work for me," Lachlyn replied, panic coating her throat and words. He'd be there when she woke up, when she went to sleep, in her face. All day. "It's not feasible. You have a company to run. You can't trail after me on an hour-to-hour basis."

Her suitcase hit the floor with a heavy thud. Reame folded his arms across that continent-size chest and tilted his head. "You're nervous."

Well, duh.

"You don't need to be," Reame told her, using a voice that could sooth wild horses. "Despite what happened earlier, nothing is going to happen between us. You're now my client and that means that you are untouchable.

"If my employees crossed a line like that with their principals they'd get fired. I hold myself to the same standards I do them," Reame said, avoiding her eyes. His words were meant to reassure her, so why was she feeling thwarted? Really, none of this made any sense. "Besides, if it makes you feel any better, you're not my type."

God help the women he kissed who were his type. "I'm not?"

"Firstly, you're Linc's sister and I don't fool around with my good friends' sisters because brothers tend to get pissed off. Secondly, I don't do commitment and I only fool around with women who fool around too, who have no expectations beyond a fun time." Linc ran his hand over his face. "That kiss earlier was a..."

"Mistake." Lachlyn filled in the word for him, feeling like she'd run a marathon or swum the English Channel.

"Yeah, it was a mistake," Reame agreed. "It won't happen again."

Lachlyn knew that she shouldn't be feeling the level of disappointment she did and couldn't understand why. This was the smart option, the sensible choice. This was what she wanted!

"Now that we've got that settled, can we go?" Reame demanded, picking up her suitcase again. He glanced down at it, frowned and pushed it away. "I'll come back for that later tonight, when the crowd goes to bed. If they see you leaving with a suitcase, they'll follow and that's exactly what you don't want. Anything in there you can't live without?"

Yes, her lingerie and her toiletry bag and her pile of books. Lachlyn gasped when Reame tossed the case onto its back, crouched down and flipped the lid open. Her lingerie, her one indulgence apart from books, was the last thing she'd packed. Lachlyn blushed as Reame looked down at her pink camouflage bra, bright purple thong and almost transparent lacy boy-cut panties.

She saw him swallow once, then twice, before standing up and gesturing to the frothy, jewel-colored piles. "Grab whatever you need and shove it into your bag. One of my guys will bring the rest over later tonight."

Lachlyn nodded, crouched down and balanced on her toes. She grabbed two matching sets of lingerie, a T-shirt, her toiletry bag and three books. She just managed to squeeze them all into her leather tote bag. She shut the suitcase, closed the hinges and stood up.

Reame held out his hand to take her tote bag.

"I can carry it," Lachlyn assured him.

Reame nodded. "After I open the door, stay behind me, keep hold on my hand. Do not speak, not even to say no comment."

Lachlyn nodded. "I know the drill. Shoot, my sunglasses!"

She needed her glasses because the winter sun was bright but mostly because she knew that she still looked like a haunted rabbit whenever she faced the press. Pulling open the side of her bag, she dug in and rootled around, unable to lay her hands on her shades. Dammit. Grabbing a handful of lingerie, she handed it to Reame to hold, then passed him two books, another bra, a T-shirt and her toiletry bag. And another book. She peered into the depths, shook her bag and saw her glasses under her purse. She pulled them out, jammed them onto the top of her head and looked at Reame, who was holding the bundle of silk and satins, paperbacks and a hard copy, her toiletry bag dangling off his index finger. Seeing his big hands holding her intimate clothing sent a bolt of warmth through her, straight to her core. Dammit, she had to stop allowing him to do that to her.

She wasn't his type and he was more than she wanted to deal with. Too big, too intense, too alive.

Too tempting, too uncontrollable, too fascinating.

Far too dangerous...

Just cool yourself and use your brain, Latimore.

Lachlyn opened her bag wide and gestured for Reame to dump her stuff back into its depths. He did and Lachlyn managed to smile, enjoying seeing him looking uncomfortable for once. "Shall we go?" she asked.

Reame scrubbed his hands over his face before reaching for the door handle. "Yeah. Remember, look straight ahead and don't speak."

"And keep hold of your hand."

Reame's eyes blazed as her hand slid into his, their fingers entwined. "I'm not going to let you go, Lachlyn."

He meant for the short walk to the car he had waiting, Lachlyn thought as he opened the front door and the crowd roared their questions. Not for anything more than that. Because, thanks to her past, that was impossible.

Five

Reame found a parking for his black SUV a block from Lachlyn's apartment. He exited his vehicle to walk around the hood to open her door for her. Lachlyn hopped down, pulling her oversize tote bag—full of the bits and pieces of silk and satin he'd been trying, very hard, not to think about—over her shoulder.

But images of the very blonde Lachlyn wearing nothing more than a vibrant-colored bra and matching panties that wouldn't fit a flea kept jumping into his head. He wanted to pull aside silky material to see her creamy nipple and push scraps of lace—designed to be panties but could be used as a weapon of distraction—down her legs.

Lachlyn slammed the passenger door and the sound pulled Reame back to the present. Great bodyguard he was... He was supposed to be watching Lachlyn's back but he was far more interested in fantasizing about what was under her clothes. The US government had spent millions training him to be aware of his surroundings to prepare for anything and everything, to anticipate situations before they arose. And here he was in fantasy land.

This had to stop...

Reame scanned the area but didn't see anything or anyone that lifted the hairs on the back of his neck. Best of all, he saw no press, which meant that his computer guy had covered Lachlyn's cyber tracks well and no one had her address yet.

Lachlyn pulled her bag over her shoulder and turned right, heading down the block. Coffee shop, tailor and dry cleaning, second-hand book shop. Deli, a Filipino restaurant. So far, so good. "How long have you lived in this area?" Reame asked her, pulling her out of the way of an incoming skateboarder.

Lachlyn pushed her heavy bangs out of her eyes and tucked the hair behind her ear. He'd loved her long, waist-length hair but this short, sassy style was growing on him. "About four years." She looked around and a small smile touched her amazing lips.

"It's cheap, diverse and safe. I can get to Midtown in thirty minutes." Lachlyn gestured to an Irish pub across the road. "Best burgers in the city."

Reame lifted his eyebrows at the challenge. "I know where all the good burgers in the city are."

Lachlyn lifted her thumb at a nondescript restaurant to her right. "Best Thai food in the city."

"You're making a lot of claims, Latimore."

"I can back them up," Lachlyn responded. "I'm a lousy cook so I eat out a lot. I'm an adventurous eater so this area suits me well."

He couldn't help wondering whether she was equally adventurous in bed. Yeah, he shouldn't be thinking about her like that but he was a red-blooded, horny man and she was five feet of undiluted sexiness.

You really need to get laid, Jepsen. One night, a few nights, weeks, pure sex, just pleasure with no responsibilities. He seriously needed to put himself out of his misery and go on a frickin' date!

Reame followed Lachlyn into an Italian bakery and the smell of butter and sugar hit his nose. His stomach rumbled, and he suddenly remembered that he hadn't had anything to eat all day except for a green smoothie after his gym session much earlier in the day.

"Ciao, bella." Reame heard the boisterous greeting and saw Lachlyn lifting a hand to return it but he veered away and headed for the display fridges, his mouth watering. Cannelloni, ricotta cheesecake, pasticiotti. There was also herb and garlic focaccia and he could easily imagine tearing the bread apart, steam rising, and eating it straight from the oven. Before his parents moved, they'd lived in Flushing, another diverse neighborhood with many mom-and-pop food businesses, and like Lachlyn, he was an adventurous eater.

He was also an adventurous lover and, judging by the way she kissed, he thought she might be, as well. Not that he'd ever get to put that theory to the test...

"Reame?"

Reame wrenched his eyes away from the bomboloni—Italian doughnuts—and saw that Lachlyn was behind the counter, waiting for him to follow her. He hurried across the room, pausing when Lachlyn introduced him to Riccardo, a tall, thin man who Lachlyn said was both the baker and owner. Reame followed Lachlyn into the heart of the bakery and up a narrow flight of stairs.

"Two flights up," Lachlyn said, jogging up the stairs.

"You access your apartment through the bakery?" Reame asked.

"Ric lives on the first-floor apartment, I'm on the top floor. There is another entrance at the back of the building but this is easier, and doesn't require me to walk around the building and down a dark alley."

"Good plan," Reame said as they hit the second set of stairs. "Did you ask Riccardo whether anyone had been by looking for you during the past week?"

"I spoke to him shortly before we left The Den and he said no," Lachlyn replied and Reame had a hard time keeping his eyes off her exceptional butt and long, shapely legs.

Strange that nobody in the bakery had contacted the press to tell them where she lived, that they knew her. Despite his guy covering her tracks, he would've expected some press to have picked up her trail. Weird, Reame thought, as, out of the corner of his eye, he caught sight of a shadow passing over the wall at the top of the stairs. Reame reacted instinctively, clamping his hand around Lachlyn's wrist and jerking her down the steps. She yelped as he pushed her behind him, creating a barrier between him and the three camera-wielding journalists at the top of the stairs.

"How much money are the Ballantynes giving you?"

"Are you moving back in?"

"How does it feel to be one of the wealthiest women in the city?"

Reame cursed, spun around and pushed Lachlyn down the stairs and they burst into the bakery, straight into a bigger crowd. Ric had set this up, Reame realized. They'd been waiting…somewhere. Reame wrapped his arm around Lachlyn and marched them toward the front door, using his height and strength to bulldoze his way through the crowd.

"I need clothes, Reame," Lachlyn said, her words barely discernible over the loud questions being fired at them from every direction.

Reame bent down to speak in her ear, tightening the grip on her arm. "I'll send someone to pack for you. Right now, I need to get you out of here."

"Who did this?" Lachlyn asked him, her eyes wide with fear and frustration.

"Who do you think, Lach? Who is the only person who would've allowed this to happen?" Reame replied.

Lachlyn spun out of his grip and he knew that she was looking for Riccardo, who was standing behind the counter. He followed her gaze and saw the smirk on his face. It was as he thought—ratting Lachlyn out was fantastic publicity. He'd have the bakery's name in every column in every paper in the morning. When Riccardo just lifted his shoulders in an "I gotta do what I gotta do" shrug, hurt swept over Lachlyn's face. *Bastard*. Reame cursed silently and slapped his hand on the door, very close to the ear of a reporter who was trying to stop them from leaving.

Reame looked down, adrenaline coursing and anger for Lachlyn heating his blood. "Swear to God, you either move or I'm putting you through the glass."

Something in his face or tone must've told the paparazzi that he was looking for an excuse to punch someone because the reporter ducked under his arm and scuttled out of the way.

Reame tugged Lachlyn through the door and hurried her down the street, the paparazzi a bunch of vultures following them all the way to his vehicle.

* * *

"Ric set me up," Lachlyn said in a small voice as they made their way back to Manhattan.

"Yep."

"I thought he was my friend," Lachlyn said, her words icy with hurt and disappointment. "Why would he do that?"

Lachlyn caught Reame's astonished look. "They offered him money or publicity, Lachlyn. The three guys at the top of the hall offered him the most."

"So he sold me out for a couple of hundred bucks?" Lachlyn asked, sounding bitter.

"Or thousands," Reame replied.

Lachlyn placed her fist in the space between her ribs, her heart still threatening to beat out of her chest. She and Ric had shared coffee and pastries, dinners, books. If one of his staff had sold her out, she could understand it, but the guilty look on his face as they left his bakery told her everything she needed to know. Her friend, one of the very few she'd allowed herself to have, had tipped off the press at her expense. It was just another reminder of why engaging with people, trusting anyone, even on a superficial basis, was a really stupid idea.

Lachlyn rested her head on the window and closed her eyes. She was so tired, emotionally and physically whipped.

Reame placed his hand on her thigh and squeezed. "Well, you need to put it behind you because we have a decision to make."

Lachlyn groaned loudly, secretly hoping that Reame wouldn't remove his hand, not just yet. It felt rather... wonderful. Despite the denim separating them, she felt heat slide into her veins. Her eyes flew open to find Reame looking at her with all the passion and need he felt for her. Lachlyn dimly realized that they had stopped for a red light and suspected that she was a heartbeat away from being hauled onto his lap and kissed senseless.

Lachlyn stayed where she was, the tips of her fingers lightly resting on the top of Reame's hand.

"God, one look at you and I forget that you are under siege from the press, that you are under my protection, that you are Linc's sister," Reame stated, his words rough and hard. "I forget that I don't mess around with my clients."

"I'm not your client—" Lachlyn began to protest but knew that she was on shaky ground indeed. Reame had been a solid barrier between her and the press. If he hadn't been there earlier she might've found herself in a situation she couldn't handle.

Their heat and chemistry was another situation she was struggling to deal with.

"Define 'mess around,'" Lachlyn whispered.

"That covers anything from kissing to raucous sex," Reame retorted, pulling his hand out from under hers to push his hair off his face.

"Okay."

"I'm serious, Lachlyn. Yeah, hooking up with you would be that easy but you are not only my client, you are my best friend's baby sister," Reame stated, his tone suggesting that she not argue.

Lachlyn knew that he wouldn't be dissuaded. And why was she so concerned what Reame Jepsen thought anyway? She wasn't going to sleep with him. She didn't sleep with random hot guys. Or any guys...

Ignoring her promise to keep herself emotionally isolated—if she didn't engage, she couldn't be hurt or disappointed—Reame was, as he kept reminding her, Linc's oldest friend. He was going to be in Linc's life for the rest of his life and that would mean seeing him occasionally, having to interact with him at the family functions she was invited to. If they did sleep together, those future occasions would be ridiculously awkward.

Awkward? They would be hell!

What was wrong with her? This wasn't like her, going into free fall because of a man. She'd, hopefully temporarily, lost her job and her way of life. She had so much to adjust to. Why was she tying herself up in knots over a man?

This was her life... She was always and forever in control of what did and did not happen in it.

"Where are we going?" Lachlyn asked suddenly, taking notice of their surroundings. They had crossed the Brooklyn Bridge and instead of heading toward the Upper West Side, Reame pointed the car toward Midtown. She sat up straight and frowned. "Why aren't you taking me to The Den?"

"That's where the press would expect you to go and they will be waiting for you there."

"So are you taking me to a hotel?"

Reame shook his head, whipped onto a side street and then into an underground parking garage. He lowered his visor, hit a button and the heavy boom in front of the car lifted.

"Where are we?"

"My place."

Lachlyn saw parking spots designated Jepsen & Associates and Reame parked in the empty space close to the elevator. The other parking space held a matte-black superbike and on the other side of that, a low-slung, German-engineered sports car. Nice.

Lachlyn released her seat belt, the back passenger door opened and Reame grabbed her tote bag before opening her door. Lachlyn hopped down to the floor and after locking the car, Reame steered her to an elevator also marked Jepsen & Associates. He plugged a code into the keypad and the doors silently opened.

Lachlyn felt panic coat her throat. This was entirely out of her comfort zone.

"Reame, I'm really tired. I'd like to find a hotel and collapse so if we could make this trip to your office quick, I'd appreciate it," Lachlyn said, slumping against the back panel of the elevator.

"No hotel, Lachlyn. You're staying here tonight. And for the foreseeable future," Reame replied, hitting a button with the side of his fist. He tossed her a small smile. "Don't worry, I'm not going to ask you to sleep on a desk. My apartment is on the penthouse floor."

Lachlyn felt her throat close while her lungs tried to crawl out of her chest. "Uh—"

"Relax, Lach, despite the craziness between us, I'm not moving you into my bed. My apartment is on the top floor and next to it I have a fully outfitted guest suite for unexpected visitors or high-value clients who need special protection. You're going to move in there for a while until this madness dies down.

"My building is super-secure, there is no chance of anyone finding you here or sneaking in without a half dozen ex-soldiers knowing about it. If you want to go out, either I or Liam, my right-hand guy, can escort you where you need to go, depending on our schedule."

Reame sounded like he was trying to convince himself as much as he was trying to convince her. While she felt calmer hearing that she wasn't going to be staying with Reame, she would feel a lot more comfortable with more space between them. Physically and emotionally. A thousand miles might work. "I think that a hotel would be better, Reame."

Reame looked at her with hooded eyes. "Better for our attraction problem, sure. But safer? No way in hell is a hotel a safer place for you to be. Your safety will always be my paramount concern."

Lachlyn forced the words out. "Then what are we going to do about our attraction problem?"

"Hell if I know. All I know is that you are driving me crazy."

Reame leaned sideways, bent his head and Lachlyn held her breath thinking that he was about to kiss her. She titled her head and licked her bottom lip, not able to resist him. Man, she was in a heap of trouble. Reame just brushed his lips against the shell of her ear and his words vibrated off her skin.

"You are so damn beautiful," Reame told her, his voice igniting sparks on her skin.

"You smell so damn good," Lachlyn told him, standing on her toes to nuzzle her nose against his jaw. "And so are you…beautiful, I mean."

Reame's mouth curved against her ear and she felt him smiling. That smile traveled down her throat, onto her nipples and wandered down…and then down some more. She wanted to feel that smile on her lips, his tongue tangling with hers. Lachlyn turned her lips and connected with his and she felt his surprise and his hesitation. Not wanting to give him time to think, her tongue swiped his lower lip before she tugged that sexy piece of him between her teeth and nibbled. His hands found her jaw and Lachlyn swallowed his groan, entranced by the fact that this man—sexy, successful, so damn hot—wanted her.

Reame took control of their kiss, his hand moving from her jaw to the back of her head to hold her in place. He tipped her head to one side to change the angle and intensity of the kiss and she could taste his frustration, his need, his banked desire.

Reame tasted hers, feasted on her for a long minute before he pulled back and rested his forehead on hers, his light eyes frustrated but determined.

"We are not going to do this. I am not looking for this."

"Looking for what?" Lachlyn asked, her brain cells trying to restart.

"Sweet, hot...you." Reame pulled away from her, his hands holding the handrail in a death grip.

"I want hot, hard, sweaty, no-expectation sex from someone who wants to give it to me. Someone who knows the score, who can walk away with no regrets." Reame sucked in an agitated breath and his tense shoulders rose and fell.

His words were like rubber bullets peppering her skin. "And you think I want more from you?"

"It doesn't matter what you think you want, Lachlyn," Reame said, his voice harsh. "I've waited for this time, Lachlyn. I damn well deserve it. I've spent the last ten years paying bills, working my ass off, trying to be the good older brother, the responsible son, putting everyone else's needs first. This is my time, Lachlyn."

Reame turned to look at her again, his eyes blazing. "You, me...we're business, Lachlyn. You remember that, okay?"

Lachlyn placed her fist into her sternum in an attempt to push away the pool of acid there. Shooting steel into her spine, she lifted her chin and narrowed her eyes. "Since you are the one who keeps touching me, why don't you take your own advice, Jepsen?"

Six

Two days later, on Sunday morning, Lachlyn awoke to a text from Reame inviting her to join him for breakfast. Although she loved her own company and Reame's apartment was set up to keep his guests entertained, she was desperate to leave the building, for a change of scenery and some fresh air. She'd even put up with Jepsen's company if it meant taking a break from the white walls and white furniture. Lachlyn tugged on a pair of dark jeans, tucked them into knee-high boots and pulled on a thigh-length cable-knit sweater, the blue of the sweater repeated in a blue-and-white-checked cotton scarf. Lachlyn worked her long bangs into two braids and pinned them back under her hair, totally changing her pixie cut from sophisticated to relaxed. Mascara, a hint of bronzer and lip gloss... She didn't want Reame to think that she was trying to impress him...

You're not being businesslike, Lachlyn chided herself. The problem was that businesslike was the last word she'd use to describe how she felt about Reame Jepsen.

"Cut it out," Lachlyn grumbled as she walked the few steps to Reame's door. Yes, he kissed like a dream. Yes, she loved his hands on her skin but, even if he wanted to, she couldn't go there. Reame was so big, so capable... such a "take charge and get it done" type of guy. He was the pillar that supported Linc and, she imagined, the rest of the Ballantyne crew. He was the tall tree in a howling wind, the place where his friends and family could always find shelter. Calm, proficient, steadfast. She might want to sleep with him, and she reluctantly—and regretfully—admitted that she needed his bodyguarding skills, but nothing else. She was an independent, strong, capable woman who didn't need emotional and mental support. She'd be her own tree, build her own shelter.

She just needed him to take her out of the building, he didn't even have to talk to her. In fact, it would be better if he didn't...

Lachlyn knocked on the door, heard Reame's shout to come in and stepped into his private space. His apartment was a lot bigger than she thought, she realized, as she walked into the foyer. Through the open door on her right she saw a laundry room and to her left was a short passageway that ended in what looked like a bedroom the size of her apartment in Woodside. Lachlyn walked into the open-plan area, which culminated in a chef's kitchen and a combined dining and living space. His oversize man couches in deep, rich jewel colors faced tall windows. Lachlyn took another look and realized that the doors could fold back and that the living area would then flow onto the good-size balcony beyond. Lachlyn walked past Reame's furniture, noticed one of her brother's paintings on the wall and his sculpture in the corner—the man had taste and money—and placed her hand on the glass door. Sunbeams from a weak March sun tried to break through the clouds. Gray day or not, his view was spectacular. Hearing footsteps, Lachlyn turned around and saw Reame walking out from a room on the other side of the foyer and, judging from the desk she caught a glimpse of, presumed it was his home office.

"Hi," Reame said, his eyes scanning her. Dressed in an untucked green-and-white-checked shirt and well-fitting jeans, he looked spectacular. All golden goodness...

Business, Lachlyn reminded herself.

"How are you? Anything you need?" Reame asked her, moving to the kitchen, his bare feet silent on the hardwood flooring.

"I'm fine, thank you."

"Coffee?"

Reame pushed a mug under the spout of his coffee machine and hit a button. Lachlyn heard the grinding of beans and the smell of coffee intermingled pleasantly with his clean apartment and Reame's just-showered scent.

"How are you finding the guest suite?"

"Fine." It was a perfectly adequate word so she'd used it again.

Reame smiled. "Liar. The guest suite is very white and very cold. It was purposefully designed like that."

Lachlyn walked over to the freestanding kitchen counter and leaned her forearms on the mottled granite. "It was? Why?"

"We occasionally use it for very high-value clients who either want to drop completely off the grid for a couple of days or clients who need to drop out of sight. But it's not a place I want people to linger in so I made it as cold and as uninviting as possible."

While Lachlyn appreciated the loan of his apartment, she knew that she couldn't spend a lot of time in it. And time was the one thing she had on her hands at the moment. If she stayed in his guest apartment, she didn't need a bodyguard—or to pay Reame for one—on a minute-by-minute basis but it did mean living in what felt like a psych ward or hospital room.

Lachlyn thanked him for the cup of coffee he placed by her hands. Beggars can't be choosers, she reminded herself. At least she wasn't sharing the space with anyone; that would be a nightmare.

"You're frowning," Reame said. "What's the problem?"

"Tomorrow is Monday and I wish I had a job to go to in the morning but my supervisor nixed that idea," Lachlyn said, still upset by that decision. Somebody else would be allocated her Parisian art critic project and would make the decisions on what had historical value.

"Tell me about your work."

Normally a command like that immediately dried up her words but they were still there, bubbling on her tongue. She couldn't understand it—why him and why now?

Lachlyn shrugged. "I'm just annoyed that I can't work. I've just started sorting through a collection of diaries and documents from the Années folles—that's the crazy years of the 1920s in Paris. The collection has just arrived and I was super-excited to work on it." Lachlyn rested her forearms on the kitchen counter, thinking about the treasures she'd had to leave behind.

"What's so special about it?" Reame asked, sounding genuinely interested.

This wasn't anything personal so Lachlyn gave herself permission to ramble on. "Maxwell Cummings-Brown was an American living in Paris. Lots of money, lots of pizzazz. He was on first-name terms with Max Ernst and Salvador Dali, and it was said that he watched Josephine Baker dance the Charleston—practically naked—at the Folie Bergère. He bought jewelry from Cartier and Frédéric Boucheron for both his male and female lovers. Best of all, he kept everything—menus, calling cards, letters, diaries… It's like a snapshot of that era."

"I actually have no idea what an archivist actually does. So you get this collection in a couple of boxes—"

"Sometimes by the truckload," Lachlyn corrected him.

"And then?" Reame asked.

"Basically, I organize and rehouse the collection, whipping it into shape. Then I describe the collection so that researchers can access information easily. I specialize in late nineteenth and early twentieth century history so the Parisian collection is, was, right up my alley." Lachlyn blew out a long breath. "So instead of doing my job, I'm wafting in the breeze or, more accurately, staring at your white walls."

Reame cocked his head and Lachlyn could see the wheels turning in his head. "What if I found you another collection to whip into shape?"

Lachlyn sent him a "you're dreaming" look. She didn't want to offend him but she doubted that Reame could conceptualize the range and depth of what she normally dealt with. She didn't sort through boxes of photographs and make timelines. "I appreciate the thought," she said, choosing her words carefully, "but you can't just rustle up a collection."

Reame sent her a smile that reached her toes. "Wanna bet?"

Later that morning Lachlyn found herself walking past the exquisitely decorated windows of Ballantyne's on Fifth, her head covered in a burgundy floppy hat, oversize sunglasses on her face. Reame, dressed in faded jeans and a battered leather jacket, kept his hand on her lower back, his eyes constantly scanning the sidewalk.

Lachlyn wanted a closer look at a magnificent pearl and diamond choker in the display window but Reame wouldn't let her stop. "What's the hurry?" she demanded. "It's Sunday, the day of rest."

"Although it's early, this is also the busiest street in Manhattan and the chances of you being recognized are stratospheric. I'd like to get you off the street."

"I'd like breakfast," Lachlyn grumbled. After their discussion about her job back at his apartment, Reame had left the kitchen, headed into his den and closed the door. Taking that as a sign that he didn't want to be disturbed, and that breakfast wasn't high on his list of priorities, Lachlyn had taken her coffee onto his amazing balcony and watched Midtown rumble to life. Fifteen minutes later, Reame had emerged and told her that they were going out.

And he still hadn't fed her.

Lachlyn tried to ignore her growling stomach as Reame took her hand and stepped up to the doorway of Ballantyne's on Fifth. The door clicked open and Reame stood back to let her walk through the door first.

Because the store was opening to the public in fifteen minutes, the iconic shop was empty, blissfully quiet, with just one staff member behind the far counter. Gemstones and jewelry glittered and sparkled from their beds in the art deco display cabinets. The lighting was subtle, expensive but most of all flattering, to the customers and to the product. Tasteful and expensive artworks lined the wall and there were vases of lilies on pedestals in each corner. Lachlyn inhaled deeply and held her breath, lifting her eyebrows when she caught Reame looking at her.

"What are you doing?"

Lachlyn released her breath and lifted one shoulder. "I just love the smell of fresh flowers." She looked around and lifted her hands. "What are we doing here?"

"You'll see," Reame replied, doing his Mr. Mysterious thing. He reached for her hand and tugged her across the store, heading for a door discreetly marked Staff Only.

"Please tell me that whatever you are up to involves food," Lachlyn begged.

He grinned. "Stop whining, woman." Reame punched in the code on the access panel and then pushed open the heavy reinforced door.

"You have the access code to Ballantyne's?"

"It's a temporary code, valid for eight hours," Reame explained as they headed toward two elevators at the end of the hallway. But she still didn't understand why she was here and, more important, why he wasn't feeding her instead of taking her on a tour of the back rooms of Ballantyne International.

Before she could make another demand for an explanation, Reame stopped in front of the smaller of the two elevators. The bigger elevator was standard, with up and down arrows, but its smaller sibling had another of those damn keypads Reame was so fond of. Reame put in a code, the doors opened and they stepped inside the small box. It was way too small for two people, Lachlyn thought, her shoulder pressing into Reame's bicep. Reame placed his hand on her hip and shifted so that her back was to his front. The doors whispered closed and Reame reached past her to hit the last button in a row.

Conscious of his hand on her hip, his hard body behind her, Lachlyn tried to regulate her breathing. She could smell his sweet breath, could feel his hard chest against her back. If she pushed her bottom back she could rub against his...

Lachlyn released a huge sigh and at the same time her stomach growled, filling the small space with its demands for food.

Reame's low laugh brushed her hair. "Hungry?"

"That's what I've been telling you!" Lachlyn spun around to glare at him. Not having anywhere else to put her hands, she slapped them on his chest. "You promised me breakfast!"

Reame lifted his hand and with one finger, pushed a bang off her face. "This is better, I promise."

His eyes dipped to her mouth and he bent his finger to rub his knuckle over the ridge of her cheekbone. "You have the most beautiful skin," Reame murmured, his voice husky. "It's pure cream."

Lachlyn pushed her face into his hand, just like a cat begging to be scratched. Reame moved his thumb across her lower lip. He pressed his thumb into the center of her lip and released a heartfelt groan. Reame rested his forehead on hers.

"You're a client, Lachlyn."

"Not really," Lachlyn whispered as the elevator stopped. She felt a cool blast of air on her back, indicating that the doors were open.

"Yeah, you are. And if you weren't, you're still my best friend's little sister."

"Not that, either," Lachlyn said. Well, she wasn't, not in the truest sense of the word. She was someone they'd just met. A sister implied that you had a history together, shared memories of a childhood spent together. She and the Ballantyne siblings would never be closer than what they currently were. She'd never allow it. She wasn't that brave. Or stupid.

"Thirdly, I only want to fool around and you're not the fool-around type," Reame said, keeping his voice low.

Lachlyn narrowed her eyes, annoyed. "That's a pretty big assumption, Jepsen. Maybe a red-hot, brief affair is exactly what I want, the only thing I need."

Such a lie but worth it if it wiped that smirk off his face…

Reame stepped back and had the audacity to deepen his smile. "So you are telling me that we could have wild sex in the limo on the way to dinner with your siblings and when we arrived at The Den, you could act like nothing happened? Cool, composed, not giving the smallest hint that I'd just had you screaming my name ten minutes before?"

Well, when he put it like that… Lachlyn scowled. "No, I couldn't pull that off." Partially because she'd never had a proper orgasm before. She released a heavy sigh, knowing that she wasn't fooling him. "I'm not that sophisticated. Is that your definition of wild sex? Limo sex?"

"I have others."

Lachlyn blushed at the undisguised passion in his eyes.

"I'm attracted to you, Lachlyn. I'm not going to deny that, but you're not what I'm looking for."

"And that is?'

"Uncomplicated, easy, someone who just wants to have a good time. I want to be able to jump onto a dating app, to call someone at ten at night, someone who would be keen to have a drink, hit a club and then her bedroom. I want to be able to leave when we're done, guilt-free, and not have to stress about calling her the next morning. Or ever again," Reame said, putting more distance between them. "Right now I need a woman I don't have to worry about, whose feelings aren't going to be hurt if I don't call or text. I want the freedom to not have to worry about her. I'm taking a break from responsibility."

His mouth was spouting one thing but behind his bravado, she sensed a sliver of fear. This man had his own demons. "That's not you," Lachlyn said, her words falling into the silence between them.

"What do you mean?" Reame barked, nudging her out of the elevator.

Lachlyn stepped into a well-lit, stark hallway and looked around. On her right, cardboard boxes abutted a heavy, partially open steel door.

"Where are we?" Lachlyn asked, her nose immediately picking up the odors of paper and age, dust and damp.

"In the basement," Reame retorted. Lachlyn started to move toward the door but Reame caught her elbow and halted her progress. "What did you mean, Lachlyn?"

Oh God, she didn't want to talk about this anymore. She wasn't a fan of people psychoanalyzing her so she tried not to do it to other people. Reame was calm and controlled, strong-willed and dutiful. He seemed to like organization and structure. He wasn't impulsive or impetuous and she really couldn't see him in a club environment, buying drinks and spinning lines.

"That club-hopping, free-wheelin' guy isn't who you are. Neither is the have-sex-in-the-limo guy. It's too chaotic."

"You don't know me."

"Fair point," Lachlyn conceded. "But I find it interesting that you use the words *I* and *want* a lot... 'I want to do this, I want to do that.' You're good-looking, rich, successful. So why aren't you doing it?"

Lachlyn pushed her hand through her hair, and the

corners of her mouth lifted. "I respect the fact that I'm
not your type and I'm okay with it. God knows that my
life is complicated enough at the moment. Can I just ask
one last thing?"

Reame's expression hardened and she saw impatience
flash in his eyes. He was fully uncomfortable with this
topic but he was too polite to ask her to shut the hell up.

"Is there food behind door number one?"

The last and only time he'd visited this basement storage area was when he was first employed by Connor, a
few weeks after he was discharged from the army. Connor had a rather fluid idea of what a bodyguard should
do and wasn't afraid to add extraneous duties to his job
description. He'd picked up dry cleaning, occasionally
acted as chauffeur to Connor's lady friends, done some
heavy lifting. He hadn't minded. Connor had paid him a
hefty salary that'd allowed him to clear the most pressing
debts his dad had left behind and allowed him to catch up
on his mom's mortgage payments for her house.

He'd accompanied Connor to this room and his boss
had told him to find a book of hand-drawn jewelry designs from the '50s. Hetty Clark-Grimbly wanted him to
re-create the engagement ring he designed for her mother,
which she'd lost while swimming off a private yacht in
the Med. *Find the book, dear boy,* he'd said.

The dear boy had searched for two days solid through
generations of Ballantyne crap before Connor blithely
told him that he'd found the book in the study at The
Den, the day before.

Reame was fond of Connor but he'd come close to
throttling him that day. The massive room was even fuller
today than back then, boxes and odd bits of furniture
scattered across the cold concrete floor. One corner of

the room held props and old window decorations, there were paintings leaning against the walls. But mostly there were boxes and more boxes.

Messy, disorganized, dusty…it offended Reame's organized military soul. But Lachlyn looked like she had stepped into the lost Library of Alexandria.

"Lachlyn Latimore, meet the Ballantynes' junk room," Reame said, leaning his shoulder into the door frame. "Your new project."

Lachlyn blinked at him, her eyes foggy. "What?"

"The idea popped into my head when we were talking about your work at the NYPL," Reame explained. "As you might have realized, I spend a lot of time with the Ballantyne siblings. Over the years, there has been a raging argument about what to do with this room, specifically the stuff in this room. They keep promising to get it done, that they have to sort this mess out, that the Ballantyne history—most of which is in here—has to be preserved. Every couple of years, they traipse down here, determined to sort it out."

"Then they take one look at it and find something more important to do?"

Reame nodded. "Exactly." Reame walked farther into the room and scowled. "God, it's a mess. I don't remember it being this bad but when I spoke to Beck earlier, he said that early last year, a container of boxes came from the Ballantyne jewelry store in London, as they were running out of space. The store above us opened in the 1890s. London opened a few months later. So some of this stuff is old."

"What sort of materials are we talking about, Reame? Letters? Accounts? Diaries?"

"I asked Beck that and he said anything and everything. Signage, designs, smalls. Personal and professional stuff from the Ballantynes' past." Reame shoved his hands into the back pockets of his jeans. "You need something to keep you occupied in the day, Lach, and that would help me. This building is like Fort Knox. There's no safer place for you to be. I can drop you off in the morning, pick you up in the evening and you can putter around in here to your heart's content." Reame kept his voice low, reminding himself not to push. "You'd also get a really good idea of the family you are now part of."

Lachlyn rocked on her heels. "And the siblings are happy about me doing this?"

Reame laughed. "Happy? Well, handing over first-born children and sacrifices to the gods were mentioned if you took on this task." Reame rubbed the back of his neck, wondering how to frame his next comment. He wasn't a subtle guy so he'd just come out and say it. "They said that they'd pay you to do it."

Lachlyn's back stiffened and those bright blue eyes turned frosty. "In addition to the forty million?"

That much? Holy hell. Reame didn't react. "Can I point out that all the Ballantynes work for the company and they all get paid a monthly salary to do that? Linc offering you money to do a job, a job you have the skills for, is not an insult."

Lachlyn lowered her eyes and he saw the pink tinge of embarrassment on her face. He'd been totally wrong when he assumed that she was just out for the Ballantyne cash; that had been a major misjudgment on his part. Lachlyn was turning out to be deeper and more complicated than he'd expected.

And far more perceptive than he'd expected. Her earlier question about why he kept talking about having this hot affair, this responsibility-free lifestyle and not doing what he said rocked him. He wasn't the type of guy who said one thing and did another so why hadn't he gone on a date yet? What was holding him back? He had the time and the opportunity…he just needed to get his ass into gear.

Make a connection, take a girl out for a drink, to dinner. Get laid. *This isn't nuclear fusion, Jepsen.*

And none of those plans had to, or would, include Lachlyn. He turned to look at her and smiled when he saw her sitting on the dusty floor, quickly sorting through a pile of papers, abruptly pushing her bangs behind her ears when they obscured what she was reading.

Reame pulled out his vibrating cell phone and looked down at the flashing screen. He opened the Ballantyne family chat group and skimmed through the multiple messages.

Did Lachlyn take the bait? Is she going to do it? Please tell me she said yes.

Reame looked at Lachlyn again and his heart skipped a beat when he caught her tracing a finger over a ragged-edged photograph. "Lach?" he quietly called.

She didn't respond so he tried again. "Lach? Breakfast time."

Lachlyn made a humming sound in response and he watched, amused, as her hand dipped into the box next to her, pulling out a wad of papers as she perused the document in her hand.

She'd forgotten about him and her growling stomach. Reame quickly typed a message on his phone.

It looks like you've got yourselves an archivist.

Seven

Later that week, Reame knocked on the door of the guest suite, expecting it to swing open and to see Lachlyn's wide smile. When the door remained closed, he frowned and knocked again. There was nothing but silence behind the walls so he turned the knob and stepped inside. He found Lachlyn sitting on the white sofa still in her pajamas, a pile of papers on her lap.

Giving her a closer look, Reame realized that her eyes were red-rimmed. She looked exhausted. "Hey."

"Hey back." Lachlyn's smile didn't hold a fraction of its normal wattage.

He crossed the apartment and sat down on the cold, white coffee table in front of her. "Did you sleep last night?"

"Not much," Lachlyn replied.

"Are you sick?"

Lachlyn shook her head and looked down at her flannel pajamas. "I'm sorry, I'm running late. Can you give me twenty minutes?" She sighed and started to swing her legs off the couch, her toes tipped in shell pink. Pretty toes, Reame thought. The middle one sported a toe ring. Sweet and sexy.

Reame felt the action in his pants and ignored his trigger-happy junk. He placed his hand on her slim thigh to keep her lightly pinned to the sofa. He shouldn't ask, he should keep his distance, but the words flew out of his mouth despite his best intentions. "What's the matter, Lach?"

Lachlyn picked up the sheaf of papers, straightened them by banging them to her knee and slid them back into the folder. "Linc hired me a lawyer to go through the Ballantyne offer, to answer any questions I might have that I don't feel comfortable asking them directly."

That was Linc, Reame thought, cool, capable and hell-bent on making the situation as easy as possible. "I have a meeting with her at nine thirty." Lachlyn grimaced. "Sorry, I meant to tell you but I forgot. If that doesn't suit you, I can reschedule."

The look she sent him was full of hope and Reame knew that she was trying to avoid the meeting, possibly trying to avoid the whole inheritance saga, as well. He was a confront-and-deal-with-it type of guy. He didn't avoid situations and conflicts.

Lachlyn, he suspected, did. She also avoided people. He'd heard that the Ballantyne women were desperate to take her out for a girls' night—though how much fun three pregnant women could have was debatable—but Lachlyn kept finding an excuse not to go. She was the most solitary person he'd ever met, content to spend hours on her own in the Ballantyne basement. After taking her home, she slipped into this guest apartment and, because he had to approve any visitors to this floor, he knew that no one had visited her since she moved in a week earlier. Her cell phone was monitored to keep track of the crazies and yeah, he'd peeked at her call logs. A few text messages from the Ballantyne women, Linc, two calls from Sage that didn't last more than thirty seconds each and a longer call from her brother Tyce.

The woman was a self-contained island…

If she couldn't talk to her future sister-in-law and brother, then there wasn't much chance of her opening up to a lawyer. And she needed to—this wasn't Monopoly money they were dealing with. "You need to meet with the lawyer, Lach."

Lachlyn shook her head. "Why? It seems pretty simple…they want to give me money and pass on a share of the assets."

"You make it sound like they are trying to give you a nasty infection, Lach. This isn't a bad thing."

Lachlyn jumped up and walked over to the coffeepot in the kitchen. Reame couldn't help noticing that she was braless and that her breasts were round and perfect. *Ah, crap.*

Lachlyn lifted the coffeepot in his direction. He nodded. What the hell, at least holding a cup of coffee would give him something to do with his hands.

Reame waited for Lachlyn to bring his coffee over before gesturing for her to sit down. She did, perching on the end of the uncomfortable-looking cushion. Reame picked up his coffee mug and held it loosely between his hands. "So, why are you hesitating about taking their offer? What's stopping you?"

Reame knew that Lachlyn was thinking about changing the subject and wondered whether she'd answer. "People think it's so easy, that I should just accept their offer and slip into their family. They think that I should just jump at the chance at being part of the Ballantyne legacy."

Wow, okay, that was a genuine answer and a whole bunch of honesty he didn't expect.

"So, what's the problem, Lach?"

Lachlyn lifted her feet up to the cushion and wrapped her arms around her bent legs. "I don't know what being part of a family means, how to act, what to do." More honesty, Reame thought. This was Lachlyn raw and unedited and he felt, yeah, touched, that this intensely private woman was opening up to him.

"Tyce and I grew up hard, Reame, like really hard. It was very tough and my mom just managed to bring in just enough to cover the basics. At any given time, we were a tiny crisis away from living on the streets. My mom would come home from work and collapse in a heap, and I'm not exaggerating. She'd fall down, onto her bed or the couch and she wouldn't move, frequently she wouldn't speak, until she had to get up the next morning for work."

Reame made a sympathetic sound in the back of his throat but kept it down. Sympathy, he knew, would not be appreciated. "Tyce got me to school and, when I was smaller, organized for me to stay with our neighbors, at the library, in shelters. Wherever he could stash me, he would—"

"There're ten years between you. Why didn't he look after you himself?" Reame asked, confused.

"Because he was constantly hustling for cash. That crack between income and expenses was sliver-thin. Tyce had to make up the shortfall. He washed windows, cars, sold his sketches…he did what he could while trying to look after me," Lachlyn explained. "Between the ages of three and maybe six or seven, I didn't know whose house

I would be going to that day, whether I would know the caretaker or not. All I knew was that I had to be good, stay invisible and wait for Tyce to pick me up in the afternoon. If he was one minute late, I would start to panic."

Lachlyn looked away, staring at a point past his head. Reame rested his forearms on his thighs, not dropping his eyes from her face. If he did, he'd lose her. There was more to this story and Reame knew that if she didn't tell him now, she might never.

"My biggest dream was for a family, some normality. I held on to that dream, lived it, breathed it, was obsessed by it. Around the age of fifteen I finally accepted that it wasn't ever going to happen and I was cool with it."

Oh, now that was a lie, Reame thought. She wasn't cool with it then and she most definitely wasn't now. He really wanted to know what happened to destroy that dream. "Twelve years later, the thing I most wanted is mine for the taking but I can't accept it. I disconnected from that dream and I can't go back there."

Her foot was a scant inch from his hand so Reame rubbed his thumb over the ball of her toe, trying to comfort her in a way that wouldn't spook her. Because this girl was already spooked to the max.

"I think that you not only disconnected from the dream, you disconnected, period. One day you might tell me what happened to cause that."

Panic flashed in her eyes and Reame cursed himself. *Too fast, too soon, idiot.* "It's easier to be alone, Reame."

"But far less fun," Reame countered.

"The Ballantynes are the most in-tune, most interconnected people I know. They communicate silently, through laughter and their eyes, their facial expressions. They all seem to operate on their own special bandwidth," Lachlyn said, waving her hands around. "You know what I mean. You do it, as well…with them.

"I can't be like that, operate like that. It's…overwhelming," Lachlyn added.

"Tyce seems to be fitting in okay," Reame stated, keeping his tone and expression calm.

Lachlyn scoffed. "He's in love with Sage. He'd do and say or be anything for her."

"Are you saying that he is faking his friendship with your brothers, with me?"

Lachlyn rubbed the back of her neck. "No, of course I'm not! I think that this is the first time he's had friends, real friends."

"So, if he has managed to overcome his crappy childhood and find his place in the family, why can't you?" Reame asked, crossing his feet at his ankles and looking at her over the rim of his coffee cup.

"Because I'm not as strong as him, as brave." Lachlyn whipped back and Reame saw her frustration.

"It's your family, Lach. It's supposed to be the one place where you don't have to be strong or brave. It's the one place where you can let your guard down, where you don't have to be a self-contained, independent entity. Someplace where someone else can take up the slack."

Lachlyn sent him a smile so sad that it raised blisters on his heart. "I know that you probably won't understand this, but the loneliest place you can be is in a place where expectations aren't fulfilled, where the people who are supposed to love you the most can decimate you without even trying."

Reame reached out to grab her, wanting to hold her, to wipe the devastation from her face. But Lachlyn was too quick for him—she scrambled away and hurried into the hall. "I'll meet you downstairs in thirty minutes."

Staring at his empty hands, Reame cursed. He jumped up and easily caught up with her, holding her delicate wrist in his big hand. He was about to speak when her eyes connected with his and he saw her embarrassment, her fear and intense vulnerability. Bombs and bullets had never shaken him but she made him weak at the knees.

"I can't talk anymore, Reame. Please don't ask me to," Lachlyn whispered, staring down at his brown hand holding her white arm.

Reame stroked her skin with his thumb before releasing her. He wouldn't force her, he couldn't. Force was not part of his vocabulary when it came to women. So he changed the subject.

"I need this guest suite back for a couple of days. I have a high-value target who needs a place to hide out while we set up a safe house for him."

Lachlyn blinked a few times. "Safe house?"

"Yeah, he's testifying against a drug cartel and he doesn't trust the US Marshal Service to keep him safe. He's an idiot, those guys are awesome, but the guy has cash to burn and he's hired us to look after his sorry ass. So you're going to move into my guest bedroom for a few nights. Can you deal?"

He expected her to run, to insist that she go to a hotel, but after panic flashed through her eyes, he saw a touch of resignation. Maybe it was exhaustion or maybe she was finally beginning to feel more comfortable around him. Her opening up had him leaning toward the latter.

Amusement flashed in Lachlyn's eyes, surprising him. She lifted a cheeky eyebrow. "Won't I cramp your style?"

Reame narrowed his eyes at her. "I think I can cope for a few nights."

Lachlyn grinned at him and he was relieved to see

the pain in her eyes dissipating. "So have you managed to have limo sex yet?"

Well, no. Nor any other type of sex.

"You're definitely a Ballantyne," Reame muttered as he turned to walk back to the front door. It was either walk away or kiss the hell out of her. "Just another pain in my ass."

That evening, Lachlyn dumped her suitcases in Reame's guest bedroom, plugged her phone in to charge and walked into the living area of his apartment. Thirty seconds later she heard the door to Reame's bedroom open and she turned to watch him cross the floor. His hunter green T-shirt accentuated his broad shoulders, the hem of the sleeves tight around his biceps. Straight-legged track pants rode low on his hips and made his legs seem longer. He looked spectacular.

He was also, obviously, going out. So why was she feeling disappointed? Being alone was what she specialized in, wasn't it?

Lachlyn watched Reame walk into the kitchen to open the stainless steel fridge. "I've got wine and beer and water, some fruit juice."

Lachlyn heard the slow roll of her stomach and waited for him to mention food. "I really need to get some food in but help yourself to anything you find." He slammed the fridge door closed and picked up a black sweatshirt that lay on the kitchen counter, pulling it over his head.

Lachlyn perched on the arm of a leather couch, feeling jittery and a little resentful. Who went out the first night they had a guest? Except that she wasn't a guest, she was an obligation, someone Reame was helping for Linc's sake. She was safe in his apartment, in this building. He'd fulfilled his end of the bargain.

Reame bent over to pick up a pair of trainers and Lachlyn was jolted out of her pity party when his pants pulled tight across his perfect, perfect ass. She touched her cheek with the backs of her fingers, felt the lava under her skin and frantically searched for the smallest drop of moisture in her mouth.

Oh...oh, wow.

Reame straightened and walked over to the opposite sofa, sitting down to pull on his shoes. He lifted his head to look at her and, damn, caught the lust on her face. His eyes narrowed, his cheeks flushed and his fingers stilled. Electricity danced over her skin, blood raced from her brain into her heart and she felt her womb contract once, then again. She wanted him, Lachlyn thought, dazed. In his hot gaze she saw his tanned hands on her light skin, could taste him on her tongue. Unconsciously, her legs spread and her core throbbed.

Reame swiped his hand over his face and released a low, dark curse. He stood up abruptly and Lachlyn saw his erection tenting his pants. He released another harsh, pithy curse before stomping toward his bedroom.

Right, so he wasn't happy about whatever was bubbling between them. She got that, she wasn't too thrilled herself. Lachlyn pushed the balls of her hands into her forehead. She was living in his space—she'd have to see a lot more of him. How were they going to keep their hands off each other? She needed to keep her distance from him—sleeping with Linc's best friend was a spectacularly bad idea.

Oh, Bitch Fate, why him and why now? What are you trying to teach me?

Lachlyn heard the hard knock against his door and dropped her hands. Since Reame had told her that she shouldn't, under any circumstances, open the door, she stayed where she was. "Get that, won't you?" Reame yelled from the bedroom.

Lachlyn stood up slowly and walked into the hall, checking her reflection in the mirror over the hall table. Bright eyes, flushed cheeks, wet mouth. Yeah, she looked as turned on as she felt. Irritated, she wiped her mouth with the back of her hand and ordered herself to get a grip.

You are not going to have sex with Reame Jepsen, she told herself. She was to live here until the press coverage died down, then she was going to exit his and the Ballantynes' lives. She turned the knob and pulled the door open. *Let's repeat this—you are definitely not going to sleep—*

"What are you mumbling about, Lach?"

Lachlyn looked up at her half brother, dressed in athletic gear. He held two boxes of pizza in one hand and Sage, as per usual, was tucked into his side.

"Uh, hi," Lachlyn said, standing back to let them in. *People*, she thought. *Damn.* "Come on in."

"Reame and I are going to work out," Tyce said, thrusting the box of pizza into Sage's hand. "Sage is hanging with you."

Lachlyn, feeling Reame's presence behind her, put her back to her brother and Sage and sent him a "save me" look. He shook his head before rolling his eyes. He placed his hands on her shoulders and dipped his head to kiss her cheek and whisper in her ear. "It's pizza. There's wine in the fridge. A little conversation with a nice person. You can do this, Latimore."

Lachlyn glared at his back as he followed Tyce into the hall. When they disappeared around the corner, she turned back to Sage, who was standing in the doorway, tears in her eyes.

"I can go, if you'd prefer," Sage stated quietly. "Reame said that there was no food in the house so I'll leave you the pizza."

Lachlyn bit her bottom lip. She hadn't meant to hurt Sage but she wasn't good at surprises. She didn't like to be ambushed. She liked to have time to prepare...

Lachlyn heard Reame's voice in her ear. *It's not war, Latimore. It's Sage, your brother's fiancée, the mother of your niece. Or nephew.*

Lachlyn shook her head and made herself reach for Sage's hand. "No, come on in. Please."

She couldn't keep ignoring the Ballantynes, they wouldn't let her, so she supposed that she was going to have to learn to deal with them. She'd have a slice of pizza, politely listen to Sage's arguments on why she should take the money, she'd agree to disagree, and then Sage would want to tell her about Connor, about the father she never knew. Lachlyn wondered where Reame kept his aspirin; she knew that she'd need a few before the night was over.

Sage's hand on her arm halted her progress back into Reame's apartment. "Lach? Can we forget, just for tonight, about the money and Connor, and me being a Ballantyne? Can I just be the girl who wants to get to know her fiancé's sister?"

Lachlyn smiled and immediately her headache receded. "That sounds so good to me."

Eight

Reame felt the feminine hand land on his thigh and looked down at the painted pink fingernails and the expensive rings decorating that hand. It was inching higher up his leg and he waited for his junk to react, his interest to form.

Nope. Nothing.

Crap.

Reame turned his head to look at his date and wondered what the hell was wrong with him. He'd met Gretchen a few weeks ago on a dating app and had invited her out for a drink. Over a couple of beers, he'd found the forensic psychologist fascinating. Intelligence and sexy was a killer combination. Within an hour, they'd both known that if she hadn't been flying out that night, they would've hooked up in her hotel room for a night long on pleasure and short on regrets. She was based in Seattle but she crisscrossed the country and would like to, she'd told him, have dinner with him the next time she was in town.

And by dinner she meant food followed by hot, no-strings sex.

Now here they were, in a taxi, headed toward her hotel. The dinner had been good, her company interesting, but his body wasn't cooperating. Gretchen was tall, buxom and confident and, he was sure, knew her way around a man's body. She was what he'd been wanting, looking for, but the thought of kissing her mouth, palming her breast made him feel a little nauseous.

Maybe he was coming down with something.

Gretchen lifted her hand off his thigh and half turned in her seat, crossing her spectacular legs. "Are you okay?"

Reame lifted one eyebrow at her very female question. "I'm fine, why?"

"Well, we had a lovely meal and we enjoyed the conversation." She tipped her head to the side, her eyes roaming over his features. "At least, I enjoyed myself."

"Dinner was fine, Gretchen."

"Fine. Just what every girl wants to hear," Gretchen replied, her tone cooling. She tapped her clutch bag against her knee in obvious frustration. "I thought we were on the same page, Reame."

So had he. Reame sighed, thought about fudging his answer and decided not to, that Gretchen's confidence deserved the truth. He pushed his hair away from his eyes and tried to smile. "I did enjoy dinner, Gretchen. You have a fascinating job and an interesting life. You're a fascinating woman."

"A month ago, if I hadn't had a flight to catch, we would've spent the night together."

"Yeah, we would've," Reame admitted.

"But that's not going to happen tonight, is it?"

Again, it would be so much easier to fudge. But she deserved better. "It could," he admitted. He shrugged and her thin eyebrows pulled together in a frown. "I'm a guy—touch me in a couple of places and it could happen."

"But it wouldn't be about me."

If they had sex, he'd make it good for her—of course he would. He'd get off and she would get off and afterward there wouldn't be anything to say because she'd know that he'd been thinking of someone else while kissing and touching her. Women were spooky clever that way.

"So, you're telling me that I'm not your first choice tonight."

Reame picked up her hand and kissed her fingers. "I'm telling you that I think that you deserve to have someone fully there in the moment with you, enjoying you. I'm not that guy, not tonight."

Reame could see the offer of them trying this again when she returned to the city hovering on her lips and he hoped, prayed that she didn't utter the words. He didn't want to tell her that he wouldn't take her call, that their moment had passed. The words were about to tumble out when Gretchen's lips firmed and she nodded once, then again.

Fortuitously, her nodding coincided with the taxi pulling to a stop outside the entrance to her hotel. "I'll walk you to the door," Reame said.

He sighed when Gretchen opened her own door, ignoring the hand he held out. She seemed to realize that asking him not to walk her to the entrance was futile so he matched her long strides to where the doorman stood, the door open for them. Gretchen turned, placed her hand on his arm and her cheek against his.

"Thanks for dinner, Reame. I'm sorry this didn't work out."

"Me too." He genuinely was. Taking Gretchen to bed would've been a hundred times simpler than dealing with the blonde bundle of craziness he'd left in his apartment.

The one he actually wanted, consistently craved.

Sitting in Reame's den, Lachlyn dipped her hand into a bag of chocolate-covered peanuts and as she lifted the handful of sweets to her mouth, she heard the slam of Reame's front door, heavy footsteps crossing the floor of his apartment. Lachlyn muted the television and looked at her watch; Reame was back early from his date.

Lachlyn had thought that she'd spend a sleepless night listening for him to return, if he returned at all. So she was very surprised to hear that he was back and shortly after ten. Hearing his footsteps approaching the den, Lachlyn rolled the packet closed and shoved it down the side of the cushion. She stared at the TV, pretending total fascination. Reame's ego was healthy enough—he did not need to know that she'd spent the past three hours in agony, imagining him eating and drinking and flirting.

Lachlyn dragged her eyes off the TV as he sat down on the couch next to her, propping his flat-soled boots up onto the designer coffee table. He looked amazing in dark jeans, an expensive white shirt and soft green jacket.

"Hi. Good night?" Lachlyn asked, proud of her vague, not-terribly-interested tone.

"Yeah."

Lachlyn felt Reame's eyes on her face and she turned, sucked up a smile and returned her attention to the television. Questions she refused to utter bounced around her brain. *Why are you home so early? Did you skip dinner*

*and go straight for dessert? Did you kiss her, flirt with
her? God, I'm sure I can smell her perfume...*

"Are you actually watching this?" Reame asked.

"Yeah, it's fascinating," Lachlyn replied.

"Really? Beginner's taxidermy? Are you kidding me?"

Ew! Seriously? Lachlyn focused on the screen where a
red-faced, sweating man scraped at an animal skin with
a flat blade. Gross. Reame snatched the remote control
from her hand, flipped over to a sports channel and held
out his hand, bending his fingers into a "give it up" gesture.

"What?" Lachlyn asked, trying for innocence. If she
handed over her bag of chocolates, he'd polish them off
in five seconds.

"The candy you are hiding."

Lachlyn widened her eyes and opened her palms.
"What candy? I haven't been eating candy."

Reame's thumb swiped her bottom lip and he lifted his
thumb to his mouth and sucked. Lachlyn's heart stopped,
fell out of her rib cage and flopped onto the floor. Unable
to keep her eyes off his, all that gorgeous green, she was
caught unaware when Reame's hand shot past her hip to
pull the packet from its hiding place. Lachlyn lunged for
it but Reame held it up and away from her, his long arms
keeping it out of her reach.

"Give it back! That's mine." Lachlyn stood on her
knees and reached for the bag, placing her hand on his
shoulder to keep her balance as she leaned across his
torso to retrieve her chocolate treat.

"C'mon, be nice and share them with me."

"That's my dinner because I didn't eat at one of the
city's best restaurants tonight." Lachlyn lunged, toppled
and Reame's arm banded around her waist, pulling her

close. It felt natural to swing her knee across his lap to straddle him.

Natural but dangerous.

"You had chocolate for dinner?" Reame asked, lowering his arm.

"You don't have much in the fridge and I still don't know what the security procedure is for deliveries. Plus I didn't want to chance it because I heard your high-value client come in."

"Sorry, sweetheart," Reame said, his hand settling on her hip. He seemed quite happy for her to sit on his lap, quite at ease with the fact that her core was resting on his rock-hard erection. She licked her lips. "What did you have for supper?"

Reame's eyes darted to her mouth and back up to her eyes. "Steak, veggies, salad."

She had to ask because they couldn't take this further if he'd so much as kissed his date. "And for dessert?" she whispered.

"Are you asking me if I had sex with my date?"

"I'm asking if anything happened earlier tonight because if it did I'm walking out and going to bed...alone."

Reame's hands tightened on her hips and the packet scratched her skin. "Nothing happened."

"Why not?" Lachlyn whispered.

"Because she wasn't who I wanted." Reame tossed the packet of peanuts onto the couch and reached up to clasp her face. "I thought about it, I admit that. I wanted to burn this crazy I have for you out of my system and I intended to sleep with her. But I couldn't pull the trigger."

Lachlyn lowered her forehead to rest it on his. "I'm glad. I know there are a hundred reasons why we shouldn't but I need to burn the crazy away, too. Maybe when we have we can go back to normal. I can spend

some time thinking of whether I want to be a Ballantyne or not—"

"You are a Ballantyne," Reame murmured.

Lachlyn ignored his interruption. "—and you can go
back to sleeping with wild women."

That was the plan but she doubted that it would work
out that way. But she didn't care. She wanted this, she
wanted Reame, she wanted *one* night exploring this fire-
hot passion that only he'd ever roused in her. She wanted
to know what bliss felt like, whether those Big O's she'd
read about were as magical as everybody said they could
be if you found a man who knew what he was doing.

Reame, she was convinced, knew what he was doing.

Reame's thumbs caressed her cheekbones, his eyebrows pulled into a slight frown. "You sure about this,
Lach?"

Lachlyn shook her head. "No. But I want this. I want
you."

Three words—*I want you*—and Lachlyn saw the capitulation in his eyes. Reame moved one hand to the back
of her skull and pulled her head down as he reached up
to take her mouth in a kiss that was as powerful as it was
sensational. Heat, red-hot and fizzing, skittered along her
skin, igniting every nerve ending. She wanted to wait,
to take this slow, but she couldn't. The sensations he
pulled from her were too insistent, too demanding to be
ignored. Wrenching her mouth off his, Lachlyn grabbed
the hem of her T-shirt with both hands, pulling the cotton
up and over her head. She dropped her shirt to the floor
and watched Reame's eyes darken as they landed on her
chest, her breasts covered by a plain white cotton bra.
She wished she'd worn her prettier lingerie, something
far sexier, but judging from Reame's hot gaze, he didn't
seem to mind or notice. His big hand easily covered her,

his thumb swiping her beaded nub, and Lachlyn groaned, instinctively grinding down on his hard length.

Needing to get her hands on his skin, her fumbling fingers undid the buttons on his shirt and she hastily pushed away the fabric and his jacket, finally connecting with warm, male skin. So different from her own smooth skin, Lachlyn thought, her hand drifting through the light hair on his chest, over flat nipples, down that ridged stomach. She heard Reame's gasp and finally understood the power of being a woman, how good it felt to make a strong, powerful, alpha male groan. And want. And need.

She wanted more, she needed more…now. This was taking far too long and she was scared she'd lose her courage. Lachlyn scooted off his lap, pushed her yoga pants down her legs and stepped out of them, using her toes to push her thick socks off her feet. Damn, but her white cotton briefs and bra would have to go, too. Lachlyn reached behind her back and was about to unsnap her bra when Reame leaned forward, gripped her hips and placed his hot mouth on her stomach, his tongue writing words on her skin. "Sweetheart, slow down."

He didn't understand; she was vibrating with need, terrified that if she stopped, hesitated, that the rush would fade away, that she'd lose the feeling.

Lachlyn wrapped her arms around Reame's head, pushing her fingers through his silky hair as his fingers danced around her back. With ease, he unhooked her bra and with one finger pulled the garment from her body. Instead of touching her, Reame blew on her nipple, nuzzled the bud with his nose. "You're prettier than I imagined, and I have a damn fine imagination."

"Kiss me, Reame," Lachlyn murmured.

And finally, he did. Reame's tongue curled around her nipple as his other hand cupped her bottom, his fingers running from her ass cheeks down her thighs and inside. Lachlyn opened her legs and felt one finger slide under the band of her panties, perilously close to where she craved his touch.

Lachlyn begged him to touch her, all pretense at pride out of the window. Reame pushed her panties down her thighs and then his fingers were in her cleft, seeking out her point of pleasure. Masculine fingers, knowing fingers, slid inside her as his thumb continued to caress her and Lachlyn felt her orgasm building, felt herself reaching for the impossible. She sucked in her breath and her chest heaved and because she had no words, she guided his mouth back to her nipple and urged him to suck. Pinpoints of pleasure danced behind her eyes, her womb throbbed and she knew she was close, as close as she'd ever been.

But she didn't want her first orgasm to be had alone—this was something she wanted Reame to feel, as well. She wanted him to share in her pleasure, for her to be a part of his.

"Condom?" Lachlyn rasped.

Reame nodded. "Inside pocket of my jacket."

Lachlyn slid her hand under his jacket—he was wearing far too many clothes—and dipped it into his pocket, finding and pulling free a strip of condoms. Ripping one off and apart, she pulled the latex from its wrapper and looked at it, her mind whirling. She shoved it at Reame. "My hands are trembling. You do it."

Reame glanced down at his pants still covering his erection. He moved his fingers inside her and Lachlyn gasped. "I'm a bit busy here. If you want me, you'd better free me."

Lachlyn licked her lips, attacked his belt buckle, opened the button on his jeans and pulled down the zipper. Sucking in her breath, she pushed her fingers under the band of his underwear to encounter him, smooth and oh-so-hard. Lachlyn felt dizzy. He was all male, so much more than she imagined.

And she had a good imagination.

Reame groaned and muttered a low curse. "Scoot." Lachlyn moved away and Reame shot to his feet. He kicked off his boots, removed his socks and dropped his shirt and jacket to the floor. Lachlyn, throbbing, every inch of her skin flushed with heat, sucked in her breath at the sheer perfection of his body. Broad chest—marred only by a scar on the right side of his rib cage—that ridged stomach, strong, muscled legs. And yeah, his beautiful, beautiful—

Reame yanked the condom from her grip, rolled it down his shaft and reached for her, lifting her up in one arm to walk her around the couch. Turning her to face it, he placed her hands on the back of the couch, his foot nudging her legs apart. Banding his arm around her midsection, he pulled her butt up and caressed her with his free hand, from spine to butt cheeks and between her legs.

So, this wasn't what she was expecting but it was thrilling and exciting.

"You are so damn beautiful," Reame murmured, his mouth dropping to kiss the side of her neck. "I'm going to make you mine now, Lach."

She couldn't wait. Lachlyn felt his head at her entrance, felt the push, felt herself expanding and thought yes, this was what she wanted.

"Relax, baby. You're so damn tight."

Reame's hand sneaked around her hips to play with her bead and Lachlyn liquefied. Instinctively, she pushed backward at the same time Reame surged and she felt a hit of pain before the world exploded behind her eyelids.

Reame stopped in his tracks. "What the hell—"

"Not now, dammit," Lachlyn told him, reaching backward to grip his thighs.

"Lach, I—"

"Not now!" Lachlyn yelled, pushing backward, trying to recapture that intense, supernova feeling. Reame hesitated, cursed her and plunged inside her, hot and hard and melting her from the inside out. Wanting more, wanting everything, Lachlyn tried to touch herself but Reame beat her to it, his fingers finding her, rubbing her as he bucked inside of her. Lachlyn's world exploded into tiny pinpricks of light, her stomach clenched and then she was falling, falling, rolling, touching the universe and everything in it.

From somewhere far away, she heard Reame's shout, felt his body tense and her name being called.

She didn't answer because she was still dancing on the stars.

A little while later, Lachlyn removed her fingernails from Reame's arm and winced at the half moon marks on his skin. She tried to sooth them away, absurdly conscious of Reame's hand between her legs, his shaft still buried deep inside her, the occasional shudder that ran through his body.

Reame touched his lips to her shoulders. "I'm sorry."

"I'm not," Lachlyn told him and it was the truth. For her first time, it had been magical.

"I don't understand," Reame said, keeping his voice low. "You're not a kid so I assumed…"

"Please don't make this a bigger deal than it is, Reame," Lachlyn said, keeping her voice low. "I've had fun with guys but I never dated anyone I liked enough to go this far."

Lachlyn felt Reame tense, heard his sudden intake of breath. "Lach—"

She heard the warning in his voice, the please-don't-read-anything-into-this tone. She patted his arm. "Relax, Reame, I know what this is and it's just sex. I know I'm not the wild woman you wanted but I don't plan to make any demands on you that you can't meet. I don't do personal connections, remember?"

Reame rested his cheek on her shoulder. "That was pretty wild, Lachlyn, for your first time." Reame sounded rueful so Lachlyn pulled away and turned to look at him. She flashed him a cocky grin because he seemed to need the reassurance. "I know, right?"

Reame closed his eyes and shook his head, a small smile touching his lips. Then he sighed. "Your brother is going to kill me."

"So, here's an idea—let's not tell him," Lachlyn suggested.

"He's going to take one look at me and know," Reame said, sounding mournful. "Then he's going to rip my head off."

Lachlyn pushed her hips back and, amazingly, felt him hardening inside her. She thought that men needed some time to recover... "Well, before you die, let's do this again."

Reame's laugh coated her skin in sunshine and she sighed her disappointment when he pulled away from, and out of, her. "Let's clean up and then—" he dropped a kiss on her nose "—we'll do this properly."

"I prefer improperly," Lachlyn said, missing his warmth and touch.

"You are definitely a wild woman in training," Reame

said, rueful. "And if your brother doesn't kill me, I suspect you will." He took her hand and led her to his room. "Shower then bed."

Lachlyn stopped in her tracks, tugged her hand from his and ran around the couch to pick up the packet of candy. She waved it at Reame. "I'm still hungry."

"We'll order pizza later." Reame snagged her by the waist and swept her into his arms, laughing when Lachlyn opened the bag of candy and popped one into her mouth. He watched her eat as he walked her into the bathroom. "Are you going to share?" he demanded.

He was trying to act blasé but Lachlyn could see his brain turning, knew that he was trying to work out all the angles. She meant what she'd said earlier; this wasn't a big deal. Well, it was, in the sense that the sex had been utterly delightful, but not in a what-the-hell-have-I-done? way.

"I gave you my virginity, what more do you want?" Lachlyn teased him and was relieved when his mouth quirked up. "Great sex doesn't earn you candy."

"Brat," Reame said as he lowered her to her feet.

Reame shoved his hand into the shower, flipped on the taps and covered her mouth with his. Lachlyn felt him lift her up and then he dropped her under a cold spray of water, snatching the bag out of her hands while she danced around trying to avoid the freezing deluge.

Reame tossed a handful of candy into his mouth before placing the bag on top of the bathroom cabinet, out of her reach, before turning away from her to deal with the condom. Even as she cursed him—using his height was so unfair!—she admired his broad, muscled back, his narrow hips, his truly fantastic butt.

"This water is freezing, Jepsen."

Reame turned back to her, reached past her and flipped

on the hot tap. *Right*, Lachlyn thought as hot water poured over her head, her back. She could've done that, too.

Being around Reame fried her brain and judging by the predatory look on his face as he stepped into the shower and pulled her into his arms, he was about to do it again.

She couldn't wait.

Nine

Finding his bed empty the next morning, Reame pulled on a pair of sweat pants and a ragged sweatshirt and padded out of his bedroom in search of his not-so-reluctant, no-longer-virginal lover. He rubbed his hand over his face, a part of him still not believing that the super-passionate, incredibly lusty woman in his bed was as inexperienced as she could be.

Reame considered feeling guilty about taking her so lustfully and so often but he shrugged that emotion away. Lachlyn was no shrinking violet and had been very vocal in telling him what felt good and what didn't. She was simply a woman who'd waited for a man she liked enough, was deeply attracted to before she allowed him the intimacy of sharing sex with her. And yeah, he felt super-proud that he'd been her first, that she'd taken a chance on him.

Judging by her screaming his name numerous times, he thought he'd done okay.

Reame didn't find Lachlyn in his den or in the kitchen. Booting up his coffee machine, he felt a frigid draft and looked toward the balcony that could be accessed by both bedrooms and the living area, noticing that the sliding door was slightly open. Lachlyn was outside? Holy hell, she had to be freezing. Opening the door, he saw her huddled into a chair in the corner of the balcony, a cashmere blanket wrapped around her tiny body.

"Lach?"

Lachlyn looked up at him and sent him a slow smile. Two strips of blue ran under her eyes and her face looked drawn. They'd spent much of the night making love but he'd dropped off to sleep around 3:00 a.m., Lachlyn in his arms. He was normally a light sleeper and he hadn't heard her rise. "Did you sleep at all last night?"

Lachlyn allowed the blanket to drop and he saw that she'd pulled on his thick parka, her knees tucked up under it. "I'm not a good sleeper."

So that meant no. Pulling up a chair, he faced her and touched her cold cheek with the tips of his fingers. "It's freezing out here. Let's go inside."

Lachlyn ignored that suggestion and he followed her gaze to the familiar ring lying in her palm. He picked up the ring and looked down at the intricate workmanship, his heart bumping off his rib cage. "It's Connor's ring. Linc gave it to you?"

Lachlyn nodded in reply to his question. "He told me what the ring is made from but I can't remember."

Reame ran his fingers over the surface of the ring. "Bands of Baltic amber and meteorite, separated by thin strips of platinum. I've always loved this ring." He showed her his bare fingers. "I'm not a jewelry-wearing type of guy but this ring kicks ass. I remember him and

Sage designing and making it—they cursed the materials and each other for months." He smiled at the memory.

Lachlyn put the big ring onto her thumb and spun it around. "It feels strange that you all have memories of him and I have nothing. I have his blood, his genes, but he's an absolute stranger to me. Then again, so was my mother, for all intents and purposes." Lachlyn tried to smile but he noticed the pain in her eyes, the longing to connect.

Reame took her hand and rubbed his thumb along hers. "Connor was part of my life for a long time. I could answer any questions you have about him."

Lachlyn looked past his shoulder to stare at the cityscape. He waited for her to formulate the words, ignoring the cold wind hammering his back.

"Everyone keeps telling me that, had he known about me, I would've been part of his life," Lachlyn said, her words a whisper on the wind. "Do you think that's true or is that just something they're saying to make me feel better about the situation?"

Reame took his time answering, knowing this was a hard question for her to ask. "I think his actions speak louder than words. Look at what he did for his nephews and niece... As a single guy he took them in after their parents died. From the moment Linc came to live in his house, as the son of his housekeeper, he treated him exactly like he did the other three. He didn't need to adopt the four of them, Lach. He gained nothing legally from that action. He just wanted to tell the world that they were his. So, judging by that, do you honestly think he would've treated you differently?"

Intellectually, he knew that she understood his words but he suspected that she was having a hard time believing them. It had to be really tough, Reame thought, to reconcile the fact that she was Connor's biological daughter and had suffered a hard childhood—mentally, financially and emotionally—while her siblings had had what seemed to be a gilded childhood under the protection of a man who wasn't their real father.

"Are you angry, Lach?"

Judging by the shock that jumped into her eyes, he knew that he'd hit a nerve. "No! Why?"

He placed his other hand on her bare knee and squeezed. "Come on, Lachlyn. Talk to me."

Lachlyn pushed her hair behind her ear and tried to shrink back, pulling her hand from his and moving her knee. Because she was such a fairy, he just needed to tighten his grip slightly to hold her in place. "Are you angry, Lach?" he quietly repeated his question.

Lachlyn's eyes were pure blue fire. "What do you want me to tell you, Reame?"

"The truth."

"The truth?" Lachlyn sprang to her feet, her bare feet hitting the freezing concrete. She didn't seem to notice the cold, that his parka hit her just above her knees and that the sleeves hung a foot over her arms. "Hell, yes, I'm angry! I'm angry that they knew him and I didn't, that they had a parent who loved them enough to make an effort to be a parent. They never had a mother who'd cry herself to sleep or just cry, all the time. I've seen the photos, Reame. They went on family vacations to exotic beaches, went skiing over the Christmas holidays, had piles of presents under the tree, the elaborate birthday parties. Christmas was just another day for us, Reame. Tyce used to draw me pictures for my birthday. I never, once, blew out the candles on a birthday cake! I never sat on my father's lap, had him buy me a pony, got to design rings with him."

He got it now—Sage had lived her life and she was struggling to deal with emotions that idea generated.

"I like Sage, I do!" Lachlyn cried. "She's carrying Tyce's baby, she's going to be my sister-in-law. But it's just…" Lachlyn bit her bottom lip and stared down at her feet, her arms crisscrossed against her body. He couldn't blame her or judge her. She needed to work through her feelings toward Sage, her feelings toward Connor. And he knew that, while she might feel resentful for the life she didn't live, there was something bigger bubbling beneath the surface.

Something she couldn't, or wouldn't, share with him.

He wanted her to. Reame wanted her to spill it, to throw it at his feet so that he could help her bear the load. He wanted to pull her in tight and box away her demons, kick away her pain. Shelter her, protect her.

He was doing it again, he realized. Typical protector behavior, taking on wars that weren't his to fight, situations that didn't need his input. He wasn't anyone's white knight, not anymore. He was trying to get out of the rescue business.

That was why he wanted to date self-confident, independent women, wanted to stay free of emotional entanglements. He didn't want the responsibility of caring for someone else, of fighting their battles, propping them up and making them stronger. It took so much emotional energy.

Lachlyn needed to fight her demons herself and he needed to put some distance between them. Physically and, more crucially, mentally.

This was his time…and he'd messed up by sleeping with her and worse, allowing her to confide in him.

Reame stood up and walked toward the balcony door, gesturing to Lachlyn to come inside. Lachlyn frowned and walked toward him, her expression tight. "Is that your way of saying that this conversation is over and you're tired of hearing me whine?"

Reame rubbed his hand up and down his jaw and thought that honesty now might save some later heartache. "You're not whining but I'm not the person you should be talking to."

Lachlyn stepped into the living room and Reame closed the sliding door behind him.

Lachlyn rocked on her heels, looking ridiculously young and small in his huge-on-her coat. "You're right. Your loyalty is to Connor and the Ballantynes and you'll always defend them," Lachlyn stated, sounding a hundred years old. "All of you, including Tyce, have picked your sides."

"This isn't about taking sides, Lachlyn. It's not like they are trying to sell you into slavery!" Reame shouted, frustrated. "They are trying to do what's right, what they think is fair."

"What if I don't want what's right, what's fair? What if there is something else I want from them, something else I need?"

"What is that?"

Lachlyn just held his hot stare. "If I have to ask for it then it won't mean as much."

Reame threw his hands up in the hair, intensely frustrated. This was the problem with women. They never just came out and said what they meant, they always had to shade their words. Well, he could teach her to be brutally honest. "Well, they won't know what you want until you tell them." Reame gestured to the bedroom. "I believe in being straightforward, Lachlyn, in laying all my cards on the table."

Lachlyn lifted a challenging eyebrow. "Go on then.

Lay your cards on the table, Reame. But if you say anything that sounds patronizing about the fact that I was a virgin, that I am inexperienced, I will throw something at you."

God, he wouldn't insult her like that. She'd chosen not to share her body with anyone but that didn't mean she lacked maturity or independence. Reame hauled in a breath, looking for composure. "Last night you said, before we lost control, that it would be a onetime thing, to blow the crazy away. Do you still stand by that statement?"

God, say yes. Because if you so much as hint at wanting more, then you'll be back in my arms so fast your head will spin.

But common sense dictated that they step back and away, that making love again might lead to deeper conversations and that could lead to them feeling more than they should. He didn't want a relationship, he wanted his freedom, to be solely and utterly responsible for himself. Was that too much to ask? Really?

"I think it's better that we chalk last night up to a moment of insanity," Lachlyn said and Reame ignored the jab of disappointment. Lachlyn conjured up a smile. "We scratched an itch and we should leave it at that."

Reame nodded. "I agree with you. It's far simpler that way."

Lachlyn walked toward the guest bedroom and Reame had to fight the urge to run after her, to wind his arms around her tiny waist and kiss her neck, to inhale her perfume. The itch wasn't gone, he admitted. If anything it was bigger and more annoying than before.

Reame lifted his arms up behind his head, laced his fingers, cursed himself and the situation and headed toward his bedroom, wondering how he was going to manage being around her 24/7. Now that he knew how she felt, tasted, the noises she made in the back of her throat when she was turned on, how was he going to be able to keep his hands off her?

All he wanted was a few months free of complications. Anyone would think that he'd asked for world frickin' peace.

The following week, in the basement, Lachlyn boosted herself up onto the steel table in the center of the room and, sitting cross-legged between the piles of paper, opened the small white box next to her. Inhaling the warm, rich scents of caramel and chocolate, she slowly pulled out the cupcake, lifting it to her nose to inhale its sugary wonderfulness.

If Reame knew that she'd left him in the reception area of Ballantyne International and that she'd sneaked out and ran all the way to the bakery two blocks away, he'd be furious.

But traditions were traditions and this was one she'd indulged in all her life. So much had changed in her life but she was determined to hold on to a little of her past.

Lachlyn swiped her finger through the frosting and lifted it to her lips, whimpering when the frosting dissolved on her tongue, spreading sugar and caramel and spice throughout her mouth. Good cupcake, Lachlyn decided. *Happy birthday to me*.

She was twenty-eight today and nobody knew. Well, Tyce should but she doubted that he'd connect this day to her; birthdays hadn't been a big deal in their house. There had been no extra money for gifts and cake and her mom, well, getting through the day was enough of a struggle without having to remember extraneous stuff. As a child she'd heard her school friends talking about birthdays, about parties, gifts and streamers and cake. When she was still living her fantasy of having a family, in her imagination birthdays had been a big deal. There was always a party and she always had a new dress and ribbons threaded through her hair. There were piles of gifts and she was hugged and kissed a lot.

It was always the most perfect day.

Her reality was taking the pennies she managed to scrounge, buying a single cupcake and eating it slowly while the world continued on without her. She'd eaten a hell of a lot of cupcakes alone...

So much had changed, was still in the process of changing. She'd finally had sex, proper sex, with a man whom she liked and it had been everything she'd hoped it would be. She and Sage were talking more. She hadn't seen much of the other Ballantynes lately. Linc was, as far as she knew, still out of town and Jaeger and Beck were busy people. Cady and Piper still sent her the occasional text messages to check in, to remind her that they were free to meet if she wanted company.

She had to admit she was tempted. She'd thoroughly enjoyed talking to Sage over pizza and she imagined that the Ballantyne women were as much fun. Lachlyn put the cupcake down and placed her elbows on her knees. For the first time in over a decade, she allowed her thoughts to drift, for the movie in her head to play.

In the movie, she was racing across Manhattan, late for supper at The Den. The whole family would be waiting for her, either in the upstairs sitting room or in the great room. There would be babies everywhere, Shaw would be on one of his uncles' shoulders and Linc's and Jaeger's toddlers would be tottering around or playing on the jewel-toned Persian carpet. Sage would be on Tyce's lap, his big hands on her belly, and Jaeger and Beck would be arguing about something because that's what they seemed to do. Linc would play peacemaker, handing out wine while Tate put the final touches on supper.

She'd be kissed and hugged hello, handed a glass of wine and someone would ask her about her day, whether she'd found something interesting at work, and she'd feel warm and fuzzy because these were her people, her clan, her soft place to fall.

They'd all turn at the sounds of big boots on the stairs and Reame would step into the room, his eyes quickly moving across the room to find her. Shaw would launch himself at Reame but his eyes would stay on hers, and he'd send her a quick "missed you" smile. She could wait, just, to feel her mouth on his, knowing that she'd have all of him later, for the rest of her life...

Jesus! Lachlyn blinked and jerked upright, chills racing up and down her body. She'd had this fantasy before, a large family, a big house, laughter, love. It was like she was twelve again and still believed in the power of dreams.

She didn't. She couldn't.

God, she was losing herself, losing sight of what was important. Her protective shell was cracking and if she didn't rebuild it—if she didn't shore up her defenses— she was going to be annihilated by disappointment. She didn't need the Ballantynes—their money or their company—and she didn't need Reame for sex or companionship. She was fine on her own. She liked being on her own...

Didn't she?

"Pedro's Bakery, Latimore?"

Lachlyn spun around and saw Reame in the doorway wearing a ferocious scowl. "Please tell me that you didn't leave the building to go to a bakery for a cupcake."

Lachlyn glanced down at her half-eaten treat. It wasn't just a cupcake; it was her birthday cupcake. Lachlyn couldn't explain so she just looked at him, noticing that his eyes were a shade warmer than ice. "I am responsible for your safety, Latimore!"

"I went to a bakery, Reame, not to a crack den," Lachlyn protested, lowering her legs and jumping to the floor.

"It's my job to keep you safe and I can't do that if you sneak off behind my back!" Reame shouted. "If you wanted a cupcake, I could've stopped on the way here, or you could've asked me or Linc to organize an intern to run out for one."

But then she would've had to explain why she wanted a cupcake today, why it was important that she buy it herself. It was her small ritual, a reminder of her independence—a way to remind herself that she could still be alone.

"Your lack of gratitude is astounding. Do you know how much time and effort it takes making sure that you are okay?"

Oh, whoa, hold on a minute. That wasn't fair! "I didn't ask for a bodyguard, that was Linc's idea. You have a company full of guards. I didn't have to become *your* problem. You didn't have to move me into your apartment. That was *your* choice." The apartment she wasn't spending another minute in. Lachlyn slapped her hands on her hips, her temper bubbling. She waved her hands in the air. "You're fired. I release you from all obligations to me. I'm going back to my place—you can deliver my luggage there."

"The hell you will! A child could break into your apartment!"

She should be scared of him. With his wild eyes, clenched fists and heaving chest, he looked the warrior she knew him to be. But she wasn't scared, she was flat-out pissed. Lachlyn closed the gap between them and slapped her open palm on the thin fabric of his blue-and-white-striped shirt. "I am *not* your responsibility. I refuse to be! I can take care of myself. Always have, always will."

Reame grabbed her wrist and yanked her to him, her chest colliding with his. *You are not going to kiss him*, Lachlyn told herself. *You are not going to be a damn cliché.*

"You are the biggest pain in my ass, Latimore. From the moment I heard about you I knew you were going to be trouble."

"Then walk the hell out of my life, Reame. I don't need you, I don't need anybody!" Lachlyn shouted, trying to tug her wrist from his strong grip.

"Keep telling yourself that, honey. Maybe one day you'll actually believe it," Reame growled and then his mouth was on hers. Lachlyn willed herself not to open her mouth, not to let him inside, but it took just one slide of his tongue against the seam of her lips and he was past her first barrier. Determined not to respond, she stood rock still, fighting the battle between temptation and anger. Reame simply gripped her ass and lifted her up to close the distance between them. Holding her with his arm under her butt, he used his other hand to hold the back of her head, tilting it so that he had better access to her mouth.

"Kiss me, dammit." Reame muttered the words against her mouth and Lachlyn heard the rasp in his voice, the need below his rough command. If she was a better woman she'd stick to her guns, keep herself aloof, but this was Reame and he was kissing her, slowly liquefying her joints. Lachlyn wound her arms around his neck and pushed her tongue into his mouth, wanting to do her own tasting and feasting.

She could taste the coffee he'd had earlier, and the fresh tang of his toothpaste. His hair was silky soft under her fingers and the bone-hard erection pushing into her stomach. He felt like heaven with undercurrents of sin. Hot hands pulled her legs apart and she obeyed his silent request to wind them around his waist. Then his erection was rubbing against her core and she could feel his heat and steel through his suit pants and her leggings. His hand worked its way under her thigh-length sweater, covering most of her lower back as he pushed her closer to him.

He just had to keep rocking into her and she'd spin off on a band of pleasure. Just a little more, she thought, grinding against him, a harder kiss, another rock…

Lachlyn felt her butt hit the table and, *nonono*, he wrenched his mouth off hers. Lachlyn reached for him, but Reame threw his hands up in a *just stop* gesture. He bent over, placing his palms on his thighs, and stared at the floor.

"I don't need this in my life," Reame muttered, his words poison-tipped bullets spinning through her heart. Of course he didn't need her. She was extraneous, a distraction, a burden. She was, as he'd stated, a pain in the ass.

Reame stood up and pointed a finger at her, his expression a weird combination of pissed-off male and turned-on male. "I will be back at five to pick you up and take you home. Do not make me look for you, Lachlyn."

She couldn't stay with him. She refused to inconvenience him any more than she already had. "I'll make other arrangements, Reame. I refuse to be a burden and I am not your responsibility!"

Reame gripped her face with one hand. "Five o'clock, Latimore. Be here."

Reame spun around and weaved his way through boxes to the door. Lachlyn looked down and picked up the box holding the cupcake. Dropping down from the table, she walked to the trash bin and tossed the box inside.

She'd had a couple of crappy birthdays before but this one, excuse the expression, took the cake.

Reame's foul mood hadn't dissipated by the time he got back to his desk. Slamming his office door closed, he flung himself into his chair and stared at his blank monitor. He wasn't sure what he was more pissed about, the fact that Lachlyn went AWOL on her own or that she thought that she wasn't worth his time and effort.

Why couldn't she see her worth? Why was she so convinced that she had nothing to give? She was super-smart and, when she allowed herself to relax, surprisingly funny. The other night, after he returned to his apartment with Tyce, he'd listened to her talk with her brother and Sage. Either the wine had made her tongue loose or she was finally starting to feel comfortable with Sage, but she'd shown no signs of the loner she professed herself to be. She was a lively conversationalist and, surprisingly, quite affectionate. She'd touched Sage's arm to make a point, rested her head against Tyce's shoulder, kissed and hugged them both goodbye. He'd had a glimpse of the real Lachlyn and, crappit, he really liked her.

He also really liked her body. She was small, sure, but perfectly formed, feminine from the top of her head to that silver-ringed toe. Knowing that she was just down the hallway half-naked and that he couldn't touch her was a special type of hell. The biggest problem with Lachlyn was that she was the first woman in a long time that he could imagine dating, spending long periods of time with. He liked her steel-trap mind. Her laughter made his stomach flip. Her vulnerability made him want to slay her dragons.

She was exactly what he wasn't looking for. He was out of the business of slaying dragons, running to the rescue. While he never expected anyone to fight his battles, he just didn't want to take on another person's drama. And Lachlyn had more than most. No, he was sticking to his plan...he wanted to have uncomplicated sex with uncomplicated women.

You use the word want *a lot. Why don't you just do it?*

Lachlyn's words popped into his head and ricocheted through his brain. She was right—he'd been talking big but hadn't put any of his words into action. Truthfully, he only wanted to sleep with Lachlyn again, and again, but she was firmly off-limits. What the hell had he been thinking earlier, kissing her like that?

Her skin was like satin and he loved the sounds she made in the back of her throat when she was turned on. And the way she slid her core up and over him...he'd come close to losing his load right there and then. Reame rubbed his hands over his face. *Stop thinking about Lachlyn, moron, and get your head in the game.*

Lachlyn, for a hundred and one reasons—the best being that she was Linc's sister, inexperienced and too damn vulnerable—was off-limits. He wasn't going to sleep with her again. In fact, it was better if he did put some distance between them, find her another place to stay. Truthfully, the attention around her had died down and he thought it was reasonably safe for her to go back to her apartment. He could easily arrange for one of his agents to escort her to work and back. There was no reason for her to stay in his apartment except that he liked having her there.

He didn't like that he liked having her there. It felt too much like something real, something similar to the relationships the Ballantynes were enjoying. He was happy that his friends were happy but fairy tales didn't last forever. He should know—he'd watched his parents' marriage detonate without rhyme or reason. Love didn't last, and the country's divorce statistics proved his case. And if it didn't last then what was the point of even trying? And what if he messed it up? What if he failed?

The rewards, companionship and sex, weren't worth the risk and failure was never an option. Sex was easy to find and he had good friends who kept him entertained. So he'd stick to the plan.

Reame pulled his phone out of his suit jacket and scrolled through his dating app. He chose and then dismissed a dozen women before cursing himself. This should not be that difficult. These were smart, nice, hot women who were on the same sex-only page. Reame stared down at a brunette, trying to make sense of her profile. Professional, intelligent, not looking for anything permanent. Perfect. He swiped right and because she'd already indicated that she was interested, sent her a message suggesting drinks. She suggested dinner and Reame agreed.

See, what was so hard about that? Nothing really, if he ignored the acid-inducing feeling that he was cheating on Lachlyn.

Cora rapped on his door and, grateful for the distraction, Reame called for her to come in. She held a cup of coffee in one hand and a stack of files in the other. "Is it safe to come inside?"

Reame sent her a sour look as she placed his cup of

coffee next to his elbow. "Thanks. Can you make a reservation for me for dinner for two tonight? Someplace nice."

"Sure. Glory's make a fuss of ladies on their birthday, they make this wonderful cocktail which you can only order if it's your birthday."

What the hell was Cora talking about? "Why are you going on about birthdays?" Reame demanded, flipping through the files. More expenses, staff rotations, background checks. Staff reviews. The fun never ended...

Cora looked puzzled. "I presumed that you were taking Lachlyn to dinner because it's her birthday."

Reame's stomach felt as heavy as a boulder. *Please tell me that you are joking*, he silently begged Cora. But he knew that he was out of luck. That explained the cupcake. Her solitary celebration cracked his heart.

I never, once, blew out the candles on a birthday cake.

Reame dropped the folders, feeling sick to his stomach. Reame was damn sure that nobody, not even her brother, remembered that it was her birthday. He'd had his a few months back and his mom and sisters all called him before he'd had a chance to wipe the sleep from his eyes. Throughout that morning he'd taken calls from every Ballantyne who could speak on a telephone. Cora ordered pizza for lunch and he'd eaten with his staff in the break room. That evening, he and the Ballantyne men had hit a couple bars for an evening of beer and pool.

It had been a great day.

Lachlyn had bought herself a cupcake. And he'd chastised her for it. Reame shuddered and held his head in his hands.

Lachlyn pressed her cheek to Tyce's heart and closed her eyes. Her big brother bent his knees and tightened his arms around her. It was the best hug she'd ever received from him and a great way to end what she was sure was the best evening of her life.

"Sorry I forgot, Lach," Tyce muttered and she heard the regret in his voice. It was past eleven and they were standing at the entrance to the basement of the Ballantyne building. The rest of the family had left and Reame and Sage were standing by the elevator giving her and her brother time to talk.

Lachlyn dropped her head back to look up at him. "It's fine, Tyce. We were never good at birthdays."

Tyce tucked a strand of hair behind her ear. "And I'm also sorry for that."

Lachlyn blinked away her tears. "You were trying to keep us fed, keep a roof over our heads, while still going to school. There is no blame, big brother, only gratitude that you were there."

Tyce kissed her forehead before cupping her face in her hands. "You have an opportunity to change your life, baby girl."

"It's too much money, Tyce."

"We're not talking about the money, Lach, and you know it. I'm talking about giving yourself a chance to love this family. To love a man."

Lachlyn shook her head, instantly in denial. "He doesn't want a relationship and neither do I. He's just looking after me because Linc asked him to."

"Oh, BS, Lachlyn! He has a hundred employees. He could've asked any one of them to guard you. He moved you into his apartment when he could've put you into a hotel. He organized a last-minute surprise birthday party, threatening death if we didn't cancel whatever plans we had this evening and get our butts down here to this basement."

Lachlyn looked behind her and saw her steel table covered with a pretty tablecloth, takeout containers scattered across its surface. Empty bottles of wine sat on the floor and the wingback chair was piled high with presents. Nothing terribly expensive, just thoughtful gifts from thoughtful people.

Reame hadn't given her a present but organizing this party was the best gift he could've given her. All four Ballantynes and their partners attended her ad hoc party, plus Linc's mom, Jo, and Linc's PA Amy and her wife. They'd all walked into the basement shortly after six, carrying wine and takeout, presents, dropping birthday kisses on her cheek.

"Tonight I felt like I was part of the family," Lachlyn admitted, picking a piece of lint from Tyce's shirt.

"Honey, you *are* part of the family. The only person who doesn't realize it is you," Tyce told her. "This was what you wanted, Lachlyn. All your life you've wanted this. It's yours for the taking. *Take it.*"

"I'm scared, Tyce."

"I know, Lachlyn. I was scared, too. I get it, I do. It's so much easier being alone but it's also so damn selfish and far *too* easy." Tyce held her hand between both of his, his dark eyes filled with emotion. "Mom, she was selfish, Lach. She liked being depressed. She enjoyed being useless—"

Lachlyn tried to tug her hand away but he held tight. "Don't say that. She was sick!"

"Sure, but she had options to get better. Taking her damn antidepressants would've helped but she chose not to, Lachlyn. She chose to check out, because getting better, interacting, loving us meant work, hard work. It was easier to hide, to sleep, to fade away. By not raising us, she made us selfish, Lach. She made it seem okay to hide, to not try." Tyce squeezed her fingers. "You've got to *try*, Lach."

"I just wanted her to love me, Tyce," Lachlyn said, the tears that had been so close to the surface all evening finally released and rolling down her face.

"And the fact she couldn't was her problem, not yours. No one, except Mom apparently, gets out of this life without having dirty knees and a broken heart. When are you going to break up with your childhood, Lach? When are you going to release its hold on you? Because no matter how independent you are you still need, and deserve, to be taken care of sometimes. This family, and Reame, seem to want to do that."

"Tyce, you ready to go?" Sage called from down the hall.

"Yeah, on my way." Tyce gave her another long hug and when he stepped away, Lachlyn looked at Sage who blew her a kiss. Then her eyes slammed into Reame's and Lachlyn barely registered her brother and Sage's last goodbyes.

Reame stalked over to her and clasped her face in his hands. "Happy birthday, honey. I'm sorry for earlier."

Lachlyn's fingers encircled his wrists and her heart stumbled and sighed. "Thank you for my fabulous birthday party. Best gift *ever*."

Reame dropped his hand and led her back into the messy room. "Linc asked me to tell you that he instructed the night supervisor to send the cleaning crew down in thirty minutes to clean up after us."

"I was going to do it," Lachlyn protested, picking up a container containing a lone slice of pizza. She started to pile the Chinese takeout containers on top, jamming paper napkins into the containers. She wasn't sure what to say, or how to act. Earlier today she and Reame had been yelling at each other and she was pretty sure she'd fired him at one point. But, despite the ugly words they'd exchanged, he'd organized a surprise party for her.

She was both touched and confused.

Where was she going to sleep tonight? Back at Reame's place or in her own apartment? Would he take her to work in the morning or would she have to go back to using public transportation?

Lachlyn suddenly felt exhausted and oh so emotional—although her conversation with her brother about their mother had been brief, it had been intense. She wanted time to think, to mull over Tyce's words, to take them apart and examine them. Lachlyn jammed the boxes into the trash bin and looked up to see Reame propping his phone against a pizza box. A haunting melody filled the room.

Reame held out his hand, his eyes on her face. A small smile touched his lips. "We have half an hour... Dance with me?"

Lachlyn placed her hand in his, her soul sighing when she stepped into his embrace, his big hand between her shoulder blades. His chin rested on her temple as he moved her in a slow circle around the room.

"I didn't buy you a present." Reame's words rumbled across her temple, down her neck.

"I don't need a present, Reame. I had this wonderful evening and you're dancing with me."

Reame tightened his grip on her and she heard his sharp intake of breath. "I don't want to hurt you, Lach. I can't give you what you need."

Lachlyn brushed her thumb against the cord in his neck and felt him shudder. "I'm still figuring out what I need, Ree. Will you take me home? Can you give me tonight?"

Reame's lips moved against her hair and his hand pulled her closer to him so that there was only a paper-thin gap between them. "Yeah."

"Then let's take tonight and tomorrow can take care of itself."

Ten

"The brothers are getting restless."

Sage was sitting on one of the three steel tables in the cavernous storeroom, sandwiched between piles of Ballantyne documents and photographs dating from the 1920s and 1930s. Since her impromptu birthday party ten days ago, the Ballantynes and their partners had taken to popping down to the basement on odd occasions but Sage was her most frequent, almost daily visitor. On the days she didn't see Sage's lovely face, Lachlyn felt cheated. Sage wasn't only the love of her brother's life, she was fast becoming her closest friend.

So much for keeping her distance…

Lachlyn, digging into a box, pulled out another leather-bound diary and, seeing the initials on the cover, frowned. "How did your great-grandmother's diary from 1928 end up in a box holding mostly correspondence from the 1950s?" Lachlyn demanded, frustrated. "The Ballantyne filing system is appalling, Sage!"

"So you've told me, a time or twenty," Sage replied before biting into her half-eaten apple. "Are you ignoring my comment about my brothers?"

I'm trying to, Lachlyn silently admitted.

"None of us understand why you are hesitating, Lachlyn. And the brothers want a decision by the end of the month. That's in ten days."

"I have ten days to decide?"

"No, you have a week. We need some time to tell the accountant what we plan to do so he can factor in—" Sage wrinkled her nose "—what needs to be factored in."

Like Lachlyn, Sage did not have a head for numbers. "I don't know if I can make a decision by then," Lachlyn said, carefully placing the diary with the others she'd found.

"You're going to have to, Lach," Sage said, hopping off the table and holding her stomach with one hand. The sound of the heavy door opening interrupted their conversation and Lachlyn spun around, eager to welcome anyone into her basement space, particularly if that person wasn't a Ballantyne and wouldn't talk about her becoming one in name and money.

It was Reame. Lachlyn glanced at her watch and saw that it was past quitting time and Reame was late to collect her. She hadn't noticed because she'd been so fascinated by the history in this room. Not only was she getting a thorough education on all things Ballantyne, she'd also discovered various items and documents that allowed her a glimpse into how the city had changed over the past hundred and twenty years, and how norms and

culture had altered. This history should be collated, re-
corded and shared with the world.

Lachlyn pulled her attention back to her brother's fiancée. Sage patted Reame's big arm as she passed him
on her way to the door. "Try to talk some sense into her
about taking our offer, Ree."

Reame nodded, shut the door after Sage left and immediately walked over to the stuffed chair in the corner of the room, sinking into it like he'd been awake for
days. "Hey."

"Hey back," Lachlyn said, remaining by the steel
table, her hand on a tower of black-and-white photographs. "You're late."

Reame didn't reply, he just tipped his head back and
stared up at the unpainted ceiling. Lachlyn did a tip-to-
toe scan, starting at his expensive shoes, up his muscled
legs covered by gray suit pants. He wore a white, open-
collared shirt and a jacket matching his pants. One end
of his pale blue tie peeked out from his suit pocket.

His shoulders were hunched halfway up to his ears and
his jaw was rock-hard with tension. Lachlyn opened her
mouth to ask him what was wrong but bit back the words.
It wasn't the time. She recognized his need for quiet, to
be alone with his thoughts and to work through whatever
was tying him up in knots. Reame was even more spooked
by relationships than she was, so they were trying to keep
things uncomplicated, making love but avoiding conversation that dipped below the surface of politeness.

Since Reame didn't want to talk, Lachlyn turned back
to the box she'd been making her way through, rapidly
sorting through the paperwork previous Ballantynes had
left her to find. Lachlyn picked up a bundle of letters secured with a silk ribbon and pulled one from the bundle,
opening it up with gentle fingers.

February 1926,
My darling Matthew…
It is snowing again and I am bereft without you…

Lachlyn read three letters before Reame pulled her
back into the present by standing up and walking over to
the tiny bar fridge in the corner and pulling out a water.
He slammed the door shut, cracked the top and took a
long pull, draining half of the bottle within a matter of
seconds.

He looked exhausted and so very alone. If there was
ever an emotion she could easily recognize, it was lone-
liness. How best to get him to open up, she wondered,
carefully folding one of the letters. She hated it when
people prodded and probed, bugged her to talk, so she
kept her statement short. "If you want to talk, I'll listen."

Reame stared at his feet, finished his water and crum-
pled the plastic bottle in his hand. "I had a craptastic day,"
he admitted, his low voice drifting over to her.

"It happens," Lachlyn stated, knowing that Reame
wouldn't appreciate sympathy. Narrowing her eyes, she
looked around for a particular box.

Lachlyn zeroed in on the box and, pulling a box cutter
from her back pocket, sliced open the tape. Inside were
six bottles of ten-year-old whiskey that she knew were a
Christmas gift from a Scottish laird to Connor.

Since nobody but she knew the box was here and
thinking that Connor wouldn't mind her filching a bottle,
she pulled one out and, walking back to Reame, cracked
the seal and removed the top. She held it out to him and
smiled at his grateful look.

"I can find you a cup if you want one," Lachlyn said
as his fingers wrapped around the neck of the bottle.

Reame snorted his refusal. "Please." He took a hit and

then another one before offering her the bottle. "This was Connor's favorite whiskey. He got a couple of cases delivered every few months."

Lachlyn refused his offer and looked around. "I can't believe what I am finding in this storeroom, and that is one of the less weird items."

Folding her arms, she looked up at Reame and saw that the whiskey had chased a little of his anger away. "So, why did you have a—what did you call it?—craptastic day?"

Reame took her hand and pulled her onto his lap, one hand on her thigh and the other still holding the bottle of whiskey.

"My mother left today on a cruise. As she was preparing to board, she realized that she forgot her passport and ticket on the kitchen counter. She lives in South Orange," Reame said, placing the bottle on the floor.

"Nice," Lachlyn said, thinking of the New Jersey neighborhood, with its quaint houses and gaslight-lined streets.

"I wanted to send Cora but no, I had to go because she doesn't want strangers in her house. Cora has worked for me for five years and has met my mother twenty-plus times. So I belted out to South Orange, picked up the documents, eventually found her at the cruise ship terminal, where I listened to her twenty-minute monologue about why this trip wasn't a good idea before making my escape."

Lachlyn ducked her head, trying to hide her smile. Under his irritation she heard his affection for his mother in his voice. "As I hit the office, I receive a message from my younger sister, Lara, telling me that she hates her job and has resigned. She's now jobless and homeless and doesn't think accounting is for her."

"Do you want me to move out of your place so your sister can move into your second bedroom?"

Reame looked horrified. "Hell, no! But could she not have decided this earlier and saved me a crap-load of college fees?"

"You paid for her education?"

"Somebody had to," Reame snapped. "I have three younger sisters and when the oldest got to senior year, my dad walked out on his twenty-five-year marriage, cleaned out all his bank accounts and bailed."

Lachlyn saw pain and disappointment wash across Reame's face. "What happened then?"

"I was twenty-five, in the military and loving my life. Yeah, war was hard and the tours were tough. We were an elite unit and the pressure was intense. I made life-or-death decisions on a daily basis, but I believed in what we were doing and I believed in my men. We were tight.

"My mom told me what happened and said that she couldn't cope. She had no money and my sisters, ages fifteen to seventeen, were beside themselves. I had to go home. When I got Stateside, my mom was a walking zombie and my sisters were all acting up in different ways. One was studying herself to death, another was sneaking out at night, the youngest was all but living at her boyfriend's house. I couldn't go back to my unit. They needed me."

"Then Connor stepped in," Lachlyn guessed.

"Yeah. He gave me a job as his bodyguard, then as his head of security. Then he suggested that I go out on my own. He provided the capital I needed, and between the business profits and student loans, my sisters all got a decent education."

"And your mom?"

"She found a job and between her salary and me helping out, she got back on her feet. Emotionally, she never recovered. She thought she had this perfect marriage, that everything was amazing between her and my dad, she just never saw him for who he really was."

"Who was he, Reame?"

"An intensely selfish man who felt confined by his circumstance, by marriage, by the kids who demanded time and money and attention from him."

Lachlyn toed off her sneakers and tucked her feet beneath her, curling up in his lap. "What else happened today, Reame?"

Reame lifted an eyebrow. "That isn't enough?"

"You're a Special Forces soldier, and while your sister's actions are annoying and having to retrieve your mom's documents was irritating, that wasn't enough to put you in such a foul mood."

"We moved the high-value target out of the guest suite and into his safe house today. He and my guys were ambushed on route because my client leaked his whereabouts to his mistress," Reame stated quietly, fury coating every word. "I was supposed to be riding along but I asked Liam to go along instead of me, because I was chasing down my mother's missing passport. A passing car opened fire on them."

"Was anybody hurt?" Lachlyn asked, dreading the answer.

Reame shook his head. "No and the client is fine." There was no blood left in Reame's clenched fists. "It could've ended badly, Lachlyn. Really badly. All because he couldn't keep his mouth shut."

Lachlyn rolled the fat body of the whiskey bottle between her palms. "What a moron."

"Tell me about it. He put my guys at risk so I terminated his contract." Reame tipped his head back to look at the ceiling. "I am just so sick of responsibility, Lach. Liam has a wife, kids. If he was killed, I don't think I could live with myself."

Lachlyn looked at him and saw stress—the tension in his arms, his tired eyes, the grooves down the side of his mouth so much deeper than normal. His fantastic eyes were a flat green, almost as if they were too tired to show emotion. People entrusted their property and lives to him and his men and he, as head of Jepsen & Associates, was ultimately responsible for every life, every business, every piece of property. That was a hell of a load to carry.

"Do you ever feel like you want to throw up your arms and lie down and be taken care of? Just once?"

Reame rolled his head to look at her, his eyes speculative. "Yeah. I sometimes wish that someone would step in and make some decisions, *any* decision."

So not the tough-guy, I-can-handle-it response she'd expected. Well, then, she might be able to help him out. "Being an adult sucks," Lachlyn murmured before standing up and moving to the door. She twisted the lock closed, effectively locking them into the storeroom. She could do this, she thought. She could make the first move. She'd lead and God, she hoped he'd follow.

Lachlyn played with the buttons of her shirt as she made her way back to Reame, fighting the urge to bite her lip. *You have to look at him, Latimore. This can't happen without eye contact.*

"What are you doing, Lach?" Reame's voice was a low rumble.

"Making a decision for you," Lachlyn said, her fingers working the buttons on her shirt. "Taking care of you."

"I thought we were keeping this on the surface, keeping it simple."

Lachlyn shrugged out of her shirt, her eyes on his. She flushed as she stood in front of him in her rose-pink bra, her skin pebbling with anticipation. "Shh, that sounds like you are thinking. Don't think, just feel. Step out of your life, your head and let me love you," Lachlyn said, straddling his legs and placing her hands on his shoulders.

"Lach, do you think this is a good idea?" Reame demanded as his big hands settled on her waist, his thumb swiping her skin.

"It's not your decision but mine. You don't have to think, or run options or scenarios... You just have to enjoy." Lachlyn placed her hands on his cheeks, enjoying his stubble under her hands. He smelled of mint and whiskey, like a turned-on man. "Let me do all the work—consider this my gift to you."

Reame's eyes drilled into hers and she could see him fighting temptation. Lachlyn dropped her head and her mouth drifted over him. "Let me give you this, Reame. Please? Relax, enjoy."

"It's a dusty storeroom in the bowels of the Ballantyne building," Reame protested.

"The door is locked." Lachlyn curved her lips against his. "We have a chair and I know that you have a condom in your wallet. Stop thinking, Reame. Let go."

"Lach—"

Lachlyn saw the capitulation in his eyes and her mouth dropped onto his, her lips playing with his, exploring, tasting, feasting. She sensed him losing control, knew that he was on the verge of taking charge of this encounter, so she pulled back and picked his hands off her waist and placed them on the arms of the chair. "This is about you, not me," Lachlyn told him. "Keep your hands there."

"I don't think I can," Reame said, his voice hoarse.

"You can," Lachlyn replied. "Let me play, Reame."

Reame groaned, dropped his head back and closed his eyes, and Lachlyn knew that she'd won this battle. Knowing that Reame was naturally impatient, she kissed him again, tracing her tongue over his bottom lip, nibbling her way up his jaw, nuzzling her nose into that delicious space between his jaw and neck. She sucked, gently, before soothing the skin with a tiny lick. She heard his low, masculine rumble of appreciation and her soul smiled. Lachlyn kissed her way across his collarbone, her hands on his chest, conscious of his elevated heart rate. It made her feel strong and powerful, so intensely feminine, that such a man—an alpha to his core—wanted her, burned for her. For *her*, inexperienced and unknowing, but so, so willing to learn. Lachlyn fumbled with the buttons of his shirt, sighing when she pulled the sides apart to reveal his muscled chest.

"I'm so glad my first time was with you," Lachlyn murmured, her fingers dancing across his flat nipples, her eyes locked on his. "Thank you for letting me do this, for letting me touch you."

Reame's eyes flared with passion and he licked his lips. "That's never a problem, sweetheart. But I have to say, you are driving me crazy. Not being able to touch you is both hell and heaven."

Lachlyn was content to look at him, her fingers skating across his ridged stomach, across the top of his hard thighs. She looked down and saw his erection straining the fabric of his suit pants. She lifted hot, heavy eyes. "That looks uncomfortable," Lachlyn said, sounding a little wicked.

"You have no damn idea," Reame retorted. "Can I touch you yet?"

Lachlyn shook her head. "I'm not done exploring."

Lachlyn scooted off his lap and bent down to pull off his shoes, then his socks. Standing up, she leaned over him, her blond hair falling into his face. She tucked it behind her ear as her hands went for his belt buckle. Reame protested but she cut off his words with a kiss, pushing her tongue into his mouth to tangle with his. He was as into the kiss as she was. She could feel the passion rumbling beneath his control as he allowed her to take the lead, as she advanced and retreated. His trust in her both warmed and emboldened her, and her hands steadied as she flipped open his belt and unhooked the snap on his suit pants. Now owning her confidence, she placed her palm on his erection, sighing at the evidence of his desire.

For her. Only for her.

Reame cursed, then sighed. "Get naked," he muttered.

Lachlyn raised a sassy eyebrow. "Uh, my show, remember? This is about you, not me."

Reame frowned, uncomfortable. "I can't do this unless you are with me, Lach, every step of the way. That's not the way this works."

So honorable, Lachlyn thought. And that was the problem. Reame had no idea that he could occasionally put his needs first. He had no concept of how to take, only how to give. "Right now, this is exactly how it works."

Through the soft cotton of his underwear, Lachlyn stroked him, rubbing her thumb over his tip, feeling him shudder, jump, with every touch. She wanted to kiss him, to lose herself in his mouth, desperate for his hands between her legs, but she knew that if she did, she'd lose him, lose control of the situation.

"Where's that condom, Ree?"

"Inside jacket pocket. Wallet," Reame said, his eyes glazed with passion.

"Get it," Lachlyn ordered.

While Reame fumbled through his wallet, Lachlyn, still dressed, pushed her hands beneath his underwear and suit pants, urging him to lift his butt. Pulling his pants off him, she stood back to look at him and sighed. Reame looked magnificent in just an open jacket and shirt. "Man, you're hot," Lachlyn told him, her eyes traveling up his muscled legs, over his impressive groin, that wide chest and to that face that stopped traffic. "I want you so much."

Reame had the condom halfway to his mouth and his eyes flew to hers, pure green fire. Three words—*I want you*—were enough to push him over the edge, to snap his control. Letting out a muted roar, his arms shot out and wrapped around her waist, pulling her onto him. He stood up, holding her with one arm as he ripped the packet open with his teeth. Thrusting the condom into her hand, Reame lowered her to her feet, his mouth hot on hers as he shrugged out of his shirt and jacket.

"What are you doing?" Lachlyn asked, her voice trembling, as he expertly flicked open the button to her jeans. He then sneaked his hands down the back of her jeans, underneath her panties, and Lachlyn felt cool air on her butt and thighs as the material fell to the floor. "I was going to make love to you!"

"Yeah, well, crap happens," Reame retorted, before unsnapping her bra and pulling her naked chest flush against his. He clasped her face in both his hands, dropping hot, open-mouth kisses on her cheekbone. "I can't stand not being able to touch you. I need to touch you."

Lachlyn closed her eyes as his sexy words sent her already high internal temperature rocketing.

"That condom on yet?" Reame asked against her mouth.

"No space to work." Lachlyn managed to find and

utter the words, a minor miracle because she'd lost all power to her brain. Her hands were trapped between their bodies so Reame moved backward. While Reame traced the shell of her ear with his tongue and lips—man, that felt amazing—Lachlyn fumbled with the condom, her hands shaking.

Reame placed his hands on hers and together they rolled the condom over his hard, hot skin. Reame showed her how to touch him, how to roll him in her hand. And the more she touched him, the hotter she got, her own need for him clawing at her from the inside out.

"I can't take much more," Reame told her, his voice low and guttural. "You ready for me, baby?"

Lachlyn managed a low "Yes."

"Think I better check," Reame teased and slid his fingers between her legs, and Lachlyn sucked in her breath at his desperate groan.

Reame rested his forehead on hers, his breath shallow. "So hot, so wet." Lachlyn felt all the air leave the room so she did the only thing she could think of—she kissed him. He was all she needed.

Reame inhaled her, sucked her inside him and Lachlyn felt herself falling, whirling. Boosting her up his body, her legs encircled his waist and then Reame was inside of her, filling her, making her whole.

Walking her backward, he somehow managed to find a steel table and not even the cold metal against her backside managed to shock her out of her Reame-induced stupor. Nothing else existed but Reame's touch, his smell, his tongue in her mouth and his hands on her hips as he poured himself into her.

"Need you, need you, need you," Reame chanted in her ear.

Lachlyn, unable to speak, arched into him, tightening her legs around his waist as he took her on a roller coaster ride of passion.

He pushed into her, she sighed, he pushed again, she cried out. Passion built and built, pulling her up to where nothing mattered but this, him, the world they'd created together.

"Now, Lach, dammit. Do it," Reame ordered her, his voice harsh in her ear.

Lachlyn splintered into bright, jewel bright shards as she dimly felt Ream's tension, his utterly still body, before he shattered in her arms. Slowly, so slowly, her mind started to stitch itself back together again and she became aware of Reame's heavy breathing, his weight, the cold table beneath her skin, the fact that he'd swept piles of carefully sorted papers onto the floor.

It didn't matter, nothing mattered. Reame was holding her, and as long as he did—like she was the most precious mineral in the world—she was content.

Maybe even happy.

Eleven

Lachlyn looked up at the sound of footsteps, thinking Reame had returned to collect her. After making love, he'd told her that he'd take her home but first he had to meet a client for a drink and that he hoped it wouldn't be a late night. Feeling wired from their lovemaking and not wanting to sit in an empty apartment by herself—wow, first time she'd felt that—Lachlyn told him she preferred to work in the basement. He could collect her later but he'd better bring her some food.

Making love made her hungry.

But, sadly, it wasn't Reame with food but one of the nighttime cleaning staff, pulling her cart. She sent Lachlyn a tentative smile and softly asked whether it would be a good time to clean.

Lachlyn waved her in, thinking that her mom, nearly thirty years ago, might've worn that same green-and-blue uniform, worked these same hours.

On the tag clipped to the woman's uniform Lachlyn saw the name Greta. The cleaner coughed and with her red nose and bright eyes, looked like she might be fighting the flu. She was probably at work because she had children to feed, rent to pay.

Lachlyn walked over to her, placed her hand on her cart and nodded to the wingback chair. "Why don't you sit down for five minutes? You look like you could use the break."

Greta shook her head so hard that her gray-streaked bun threatened to fall apart. "I can't. I have work to do, a schedule to follow."

"How long are you allocated to clean in here?"

Greta sent a longing look at her chair before sending a quick look at her watch. "Thirty minutes."

"Then you can sit down for thirty minutes," Lachlyn insisted. "My work area was cleaned last night—it doesn't need to be done again."

"I don't think—"

For the first, and most likely the last, time Lachlyn pulled rank. "I'm a Ballantyne, Greta, and I say you should."

Surprised gratitude flashed across her face and the tiny woman sank into her chair, closing her eyes in relief. She really wasn't well, Lachlyn thought. Walking over to her makeshift kitchen—coffeepot, kettle and microwave—she poured Greta a cup of coffee. Asking how she preferred it, she added the last of her cream and two sugars, hoping that the sugar would give the older woman an energy boost.

"Are you sick?" Lachlyn asked, pushing the cup into her shaking hands.

"A persistent cold," Greta replied, before lifting the cup to her mouth.

Lachlyn hooked a small wooden stool with her foot and sat down in front of Greta, noticing a fine sheen of perspiration on her brow. That wasn't good, Lachlyn thought; it looked like she was running a temperature.

Greta looked sick and miserable and, worst of all, uncomfortable with being waited on by a Ballantyne, so Lachlyn attempted to put her at ease. "My mother was a night cleaner, in this very building," Lachlyn said softly. "That's how she met Connor Ballantyne."

Greta's thick eyebrows lifted. "I thought that was fake news, something the newspapers wrote to sell papers."

"No, it's true. She worked here for a few years and she used to clean Connor's office."

Greta rested her cup on her knee, her faded blue eyes thoughtful. "I can't believe Mr. Connor has been gone for nearly four years now. Before he got sick, he was often in the building late at night. He was a friendly man who talked to everyone. He was larger than life, happy, you know?"

Unfortunately, she didn't, but Lachlyn smiled anyway.

"He didn't like quiet. We always knew when Mr. Connor was working late because he'd play his stereo very loud or he'd sing. Sometimes both at the same time. He couldn't hold a tune."

Lachlyn grinned at the image. She leaned forward as if to impart a great secret. "Neither can I."

"I'm sorry you never met him." Greta tapped her finger against her mug. "But your mother would've told you about him."

That was a reasonable assumption but...no.

"Your mother should be very proud of you, Miss Lachlyn."

It was such a simple statement but it rocked her to her core. Feeling off balance, Lachlyn stood up, told Greta to rest, walked back to her steel table and lifted the photograph she'd been examining before Greta had arrived. The image refused to come into focus.

She'd spent far too much time and energy thinking about her mom and what she had and hadn't done and that small statement from a stranger struck a chord deep inside of her. The wall to her emotional dam cracked and split open, flooding her system with anger, regret and resentment. Tyce was right—Carol hadn't tried. She hadn't attempted to get better, hadn't tried to be a mom. While Lachlyn knew that depression was debilitating and soul-sucking, she also knew that Carol hadn't made any effort to feel better, to do better. The full bottles of antidepressant medication and empty boxes of sleeping tablets had told that story well. She'd wanted to stay sick and so she had.

Instead of fighting the negative emotions like she normally did, Lachlyn let them wash over her, knowing that they would pass. And when they did, a few minutes later, she felt cleaner for the dousing, able to see that understanding and relief were waiting to soothe her, a warm bath as opposed to a raging torrent.

Your mother should be very proud of you...

Had she lived, would her mom be proud of her? Lachlyn wasn't sure. She'd been so consumed by her illness, so wrapped up in being ill. She should have been there for her, she should have tried harder to get better, she shouldn't have let her down over and over again. But Lachlyn was still standing. *You have to let go of her*, Lachlyn told herself. *You have to, finally, say goodbye to her and your childhood.*

Ninety-nine out of a hundred women would've fought their illnesses to be there for their kids, and the same number would've stormed into their daughter's bedroom and kicked some young jerk's ass for laying a finger on her.

And while she was on the subject of parents, Connor might not have been able to restrict himself to one woman, but everyone she'd met had told her that he was an honest man who'd loved his life. He'd had an enormous capacity to love and he'd taught that to the children he'd raised as his own. He'd taught them to be kind, to be fair, to be committed, and that family was the rock you built your life upon. She wanted the Ballantynes to want to be her slab of rock.

So why was she being so damn stubborn about letting them in? Why had she avoided men and any type of relationship that smacked of emotional intimacy? Because she judged people based on the actions of a depressed, lonely, selfish woman, and that wasn't fair. To herself or to the family who wanted to claim her as their own. She was more like her mother than she wanted to admit. Instead of hiding behind her depression, she was hiding behind her independence, using her fear of leaning on others as a barricade against feeling anything.

Enough. Enough now.

Lachlyn, standing in that basement, a night cleaner dozing behind her, punched a mental fist through that thinking and decided that she wanted to live a full life. She wanted to be like her real dad who'd embraced life, who treated every day as a gift and an adventure. She wanted to love deeply and widely, to open herself up to the good and bad of life.

She needed to be honest about herself and what, and whom, she wanted in her life. Poor, rich or anything in between, she wanted the Ballantynes in her life. She couldn't wait to be able to walk into The Den and toss her coat onto the chaise longue next to the door, as was their habit, and count coats to see who was hanging out downstairs. She wanted to have more girly nights with Sage, Tate, Piper and Cady, to be hugged by her brawny brothers.

She wanted to watch Tyce's children grow up within a healthy environment, watch as they were taught to juggle their privileged life with service to others, and maybe teach her and Reame's...

Ah... Damn.

Lachlyn laced her hands behind her head. Reame was part of what she wanted, probably the biggest part of what she imagined her new life to look like. He was already an integral part of the family, even more than she was, and it felt right, so very right, for the two of them, together, to be the last cogs in the Ballantyne wheel.

Yes, she'd avoided men and relationships for fear of being disappointed, but a sliver of her soul insisted that she had been waiting for him, that her heart had known what it was looking for and had decided to be patient. Reame would never cheat on her or let her down; once he made a commitment he stuck to it like superglue. With her issues, she needed that doggedness, his unfailing and deep-seated commitment to what he believed in.

She needed him...

Lachlyn dropped the photograph and closed her eyes, wrapping her arms around her waist. *Love* was such a small word for what she felt for him. She thought that when she finally fell in love, her world would seem rosier, light-infused, celestial. It was just... Lachlyn searched for the word...*real*. Loving Reame felt real. It didn't feel perfect or easy or without its challenges. Her truth was that she'd rather be beside Reame in a violent storm than safe and warm by herself.

"Hey, I'm back."

Lachlyn jerked her head up to see her long-legged, broad-shouldered man amble into the room. *Her* Reame. His hair looked like he'd spent the evening running his hand through it and his tie was pulled away from his open collar. Golden stubble covered his jaw and his eyes sliced through her like a hot blade through butter. He slammed to a stop, his eyes narrowing and color leaching from his face.

Oh, God, he knew. Somehow, maybe because he was the other beat of her heart, he knew that she was in love with him, he knew what was in her soul.

And, judging by his tight mouth and tense jaw, he didn't welcome her silent declaration.

"You've made a decision about the family," Reame stated.

Lachlyn felt her knees soften and gripped the table, relief surging through her. He hadn't discerned her feelings of love, instead he assumed that the emotion in her eyes was a result of her deciding to be a part of the Ballantyne family.

Thank God. This way she could still be with him and pretend that they were friends who were having sex. She might even get to sleep with him again...

If she told him the truth, he'd run. They'd start avoiding each other and when they had to attend the same Ballantyne family functions, she'd be forced to endure stilted conversations with him across the dining table at The Den. Reame didn't want a relationship, he'd told her that often enough. Was it fair to burden him with her feelings, especially since the result of that conversation could affect the rest of the family?

She didn't think so.

"What's going on, Lachlyn?"

Reame's hard voice yanked her back and she quickly

shook her head, then nodded toward the wingback chair. Greta looking wide-eyed and nervous, had yet to move from her seat. She looked even grayer than she did before. "Hold on, Ree."

Lachlyn walked over to her desk and, after scanning the list of extensions taped to the wall, picked up her desk phone and punched in a number. "Security? This is Lachlyn Latimore-Ballantyne. Can you contact the supervisor in charge of the cleaning staff and tell him that I have instructed Greta to go home, as she is ill? Also, I want you to call a cab to take Greta home."

Greta let out a low wail and Lachlyn disconnected the call. "Miss Lachlyn, I can't…"

Lachlyn went down on her haunches and rested a light hand on Greta's knee. "You have to go and get well, Greta."

"It's just me and my two girls. I have to work. I need the money. If I am away for too long, I might lose my job."

The hell she would. Lachlyn was not going to allow that to happen. "I will talk to my brothers and, between us, we will make sure that does not happen." Lachlyn looked at Reame, who was now looking bemused. "Reame, would you mind helping me with Miss Greta?"

Reame stepped forward and gently helped the older woman to her feet. He held her elbow as she started to shuffle to the door. He tossed a look over his shoulder and the corners of his mouth quirked upward. "You coming, Miss Latimore-*Ballantyne*?"

The man was as sharp as a spear, Lachlyn thought, picking up her bag. She was going to have to be very careful around him.

Reame parked his SUV in his allocated space and looked at Lachlyn's exquisite profile in the low light of the car's interior. It was late and probably not the best time for this conversation—it had been a long and weird day—but he wasn't the type of guy who shoved his head in the sand.

He needed to know who, what and how and he needed to know now. And when it came to what was going on in Lachlyn's head, he needed to know *yesterday*.

Lachlyn started to open the door but he hit the lock button, effectively jailing her inside the car. She turned to look at him, resignation on her face.

"You're not going to give me any time to work this through, are you?" Lachlyn asked.

Reame shook his head. "Not when I suspect that whatever you have decided will have a big impact on my friends, personally and professionally."

"You're assuming that impact will be negative," Lachlyn said, sounding hurt.

Dammit. He half turned to face her and rested his hand on the knob of the gear shift, idly stroking the soft leather, wishing that he was stroking her skin instead. No, they needed to talk more than they needed sex. In fact, maybe they should hold off on having sex again anytime soon—the connection he'd felt earlier that evening terrified him. It was the first time he'd felt completely lost in a woman's touch. Lachlyn had swept him away. He needed to find some perspective and some distance and he couldn't do that if she slept in his bed, if she climbed beneath his skin.

God help him if she told him that she was falling for him. The quick, almost hopeful thought flittered through his brain and he quickly dismissed the notion, partly because the thought of Lachlyn loving him was fantastic and he shouldn't be feeling that way. As he'd watched his mom fall apart after a quarter century of loving the same man, he'd vowed that he would never put himself at the emotional mercy of another person's love.

His friends thought he was so damn brave for the work he did in the hot, war-ravaged regions of the world but Reame thought that, compared to love, war was easy. No, being brave was loving someone, forging a commitment, bearing the responsibility of making someone else happy. His dad had failed that acid test—he might, too. Yeah, sure, he was scared of being hurt like his mom had been, but what if he was just like his dad and couldn't be a good husband and father?

He refused to do that to Lachlyn...the only person who'd ever tempted him to think of what-ifs and maybes.

"Are we going to sit or are we going to talk?" Lachlyn demanded.

Right. Reame snapped out of his reverie and ran his hand over the back of his neck. "So, tell me what happened tonight."

Lachlyn drummed her fingers against her thigh. "I think I am going to accept the Ballantynes' offer. I think I want to be part of their family."

Okay, that wasn't a huge surprise. The only one who hadn't been convinced that she'd find her way into the family was Lachlyn herself. "Want to tell me what prompted your decision?"

Reame wished that she would look at him. Her eyelashes were dark smudges against her cheeks, and she'd chewed off any remaining lip gloss hours ago. Emotionally exhausted, she looked more beautiful than he'd ever seen her. "I decided to let go of my past and my mother," Lachlyn said, her soft words dropping into the silence between them.

Reame waited a beat before covering her hand with

his and interlocking their fingers. "I need more than that, Lach."

Lachlyn turned so that she was fully facing him, her thigh on the seat and her foot tucked under her opposite knee. She rested the back of her head on the window and pulled her bottom lip between her teeth. She looked both defiant and terrified, pissed off and...sad. Yeah, so sad.

"Our mom was hard work, Ree. She was chronically depressed but no matter how often she went to the hospital and the clinic, she never took her medication for longer than a month, maybe six weeks if we were really lucky. When I was young, she managed to work, just. By the time I hit my teens, she faded in on herself, doing the bare minimum to get through the day for the bare minimum wage. Her biggest ambition was to get home as soon as she could so she could pop a couple of sleeping pills and fall asleep as fast as possible."

His father had been a useless dad but he, at least, had been there. He'd interacted with his children.

"Tyce was amazing," Lachlyn continued. "He quickly realized that if he didn't do something, we'd either end up on the streets or in the system. He hustled for extra cash and, because he was always out beating the wolf away from the door, I was left alone. A lot." Lachlyn's eyes flashed and she held up her hand. "Don't pity me, I was fine. I spent a lot of time in libraries."

Reame just picked up her hand and rested his lips on her knuckles before placing it palm-down on his thigh, anchoring it, and her, with his much bigger hand.

"One day—it was around six in the evening and my mom had already gone to bed—I heard someone knocking on the door. It was a kid I knew from school."

Her voice had changed, Reame realized. It was now

flatter and harder. "I had a bit of a crush on him so I let him in."

"How old were you?" Reame asked, hoping the sick feeling in his stomach wasn't warranted.

"Fourteen, nearly fifteen. He asked to see my room and as soon as he entered the room, he slammed the door shut and lunged for me."

Reame knew that he had to maintain control, that if she saw the rage on his face, she'd bolt. And he needed to know what happened, who the guy was, because that kid was now an adult and Reame would love to track him down.

"Did he rape you?" Reame asked bluntly, wincing at his own blade-sharp voice.

Lachlyn quickly shook her head and Reame felt a knot or two in his spine easing. "No, nothing like that. He kissed me and copped a few feels, and I was yelling like a banshee."

"Why didn't your mom—" Reame started to ask and his words drifted off. "She didn't hear you because she was asleep."

"The walls were paper-thin. You could hear a cricket sneeze," Lachlyn snapped. "No, she was either too medicated or she heard me and didn't give a damn. That night changed everything for me."

Of course it did. "Being sexually assaulted would."

"I told you, the boy didn't get that far. I'm not trying to excuse what he did but his actions didn't cause me to shut down. I don't want you to think that I avoided having sex because of him, either. I got plenty far with plenty of guys."

"Not what I wanted to know," Reame growled, the thought of another man's hand on her causing a fine red mist to appear behind his eyes. *This is not the time to feel jealous, moron.* "Did you at least report the assault?"

Lachlyn refused to look at him and Reame gripped her jaw and gently lifted her face. "Lach? Please tell me that you reported him?"

Lachlyn pursed her lips. "You're the first person I've told, ever."

Crap. Reame dropped his hand and felt like he'd been punched by an iron fist. *What. The. Hell?*

"Are you insane? That was attempted rape!" Reame roared.

"Calm down, Reame," Lachlyn said, clearly rattled. "It was an attempted something but I handled him, without my mom's help! And that's the point that I'm trying to get to!"

Reame reined in his temper, knowing that if he continued to imagine some little reject's sweaty hands on a young Lachlyn, he might put his fist through the windscreen which would a) hurt and b) cost a fortune. He took a couple of deep breaths and nodded for her to continue.

"Up until that night, I wanted a family, I desperately wanted a big, loud happy group of people who loved me and whom I loved. My mom's nonreaction to me being in danger, her lack of a response, hurt me so much that I decided, there and then, that a family couldn't be trusted to be there for me, that a family caused more hurt than anything else. I decided to go on my own, to isolate myself, to rely on myself and only myself. I refused to be a helpless little girl anymore."

Reame's heart wept for the young girl who'd lost all her dreams and her faith in humanity in one fell swoop.

Lachlyn took a deep breath and he saw the light of determination in her eyes, a strength of purpose that he hadn't seen before. Frankly, it turned him the hell on, which was totally inappropriate given the circumstances. "Tonight, I realized that I was done with giving my mom, and that night, so much power over my life. I wanted a family. I *still* want a family. I've been offered one, a spectacular one, and it's time I sank or swam. I've decided to swim, to become a Ballantyne. It feels right."

It was right. She had Connor's enormous capacity to love—she'd just buried it for a long time. When she forgot to be shy, to keep herself insulated, she was funny and outgoing and a little wacky, in the best way possible. She was just like her dad.

Lachlyn pulled in a deep breath and Reame saw her chest rise. He looked into her determined face, saw the resolution in her eyes and knew that she was about to drop another bomb in his lap. "Since I'm spilling my guts here, I might as well keep going."

Reame wanted to beg her not to. He didn't want to hear what she was about to say, because he instinctively knew that whatever it was would change something between them.

"As you know, I never had sex with anyone before you. Not because I was scared of sex or because I was a prude or because I wanted to save myself for marriage. None of the guys felt right and I didn't feel enough for them for the intimacy sex requires." Lachlyn sounded like she was carefully picking her words and each one dripped acid onto his soul. He didn't want to hear this. He didn't want to deal with whatever she was thinking, feeling.

"I knew, within hours of meeting you, that you were the one I wanted to make love to." Lachlyn tried to smile. "You're the only one I ever want to make love to…"

"Jesus, Lachlyn," Reame groaned. "Don't do this, please."

"Don't do what?" Lachlyn cocked her head. "Tell you that I think that you are incredible, that I think we could be good together? That I'd like to explore this to see where it goes?"

Reame felt a surge of anger. Why did women always do this? It didn't matter how clear you were, how simply you explained the situation, they always, always thought they could change your mind! He didn't want a relationship! Hadn't he told her that repeatedly?

How dare she spring this on him? How dare she try this female BS on him?

But underneath the anger, the fear, something hot and bright and exciting ran through him at the thought of them trying to create a family within the bigger family they were both such an intrinsic part of.

The delight and hope that thought raised made him scared, and when he felt fear, he always, always went on the attack.

Reame gripped the steering wheel, his knuckles white in the low light of the car. "Okay, let's go through this again," He said, keeping his voice bored, flat and sarcastic. "I told you that I couldn't sleep with you, that you were a job and nothing more. When we did sleep together, I told you that I wasn't interested in the responsibilities a relationship brings, in being at someone's beck and call. I told you, over and over, that I don't want a relationship!"

Lachlyn, instead of reacting to his anger, just looked at him, her amazing eyes steady on his face. She nodded. "Okay."

Okay? What did that mean? "That's all you're going to say?" Reame demanded.

Lachlyn's eyes cooled. "Did you think I was going to beg you to be with me? Did you think I was going to cry because you said no? Okay means that I get it, that I hear you, that I absolutely and unequivocally accept that you are uninterested in anything more than sex."

Reame felt like he was standing on quicksand and sinking fast. He'd totally lost control of this conversation. "Uh—"

Lachlyn tugged on the door handle. "Would you mind letting me out of the car now?"

Reame, not knowing what else to do or say, unlocked the car and watched as Lachlyn grabbed her bag and exited his vehicle. Following her to the elevator, he noticed the tension in her back, and when she turned, her normally vibrant face was blank and expressionless.

"I'll stay here tonight but I'd appreciate it if you could arrange for me to return to The Den. Linc and Tate are back and they have repeatedly said that they are happy to have me. If you still feel it's necessary for me to have a PPO, I'll take whoever you suggest." Lachlyn's hard eyes pinned him to the floor. "And I will pay for his or her services."

Over his dead body...

He couldn't leave it this way. He didn't want to lose her, dammit. He didn't want anything to change. He liked her, he loved the sex, enjoyed having her hang around his house. Days without her would be bleak but he couldn't give her what she was asking for. "Lachlyn, look...it's been an emotional couple of weeks. Maybe you're just a bit confused about what you feel...about me and about the Ballantynes."

Lachlyn whipped around and slapped her hand onto his chest. "Don't!"

Reame jerked back as her yell reverberated throughout the cube. It was the first time he'd ever heard her raise her voice and he took a precautionary step backward. Lachlyn closed her eyes for a brief moment and when she opened them again his knees nearly buckled at the emotion he saw bubbling in those dark blue depths.

"Just don't, Reame," Lachlyn said, her tone defeated. "For the first time in fifteen years I am seeing my life and myself clearly and if you keep talking, I might be tempted to start believing you. Because it's easier not to love. It's easier not to be involved. It's easier not to make an effort. I have been taking the easy route all this time and I'm done with it. So you don't love me, you will never love me, and you know what? It's okay, I can live with it. I learned a long time ago that you can't make someone love you—they either do or don't. I never begged my mother to love me and I certainly won't beg you."

The elevator doors opened and Lachlyn pushed an agitated hand through her hair, tears in her eyes but refusing to let them fall. "Don't worry about me, Reame, I will be fine. I always am."

With those words whipping his soul, Lachlyn walked into his hallway and straight into the spare room, the sound of the lock engaging signifying that she was done talking.

Reame rested his open palm and then his forehead on the door, thinking that he'd maybe lost his only chance to be spectacularly happy.

Twelve

Standing by the window of the formal reception room in The Den, Lachlyn used one finger to pull aside the sheer drape to check to see if there was a long-limbed, broad-shouldered blond man walking down the pavement toward the building. Nope. Still no Reame.

A day after leaving Reame's apartment, accompanied by a burly, noncommunicative PPO named Jack, she'd sent a message out on the family group chat, asking the Ballantyne family for a meeting, at a time convenient for them, to discuss her future. Reame was part of that group and while her head told her that he wouldn't intrude on a private family meeting, her heart wished he would.

She missed him terribly. They'd only been apart a few days but her heart was a ball of dough being pushed through a pasta machine. She wished that there was a way for them to be friends, to have some sort of platonic relationship and maybe, sometime in the future, they could. But not now, not when she wanted what her siblings had: love, affection and, judging by their heated looks, spectacular sex lives.

Reame hadn't lied to her, he hadn't led her on and she could blame nobody but herself for her state of misery. She shouldn't have slept with him, shouldn't have fallen in love with him. He was the one person she should've kept her emotional distance from. But then she would never have known him, heard his deep laugh, been able to look behind that superhero facade to the stressed-out man behind it, seen what an amazing friend he was.

Lachlyn straightened her shoulders. She missed him but she did not regret a minute she'd spent with him. He'd done so much for her. Aside from teaching her how amazing sex could be, he'd moved her into his apartment, helped her see herself and her past more clearly.

She'd love to have any kind of contact from him, but he'd have to make the first step. Hearing footsteps behind her Lachlyn allowed the drape to drop. Today would not be that day. Pity, she thought he might enjoy what she had to say. Lachlyn smiled at Linc entering the room. She accepted the kiss he dropped on her temple. "Are you sure you want to do this?"

Lachlyn nodded.

"Okay, then." Linc frowned and rubbed his thumb over the blue stripe under her right eye. "Still not sleeping, Lach?"

"Not really."

"Reame?"

Reame and Linc were childhood friends, best friends. She was not going to come between them so she'd never badmouth him. Not that she had anything bad to say about him. He didn't love her and wasn't interested in anything more than a hookup. That she wanted more was her problem, not his. "Nothing about this is his fault, Linc. In fact, I'm the one who's to blame."

Linc frowned. "I love Reame like a brother but I have never met anyone more stubborn, and that's saying something because I have Jaeger and Beck as brothers."

"Still, I don't want you blaming him for any of this," Lachlyn insisted. "And actually, I'd like you to do something for me, if you would."

Linc nodded so Lachlyn picked up her bag from the chair where she'd dumped it earlier and pulled a small box out of its depths. Nervous, she handed the box to Linc, who flipped open the lid. Lachlyn ran a finger over the unusual band—meteorite, amber and platinum—and remembered Reame's face as he'd examined the ring on his balcony just two weeks back. "I know you gave this to me and I don't want to sound ungrateful but Reame loves this ring. He loved your Dad—Connor—and I'll never wear it. But he might."

Linc didn't say anything so Lachlyn tried to tug the ring from his grasp. "Sorry, I've offended you. You gave me the ring and I should keep it. Just forget I said anything, okay?" she gabbled, her face flushing.

Linc snapped the lid closed before shoving the ring into the inside pocket of his jacket. He smiled at Lachlyn, wrapping a strong arm around her shoulder. "I love you because you are Connor's, Lach, but better than that, I like you. You are a rather amazing human being."

Lachlyn felt tears burning the back of her throat and she rested her head on her brother's shoulder, content to stand next to him and soak up his strength, because God knew, she would need it for the days and weeks ahead.

Despite recording the Ballantyne siblings' interview on the city's most watched morning chat show, Reame had no intention of watching it. He didn't need to know, as most of the city did, the intricacies of the financial settlement that the Ballantynes came to with their new sister.

He'd resisted temptation for two solid days before cursing himself to hell and back and pulling up the segment. He skipped through the footage until he saw Lachlyn and leaned forward in his chair, drinking her in. She wore a reddish-pink sheath that skimmed her tiny body and a matching shade of lipstick. The stylist had made her normally smooth hair look a little edgy and he liked it. Her eyes looked, as they always did, endlessly wide and deeply blue. Sage sat on one side of her and Linc on the other and, zooming in, he could see the fine tremble in her fingers.

She was terrified but hiding it well.

He should have been there, Reame realized, he should've been with her in the green room, rubbing her back, trying to distract her. He should have been standing off to the side, beyond the cameras, in her line of vision so that she could have an anchor, someone to talk to beside the pretentious interviewers and the cold cameras.

He hadn't been there because not only was he a scared wuss but a crappy friend. But being Lachlyn's friend was out of the question. He liked her, was possibly in love with her, but he didn't trust that what they had could last, that a relationship with her would stand the test of time. It was too big of a risk.

Being alone was, as she'd said, so much easier. Cowardly, but easier.

"So, tell me about the money."

Sage took Lachlyn's hand and squeezed it in encouragement and none of the Ballantynes leaned forward to answer the interviewer's forthright question. Lachlyn cleared her throat and Reame held his breath, feeling inordinately proud that she was stepping up and claiming her place as a Ballantyne.

"We're not prepared to go into details about personal family business, Lora, but my siblings and I have decided to start a foundation to support children from low-income families who live with parents suffering from depression. Apart from my work as the Ballantyne archivist and historian, I will be running the foundation, with the help and support of my siblings."

Reame swallowed the emotion in his throat. He could read between the lines: the money they'd offered her as part of Connor's estate would be channeled into the foundation. Linc would've only done that if Lachlyn accepted that she was part owner of the other Ballantyne assets. Linc would've also insisted that she take a cash settlement.

God, he was proud of her.

So proud that she could grasp love when it was offered to her, that she could look fear in the eye and kick its ass. He could keep his cool on the battlefield, fire and be fired upon, but he, despite his medals for bravery, didn't have a fraction of the courage his woman did.

Reame felt acid burn a hole through his stomach. Yeah, he loved her, he was pretty sure he did, but love wasn't enough.

He wanted a goddamn guarantee. He pointed the remote control at his TV and viciously jammed the button, replacing Lachlyn's exquisite face with a black screen. And if he couldn't get one of those then what was the point of sitting in his empty apartment feeling miserable? He might as well go out and try to find a distraction.

It wasn't going to work, he knew this, but he grabbed his coat and keys and headed out anyway.

* * *

Hours later, in a club called Burn, Reame took a tiny sip of the whiskey he'd been nursing for two hours and told himself to go home. He wasn't having any fun and the bartender kept sending him dirty looks for taking up a prime space on the corner of the bar. The strobe lights felt like they were slicing his brain.

He was tired, he was miserable but he didn't think he could go back to an empty apartment. He'd rather sit here and people watch and bat off occasional requests from women to buy him a drink or dance.

Reame felt movement at his elbow and the sweet scent of clean hair drifted over his shoulder. God, not another one. "Thanks but I'm not interested," he said, not bothering to look over. Eye contact always led to more conversation so he didn't bother.

He just wanted to sit here and get hammered. Unfortunately, getting hammered also required more than two drinks in two hours.

"Please, as if I would be interested in buying your sorry ass a drink."

Reame spun around on his chair to see Sage leaning against the bar, her Ballantyne eyes on his face and, worse, deeply unhappy with him. He looked around for Tyce, didn't see her tall, ripped husband, but did see the very pregnant Piper and the just-a-little-less pregnant Cady waddling toward him, causing the crowds to part. Tate followed in their wake.

Reame groaned. "What the hell are you doing here?" he demanded, after Sage ordered soft drinks and wine for Tate.

Sage cocked her head to the side and sent him a slow smile that shriveled his balls. "Well, we decided to come and help you with your quest to have wild sex with a wild woman."

Yeah, right. And he just saw a purple pig flying past. Man, his friends had very big mouths, Reame thought. And the only woman he wanted to make love with wasn't here.

The pregnant fairies reached and flanked him, dropping kisses on his cheek and staking their claim. Even if he did want to pick someone up, there was no way anyone would be brave enough to push their way through the barrier the four Ballantyne women had created around him. Good thing that sex with a stranger was the last thing on his mind.

Sage jammed her sharp elbow into his side. "There's a blonde eyeing you at ten o'clock."

Reame had noticed and dismissed her. "Why are you here?" he demanded, knocking back his drink and ordering another. "And how did you find me?"

"GPS locator on your phone. You know how Linc likes to know where all his chickens are," Sage replied.

"And we're here because our men think that they should stay out of your and Lachlyn's business," Tate added, frustration lacing her voice.

He agreed but he was smart enough not to say that aloud.

Sage poked her fingernail into his bicep. "They have all conveniently forgotten that they'd all needed help to get the fabulousness that you see before you."

Reame grinned. The Ballantyne women were pretty fabulous.

"Personally, I think that they are just a little scared of you and your Special Forces skills," Piper said, climbing up onto a bar stool and holding her enormous belly. Reame eyed it, worried.

"You're not about to go into labor are you?"

Piper looked at her expensive wristwatch. "In a few hours."

Reame felt the blood drain from his face. God, he was so dead. Jaeger was going to kill him. Then the four witches exploded into raucous laughter and he knew he'd been had. When they stopped cackling, Piper told him that he was safe, she still had six weeks to go.

"Twins. Bigger than normal," she explained between waves of laughter.

Thank God. "Not funny," he muttered.

"Oh, it so is," Sage replied. Then her face sobered and she walked to stand between his legs, holding his face in her hands. "You, however, are not. Why are you doing this to yourself? Why are you doing this to Lachlyn? Any fool can see that you are perfect for each other. Whenever you're together the air crackles. You love her, she loves you."

"I don't love her," Reame said, his heart cracking on that huge lie.

Sage dropped her hands and folded her arms, tapping her foot. It was a sign that she was getting mad and he tried to avoid Sage when her temper was up. "Fine. Then go and pick up that blonde and take her home for some wild sex."

Dammit. She had him there. "Don't want to do that, either." Reame ran a hand through his hair and decided to be honest. "Look, I'm just scared that what I'm feeling now, what I could feel if I let myself, won't last. That one day I'll wake up and she won't be in love with me and I won't be in love with her and we won't feel what we are feeling now."

Four wise sets of eyes looked at him with complete compassion and heartfelt acceptance. Tate leaned forward and placed her cool hand on his arm. "Because of your folks?"

"Yeah," Reame said, his voice gruff. "My mom, she collapsed in on herself. I don't want that to happen to me or Lachlyn. She became a shadow of herself and I don't want that for us, either."

Sage wrinkled her nose. "I know your mom, Reame, and you know that I love her but, God bless her, she's not the strongest branch on the tree. Your dad took care of her, you take care of her, she's never had to make a decision in her life. Lachlyn is fully capable of looking after herself and if you did split up later she'd cope. It would suck but she'd be okay. You're the toughest guy I know, so you'd be fine, too. Using your mother as a yardstick is not a good idea, bud."

Reame was still trying to process her wise words, when Cady spoke for the first time. "Reame, you are also forgetting that love isn't just a feeling, it's a choice. When problems or tough times appear, the giddiness of love evaporates. You have to choose love. You have to choose to ride out a temporary lack of feelings, and believe that when the problem resolves itself—through honest communication and hard work—they will return."

That made sense, Reame thought, hope sliding into his soul. If he took their advice, he could almost, maybe, start thinking about approaching Lachlyn, about taking it slow, not looking too far into the future.

Tate opened her bag, shoved her hand inside and pulled out a small black box. She tossed it into the air and Reame snapped his fingers around the velvet square. "What's this?"

Tate shrugged. "No idea. Linc-the-wuss asked me to give this to you." The song changed, the volume increased and Tate's attractive face split into a wide smile. "Oh, I love this song. Who wants to dance?"

Cady and Piper both nodded enthusiastically and Reame sent them both an anxious look. "No labor-inducing moves, okay? Please? I'm on my knees begging here."

"No promises," Piper said as she walked—waddled—away.

Reame was considering yanking them from the dance floor—how, he wasn't sure—when Sage bumped her shoulder into his. "Open it, Ree."

Reame sent another look toward the dance floor, saw Piper and Cady swaying gently and Tate dancing like a mad woman, and then looked down at the box in his hand. He lifted the lid and saw Connor's ring, the one piece of jewelry he'd always loved. His heart tried to climb out through his ribs, and he fell utterly and completely in love.

"She loves you, Ree," Sage said softly.

"I know. I love her, too," Reame replied, taking the ring out and sliding it onto the ring finger of his right hand. It stuck at the knuckle so he tried the ring finger of his left hand. It was a perfect fit.

"Yeah, that works," Sage said, sliding her hand under his arm and linking her fingers with his. Sage sent him a sappy smile. "So what are you going to do about it?"

"Something. But not tonight." Reame sighed, knowing that he had to get his friends' women home safely before he could pursue his own.

Sage looked at the dance floor and then raised a cocky eyebrow in his direction. "You do know that they are going to be out there for hours, right? Or until Piper's water breaks," Sage said, amusement lacing her voice.

Shoot me now.

Sage tugged his hand. "Come on then, we might as well dance."

Reame slid the empty black box into his jacket pocket and sighed. Might as well, he thought.

"This building is a renovated prewar condominium. This particular apartment is sixteen hundred square feet and the ceilings are at ten feet. There are tilt-and-turn windows, oversize and facing north and east."

Lachlyn walked across the hardwood floors in the empty apartment to stand by one of those turn and tilt windows. Tuning out her Realtor, Marla's, voice, she started envisioning the space as an expansive lounge and dining room. Still, this condo building on the edge of Midtown wasn't where she wanted to be.

The Den wasn't ideal, either. She loved her new family but needed her space. She could go back to her apartment in Woodside but that wasn't practical. Her apartment was too accessible, she was still mad at Riccardo and she didn't want to go back to having a thirty-minute commute to work.

She needed, wanted, a place in Manhattan. When she'd agreed to officially become a Ballantyne, Linc had been surprisingly intractable about the financial aspects of their deal. Yes, he'd agree to a portion of the forty million being funneled into the Latimore-Ballantyne Foundation but she had to keep at least 50 percent for herself. She would also receive dividends from the company, director's fees and if they sold any assets, a fifth of the proceeds. Her bank account was ridiculously healthy and she could afford to buy a swish apartment anywhere in the city.

She'd looked at over twenty apartments and none of them had caught her fancy. Lachlyn knew that was only because they weren't on the top floor of the Jepsen & Associates building a dozen blocks from here.

"There's a sound system that runs through the house," Marla said, and Lachlyn tried to look like she cared. Judging by Marla's eye roll, she failed on that score and the real estate agent walked back into the hall.

Gripping the edge of the open windowsill, she closed her eyes and ordered herself to find her enthusiasm. Reame didn't want her with him, he didn't want anything from her—including her friendship—and the sooner she wrapped her head around that fact, the happier she would be. Well, she'd start the process to becoming happier...

This was a pretty apartment, Lachlyn thought, forcing herself to look around. Light, airy, new. It was probably the best she'd seen and she could come to like this place if she wasn't so hung up on that other place.

And that man.

"What do you think, Jack?" Lachlyn called out, knowing that Jack was standing in the hall guarding the door. She didn't expect a reply; in a week Jack had said less than ten words to her.

"I prefer mine."

Reame. Lachlyn's heart flew up her throat and a great shiver racked her body from tip to toe. Her instinct was to turn around and fly into his arms, but she kept her back to him, her eyes staring, unseeing, out the window.

"Yours isn't available to me," Lachlyn whispered, aching. "What are you doing here, Reame?"

Lachlyn heard his footsteps on the bare floor and then he was standing next to her, his back to the window, so close she could feel his heat. Lachlyn lifted her eyes to look into that face she loved so deeply and her eyes connected with his, but, as per usual, she was unable to read the emotion churning in all that green.

"Hi," Reame said softly, sitting down on the sill, his hand gripping the edge, his pinkie finger intertwining with hers. Lachlyn felt sparks run up her arm and across her shoulder blades and it took all her willpower not to jerk away from him.

"Hi."

"As for what I'm doing here," Reame said, his voice low, "I have a few things to say to you."

He probably did, but nothing she really, really wanted to hear. "Okay."

"Firstly, congratulations on establishing the foundation and on doing that TV interview. That couldn't have been easy and I'm proud of you."

Lachlyn nodded. Yep, that she'd expected. Now he would say thank you for the ring and he'd wander out of her life again. Could she stand it? Did she have a choice?

Reame didn't speak for a long time and Lachlyn was tempted to fill the awkwardness with inane chatter. She held back and eventually Reame pushed his hand through his hair before rubbing his chin. "You are so much braver than I am, Lach. I am in awe of you."

Lachlyn frowned at him, utterly surprised. "But you're the soldier. You got the medals and everything."

"I have no problem risking my body, but my heart? Not so much. Until you, it was easy to dismiss love, to say that I didn't want it, that it wasn't worth the risk." Reame's finger tightened around hers. "But it's so worth the risk, Lach. You are worth the risk."

She was terrified to trust what she thought he was suggesting. Lachlyn searched his face for an answer and saw his love for her in his eyes. "I love you, Lachlyn, whether you are a Latimore or a Ballantyne. Whoever you are is the person I want to be with, wherever you are is where I want to be. Is there any chance of you forgiving me for being a moron and giving me a second chance to see where this goes? Your pace, your choice."

Lachlyn rested her forehead on the ball of his shoulder, completely overwhelmed. Words of love bubbled in her throat but burst as soon as they hit her tongue.

It took her a while to string some words together. "About this apartment."

Lachlyn felt tension run through Reame's body and his shoulder slumped beneath her forehead, as if he were disappointed. Lifting her head, she kissed the side of his jaw. She couldn't wait another moment to embrace their happy…

"I hate this apartment and every other one I've looked at because it doesn't have you in it. I want to fall asleep in your arms, wake up to your smile. I want you to be my best friend, my lover, my emergency contact number."

Reame wound his arms around her waist, pulling her between his legs and tucking her into his chest. "Your husband? Any chance of that happening? I already have the ring."

Reame lifted his left hand and she saw Connor's ring on his wedding finger. She did a small, excited dance. "You're wearing the ring."

Reame smiled and Lachlyn's heart rolled over. "It's the only finger it fits. I thought about taking it off but since my heart will only ever belong to you, what's the point?"

Lachlyn felt her eyes prickle and burn. "Will you take it off for our wedding day when we say our vows?"

Reame held her face in his big hands, looking younger and softer and happier than she'd ever seen him. "Yeah, I can do that." His thumb caressed her bottom lip. "I suppose you'd like a ring, too?" he teased.

Lachlyn smiled. She pretended to think. "Man, I wish we had a gemstone hunter and a jewelry designer in the family."

Reame laughed. "It would help if we knew of anyone who owned a jewelry store or two."

Reame's mouth curved against hers and his kiss was full of promise, a taste of the future. Emotion whirled and swirled and Lachlyn felt an irrational burst of fear, thinking that if she didn't step back now, she never would. Old habits, she thought, pushing the fear away. *You're not going to spoil this moment.*

But she still felt the need to pull away from Reame, to look him in the eye. "It's not going to be easy, Reame. We're not easy people."

Reame nodded. "I know that but I don't want easy, Lach, and neither do you. I promise to fight for us, to surf every wave big enough to drown us. I need you to do the same. I don't want easy. I've had easy. I want multidimensional, I want real, I want every layer and level of you."

Oh, God. Words to buckle her knees, to melt her heart. Lachlyn curled her arms around his neck and stood on her tiptoes to push her nose into the side of his throat, to inhale him, wishing she could step inside him. Her words, by contrast, were small and succinct. "I love you, Ree. So much. Always."

Reame stroked her back. "So, does that mean that you're not buying this apartment?"

Lachlyn stepped back, her eyes welling with happy tears. "I still need a place to stay."

"Funny, I know a place..."

Lachlyn smiled. "Does it have room for a bodyguard?"

"Sweetheart, trust me, I intend to guard, and worship, your body for the rest for my life."

Epilogue

Walking down the stairs to The Den, Lachlyn lifted the material of her chiffon dress—as close to the shade of Reame's eyes as she could find—so that the hem didn't drag on the floor. She peeked over the bannister to see the entire Ballantyne clan, formally dressed, filling the ridiculously big hall.

Outside, four limousines were waiting to transport the family to the Forrester Hotel where they, as a family, were hosting a spring ball to raise funds for the Latimore-Ballantyne Foundation. It was also her and Reame's informal engagement party and, unlike that ball she'd attended three months ago as a newbie Ballantyne, she didn't feel like she was walking up to the executioner's chopping block.

Before walking down the next flight of stairs, she took a moment to look at her family. Apart from the next generation of Ballantynes, everyone important to her stood in the hallway of The Den. Tyce and Sage, her baby bump looking like a bowling ball under her designer gown. Her Ballantyne brothers, hot and urbane as they traded insults in a way that was all affection and pure habit. Tate, effortlessly beautiful. The new mothers, Cady and Piper, neither one looking like they'd recently given birth, Piper to twin boys and Cady to a red-haired little girl.

Her eyes danced over her family, love and affection filling her up and making her feel a little sappy and a lot grateful. She almost didn't want to look at Reame, because if she did emotion would get the better of her. Happy tears would slide down her face and she'd ruin the makeup she'd spent far too much time applying. But she couldn't *not* look at him. He was the beat of her heart, the pull of the moon, the bedrock of her life. Reame stood at the bottom of the stairs, looking ludicrously hot in a plain tuxedo and black tie. Reame's eyes darkened and she knew what he was thinking because, well, she was thinking it too.

Let's blow this off and go back to bed.

Lachlyn grinned and rolled her eyes—silently praying they never lost the passion between them—and Reame smiled, warming her from the inside out. Resuming her descent down the stairs, she held his eyes, so happy to be walking to him, into his arms, so grateful to be loved by such a spectacular man. Pulling her eyes from Reame, she flicked a glance at Connor's portrait and blew him a mental kiss.

Thanks, Dad. I wish I knew you.

Connor's voice, low and amused, drifted through her head. *You do know me, Lach. I'm Linc's capability, Jaeger's adventurous spirit and Beck's big brain. I'm Sage's creativity and I'm your bravery.*

Before she could process his words, Lachlyn felt the air move next to her, saw the streak of pajamas passing her at full tilt. Shaw released a banshee yell as he flung himself off the stairs into fresh air. Again.

Reame stepped up, snatched Shaw out of the air and tossed his godson over his shoulder. Lachlyn rolled her eyes but, as per usual, none of the Ballantynes batted so much as an eyelash.

As she tucked herself inside Reame's side, Lachlyn felt compelled to look at her dad's portrait again. She felt Reame kiss her hair, her temple. "All gorgeous, always mine," he said softly.

Connor would approve, Lachlyn thought. He'd loved Reame so much. She looked at his painted face again—the masculine version of hers—and furiously blinked away her happy tears. Then Connor's deep voice drifted through Lachlyn's mind again.

Think of me as the Ballantyne guardian angel. I'm in you, with you, around you, always protecting you. Then she heard her father's long-suffering sigh. *That being said, it pains me to admit that I might not be able to keep up with Shaw. That kid runs faster than I can fly.*

* * * * *

THE TWIN
BIRTHRIGHT

CATHERINE MANN

"A daughter may outgrow your lap,
but she will never outgrow your heart."
—Anonymous

To my daughters, Haley and Maggie.
It's been a joy and honor having watched
you both grow into miraculous women.
I love you!

One

Some women dreamed of giving birth in a hospital, husband holding her hand.

Some visualized delivering at home, man of her dreams breathing alongside.

No one fantasized about bringing a new life into the world in an SUV, in a snowstorm, with her ex-fiancé playing "catch the baby." Or in Naomi Steele's case, *babies. Plural.* Two of them. The first of which was due to make an appearance with the next…

"Push! Push, Naomi, push," Royce Miller's soft, deep voice radiated confidence in the confines of his Suburban, heater blasting inside, snow pelting the vehicle outside.

"I am pushing, damn it. I've been pushing." Because there wasn't any need to wait. No help was on the way. Cell phone reception was almost nil on a deserted highway north of Anchorage, Alaska. Sporadic bursts of connectivity offered only minimal reassurance that anyone had heard their pleas for rescue when she'd gone into labor a month early.

Even if help could make it to them through this Alaska blizzard.

The seats of the SUV had been flattened, blankets under her, an emergency kit including first aid spread out beside her. Thank goodness he'd kept his vehicle well stocked in the event of being stranded in a storm. But then of course he had. He was always analytical, organized, the brilliant scientist and professor who planned for any—and every—contingency.

She had her own analytical side as an attorney, but was more known for her flair for the dramatic, which had served her well in the courtroom more than once.

Royce knelt on the floor, his muscular body wedged in, but he still managed to look comfortable. At ease. In control.

Pain ripped through her, her whole body locked in one big muscle spasm beyond anything she'd read about or heard about in child birthing classes. She understood intellectually that a couple of pushes wouldn't get the job done, especially for a first-time mom, but she was so done. Ready to quit. Close to tears and burning to scream, but she didn't want to put any additional burden on Royce when he had to be afraid, in spite of his calm demeanor.

Beads of sweat rolled down his face.

And she knew she wasn't going to get any relief with this contraction. Disappointment stung even as the pain eased. She exhaled and sagged back. Taking the moment to store up every kernel of energy as best she could.

Light from outside grew dimmer with the ending day and thick storm. Their car lights provided minimal illumination. Royce had hung two flashlights with bungie cords. She didn't want to think about what would happen if this took too long and they ran out of gasoline.

After months on bed rest for her blood pressure, Naomi had been released by the doctor *today*. Once they'd finished the appointment, all she'd wanted was a simple afternoon drive and to celebrate a less restricted final month of her pregnancy. She was sure about their due date, since hers had been an in vitro fertilization, with a donor sperm. When she'd made the decision, she'd been worried her chance to be a mother was passing her by; that was before she met eccentric research scientist Royce Miller. Their relationship had been doomed from the start. She'd been just over two months pregnant and it had been too easy for him to use her babies as a substitute for his unresolved past.

Royce patted her knee with his broad hand. "Are you warm enough?" The wind howled, nearly drowning out his words. "I've got my coat ready for the babies, but I can give you my shirt."

She knew those beads of sweat on his forehead had nothing to do with the temperature in the vehicle.

"I'm fine, really." Even if she had been cold—which she wasn't because currently her body was on fire with pain—she couldn't take anything more from Royce. He'd given up so much of his life for her, even after they'd ended their engagement. He'd seemed to feel obligated to stay by her side until the babies were born. Every day since the breakup had been bittersweet torture. Being with him filled her with regret, sadness but—ultimately—resolve.

And she'd needed that resolve to stand her ground— she'd made the right decision in ending things—and stand up to this silently stubborn man. He'd steadfastly continued to show up with his own agenda.

Like insisting on driving her to the doctor's office today even though she had over a dozen family members who would have stepped in to help. After the smooth-as-silk OB visit, Royce hadn't driven far and the weather report had been clear as a bell. They'd been doing everything right—

Another contraction hit her hard and fast, with minimal buildup to warn her. She held back the urge to shout, and forced even breaths in and out—well, as even as possible. The distant sound of Royce counting to ten grounded her until, finally, the contraction subsided and she could relax again.

He was always so careful and precise. Unlike her reckless self. They'd broken up twice, and the second time had stuck. Well, stuck in that they stopped sleeping together and any mention of the love they'd once shared was off-limits.

And like karma laughing in her face at supposed boundaries, here she was, stuck in a snowstorm with him, just like the day they'd met nearly six months ago. Theirs had been a whirlwind romance, with an engagement that had ended nearly as quickly as it had begun.

They were just too different. They wanted different things.

At first, they'd struggled with her need to prove her strength and independence, a by-product of her teenage battle with cancer. His overprotective ways had been stifling. But eventually they'd found a balance in that. Even so, in the end, there'd been another, larger problem lurking, one core to their personalities. Something they couldn't change.

He was a brilliant, reclusive man who thrived on his work, but battled emotional insecurity, searching for a "replacement" family. She was an extrovert who flourished in the courtroom and in the company of her big, boisterous family. She'd nearly gone stir-crazy in their secluded cabin. And he'd been climbing the walls when they'd tried living in the city. She couldn't bear to see him lose what made him so special in the first place. They'd had to admit they were just too different.

And he was an admirable man. That ripped at her most of all. Still, she'd tried to push him away, but no matter what she'd said and done, he wouldn't go. His stubbornness only solidified her opinion that any emotion he'd invested in their time together was all about the babies.

He had insisted on staying in touch during her pregnancy, helping, even though the babies weren't his biological children. Seeing him was beyond difficult. Her heart broke over and over again. But given that he consulted for her family's oil business, there was no avoiding each other completely. They had to learn to coexist peacefully.

She just hadn't expected that coexisting to include him parked between her bent knees delivering her twins—

Another pain gripped her, and as hard as she tried to force those breaths in and out, panic built. "I'm scared," she gasped, fighting against the pain, which only made it worse. "What if something's wrong? We're out in the middle of nowhere—"

"Breathe, Naomi, breathe. Everything's going to be okay."

"Like you have—" she huffed a half-hearted breath "—any choice—" another gasp "—but to say that."

"All was well at your last checkup…" He paused, then continued, his voice intense, "I see the baby's head coming closer. You're doing it. Come on, Naomi."

"How do you know?" she groused, while pushing, gripping the door handle.

He rested a hand on her knee, catching her gaze with his deep brown eyes as the contraction subsided. He was steady. In control. "I've actually delivered a baby before."

"Really?" She wanted to believe it. So much.

"I never told you that?" The smile on his handsome face lit hope inside her.

"No, you didn't." But then they hadn't known each other even a year yet. So much passion—and then heartbreak—had been packed into a short time. They hadn't been able to keep their hands off each other from the start. They'd let that sexual connection take precedence over getting to know each other.

"Let's get these babies into the world and I'll tell you all about it."

The next contraction cut short anything she might have thought about saying, if she could even remember words. Pain gripped her. More powerful than any of the others. Pressure built, intensified until she lost track of counting. It surely had to be more than ten—

The pressure released and the vehicle filled with… cries. Her baby. Tears welled in Naomi's eyes, blurring the vision of Royce holding her newborn child up for her to see.

"It's a girl," he said, emotion clogging his voice as he confirmed the gender ultrasounds had shown.

But hearing it now still carried such a momentous thrill.

"She's okay?"

"A healthy set of lungs, ten fingers and ten toes."

Once Royce tied off the cord and wrapped the infant in his parka, he passed the bundle to Naomi, who held out her arms. She cradled the precious weight against her, marveling in gazing at her child for the first time. Love swelled in her heart and she looked at Royce. Just as another contraction gripped her. He reached over her to settle the baby at her side.

Naomi gasped, "I guess…now… I know with absolute…certainty that you have…delivered a baby before."

His low chuckle filled the SUV just before the pressure built again, until she felt the familiar release. Followed by another infant cry.

"Naomi, you have another healthy baby girl." Royce's joy was mixed with a hint of a tremble that relayed yes, he must have been more nervous than he let on.

How could he not have been?

But all that mattered now was that her twins were alive. Safe. She sagged back in relief, holding her first child against her side and reaching out her arm for the other.

Royce wrapped the second newborn in her pink parka and passed the baby over. Naomi stared into those wide curious eyes and thought of her sister, Breanna, who'd died over a decade before, along with their mother.

The connection between Naomi and her sister had been strong. They were fraternal twins. Although people had often thought Breanna was Marshall's twin since she favored him so closely when they were young, and they were inseparable. Who knew how her sister would have looked as an adult since she'd died so young. Naomi swallowed back a lump of emotion and focused on the present. This joy.

Royce settled her legs and rested a blanket over her, before stretching up to lie beside her. "I've sent out texts for help. Let's just enjoy the babies and stay warm while we wait."

He climbed onto the reclined seats, curving his muscular body against her, somehow making room for himself in spite of the seat belts draped overhead and flashlights suspended from bungees. He was so familiar, and Lord, how she'd missed the feel of him, this closeness. She'd once dreamed of them like this, except spooned together in a hospital bed with the babies, all of them a family.

She looked over at him and found him studying the babies, which allowed her to stare at him longer. He was so much more than broodingly handsome good looks. The appeal was more than his leanly muscle-bound body on display in his chest-hugging T-shirt. And yeah, he got bonus points for the thick dark hair a hint too long, as if he'd forgotten to get a haircut, tousled like he'd just gotten out of bed.

All enticing. Sure.

But it was always his eyes that held her. Those windows to the soul. To the man. A man with laser-sharp intelligence in his deep brown gaze that pierced straight to the core of her and seemed to say, *Bring it, woman. I can keep up.*

And he had. He'd been willing to make every compromise to secure her—and her babies—in his life in a sad effort to recreate what he'd lost when his former fiancée had miscarried, then walked away.

Naomi couldn't risk hoping for a future with him, now more than ever, with the stability and well-being of these two precious little lives counting on her. If only they could all four stay just like this forever, warm and secure together while the storm raged outside.

A crack echoed, interrupting her thoughts, and she glanced up sharply to see an ice-laden tree fall across the hood of Royce's SUV.

Compartmentalizing was easier said than done.

Royce Miller wanted to be the cool scientist, detached. But this was Naomi. Her babies.

Not his.

His chest ached as if he'd sucked in a gulp of frozen air. He tucked his arm around her tighter as she catnapped, the babies sleeping against her chest.

Earlier, while she'd nursed the babies, he'd sent out a slew of additional texts, hoping one would make it through the storm. The SUV was still running, and he had extra fuel in the emergency kit. But once they needed that, he would have to try to move the tree off the hood. Hopefully, the SUV would be in shape to drive, although that was a last resort in this weather. Especially with two infants and no car seats.

He'd turned off all but one of the flashlights now to preserve batteries. His heart still slugged against his ribs in the aftermath. He could still barely wrap his brain around the fact that he'd delivered the babies. That Naomi was okay. Relief mixed with the reality that until he had them all in a hospital, he couldn't breathe easy.

After scanning the babies, checking that their chests rose and fell evenly, he glanced at the pulse in Naomi's neck. He grounded himself in the steady rhythm.

"Royce?" she whispered.

Her soft voice drew his gaze to her face. The look in her tired but beautiful eyes was…incredible. Shining brighter than the flashlight overhead.

He'd had her, and she'd slipped away from him.

It still grated deep in his gut how she'd pushed him away, given up on what they'd shared, what they could have had in the future. It was hard as hell to forgive how she'd just let go.

He brushed back her hair from her forehead, the softness of her skin soaking into him. "Here we are again, stuck together."

"Your SUV is almost as big as that little cabin you were staying in." She smiled at him wryly. "Somehow, we always manage the craziest scenarios. The way you chased that bear off my car when we first met."

Memories of that day filled him. How she'd bluffed her way into his cabin retreat to convince him to sign on his research with her family's oil business—Alaska Oil Barons, Incorporated. He'd been resistant, but man, how she'd won him over with her lawyer skills—and her smile.

And her bravado in the face of an unexpected grizzly climbing on the hood of her vehicle when she'd arrived at his cabin. "I suspect you could have handled that massive Pooh Bear yourself."

"I'll take that as a compliment."

"It was intended as one."

She was a gutsy woman with an indomitable spirit he admired. Pulling his gaze away from her intoxicating whiskey-brown eyes, he looked out the window. The snow had turned to sleet, pinging on the rooftop in the silence between them.

Naomi shifted and settled. "Now you've saved me again. And my girls. Maybe I could have handled that bear, but I couldn't have delivered my own babies."

"Happy to help. And even happier everyone's okay." Relief still burned through his veins. So much could have gone wrong. Still could, if help didn't arrive soon. "As much as it seems we have these somewhat similar crazy turns in our lives, a lot is different."

She chuckled hoarsely. "Like the fact that there's not a chance we'll be having sex this time."

He tapped his temple. "I'm intuitive that way."

Except he hadn't been so intuitive at the start. He'd fallen for the deception that brought her into his life. She'd hidden her identity as a Steele, hoping to get an inside scoop on his research, and ultimately lure him into signing on with her family business. He'd seen only her, wanted her, was determined to have her. And he'd ignored all the warning signs. In fact, he could see now how they'd both used sex to avoid talking about the deeper issues that would later tear them apart.

Resting her head on his shoulder, she sighed. "Thank you, so much. You were amazing and calm. I can't believe everything went okay. They're healthy and alive and I'm still here."

"Yes, you are." He swallowed hard.

"They're beautiful." Her voice rang with awe and love.

"That they are." Like their mama. "Have you settled on names yet?"

"Mary for my mother…" She pressed a kiss to the forehead of her firstborn, still wrapped in his jacket. "And I was thinking Breanna and call her Anna—" she kissed the clenched fist of her baby wrapped in her pink parka "—in honor of my sister."

Both of whom had died in a plane crash.

He knew well what a mark her sister and mother's deaths had left on her ability to believe happiness could last. Her teenage bout with cancer had piled onto that doubt, chipping away at what remained of her capacity for trust in happy endings.

"That's a lovely tribute. What about middle names?"

"Mary Jaqueline, after both of my parents, Mary and Jack. And I hope you won't mind if I name the other Breanna Royce." Naomi's eyes filled with emotion and a sheen of regret. "You've been here for me, but I understand if—"

"That's perfect. Thank you. I'm honored." Emotion, too much, threatened to steal his focus. He sealed it off and looked for tangible, logical facts. "I would guess they each weigh nearly six pounds. That's remarkable for twins a month early."

She studied him for an intense moment before blinking and glancing away. "No wonder I looked as big as a house."

"You were—and are—beautiful."

She rolled her eyes. "It's nice not to be arguing with a woman who just gave birth in a car."

"I don't fight."

"True." She crinkled her nose, shadows chasing across her face. "But you seethe, holding it in either out of some reclusive habit, or fear of spiking the blood pressure of the pregnant woman." She touched his arm lightly, her nails short and painted a pale pink. "I mean that nicely. You've been kind when you had every right to hate me."

Her words stabbed him clean through. "I could never hate you."

"We're just wrong for each other."

He couldn't deny that, as much as it hurt to admit. Things had moved so fast with them. And then they were done.

"Life's complicated." He studied each baby's face, their features imprinting themselves in his mind. In his heart. "But right now, it feels blessedly simple."

Or at least he wanted it to be. Here in the dimly lit car, the whistle of the wind cutting through the Alaska night. A dream he'd entertained more than once in the past. Before. A whimsical thought that wasn't like him.

She'd insisted he was trying to replace the fiancée who'd walked out on him after miscarrying their child years ago. That he'd been trying to replace that baby, as well. He couldn't deny those losses had hurt like hell. But the breakup with Naomi had been exponentially worse.

Maybe she was right about his need to fill a hole in his life that had never healed after the baby he'd lost. But all he'd known after breaking up with Naomi was that no matter what had happened between them, he needed to usher the twins into the world before he could walk away.

Light sparked behind his eyes. Becoming stronger and stronger until he couldn't blink it away. He frowned, sitting up, looking outside.

Car lights approached, twin beams streaking ahead, an emergency light strobing. Help had arrived. Thank God. Yet with that help came another realization.

As much as he'd thought he could cut ties once the babies were born, he still couldn't walk away. Not tonight.

Two

Naomi shivered under the blankets in the ambulance as she stretched out on the gurney. She had no reason to be cold. The heater was blasting and the emergency technicians had piled blankets on top of her.

Supposedly it was the aftermath of childbirth making her teeth clatter together. That and relief. Her two little girls—Mary and Anna—had been checked over thoroughly and both declared healthy miracles.

Twins, born in a car, in a snowstorm.

Amazing.

Both her babies were bundled up and being secured by the younger of the two techs in preparation for the ride to the hospital. A pediatrician would be waiting for them there.

Her teeth chattered faster and she searched beyond the open back door for Royce. He stood a few feet away, under a spotlight the techs had placed outside. The halogen beam shone down on his hair, made all the darker by the dampness from a fresh sprinkle of snowflakes collecting and melting. She heard the low, confident rumble of his voice. The tones grounded her with reassurance far more than the blankets. Holding strong to keep him at a distance proved hard right now, with her emotions so close to the surface.

"Thank you," he said to the older of the two techs. "I appreciate your coming out on roads as messy as these."

"That's what we're here for." The medic tugged his knit cap more firmly over his head, wind whipping flurries sideways.

"And they're all really okay." Royce's broad shoulders rose and fell with a sigh so heavy she couldn't miss it.

"Mom's blood pressure is a little higher than we would like, but we're monitoring her and we'll be on the road shortly." He nodded. "You handled everything very well, especially considering the circumstances. The babies both have a ten Apgar score."

"That's good to know. When they were born, they both had blue hands, but they came out crying, actively kicking."

"That's excellent. You did a great job in a tough situation. There's really nothing more anyone could have done in those circumstances."

Royce scrubbed the back of his neck, a gesture she recognized as weariness. "Other than not go for an impromptu scenic ride with a pregnant woman."

"You can beat yourself up later, Dad." The older man clapped Royce on the shoulder.

Dad? Naomi's throat closed and she bit her lip against a tremble.

Royce shrugged. "I'm not...their dad."

The pain in his voice tore at her heart. For him, for herself and for her children. She and Royce had made such plans for the future. He was a good man who would have loved her children as much as if they were his own. If only she could have escaped the feeling he was filling a void left by the loss of his own child.

By the loss of his fiancée, a woman he'd known so much longer than his and Naomi's few, intense months together.

Turning, he walked toward the ambulance, stepping up on the bumper and then inside, his eyes trained on Naomi, his broad shoulders nearly filling the opening.

The ambulance shifted again with the arrival of the other tech, angling past him. "My bad, man. I assumed you two were married."

Royce shook his head. "Not married. Not a couple. Not the dad. Just a…friend."

"Then I'm sorry, sir." The man smiled apologetically. "You'll have to step out of the rig. You can follow us in the tow truck."

Royce's face went tight for a moment before he shot her a forced smile. "Naomi, I'll see you and the girls at the hospital. I promise."

He stepped back out and the void where he'd been seemed to expand. Naomi's stomach sank as the doors closed, sealing Royce out. He dropped out of sight.

She thought she'd gotten used to the idea of doing this on her own, but having him with her through the birth of the babies had felt so right, the connection between them fragile, but there.

The door to the rig slammed, and they pulled onto the road, taking with them the last hint of how things might have been.

* * *

Royce couldn't will his feet to move, eyes fixed on the glass that separated him from the nurse's station where the twins were being settled. He watched the staff cradle the girls, tugging a tiny T-shirt and cap on each newborn before swaddling them in a blanket. Try as he might, he couldn't avert his gaze now that he'd finally made it to the hospital.

The trek here looped in his mind as he remembered the sinking feeling in his chest, being stuck in a damn tow truck with no rights to Naomi or the babies. He'd called to postpone his guest lecture series at the university. He'd also arranged for a car to pick him up in the morning, and sent an email to his administrative assistant at the oil company to start the paperwork for a replacement SUV. A new version of the one he'd had. He didn't like change in his life. From a make and model of a vehicle to a brand of boots.

At least he hadn't been stuck finding a ride tonight. The driver had taken pity on him and brought him all the way to the hospital before leaving with the demolished SUV.

Monitors beeped, briefly calling his attention away from the smells of disinfectant and stale coffee. Even late at night, the hospital hummed with activity here in the maternity ward. The low din of a family huddled together waiting to hear the news. A couple of grandparents at the window, tapping. A cart rattled by, pulled by a nurse. A mother walked slowly down the hall, pushing a wheeled hospital bassinet.

A rush of cold air pricked the hairs on the back of his neck as he registered the sound of doors opening. Barely enough time to digest the herd of people flooding in. Naomi's family filled the room, rushing toward him and the glass window pane. Concern became a common, identifiable feature on everyone's brow.

So. Many. Brows.

Her sister, Delaney; two of her brothers, Broderick and Aiden. Broderick's wife, Glenna, and a slew of other Steeles and Mikkelsons, whose faces all started to become a blur after a while, there were so many of them.

So many people here to support Naomi and the girls. That was a good thing. He should be fine with leaving. She didn't want him here. She'd pushed him away.

But he wasn't anywhere near okay with turning his back on them. He needed to see her settled in with the girls after the tumultuous delivery. He could provide a buffer between her and her overprotective family. He'd already sent out messages to excuse himself from work for a few days, his research taking a back burner to this.

Delaney—a shier version of Naomi—tugged her dark ponytail tighter, her eyes welling with tears that glistened even brighter than her diamond stud earrings. "Ohmigod, Royce, what happened to my sister?"

"The babies?" Glenna's gaze was direct.

Broderick stepped up behind his wife. "In a snowstorm?"

The Steeles and Mikkelsons were out in full, overwhelming force.

In days past, they would have been at each other's throats. Now they were a unified wall of huge personalities.

Royce shifted toward them, while keeping his body angled enough toward the window that he could still see the infants out of the corner of his eye. "We had just left the doctor's appointment. She got a clean bill of health, so we took a drive to get a bite to eat. The storm came out of nowhere right as she went into labor." He gestured toward the side-by-side warmers, with pediatricians and nurses gathered on the other side of the partition glass. "Those are your nieces."

Delaney stepped closer with a soft, "Oh, my."

Glenna pulled her cell phone from its monogrammed leather case, smiling, her CFO, no-nonsense demeanor fading. "We need photos. Lots. Mom and Jack are already texting me like crazy for updates."

The Steele patriarch and Mikkelson matriarch were on a belated honeymoon.

Broderick, the oldest of the Steele siblings—and a numbers person like his wife—gripped his Stetson. "Well, you certainly came through. I can't thank you enough."

Glenna stepped nearer to her husband, her phone in her hand and her eyes still fixed on the window. "It had to be scary for you."

Teenager Aiden Steele didn't even look up from the screen of his social media feed when he snorted, then said, "Like any guy's going to admit that."

Royce exhaled hard, muttering, "It was scary. As hell."

Broderick's stern face went taut. "Damn straight, it was." He pinned his youngest brother with a quick stare. "Only young fools don't know when to be afraid." He looked back. "Being scared and pushing ahead, that's bravery."

Royce cleared his throat. "I'm just glad everyone's all right," he repeated, for what felt like the millionth time, but knew it could never be said enough to ease the chill inside him. The room started to close in on him with all these people.

Glenna wrapped her arms around herself, visibly trying to calm down as she rubbed her hands over the elbows of a cashmere cardigan. "Marshall—" the middle Steele son "—flew out to get Mom and Jack and bring them back here."

"I'm sure Naomi wouldn't want to interrupt their honeymoon." Royce waved a hand. Despite the difficulties between them, he knew Naomi could do without the fanfare. She wanted to prove she was capable all on her own. And the last thing he wanted was for her stress level to rise right now and have her blood pressure spike as a result.

Jack and Jeannie had certainly waited long enough for a real honeymoon. They'd had to delay their wedding and their trip after Jack's spinal injury in a horseback riding accident. Luckily, he'd made a miraculous recovery after the surgery. They'd gotten married shortly after he'd gotten the neck brace off, but their celebration trip had been further delayed.

Broderick shook his head. "Like Dad was going to take our word for it that his little girl's okay?"

"Fair enough." Royce scrubbed a hand over his bleary eyes. The magnitude of the night's events threatened to overwhelm him until he rocked back a step. "I'm going to find the coffee machine. Text me if you hear any news."

He wouldn't have been able to sit idly by, twiddling his thumbs, until he'd seen Naomi and the babies. He still needed to clamp eyes on them again.

Then he could walk away.

Naomi's shakes had waned, but reality was just as rattling now that she was tucked in her hospital bed.

The magnitude of all that could have gone wrong kept pounding through her head. She'd faced the possibility of death as a teenager with cancer, bringing memories too close to the surface anytime she visited a hospital. But the thought of something happening to her babies?

That scared her more than anything she'd ever experienced.

Hospital beds, even in the maternity ward, never did Naomi's back any favors. The hospital decor spoke of an attempt at making the place seem more like a homey living room, but fell short of the mark. Doing her best to adjust her position, she sat straighter, determined to make a rapid recovery. The interminable bed rest of her pregnancy had made her stir-crazy. She blinked against the harsh lights of the room as her doctor and the pediatrician exited into the too white hallway.

Despite the roadside delivery, the pediatrician had given her a positive report that ought to have put her mind at ease. Instead, Naomi fidgeted, rubbing her fingers together as the redheaded nurse with freckled constellations on her cheeks adjusted the covers and set a glass of room-temperature water on the rolling bedside table.

The nurse closed the door behind her as she left, and the hushed sounds of hallway conversation dimmed.

But Naomi's heart was with her babies. She felt like the exams had taken longer than if she'd delivered the babies here. In fact, her daughters would have to stay in the nursery for observation tonight, since they'd been born in such unusual, unmonitored circumstances. The doctor had told her that once her blood pressure came down, she could see them.

The wait was driving her crazy. At least she didn't have a headache like she'd experienced during pregnancy with her preeclampsia.

Scanning the room, she steadied her gaze on the clock, watching the second hand move like molasses.

The creaking of the door cut through her thoughts, and for a sliver of a second, her heart screamed out for Royce. His calming presence.

Instead of the enigmatic man, Delaney lingered in the doorway, her hand balled into a tense fist as she held on to the sleeves of her green sweater.

Naomi didn't want to think about feeling disappointed.

Had he left? She swallowed hard and focused on her sister with a smile. Extending her arms for a hug, she drew Delaney close, breathing through the physical and emotional pain that racked her body.

"Naomi, the babies are beautiful. Glenna took a million photos already and I'm sure we'll take a million more. How are you?"

"Relieved. Eager to see my children. Grateful Royce was there to help."

"I can't believe you actually delivered in a car." Delaney tugged a chair close to the bedside and sat. "You always did have to one-up me. Two babies and now giving birth in a snowstorm. I'll never top that."

"What can I say?" Naomi shrugged, adjusting her hospital gown. "I strive to overachieve."

"I'm just glad you're all three okay. And the girls, wow. I can't wait to spoil them and buy tons of little pink outfits. I can't believe how tiny they are. So precious. You're so brave."

"I didn't have a choice." Her mind flashed to the terror she'd felt when she realized she wouldn't make it to the hospital. "They were coming out."

"I mean, to be a single mom."

Single.

Not engaged. Not married.

No future with Royce.

She didn't even have her mother to turn to for advice. Naomi fought back tears, working to remind herself of all she had to be grateful for tonight. "It's not like I don't have a ton of support, an even larger family now that Dad's remarried."

But no Royce. No father for her children. It had all seemed clear when she'd opted for in vitro fertilization with eggs she'd frozen prior to her treatment for cancer. Now everything was...complicated.

In the wake of her relationship with Royce, she better understood all that was missing in her life.

All that might have been for her girls.

"We're here for you." Delaney covered Naomi's hand with hers, careful of the IV. "What's the deal with Royce and you being out there together?"

Naomi sighed. "I should just put a sign on the door explaining, so I don't have to repeat myself. He's been helpful during the pregnancy. He cares about the babies."

"And about you. Be honest." She touched Naomi's forehead, pushing away loose strands of dark hair.

Naomi bit her lip and weighed her sister's words. "We'll always care for each other. But it was just...infatuation. Lust."

"Lust. Whoa. Friendship and lust and caring. Sounds pretty cool to me." She gave an exaggerated wink.

"Trust me," Naomi chuckled softly, "lust is the last thing on my mind right now."

"Understandable. You must be exhausted and I should let you rest." Delaney kissed her forehead. "Is there anything I can get for you? Some water? A nurse?"

"Perhaps ask the nurse to take my blood pressure again to see if I can get up?"

"Absolutely. I'll ask on my way out." She nodded to the nurse backing through the door. "You're in good hands. I'll see you in the morning."

The middle-aged nurse with silver strands in her jet-black hair barely made it five steps into the room before Naomi's question burst from her lips. "So, do we get to check my blood pressure again?"

Bowed lips drew into a smile, and for a flash of a moment, Naomi saw a glimpse of her mother in the woman. A painful thought, an ache that never seemed to ease.

"Of course, dear. Let's see what your number is now."

Naomi took a deep, steadying breath as the nurse set up the blood pressure machine. *Low. Low. Low.* The wish looped in her mind like a mantra. Her body needed to respond to the command.

An eternity seemed to pass as she stared at the nurse's equipment, waiting for the verdict.

"Well, there, Miss Naomi, I have some good news for you. Your blood pressure is back to normal."

"I'm going to see my babies." Flinging back the sheets, Naomi prepared to swing her legs off the bed.

A gentle hand met her wrist. "Hold on there, dear. I know your pressure's back down, but doctor's orders—you get a wheelchair until he says otherwise."

"As long as I see my children." Naomi took a deep breath, the kind she reserved for stepping into a trial, the type that filled her lungs and soul with determination, then she eased her feet to the floor. She was a little wobbly, but overall better than she expected.

"This is my favorite part of my job, dear."

Naomi craned her head back to examine the nurse. Faint smile lines adorned her cheeks, and the nurse's green eyes were alight.

"Wheeling people around?" Naomi asked, wringing her hands in anticipation. Doctors and nurses rushed past them, carrying charts and chatting hurriedly.

"No. Uniting mother and child. There is nothing as rewarding."

Her pulse pounding like she'd ran a marathon, Naomi swallowed, a lump of nervous anticipation welling in her throat, rendering her unable to speak. As they turned the corner to the nursery, her heart did a cartwheel. Royce. He stood near the babies, decked out in borrowed green scrubs. Looking handsome as ever, as he spoke to the pediatric nurse in a tone so hushed and gentle Naomi couldn't make out a single word he said.

He hadn't left, after all.

Even though she knew he was here for the babies, she still couldn't deny how glad she was to see him. He was a part of her past, but he'd also been a part of this miracle.

She couldn't help but wonder if she was feeling too drawn to him, weakening in an emotional moment. If anything, the other nurse's presence, with reminders of Naomi's mother, made her think of how she should be turning to the relatives she still had. She shouldn't rely on Royce. She wanted to be independent. Even leaning on family would need to be short term—just until she recovered physically—or they could all fall back into the overprotective ways she'd found so stifling as a teen with cancer. She walked a fine line with them in making sure her girls had the joy of the love of a big family.

She smiled her thanks at the nurse who'd helped her down the hall, then rolled the wheelchair toward Royce. "Where is the rest of my family?"

He looked up, lifted an eyebrow and smiled. "Hey, Mama. Good to see you up and about."

The pediatric nurse at the bassinets grinned before turning away and busying herself with another newborn.

Naomi gestured to her wheelchair. "If you can call riding in this 'up.'"

He knelt in front of her. "Your blood pressure's down?"

"Yes. And now I want to see my babies."

"Of course." He reached for the first bundle, Mary, and settled her in the crook of Naomi's arm. Then followed with Anna.

Naomi soaked in the sight of them, clean and sleeping. And beautiful.

She looked up at Royce, finding his eyes locked on hers. She resisted the urge to fidget nervously and reminded herself of who she should be depending on now. "Where's my family? Delaney said they were all here."

She'd especially wanted to see Isabeau who was expecting a baby with Trystan Mikkelson.

"They fawned over your babies and then headed home to give you rest."

"Oh, they just left?" She frowned. That wasn't like them.

"Your blood pressure was up. I sent them away."

She sat up straighter, stunned...irritated. "You did what?"

"It's late. I told them we've got this covered. And they said they'll be back in the morning."

She looked around at the busy staff and kept her voice low. "What gives you the right to decide who stays with me at the hospital?"

"There's another weather warning out, so they left to get ahead of the storm," he said, with such practical calm it set her teeth on edge.

But then she'd always been far quicker to lose her temper than he was.

"And if they'd wanted to stay?"

He stared back at her silently.

Reason trickled through her anger. Nothing could have made her family leave if they hadn't wanted to—or unless they had an ulterior motive. "They're all hoping we'll get back together."

"Maybe. Regardless, I want to help. Is that so bad?"

"I have help. Or rather, I did until you gave them all their marching orders." She tamped down her anger. "Who's watching your dog?"

His Saint Bernard, Tessie—named in honor of the scientist Tesla—was his big, lovable, constant companion.

"My neighbor's got her. She fine. Don't worry. Just rest."

Sagging back, Naomi relented. She had been surprised at how much it hurt saying goodbye to Tessie when she'd packed up her things at Royce's place. She'd cried more than a few tears into the soft fur.

So many tears. So much grief. She was weary with the hurt.

But it was for the best, because she couldn't risk falling into a relationship with him again.

Naomi cradled her babies, upset, but not wanting to

let anything spoil this first night with her girls. And Royce really had been there for her today. They had meant so much to each other once, even if for only a brief time. "I guess this was our plan, back before."

"That it was. I spent a large part of your pregnancy expecting to be their father. It's not so easy for me to just shut that off."

Tears became heavy in her eyes, compromising her vision, as all the words she knew seemed wrong, inadequate. "I'm so sorry for any pain I caused you. I should have known sooner that—"

"Stop. This isn't the time to rehash that." He slid an arm around her, the strength and heat of him so familiar. So missed.

She shrugged off his arm and the temptation it held for her to slide into their prior routine. "No offense. But touch me and I'll cry. It's the hormones. And I wish they were in my room with me and everything was…normal."

"Understandable. How about we sit together, you put your feet up here—" he pushed a chair in front of her and lifted her legs to rest on it "—and we'll hold the babies all night long."

She looked up from her daughters into his deep brown eyes, finding his gaze full of emotion, of memories. *Their* memories. And this time there would be no escaping them or hiding from each other. Not now.

As they spent the night together, pretending to be the family they never could be.

Milla Jones pushed the flower cart down the quiet hospital corridor, careful not to wake the sleeping patients, the babies and their families.

One family in particular. Her reason for being here tonight. She'd been unable to stay away, even though she would have a legitimate reason to see them all in two weeks. Revenge required patience, and God, she'd waited for so long. Surely she could allow herself this small indulgence after all that had been taken from her. All the reasons she had not to trust anyone.

Milla wheeled past a janitor mopping up dried mud and stains from people tracking in wet snow, and stopped outside Naomi Steele's door. The cart held four arrangements for the new mother of twins, and a cluster of pink balloons. Milla didn't plan to make this a full-time job. It was a one-time gig with a purpose.

She hadn't been able to resist the chance to scope out the Steeles and Mikkelsons. She'd heard about the twins' birth and had conned a hospital volunteer into letting her deliver arrangements to the patients. Which technically wasn't cool on so many levels, but Milla had long ago given up playing by the rules. Life had been too harsh. She'd fought hard to build a future for herself, independent of anyone.

So she refused to feel guilty for pushing the door open and peeking inside the room. The empty room. No one lay in the bed, though the sheets were rumpled. No sounds came from the bathroom and the recliner was unoccupied.

Sighing in disappointment, she unloaded the four arrangements, placing them around the room wherever there was space—two on the window ledge, one on the rolling cart and the last by the sink. Scanning the room once more, envisioning the family that should have been in here, she tied the balloons to the end of the bed.

Her time would come. She wasn't backing down. She

had two more weeks to scope out both families before she made her move.

For years, she'd hidden out in fear of her enemies. But when she'd almost died in a wildfire last summer, she'd decided the time had arrived. She had to look out for her own safety. She'd come here to uncover the truth. The reason she'd left Canada and moved to Anchorage. To find out who was responsible for the destruction of her life—the Mikkelsons or the Steeles.

Three

Sprawled in the burgundy recliner, Royce reached overhead to stretch out his tense back. He kept his eyes trained in front of him, watching the steady rise and fall of Naomi's chest as she slept. Somehow those breaths steadied his own after the adrenaline. The fragrance of flowers throughout the room covered the antiseptic scent and reminded him of her shampoo. Her dark hair pooled around her, halo-like. Peaceful.

But this peace between them was a temporary thing. He understood that all too well.

Hospital staff had told him he could sleep on the pull-out sofa, but he'd been too restless. Once he'd texted his neighbor for an update on Tessie, he'd reached for his tablet and got to work.

The room was still dark, even though morning crept closer. Alaska days were lengthening. Naomi was tough and independent, but he hadn't thought about her handling two infant seats on an icy walkway.

Or what if she'd been trapped in that storm, alone, with the babies?

Those two tiny girls already had him wrapped around their little fingers. The breakup with Naomi had been hell, so much so he hadn't given much thought to the twins. What it would feel like to lose them. He hadn't realized how much he already cared about the two of them. That he was gutted at the thought of losing them.

Royce rubbed a crick at the back of his neck. He and Naomi had been up most of the night. The hours together reminded him of nights they'd spent in bed planning for the twins' arrival, sharing dreams for the future.

None of their discussions bore any resemblance to the way things had turned out.

Neither of them was willing to leave Anna and Mary. The pediatrician wanted them observed for the night since they'd been born early and in such unusual circumstances.

Quite frankly, Royce hadn't wanted to leave Naomi, either. Sure, her family could have stayed, but he'd seen her assert her independence with them mighty damn effectively, and hadn't trusted she would ask for help. Or that they would see what she really needed.

So he'd stayed and kicked her family out.

And yes, he'd also chosen to stick around because the glow on her face mesmerized him. The soft, soothing sound of her voice as she spoke to her babies surpassed any song.

Finally, when Naomi couldn't keep her head up any

longer, a nurse had gently reminded her she would be no good to her children exhausted. She should rest while she could.

Royce had helped her back to her room and watched over her while she slept. The babies were in good hands. Someone needed to look out for Naomi. The best thing would be to walk away, but damn it all, he kept buying in to lame reasons to stick around.

He sure as hell wouldn't be able to hold off her family for long. They would all be back here en masse soon enough. For now, before the sun rose, he could imagine things were different between them.

Her feet shifted under the sheet in that way he'd learned she did just before the rest of her awoke. Back in the days when they'd shared a bed, when he'd made love to her through the night. When he'd had the right to slide his arm around her and draw her to him. To bury his face in her hair and breathe in the scent of her shampoo.

Naomi stretched her arms overhead, then swept back her hair before gingerly sitting up in bed. "The girls?"

"Anna and Mary are fine. The nurse said they would be brought in after the shift change, which should be happening right now."

"Did you sleep at all?"

"Catnaps. I'm fine." He set his tablet aside and poured her a cup of ice water.

"Thank you." She took it and sipped. "Catnap, huh? I bet you worked."

He didn't bother denying it. The chart he'd been calculating still glowed on the screen.

"Royce, you should rest."

He could sleep later. She would be taking care of twins. "I will. How do you feel?"

"Like I gave birth to twins in a car."

"I'll get the nurse to bring your pain meds." He started to stand.

"I was joking." She gestured for him to sit again.

"Right. Guess my brain's still on stun from everything that's happened."

"Understandable." She picked at the sheets, glancing at him, then away, blinking fast. "I'm sorry if this brought back upsetting memories for you."

Yes, the delivery had brought back the past, thoughts that would haunt his sleep. But he didn't intend to worry her with that.

"My thoughts are fully on you and the babies. What about you?" He touched her hand, paused, his thumb caressing the inside of her wrist out of habit. "Is everything else, um, okay?"

"Are you referencing hormones?" She skimmed a knuckle under each eye. "Because that could be seriously dangerous to your health."

He froze, then relaxed. "You were making a joke, right?"

"Teasing you." She squinted, sizing him up with a playful grin. "Not a joke exactly."

"Got it." He tapped his temple, missing this ease between them, not knowing how to keep it beyond sunrise. "I'm working on developing a sense of humor."

"You've always had one. You're just more literal when you're stressed." She bit her lip. "I'm sorry you had to go through that."

The pain in her words cut him to the quick. "There's nothing for you to apologize for."

"And yes, to answer your question, I'm thinking about my mom and my sister." She shrugged, the green hospital gown sliding down one shoulder. "I wish they were here to see the girls, to offer advice. Just to hug."

He covered her hand with his, stroking lightly.

Ah, there it was. An old familiar spark. The feeling of an electric current running between them, gaining voltage as her eyes caught his.

Memories catapulted through his mind, threatening to tear down the wall between them.

But the moment was short-lived, interrupted by a squeaky hospital door. Back to the present. To the babies being lifted out of the bassinets and into the arms of the nurse.

A cooing noise erupted from the pink lips of one of the girls as the nurse carefully cradled the tiny pink bundle.

"Are you ready, Momma?" the woman asked brightly, her ponytail swinging as she moved closer.

Naomi's heart was in her eyes as she looked at the nurse and nodded emphatically, her dark hair tumbling forward.

Damn.

Naomi practically glowed with maternal love and happiness. The sight of her reaching for her babies, cradling one and then the other to her chest, nearly knocked him to his knees.

"Are you sure you have them?" the nurse inquired, propping pillows under Naomi's arms to give her support.

Two babies, even at this young age, were a lot to juggle. Royce hovered. Wanting to help.

Needing to help.

"I'll make sure," he answered the nurse, easing past her to give Naomi a hand.

Seeing for himself how much she needed help meant only one thing. He had to be there for her these next six weeks as she recovered and settled into motherhood, or he would never be free of regrets.

Naomi wrapped baby Anna in her blanket, swaddling her the way the nurses had taught. Mary already slept, her sweet Cupid's bow mouth moving silently as she dreamed. So far nursing the twins was going well. At least that's what the staff said. Naomi found it more difficult than she'd expected, but she was determined to try.

It had taken all her skills as a lawyer to convince Royce to step out of the room long enough to visit the cafeteria. She'd convinced him she had to have a burger.

She carefully adjusted the pink cap on Anna and the purple cap on Mary before relaxing in the recliner by her bed. Sitting in a real chair made her feel more like a regular person after all the weeks on bed rest before she gave birth. And after the ordeal of doing so in the SUV. Usually, Naomi thrived on drama and high emotions. But was it too much to ask to have a second of peace without all these feelings crowding her? She'd given birth in a freaking car. She deserved—her babies deserved—a few minutes of calm.

The reactions stirred by Royce were anything but peaceful.

She knew the two of them were over. They had to be. They weren't good for each other. It had just been infatuation. But he still sent her hormones into a tailspin whenever he walked in the room.

And when he walked out. Even to go get supper.

What would it feel like when he left forever?

As the lump in her throat swelled to an almost un-manageable size—so much for peace—the door cracked open.

Again, anticipation hummed in her veins, made her heart race—*hope*—to see the eccentric scientist appear.

And yes, there was a man in the entry. But it wasn't Royce.

Her rugged father, an unwavering—albeit gruff—teddy bear of support through the years. He carried a vase of pink roses.

"Daddy? I can't believe you're here." She pushed on the arms of the recliner to stand.

With a hand on her shoulder, he gently eased her back, then wedged the painted ceramic vase on the counter between a spider plant and a pair of rag dolls. "Of course I'm here to see my girl and her babies. Jeannie's here, too. She's just outside the door with the family. She said I should have some time alone with you first. She's thoughtful that way. Always try-ing to be considerate when it comes to the blending of our families."

Naomi shifted to face him as he pulled up another chair to sit beside her. She was happy for her father, truly, but right now, with an ache in her heart from wanting her mother to share this moment, it was dif-ficult to think about her father's remarriage. Selfish of her? Probably. But emotions weren't easy and she'd al-ways been the volatile one in the family.

Still, she tried her diplomatic best for her dad. "I didn't mean to bring you back from your honeymoon."

"We wouldn't miss this for anything. I want to hold

my granddaughters once they wake up." He peered into each bassinet, touching the newborns' tiny caps reverently. "Lordy, girl, they're beautiful."

"I won't disagree with you there." Love filled her heart for these two lives. The swell of emotion was so deep and wide she could barely contain it.

"I had to push my way to the front of the line. There's quite a train of people out there waiting to see these little ones." He paused, eyeing her. "I saw Royce on my way in. Are you two back togeth—"

Swiftly, she held up her hand, cutting him off. "No, Dad." She didn't have the strength to fight rumors or explain yet again why they'd broken up, especially not now when her emotions were turning somersaults inside her. She could repeat only so many times that they were just too different. Sharing anything more about their breakup felt too personal, even to tell her family. "He just happened to be there when the babies were born."

"How so, exactly?" Jack narrowed his brows, his weathered face furrowing.

Hadn't he heard? Of course he would have questioned the others. She searched her father's face and decided this was another battle not worth fighting. He clearly wanted to hear her side, to see if she was weakening in reuniting with her ex-fiancé—who also happened to be her father's new golden boy consultant in the company.

Fine. "Royce took me to my OB appointment, where I got a glowing report, so good I was let off bed rest. Then we drove around for a while to celebrate. We talked about heading to Kit's Kodiak Café, because I had a craving for their Three Polar Bears special—"

"Like when you were a kid. I look forward to taking the girls there one day, along with Fleur." Broderick and Glenna's toddler. "This grandpa gig is a good thing. Now finish telling me how these nuggets entered the world in Royce's car."

"While we were out, it began snowing. Labor started…and the next thing I knew, I was giving birth on the side of the road in his Suburban." She grimaced.

Her dad chuckled. "I was there when each of you were born, you know." His eyes took on a nostalgic glint for a moment before he blinked it away.

"Please say you're going to finish your trip, though."

"Jeannie and I want to welcome you home first. Then we'll fly back out and resume the rest of our belated honeymoon."

Exhausted and emotional, Naomi inwardly winced at the thought of a big to-do. She loved her family and would need their support. Still, she yearned for bonding time with her daughters.

Even so, being a parent now gave her a new perspective on her father, and she didn't want to hurt his feelings. So she simply smiled and said, "That sounds perfect. I'll be sure to send you lots of photos of the babies."

He fished his smartphone out of his jeans pocket, waved it in the air with a wide, bright smile. "Please do. I'll be passing my phone around for everyone to see."

"You'll be back before you know it for your big wedding party." Her father and Jeannie had been married in a small service with all their children present, but given their business connections, they'd planned for a large gala after they returned from their honeymoon. After which the pipeline modifications would kick into high gear, as would Royce's workload.

"The twins will be six weeks old then." His face took on a nostalgic air as he traced the edges of the pink cap. "Little Anna here looks like you."

"Or like Breanna, you mean."

He nodded, his throat bobbing, his gaze still locked on the newborn.

"Are you sure you're all right with the names?" Naomi squeezed her father's forearm. "I don't want you to feel sad when you see them."

"I'm happy. I mean it. Seeing these two little granddaughters reminds me of my twins in all the best ways." He scrubbed his wrist across his eyes, a wide smile replacing any pain that had been on his face. "Thank you, Naomi."

"I love you, Dad." She leaned across the arm of the chair to hug him.

He folded her into a familiar embrace, patting her back rhythmically, like...a dad. "Love you, too." Finally, he angled away, standing. "Now I'm going to get Jeannie before she goes crazy waiting."

That brief sadness on her father's face and in his voice made Naomi's heart ache more than she could remember since she'd been a teenager. Scared. Unsure of the future.

Well, except for when she'd broken things off with Royce. She could still remember the shock on his face, the denial. She hadn't been able to handle his smothering, his lack of understanding when it came to her need for independence, his unwillingness to acknowledge her strength. She realized he responded that way because of his former fiancée's miscarriage, but still, Naomi had fought too hard to climb out of the cocoon her family had put her in during her bout with cancer.

Royce had accused her of being so stuck in the past she was afraid to embrace the future.

Likely they both had valid points, but bottom line, they'd jumped into the relationship too quickly.

That didn't make the breakup hurt less.

He was a good man. Almost too good—if there could be such a thing. Even while she realized theirs had been an infatuation—a hefty dose of infatuation—she'd known without question he never would have broken things off with her once he'd committed to be there for her, for her children. That honorable nature had made it all the tougher for her to do the right thing and let him go.

She rubbed at the sore spot on her wrist where the IV had been, the lingering ache reminding her of so many other pains, losses.

Royce could sit and crunch numbers, work equations and create charts for hours without feeling the least bit drained. He liked to think he had grit and stamina by the bucketful. But a day spent with inquiring and nervous family members reminded him of another skill he had to work on—resilience. Tension in his jaw conveyed his overexposure. But it was worth it for Naomi and the babies.

She was washing her hair. The sound of the showering water through the door had soothed the girls to sleep. He had to admit to being moved when Naomi had trusted him with them after her family left for supper.

The Steele-Mikkelsons never ceased to surprise him. Such as how this family worth billions, who'd wined and dined with world leaders, still chose Kit's Kodiak Café as one of their favorite watering holes. Sure, the food rocked, but he thought maybe it fit more with their pace, all of them having grown up near oil fields.

They were used to a big clan, but he was more comfortable in the solitude of his cabin with his dog Naomi had sensed that, no matter how hard he'd tried to hide it. And he had tried, because he'd wanted things to work between them.

He'd failed. And no amount of Mensa IQ points could help him figure out how to fix things so they worked together as a couple.

But that wasn't the task at hand.

Instead he'd create a perfect system that would enable a smooth transition for her and the girls. Rather than second-guessing every waking moment, he'd enjoy his time with Naomi, help situate her for success in the future.

Goals and objectives. Now he had something to work for—to help Naomi—and even a deadline. He would be there for her until her father's return from his honeymoon.

Royce made his way to the curious-eyed infants, who blinked up at him, stealing their way deeper into his heart.

"Hello, beautiful girls," he said softly. Anna crinkled her nose at the sound of his voice. "Did you know that matter is never destroyed, only converted? We have to make sure you two are at the top of your class. Yeah-huh."

A female doctor with a gray ballerina bun entered the room, cutting the science lesson short. He turned to face her, and the male nurse with a crew cut who followed, introducing themselves. Her regular OB, Dr. Odell, had gone on vacation, so his partner was making rounds.

"She's in the shower," Royce explained, just before the water stopped. "But as you can hear, she's finishing up."

"That's fine. We're about to undergo a shift change, but are also in the process of releasing patients that are able to be discharged this evening."

"Oh. Well, uh, I'm not sure how she feels."

"That's quite all right. We can wait to ask her." The doctor gestured to the darkening window. "Full moon tonight. And that means a lot of women in labor."

Naomi emerged from the bathroom in a plush pink robe and nightgown, looking pretty with her hair gathered in a damp braid.

The doctor smiled, shifting her clipboard from one hand to the other. "Well, Momma, I am prepared to release you—if you feel comfortable, that is."

Relief flooded her face. "Yes, please. I would like to go home."

Home. Royce's gut clenched. There'd been a time when they'd shared his house, talked of buying a larger place with space for the babies. That scenario had passed.

The doctor pushed her glasses up the bridge of her nose, then passed the clipboard to the nurse. "I'll have him start your discharge paperwork. You have infant car seats?"

Naomi pointed toward the corner. "My family brought them today."

"Good, good." The nurse penciled a check mark on the papers before tucking the clipboard under his arm.

The doctor touched each baby's head lightly before squeezing Naomi's shoulder. "We have plenty of guides and emergency numbers in your baby welcome packet. Don't hesitate to call if you have any questions."

The nurse pulled the papers off the clipboard and tucked them into a sack with the hospital logo on the side. "Congratulations. To both of you. All four of you, actually. I never grow jaded about the joy of releasing a family."

A family. Royce didn't bother correcting the nurse. He'd actually given up on correcting that assumption at all—and apparently so had Naomi—after the second shift change had brought in yet another wave of well-wishers who assumed he was the father.

"Wow, I can't believe we're leaving. It's all happening so fast." She opened the cabinet and pulled out the clothes her sister had brought. "Thank goodness Delaney brought a bag for the babies and me. And their car seats."

"Lucky to have all that here. Makes things easier. Although you could wear your boots with the nightgown and coat. No need to tire yourself out." He couldn't miss the furrows creasing her forehead. "Naomi?"

She shook her head, pulling out the loose sweater dress. "It's just a little overwhelming. Not the way I envisioned it. Although I will go home in this, like I planned."

"Right. And I'll get the girls in those little outfits you picked out for them." At least he hoped he could. Figuring out how to build modifications for a safer, more efficient oil pipeline sounded easier at the moment than wrangling those spindly baby arms into miniscule matching clothes. "Take your time getting dressed. I'll be sure to snap plenty of photos. Your girls are going home. You're a mom."

Going still, she held the dress against her, her eyes sad again, in that way that twisted him up inside.

"Naomi? What's wrong?"

Her mouth opened and closed twice before she finally blurted out, "I know there was a time when you opened your heart to be their father. I realize this can't be easy for you. You can come see them if you wish."

And just that fast, the thoughts that had been churning in his head all day took shape into a plan. An unwavering sense of direction. He shoved aside her concerns that he was just filling a void in his life. They weren't a couple anymore, but he could still do this for her. "Oh, I'm going to be seeing plenty of the girls and of you."

"Um, what?" She angled her head to the side, her damp braid swishing forward.

Maybe he should have waited until later to tell her, once he pulled up at the Steele compound and unloaded her and the girls in Naomi's suite of rooms. But hopefully the car ride would give her a chance to settle into the idea.

Or give him more time to convince her he wasn't budging.

"Because for the next six weeks, I'm moving in to be your nanny."

Four

This place was a sight for sore eyes. Or rather more accurately, a sore heart.

In her family's six-bay garage, Naomi cast a glance at Royce, the silent giant who'd taken over her life.

For a man who wanted solitude, he'd sure thrown himself into the fire, signing on to be here with her girls and her family. She had help. Sure, they all worked and she didn't want to impose. But she had a wide support system.

Yet she hadn't been able to tell him no. She needed to know what was really behind this crazy offer of his to be the girls' temporary nanny.

She fumbled with the diaper bag, trying to remain as quiet as possible. Waking up the sleeping babies fell low on her list of things to do. The massive garage ran the entire length of the back of the house, and sounds tended to reverberate off the top-of-the-line SUVs and snowmobiles in the space.

Exhaustion gnawed on her as she made her way around the SUV Royce had rented. Royce. A nanny. *Her* nanny. For better or worse.

"Royce," Naomi whispered, shrugging her damp braid over her shoulder. "Just so we're clear, this is temporary. Tonight only, because it took us so much longer to sign out of the hospital than I expected—and longer again to get here with the sleet outside. I don't want to wake up my family. If they all roll out of bed, it will be forever before we can get to sleep."

And she knew she was making excuses, but as far as excuses went, it was a solid one.

He simply nodded, hefting both baby car seats and then shouldering the vehicle doors closed. Anna snoozed on, but Mary flinched in her seat. Royce froze.

Naomi didn't dare breathe.

With a tiny sigh, Mary settled back to sleep again.

Naomi picked her way down the hall, making sure they didn't disturb the sleeping household. She could practically do the walk to her room in her sleep. The familiar path was as natural to her as breathing. She led him up the stairs, past a great gallery wall of childhood photographs. A repository for all that was familiar.

But as she approached the elevator to her suite, she noticed more photographs. New ones, of Jeannie and her family. Naomi's world was expanding and fracturing all at once.

She heard a voice drifting softly from the study. Her sister's voice. Someone was awake, after all. Naomi could send Royce on his way.

The disappointment hit her hard, right in her riotous hormones.

Then Birch Montoya's voice joined Delaney's. The man was a new investor in their family's oil company, a shark who had butted heads with Delaney on her environmental concerns. "You don't have to disagree with everything I propose."

"Well, Birch…" Delaney's voice rose. "If any of it showed a care about the environment, then I wouldn't argue."

Royce's eyebrows shot up. He tipped his head toward the home elevator leading to her suite. Naomi eyed the door to the library where her sister was working…

Or rather arguing. Loudly. She looked over at the babies, then up at Royce. And she couldn't deny she was using the argument behind that library door as an excuse to do exactly what she wanted.

To spend this first night playing house with Royce.

Royce adjusted his grip on the car seats, evaluating the weight of the babies. How strange it felt to hold them as he moved into Naomi's suite. How silent the elevator ride had been, his head filled with memories of a time he'd expected to bring his own child home. Plans and dreams made. Nightmares that followed. And lingered.

He rubbed his bleary eyes to clear his thoughts. He needed to keep a level head and be present for Naomi. He'd half expected her to call her family to drive to the hospital to transport her and the twins, but the lengthy checkout time, lateness of the hour and desire to go home had apparently won out.

A nursery had been added to the suite since he'd been

here last. Gray and pink accent colors surprised him, though the logical part of his mind knew there'd have to be an addition made to her living quarters. Still, the newness caught him off guard. The babies' room hadn't been here when they'd broken up. When he'd left here for the last time.

Back when he'd stayed here, the nursery had been an enclosed balcony where he and Naomi had spent a lot of hours together talking. And more.

Now, two pewter-colored cribs flanked a plush glider. Bookshelves were decorated with overstuffed toys and tons of books. There was no trace of their former life.

Did she think of those times anymore?

Better not to think of the past at all. Best to focus on the future.

He turned away from the nursery and thought of how this coming home could have been so very different. Peering into the car seats, he saw that the twins still slept. Good. He made his way to the double bassinet in Naomi's room, where the girls would sleep for the time being. "I'm going to run down and get the rest of your luggage."

And a bag he'd packed for himself.

"Are you sure you don't mind? I feel like I'm imposing."

"I wouldn't have offered if I minded. I'll be right back."

He jogged down the steps, finding all quiet in the waterside mansion. Unusual, to say the least. Even the study had gone silent. Birch and Delaney must have settled their argument. The two were at constant loggerheads. Birch kept his focus on the company's financial bottom line. Delaney had her eye solidly on protecting the environment.

Royce entered the garage and pulled the two cases from the rented SUV, then turned to head back to Naomi's suite, where he'd once stayed overnight often. But now they'd grown so far apart she hadn't even shown him the nursery.

Shuffling one of the bags under his arm, he reentered, elbowing the door closed again behind him.

Returning to Naomi's quarters, he found her bent over the bassinet. Her dark hair fell in waves, an aftershock of her earlier braids. The glossy silk framed her radiant face as she watched Mary sleeping. Cradling Anna in her arms, she rocked back and forth, hips seeming to glide against the fresh sea green nightgown.

A pull of familiarity. Of normalcy.

Being together this way was almost like they'd once imagined the aftermath of the girls' birth. Well, except they'd planned to have their own house and be married. So really, not much that mattered was the same.

Naomi eased into her glider chair and toed it into slow motion, patting Anna's back. "The house is so quiet. I guess Delaney and Birch must have finished up their work."

"Do you want me to get your sister?"

"No, don't bother her. Everyone else will wake up and… Honestly, I prefer this to a big to-do. There will be plenty of attention in the morning. I'll be more rested then." She looked at the babies. "Well, I know they'll have me up through the night, but at least I won't have the nurses coming in all the time, too."

"I'm here to help you as much as you need. You know

that." He wondered what her family would say when they saw him in the morning.

What did he want them to say? To think? Damned if he knew, beyond figuring out some way to settle the raw, torn-apart feeling between them. Neither of them could continue working together this way.

"For tonight. Just tonight. That nanny business was a cute line, but really?"

"Really. We shared an intense time, and you know as well as I do there hasn't been…closure. We still have to work together."

"Closure, huh? That's what this is about?"

"What else would it be about?"

She stared at him through narrowed eyes before finally shaking her head, then yawning, her hand over her mouth.

"I'm too tired to discuss this any longer. Thank you for the help tonight so I didn't have to impose on my family more than I'm already going to be imposing these next few months." Her face changed from exhaustion to something lighter, happier as she put Anna down in her bassinet. She lingered over her child for a moment before turning to face Royce.

The weariness flooded her eyes again as she looked above him to the ceiling, wooden beams stretching the width of the room. "You and I can talk in the morning right before you go back to your place."

"Uh-huh." He checked Mary in the other bassinet, watching the even rise and fall of her chest, avoiding Naomi's reference to the morning.

Naomi cleared her throat softly. "I'm not going to be distracted."

He wished he knew a way to dissolve all the tension

between them. Royce pulled back the comforter on her bed before cupping her shoulders, fighting the urge to linger, to stroke his thumbs along the silky skin of her neck. "Rest."

"Why is it I win in the courtroom—" she sighed, sinking to rest on the edge of the mattress "—but you always manage to outtalk me with just a handful of words?"

"Not always."

Her eyes filled with sorrow and she clasped his wrist. "I'm sorry."

"Me, too." And he was. He just didn't know how to fix things. And he sure as hell didn't want to move her hand from him. He'd missed her touch. More than he'd realized.

She eased her hand away, clenching her fist in her lap. "I still feel I'm being selfish in keeping you here."

"I wouldn't be here if I didn't want to be." He patted the pillow. "Are you going to use this bed? Because if not, I will be more than happy to sack out—"

Chuckling, she swung her feet up. "Fine. And thank you again for everything."

"You're welcome. I'll be right out there on the sofa if you need me."

She sat up straighter, winced, then said, "On the sofa? So you really mean to stay the nights here, too?"

"I'm a very dedicated nanny." He grasped the door handle. "Now sleep."

No one had warned Naomi how exhausted she'd be after giving birth. Okay, maybe people had, but she clearly hadn't grasped the full depth of the bone-weary feeling that would overwhelm her. A part of her wondered if the fatigue came from her exposure to Royce. To that future she'd missed out on when their relationship fell apart.

Despite all that, she managed to sit at the breakfast table with her family, take in all the chatter like it was just another average day.

Delaney held Mary, while Glenna and Broderick introduced their daughter, Fleur, to her new cousin Anna. The rest of her family made diplomatic small talk at the other end of the table—and avoided mentioning the fact that Royce had filled a plate of food and gone back upstairs with the excuse he needed to catch up on work. She saw well enough how the crowded dining room made the corner of one of his eyes tic.

The night had been a blur of waking up to feed the babies, then falling asleep again, only to wake up what felt like seconds later. Royce had been such a help throughout, making things go faster by changing and burping each girl while she fed the other.

"Did you and Birch settle the work issues last night?"

Delaney looked up fast, then set her fork down slowly, Mary cradled in her other arm. "What do you mean?"

"I wasn't eavesdropping, but when I got home last night I couldn't help but hear the two of you arguing, something to do with business."

"You shouldn't have to worry about the office right now. Just focus on recovering and enjoying those adorable babies."

Naomi waved her hand dismissively, then tapped her temple. "I still have a brain—albeit an exhausted one. I care about the family business. And I feel guilty that so much is falling on your shoulders."

"Glenna and Broderick are helping. And Trystan Mikkelson has been a surprise thanks to Isabeau's good influence. I bet fatherhood smooths those rough edges on him even more." Delaney picked her fork up again to chase food around her plate.

"I just want to make sure our interests are protected."

"You'll be back at the office soon enough." Delaney shot her sister a sidelong glance.

"And are you sure things are okay? He can be quite… a shark."

"I have a handle on him." Delaney refilled her china coffee cup and set down the silver carafe, leaning forward to whisper, "What about you and Royce?"

Loaded question. With all the calmness she could muster, Naomi said in a flat voice, "He says he plans to be the nanny for the next six weeks."

Delaney's eyes went wide, and she placed Mary carefully in the portable bassinet, her attention now 100 percent on Naomi. "Nanny?"

"I know, right?" Shoveling some scrambled egg into her mouth, she bought herself some time before talking. "The breakup was difficult for both of us. I think he sees this as closure. Or obligation to the babies. That's been a worry all along, actually. I figure he will give up in a week. Two weeks tops. The lure of a full night's sleep with no diaper changes will win."

Even thinking of him walking away hurt.

"Maybe," Delaney said skeptically.

"Definitely."

"It's romantic that he offered."

Naomi's heart thudded in her chest, painfully so. "There's no romance. I just had twins. And I did deliver them right in front of him." Now that the rush of the moment had passed, she couldn't help but feel…embarrassed? Unveiled? "It's different somehow than if he'd just been there holding my hand in the delivery room."

Although he had been mighty amazing, considering the situation. A rock.

"Romance is about more than sex." Her sister sounded very definite about it.

"I know that." And in some ways, that's what made Naomi the saddest about the breakup with Royce. Wondering if all they'd had was physical. That her heart had been so…confused by attraction. She considered herself a woman of logic and she'd been led by her libido.

"Just checking."

In spite of everything, something spurred her to blurt, "The sex was really good, though."

"Then I guess it's a lucky thing you can't be tempted by Royce, since you're looking at six weeks of postpartum recovery." Delaney raised the coffee cup to her lips, appearing utterly unconvinced.

"Thanks for the reminder I have a flabby body and lactating breasts. Definitely not a temptation for him." More of that embarrassment stung her.

"That's not what I said. I meant that this is a time the two of you can get to know each other better—without sex clouding the issue like it did before, when you two jumped into a relationship too fast."

"That sounds judgy."

"Trust me, I'm the last one to pass judgment on that subject." Delaney attacked the food on her plate.

Naomi tried to read her sister's expression, but that was tough to do when she kept her eyes averted. Interesting. "Delaney? Do you have something to share to distract me from the fact that I'm exhausted and my former fiancé has moved in to be my temporary nanny?"

She glanced up, a blush spreading across her cheeks. "Nothing."

Apparently there was more than one person keeping secrets in this family. "The least you could do is help distract me from my exhaustion and wrecked love life with some juicy tidbits from your world."

Delaney crinkled her nose. "Nothing to share," she insisted, clearly lying. "How about we cuddle these adorable babies of yours some more? By far the most interesting event going on right now."

Naomi relented, unable to argue with people pouring love out for her children. She reached into the bassinet by the table and passed Anna to Delaney.

Seemed that everyone had secrets and a love life.

And Naomi had a sexy male nanny she couldn't sleep with who only wanted her for her babies.

Five

When Royce signed on for the nanny gig two weeks ago, he hadn't expected that would take them to the Steele corporate headquarters with the twins in tow.

Naomi had gotten an emergency call from the office asking for information to deal with a handful of crises. He could see how torn she was between work and her children, so he'd suggested taking the babies to the workplace, where he would help with them while she handled business.

The relief on her face had been so intense he managed to stifle frustration over having to trudge with her to the company headquarters. With luck, he could use the opportunity to throw in some hints about the benefits of a home office. Absolutely his preferred work environment.

Naomi was using Glenna's desk, since her sister-in-law was working from home today. The space was also larger than Naomi's—and already stocked with baby gear for Glenna's daughter. The setup surprised Royce, but then he'd made a point to spend as little time as possible here, doing his research off site and coming in only for boardroom reports.

How was it that he'd spent so little time in Naomi's workplace?

Royce held Anna against his shoulder, patting her back, while Naomi nursed Mary and handled her business call simultaneously. She'd already addressed legal issues with firing an employee. Then she'd scanned documents from some drama-causing Florida investor.

None of which could have been easy, since Glenna's assistant had retired and the replacement had only just started. Naomi's assistant was out for major surgery, so she and Glenna were sharing.

So much upheaval, yet Naomi made it all look effortless.

She was such a dynamo. A mesmerizing dynamo.

"Dwight," she said into the phone, patient but firm, "the contracts were emailed a month ago, with hard copies sent, as well. You were out of the office for quite a while before I went on maternity leave." She paused, nodding her head, her lips getting tighter. "I only received your questions today. So let's work on addressing them—"

She went silent again as the voice on the other end of the phone rose, talking faster. Ranting. Naomi tucked the phone between her ear and shoulder and passed the baby over to Royce, mouthing *thank you*.

Balancing a now sleeping Anna, he set her down in the work space crib. The little girl stretched out slightly, reaching as if to yank on his heartstrings. He placed drowsy Mary in the white crib beside her sister, her little fingers curled into something that looked like a wave. One that could sweep right over him too easily.

He walked to one of the white sofas, settling into the surprisingly firm cushion. The wall of windows showcased the autumn sky. He'd thought nothing could be more majestic than a Texas landscape—until he'd come to Alaska.

Light snow coated the mountaintops in the distance, beautiful, regal. Just like the woman in this office who juggled motherhood while putting out legal fires as if she'd been managing the combination for years. He glanced back at Naomi just as she absently shook her head again, the echoing buzz of Dwight's voice still filling the silence.

Finally, the ass on the other end of the line seemed to run out of steam.

Naomi adjusted the phone against her ear. "I hear your concerns. Loud and clear. We can address them calmly at four o'clock this afternoon, eastern time, when I've had time to consult at length with the rest of the legal team." Her voice was all business, leaving no room for argument. "At which time you can decide if you wish to complete this deal and be a part of Alaska Oil Barons' ecofriendly pipeline to the Dakotas—along with all of the positive press that entails. Or you are welcome to roll the dice with Johnson Oil."

Cal Johnson was in a tailspin over his competition's upgrades. Even Johnson's CEO, Ward Benally, had resigned. And clearly Naomi knew this gave her an edge to use.

Royce couldn't help but think of the day they'd met, when she'd tracked him down to a remote cabin to persuade him to share his research with her family's company. He'd been skeptical about joining Alaska Oil Barons, but the Steeles and the Mikkelsons had proved themselves to be strong advocates for his vision. He appreciated the fire and conviction in her voice.

Whatever Dwight said brought a victorious smile to Naomi's face. She nodded, then said, "Glad to hear you're feeling reassured. And yes, tomorrow is fine with me, since you're busy this afternoon. Happy to accommodate. Have a nice rest of your day. We'll speak soon."

She disconnected the call and exhaled hard. "Jerk."

"He's a jerk who apparently lost whatever edge he expected to gain."

Her fingers lingered on a glass swan figurine that looked as if it were carved from ice. Steel entered her voice as she straightened papers on Glenna's desk, then swiveled in the plush black chair. "He deserves to lose a lot more."

"I agree." Royce let his gaze wander from her angled face. Natural sunlight filtered into the office, framing her at the desk between the two towering bookshelves behind her. "Your firm sense of right and wrong is very attractive."

Damn, but she mesmerized him. Loose waves of her hair gathered just above her breasts, feathering out against her flowy blue dress. She stood, moving around the desk, her leather boots softly pressing into the off-white carpet.

"Thank you." She smiled, her cheeks pink, color returning to her face after being pale for a few days. "And thank you for pitching in with the babies so I could take care of this problem. I hope I'm not taking advantage and detracting from your own work?"

"Nothing to worry about. I took some time off from lecturing at the university. And flexibility is the benefit of being a consultant. I can set my own schedule, plus any tweaks to the current project with the pipeline can be done remotely while the babies sleep." The success of his patents afforded him the luxury of never working again if he so chose. Not that he saw himself ever retiring. He enjoyed inventing, helping the work, and delivering the occasional college seminar to teach future generations. All of which left him with the creative freedom to pursue research grants as inspiration struck.

"Regardless," she said, "you've gone above and beyond. And I have to admit, it was helpful to have the paperwork in front of me today."

"You could have things couriered to the house."

"I could have…" She scrunched her nose, exhaling as she made her way to the sofa. She sat on the arm of the adjacent couch, looked over her shoulder to the window. Naomi took a deep breath before turning to face him. "Okay, truth? I needed to get out of the house and this was the perfect excuse. Thank you for helping make it happen in a way I didn't have to worry about the girls."

Coming here hadn't been as much of a chore as he'd initially thought. The stillness of the office surprised him. Solitude seemed to settle in the room—the kind he craved, and the kind that didn't permeate the Steele family compound. Attraction heightened in the solitude.

Royce cleared his throat, needing a physical act to disrupt his intense eye contact with Naomi. Eye contact that reawakened all sorts of desires in him. He needed to pull on his professional skills to help him now. "I meant it when I said I wanted to help…and before you go ballistic, wondering if I'm trying to use the twins as

CATHERINE MANN 69

a replacement family, let's just settle on a compromise. You and I both have issues to work through. And in letting me help you, you're helping me."

"You make that sound too easy. There has to be a catch." Naomi moved from her perch to sit next to him.

"Quit thinking like a lawyer."

She sagged into the couch, her skirt pooling around her knees, exposing her shapely calves. "A tired lawyer. Thank goodness Dwight didn't take me up on my offer to get everything together today."

"The girls are sleeping, so let's not risk waking them up by carrying them down to the car." He touched the small of her back, and damn, but the familiar feel of her soaked right into him. Not that anything could happen between them. She'd broken his heart. He was here for closure, not to fall back into old patterns of leaning on their sensual connection.

Clearing his throat again, he pulled his hand away and motioned to one of the sofas. "Stretch out on the couch, put your feet up and eat something. I have to confess, I wouldn't mind doing the same."

"You've been too kind to me."

"We have to work together. Unless you want me to quit consulting—"

"Bite your tongue. My family would kill me."

Chuckling, he settled onto the sofa across from her and studied the coffee table sporting a platter of food they'd ordered up from the headquarters' five-star restaurant. He loaded up a plate from the antipasto selection of cured meats, cheeses, olives, crostinis and a fruit spread. "Well, we can't have that."

She plucked an olive from the plate he handed her and nibbled it.

"What are you thinking?" he asked, trying to ignore the low buzz of his phone with an incoming text.

"Just remembering some old times. This was a favorite snack when we were kids—minus the olives back then." She swung her feet up onto the sofa, sitting up against throw pillows with her plate of food. "Life was so idyllic before the accident. Camping trips. Family dinners. And yes, it was noisy, but so happy. Even when we weren't getting along, it was funny, because it wasn't mean-spirited. Does that make sense?"

"Knowing your family? Yes." Having grown up an only child, he was intrigued by their dynamics, the ability to coexist in a crowd.

"Marshall and Brea loved trekking in snowshoes."

"I'm assuming from the tone in your voice that you didn't feel the same?" His phone buzzed again and he checked quickly, finding a work text that could wait. He switched off his cell and turned his attention to Naomi.

"I wanted to curl up with a book at the cabin."

"Seriously? You wanted to be alone?" He couldn't resist teasing her on that count.

"I wasn't totally alone. My grandmother was there—my mother's mom. She said she stayed at the cabin in case one of us kids needed to come back, but she had COPD and couldn't handle the long walks anymore. I cherished the time alone with her, not competing with the others."

"She was a strong influence in your life."

"I don't know what I would have done without her when I went through cancer treatments. I don't know how she held so strong so soon after her daughter—my mom—died." Naomi looked over at the crib with her sleeping babies. "I can't even imagine the pain she must have felt. But she was there for me. Telling me endless stories in the hospital. I can still hear the sound of her voice."

"What kinds of stories?"

Naomi smiled more to herself than to Royce. Her eyes took on a faraway, nostalgic look, and suddenly he found himself even more invested in their conversation.

"My grandmother made sure we heard the legends directly from her, not from a book. Like the tale of the Qalupalik—one of our favorites. She was green and slimy and lived in the water. She hummed and would draw bad children to the waves. If you wandered away from your parents, she would slip you in a pouch on her back and take you to her watery home to live with her other kids. You would never see your family again."

"Your grandma sounds like a tough cookie."

"She was. That story actually used to scare all of us to pieces when we were younger. Delaney cried the first time she heard it. But then the story was familiar and a part of our ritual."

He saw something lurking in her eyes that prompted him to ask, "What were some of your other favorite stories?"

"There's also the werewolf legend about the Adlet. They were said to have the lower body of a wolf and the upper body of a human—"

"Like centaurs," Royce said, before biting into a slice of sharp cheese.

"Basically, yes. And apparently, they still roam. Broderick and Marshall tried to hunt one once. They had to turn back because I tagged along, and Aiden followed me…" She straightened, setting her plate down on the couch cushion beside her. She tensed and Royce could practically see the walls fly up as her voice took on a decidedly more defensive tone. "Are you just being polite? You have to have heard all of this about the werewolf legend. It's a well-known one."

"I haven't heard it this way. Not from you." She narrowed her eyes as if trying to discern his intent. "What are you trying to tell me?"

"Marshall and Brea were always close. People worried more about him after we lost her, and I understand that. But she and I were close, too." A pained smile tugged at her mouth. "She was my sister. I was supposed to protect her."

"Naomi, you were still a kid. That's a heavy burden to put on yourself."

"I know that in my mind, but in my heart?" She blinked back tears. "Since my sister Brea died, it seems like the family is missing a part—like the Adlet legend."

"It's understandable that she's on your mind now."

"I keep thinking about how my girls will never know her."

Ah, hell. Objectivity and distance weren't even an option. He set aside his plate and moved to the other sofa. He shifted her until he could pull her against his side and hold her. She didn't resist. In fact, a shuddering sigh went through her that rocked him to his core.

They both grew silent and he stroked her hair, breathing in the scent of *her*. Every breath pulled temptation tauter inside him.

Her curves molded to his side, the swell of her breasts a sweet temptation. She was drifting off, but he was very much wide-awake. Her breathing eventually slowed even as his heartbeat thudded harder in his ears. And lower.

Sitting here, holding her, was torturous. Apparently, he was a masochist, because he couldn't bring himself to move.

Gathering bottles into a black diaper bag with polar bears stitched on the handles, Naomi took a moment to breathe. And man, did she need to after the last hour of her life.

Having Royce nearby had been a godsend. She moved through work, felt less wiped out than the day before. But she needed to get out, away from the sweet domesticity of playing house with Royce. Dividing up the tasks also made transitioning into her professional life infinitely easier.

But as for her heart? Another matter entirely.

This time with Royce had been too enticing. Too much like things were before, except with two sleeping infants in the room.

Well, and the fact that they couldn't have sex.

Which, now that she thought about it, actually made today different from before, since they'd spent most of their past jumping into bed together. Often. So why was he sticking around?

The obvious answer stung all over again. That he was looking for a replacement family. Or closure for that lost family.

Her heart hurt—and a fierce protective feeling flowed through Naomi. Her children would be no one's replacement.

She would not stay this vulnerable. No. She needed to channel her last name. Erect those famous "Steele" walls.

She quickened her pace, searching the room for any

lingering toys and necessities. At this point, Naomi felt she was almost on autopilot. She barely registered Royce's presence. Or perhaps more accurately, tried to ignore the way he attentively searched the room for stray items.

He placed a hand on her shoulder, the warmth both familiar and new. That was confusing.

"Hey, slow down, Naomi. I've got it. You've done a lot today on your first big day out, other than for a doctor's visit."

He moved closer, the musky scent of him reminding her of the bed that they once shared while making love for hours on end. What it was like to be with him, their bodies slick with sweat and need. Then afterward, sated, resting her head on his muscled chest, listening to the heavy slug of his heart against his ribs.

The memory made her move faster as she stepped away, under the guise of picking up a throw pillow off the floor and replacing it on the sofa. "I'm fine. I'll be home soon with plenty of family to help."

There. Take the hint. She could do this without him. She had to.

He cast a look at her, but didn't take the bait. He simply grunted and tucked a stray swaddling blanket into the diaper bag, then put away his tablet, which he'd brought along to catch up on work of his own during a baby feeding.

A tap on the door stopped her before she could volley a lawyerly retort his way.

Royce called, "Come in."

Of course he did. He'd won the battle by default. And she knew she was acting prickly, but being with him was difficult and too easy all at the same time.

The door opened and a woman peeked around it, her long blond hair swinging. "Excuse me for interrupting. I have those files you asked for."

Right. The files. The main reason for coming here. Naomi smiled in gratitude at Glenna's new assistant. "Thank you, Milla. Sorry to have slipped in while you were out for lunch. We're so glad to have you working for the family company." Then she turned to Royce, grateful to have the woman in the room as an extra barrier to protect her from the crackling emotions between them. "Have you had a chance to meet Milla Jones?"

Six

Her heart pounding, Milla studied Naomi and Royce, having seen the pair only from a distance at the hospital as they'd walked down the corridor with the two bassinets. She'd been careful not to be observed during her just-before-dawn flower deliveries. Although that hallway moment had been a near miss. She'd almost been spotted where she shouldn't have been and blown her whole cover as a new employee for Alaska Oil Barons, Inc. If one of them had remembered her from her job interview…

Perhaps she'd been reckless in indulging in that night to scope out the families. But the temptation had been irresistible to see them in a relaxed moment, unguarded.

Here in the office was different. They had on their business faces, with all the walls that entailed. She was taking a risk, but having an "in" here was too important. She had access to records that she wouldn't have elsewhere. Records that could provide answers. Justice.

Peace.

Milla extended her hand to Royce Miller, glad she'd taken the time to get a manicure to lessen the ragged look of her chewed nails. "Nice to meet you." She'd met Naomi at the interview stage, but not him. "I only just started officially today, although I shadowed my predecessor last week. I understand you've all been busy these past couple of weeks with those two adorable babies."

Royce Miller was a scientist of formidable reputation. She'd done her research on that score. But she'd been unprepared for the full effect of his appeal close up. He was tall and lean, his shoulders stretching the fabric of the simple cashmere sweater he wore over a T. Casual clothes, yes. But the fabric was rich, the tailoring custom. People like Royce and Naomi moved in a whole different world.

The towering guy had shutters in his eyes, a guarded, brooding aura. "Welcome, Ms. Jones."

"Thank you. It's been a wonderful, busy first day." She passed the file and disc to Naomi.

Milla couldn't help but notice Naomi wore embroidered leather boots without a care for the brutal Alaska weather, no doubt because she could afford to replace them at will. Her Italian leather handbag was the kind shopkeepers kept behind a locked counter. Milla thought she remembered it from last year's fashion magazines, not that she'd ever been able to afford anything from the pages.

Naomi took the data and slid it into her briefcase. "Royce has been a tremendous help to the company—and to me."

Gossip about Royce and Naomi had flowed through the break room at lunch earlier. There was even a betting pool over whether they would reunite. "I imagine twins are quite exhausting."

Naomi's tired face lightened with a smile. "And a blessing."

"Of course," Milla answered, curious, needing to get a solid read of the major players here, to effectively achieve her goal of sabotaging the merger. The six Steele offspring and four Mikkelsons would not be joining forces, not as long as she drew breath. "I don't have children of my own, but I can imagine."

Naomi waved to the crib tucked in the corner. "Would you like to see them?"

Milla stifled a wince. She didn't doubt her mission here, but she didn't want to think of innocents. That only complicated things. She preferred to keep her focus on the guilty. Ultimately, the most effective way to protect the innocent. "I wouldn't want to wake them."

No way around this.

Smiling, Naomi walked toward the crib. "We're about to put them in their car seats to leave, anyway."

Milla surrendered to the inevitable and crossed the room, her high heels sinking into the plush carpet. She peered into the crib, where the two infants slept side by side, their heads touching. "They both have a full head of dark hair." She clutched the side of the crib, clenching her hands to keep from reaching inside. From making a connection, its own sort of sabotage. "They're beautiful."

Even as Milla glanced at the sleeping babies, her throat went tight. To see this through, she needed to remain apart. Distant. She concentrated on the designer blankets instead of those sweet faces.

"Thank you." Naomi stepped closer, stopping beside her. "They look like my mother. In fact, Mary is named for her."

"That's a lovely tribute." Milla backed away, needing space and air to regain her conviction. "I should get to work, and I'm sure you're ready to head home. Feel free to call if you need anything while your assistant is on vacation."

Milla spun on her heels and left, closing the door after her, then sagging back against her desk. She'd done a lot of things she wasn't proud of over the years. Necessary, but choices that haunted her at times. She didn't regret the decision to start this path.

She just hadn't expected it would be so difficult to see it through.

Royce focused on the road ahead of him, needing a task, routine, control to keep him from being too aware of the woman next to him. He had to keep his head if he expected to make the most of his time with her and the twins. Easier said than done when Naomi had a way of making his go-to logic tough as hell to find.

He gripped the leather-trimmed steering wheel of his new SUV. Of course, this vehicle was nearly identical to his previous one, just a year newer. This version boasted the same attention to detail. The same precision engineering that he'd researched thoroughly the first time he'd purchased one. A methodical man, a scientist, Royce liked repeatable, predictable patterns. The uniformity of results gave him an anchor in an otherwise chaotic world.

And as he guided the new SUV around a tight moun-

tainside curve with Naomi and her daughters in tow, he
wanted something reliable.

No extra surprises. Royce had a general idea of how
this model would handle in difficult terrain. Which was
a good call, considering the snow-capped mountain they
were winding around still had evidence of the mud-
slide from a storm a few weeks ago. The sludge-cov-
ered roads stirred a deep worry in his gut, momentarily
flashing him back to the moment the twins were born.
How that night had been everything but predictable.

It had required all his willpower to shut down the
gut-deep fear for Naomi and focus on keeping her calm
while guiding the babies into the world.

Nightmares plagued him about all the things that
could have gone wrong. The hell that would have
haunted him if she or the babies hadn't made it.

Snowflakes melted as soon as they hit the heated
windshield. Glancing quickly in the rearview mirror,
he let out a sigh of relief. The road was theirs. No one
in sight.

A strange sense of calm washed over him. Being in
the car with the twins and Naomi felt so damn natural.
Even more so since they'd taken a detour to get his Saint
Bernard. Tessie rested in the far back, curled up on a
quilt. They'd placed two baby blankets there as well,
one from each of the girls so the dog would grow accustomed to their scent. She rested her big head on the
seat, staring at the babies, sniffing the air, but unable
to reach them because of her seat belt tether.

And sure, Royce found his attention drifting to
Naomi more than he should, the creamy line of her
jaw as she relaxed back in her seat. That easy smile she
wore. Her hair flowing in deep waves.

Turning her gaze from the window, she checked on the sleeping girls behind them. Then called out soothing words of praise to Tessie before glancing at him.

"Royce, thanks again for helping today."

He kept his eyes firmly on the road, all too conscious of the precious cargo in the vehicle. "You've thanked me already."

"I couldn't have done it without you."

"I beg to differ." He shook his head as the road dipped around a cluster of pine trees. "You would have managed with your sister or a nanny."

"Maybe I could have." Sighing, she turned toward him, her forehead furrowed. "Are you regretting volunteering for this unconventional setup? Because if you are, I understand. I really can ask my family for help. Maybe you should go to your place for a while."

The thought of trusting the safety of her and the twins to someone else? No. He couldn't, and he didn't want to analyze the why of that. "You're not getting rid of me that easily."

"I wish I understood better why you're insisting on us spending time together. Maybe I'm just too brain tired, but this doesn't seem to be bringing closure."

He wished he had the answer to that. But he was sorting it out. Still, she clearly expected him to respond, so he opted for something that would buy him more time. "I thought these girls were going to be mine. I'm learning to say goodbye."

Exhaling hard, she sagged back in her seat. "I thought that might be the case, because of what happened with your ex-fiancée." Her throat moved with a hard swallow as she blinked fast. "I appreciate your honesty."

Hell, he hadn't meant to hurt her—again. Communication wasn't his forte, even more so when dealing with Naomi. In the past, he'd relied more on their intense physical connection. Although backtracking to repair their communication would only make things worse, since he didn't have a better answer on how to try.

Regardless, they were locked into seeing each other for the remaining year on his contract consulting for her family's oil company. A year of wanting her. A year of remembering what it had been like to have her in his arms, in his bed.

He winced.

The best course? Dig in for the next four weeks and hope they both found what they were looking for to put the past to rest.

Naomi couldn't believe she was back at the office again.

Her maternity leave was not turning out the way she'd planned. But with the merger in the works and the future of her family's business at stake, she had to balance it all. For the past ten days, she'd fallen into a rhythm of coming to the office for an hour a day to take care of business that needed addressing in person. The hour also gave her a break from the connection with Royce that she absolutely could not surrender to. She'd let him go for both of their sakes, and with him underfoot, she needed an excuse to break the spell her mind wanted to weave.

She unpacked her briefcase onto the desk, time being of the essence. The babies napped long enough in the afternoon that she could be away for a short period of time without hauling them from home. Royce swore he enjoyed the quiet time while the babies slept to accomplish work of his own.

She could see that her huge family was starting to wear on him, yet he wasn't budging. And she couldn't bring herself to boot him out. God, they were a messed up ex-couple.

Shaking off the distracting thoughts, she settled in front of the computer. Slipping into work mode, she embraced feeling in the zone. Her fingers flew at the speed of light across the keyboard as she plowed through the work in front of her, to be ready for her meeting with Chuck Mikkelson. Officially her stepbrother now, but also a force to be reckoned with in the Mikkelson empire. She couldn't afford to assume someone didn't have a hidden agenda just because they were family now and merging the companies.

Taking a deep breath, she pressed the button to buzz for Glenna's new assistant, Milla Jones.

Deep down, Naomi knew she needed to delegate. But admitting she needed help went against all she'd worked so hard to become. Still, exhaustion crept in. She buzzed again.

"Is there a problem?" A soft voice with a trace of a Canadian accent filtered through the sleek speaker.

Tucking a pen behind her ear, Naomi scanned the desk again. Nope. No sign of the much needed files. She let go an exasperated sigh. "I can't seem to locate the files I need for my meeting with Chuck Mikkelson."

"What files would those be?"

Removing the pen from behind her ear, Naomi leaned forward on Glenna's desk. Dropping her head in her palm, she rubbed her temple, stress mounting.

"The numbers Glenna and Broderick worked up on the improvements to the pipeline to North Dakota."

"I have them right here on my desk. Give me two seconds." The speaker went silent and moments later the door opened. Milla pulled a stack of files from under her arm. "They're in here."

"Oh, thank you." Naomi reached for them, unable to help but notice how chic and put together the blonde looked, with perfect waves in her hair and not a wrinkle in her pencil skirt. "I was concerned I left some brain cells at the girls' 3:00 a.m. feeding."

Naomi resisted the urge to smooth a hand over her leggings, one of the few things that fit, along with one of Royce's cotton button-downs she'd grabbed off the back of a chair. She'd been running late, so hurriedly threw on a chunky necklace and leather boots. She needed to go shopping, but time was limited these days.

"I'm in awe you're here." The assistant tapped the two files. "I've emailed copies, as well."

"You're efficient. I appreciate your help."

Milla tipped her head to the side, surveying the office with great intensity before shrugging on her way out. "Just learning my way around, getting to know all the people."

The door clicked closed, leaving Naomi alone again. The hair on the nape of her neck prickled. Something about the new assistant felt…off. Something she couldn't quite articulate or grasp, but the same spidery sense that sometimes tingled during court cases.

Shaking her head, she decided it must be the lack of sleep playing with her instincts. She should be digging into the files rather than letting her mind wander.

Just as she reached for them, a tall, ruggedly handsome man with sandy brown hair walked into her office without being announced. Chuck, her once rival turned stepbrother. She and her family hadn't seen much of Chuck lately, since he and his wife had been having marital troubles. During Jack Steele's recovery from surgery, they'd all been so overwhelmed, they'd had to recruit the younger Mikkelson brother—Trystan—to be the face of the blending companies at a major fundraiser. It had required one helluva media and mouth makeover to get the volatile, outspoken, rugged rancher camera ready.

Of course, Trystan's attraction to the media consultant had provided a hefty motivation to succeed. Now they were engaged and expected a baby.

Chuck was back at the helm now, though. And early for this meeting, to boot. A sinking feeling tightened her chest. She hadn't even had the opportunity to crack open the paperwork and skim. Too late now, however. She would have to wing it.

Naomi stepped from behind the desk. "So, hello… *stepbrother*. How crazy is that?"

"Completely." He set his briefcase on the coffee table between the two sofas, looking professional as always, but also like he had the weight of the world on his shoulders. "I think it's going to take us all a while to get used to this unlikely blended family. Everyone sends their best on the babies' safe arrival."

"Blessings doubled and troubles shared. Thank you for all the flowers and the hospital visit." Office talk could wait for a moment. She'd deposed enough witnesses to know that things went smoother when they were at ease. She went to the wet bar and tapped the carafe. "Coffee?"

"Yes, thank you," he said. "Although I'm not so sure I've done my share with helping."

"Trystan and his image consultant pulled off a top-notch coup at the Wilderness Preservation fund-raiser."

"Surprised us all, quite frankly. I knew he could do it, but he exceeded expectations."

Trystan had a reputation for being brusque and anti-social. He'd been adopted by the Mikkelson family—a cousin with a rocky start in life.

"Together, we'll all make this happen. Thank you for being flexible about the time today. I, um, realize your plate's full. I'm sorry about the trouble you and Shana have been having…" Naomi paused, setting aside the carafe. "I hope that was okay to say. I didn't mean to get too personal."

"Everyone knows we've been struggling and how much time I've had to take off work." He took the china cup without adding cream or sugar.

She certainly understood the hardships a rocky relationship brought to every other aspect of life.

"If there's something I can do to help, let me know. Even if you just need a sympathetic ear." She poured herself a glass of sparkling water and sat on one of the sofas, bright light pouring in the huge wall of windows beside them.

"Unless you can change the past, I'm afraid not." Sitting across from her, he blew into his coffee before taking a hefty swallow.

"I heard she had a difficult time with her father." Vague details, but enough to make Naomi so grateful for her own steady dad. Jack Steele had been a rock for his children, even when suffering from a deep grief over losing his wife and one of his kids.

"That's putting it mildly." Chuck stared down into his cup of java. "I'm sure you'll hear eventually, now that our families are so tangled up. When Shana was a teenager, she found out that her 'hero' dad was a fraud. He wasn't some undercover detective. He was a rent-a-cop who had a second family tucked away a couple of counties over."

"Ohmigod, that's…awful." She'd heard about Shana's father walking out on his family, but not a whisper about this level of betrayal. And for some reason this was prevalent in Chuck's mind right now. Naomi stayed silent, letting him decide if he wanted to tell more or shift to work.

"Cheating is bad enough, but he deliberately posed as husband-and-wife with the other woman. Poured out his inheritance on her and her children at the expense of his own—not to mention the time he chose to be away from his own kids."

"Shana must have been crushed. I can't imagine what kind of person would do that to his own child."

Chuck forked his hand through his hair, a trace of anger sparking in his eyes. "A raging narcissist who's only interested in looking good in front of others, who feeds off emotions. It's all about manipulating life to what serves him best. That has made it difficult for Shana to trust."

"Her father's still alive?" Naomi rubbed her arms, goose bumps rising. She couldn't imagine hurting her children that way.

"He lives down in San Diego with his new wife, in a house on the beach that was bought with all the money he funneled into her name." Chuck held up a hand. "I'm sorry for unloading all of this on you. It's just fresh on my mind, since we heard from the guy yesterday."

The legal eagle part of her wanted to find a way to nail the guy, to get justice for Shana. "Um, what stops you from—"

"Killing him for crushing my wife?" he asked tightly. "For destroying her mother? For being the lowest form of scum on the earth?" His jaw went tight. "I get by knowing that karma will nail him. Knowing he lost amazing people in his life and he's now with a person who thought nothing of living a lie and destroying a family." Shrugging, he smiled. "And I don't want to go to jail."

She laughed softly. "There is that."

"Yeah, seriously, though, Shana says attention is what he craves, so she ignores him. He pops his head up for air every now and again to try to stir things up."

"I'm so sorry."

"I'm sorry he hurt my wife, that he has made it so difficult for her to trust. She deserves good things in life." Chuck reached for his china cup on the coffee table.

"Trust..." Naomi shook her head. "I wrestle with that and I haven't faced near what she did. I know my family loves me."

"You lost your mother and sister. You've battled cancer. You've had your fair share of kicks from life. It's not a game of whose pain is worse. Pain is pain." He cricked his neck from side to side, his face going neutral, as if he'd placed all that anger into a box and sealed it shut. "We should get to work."

"Of course, you're right. I'm sorry for prying."

He waved dismissively. "You weren't. You're just

good at asking questions and listening." His eyes narrowed wryly. "I imagine it comes with your job."

"I'm no expert at relationships. I think in listening to how other people sort through things, I'm trying to find answers for my own life." She nudged the files on the coffee table toward him. "So, back to work. I haven't had a chance to look over these numbers from Glenna and Broderick. How about you tell me your take on things before I do."

Royce's ecological innovations put every other version of oil production to shame. They could not and would not risk the wilderness they loved so much. Now there was the teeny-tiny matter of making Royce's design financially feasible.

Chuck reached for his briefcase. "There's no way around it. The numbers just don't work."

Finally, he had some much needed solitude to lose himself in business, and yet he was still tense as hell.

Royce drummed his fingers next to his computer on the teak desk, his dog napping at his feet. He'd taken time off, but his work was about more than clocking in hours for a paycheck. His occupation as a research scientist was a calling for him, a way of life to protect the future for children like Anna and Mary.

Which meant working with the Steele-Mikkelsons at Alaska Oil Barons, Inc. was his best bet for making his theories come to life. Yet another reason he had to figure out this relationship with Naomi, as they were tied together through the company. There was no avoiding each other if things went south between them again. He wasn't budging from his plan to stay until her father returned for the party that would welcome him and Jeannie.

Royce glanced at his watch and saw Naomi should be arriving home any minute now. She'd texted him when she left the office. He'd had the chef send up supper so he and Naomi could eat in her suite.

Time to stretch his legs. Which was really just an excuse to check on the girls. Sure, he had the video baby monitor hooked up, which he frequently glanced at, but seeing them with his own two eyes soothed him. Tessie stood, then loped alongside him, her tail wagging. She'd taken well to the little ones, often alerting to their coos and squawks an instant prior to the monitor picking up the sounds. Luckily, the Steeles were open to dogs, one thing he had in common with them. Tessie enjoyed romping in the snow with Glenna and Broderick's husky.

Royce looked into the bassinet, relieved that they still slept. Didn't even stir. God, they were cute, and fast wrapping him around their tiny little fingers. He rubbed the back of his neck and turned away.

A grumble in his stomach led him to the kitchen, where the chef had left a mouthwatering caribou stew, and rhubarb crisp for dessert. As he lifted the lid on the pot to stir the stew, he heard the elevator whirring closer. The doors slid open and Naomi strode inside her L-shaped corner suite.

Damn, she was gorgeous, with her legs showcased in leggings and leather boots. She was wearing one of his shirts, along with a bulky jewel-toned necklace… His mouth went dry and he reminded himself he had to stay away from her not just for physical reasons, but also for their very sanity.

He shook off thoughts he wasn't close to having answers for.

"Welcome back." He tossed a hand towel over his shoulder. "How did your meeting go?"

"Busy." She set aside her briefcase, a strand of hair slipping free from her topknot. "Let's talk about yours. How are the babies? I hope they didn't run you ragged."

"The girls napped. Then your sister came up. Some of the Mikkelsons were with her—don't ask me which ones—and they took the twins downstairs." A reminder of how soon she would realize she didn't need him. And then what? Could he just walk away? Was closure possible? "There were plenty of capable hands to hold and feed the babies."

"The wonders of a big family," she muttered, stretching her arms, the shirt pulling taught against her breasts.

"You have a pack, for sure." He stifled a wince at the mention of her large family. The last thing he wanted was to set her defenses up, but damn, his brain was on stun from taking in her curves.

"What did you all talk about?" She peeked into the pot on the stove, breathing in the aroma with a blissful expression. When she stirred it with a spoon and tasted it, her sexy moan almost drove him to his knees.

"I went to the study." He hauled his attention away and pulled a large bottled water from the stainless steel refrigerator. "Work."

"Right, of course. I'm being selfish. I know how important your research is to you."

Something shifted in her deep brown eyes that he couldn't quite place. But then his brain wasn't chugging on all cylinders with his body aching to be near her.

"It is," he said, pouring water into two cut crystal glasses. "But for this phase, I'm through with the bulk of the heavy lifting. It's about implementation now."

She turned her back to pull bowls from the cabinet, her focus on picking at the food and setting the table, his on the movement of her mouth as she licked her fingers. He recalled the day they'd first met, when they'd been alone in that tiny glass igloo-style retreat outside Anchorage. The way her eyes had roamed over him. He wanted that attention now.

She turned from the table, facing him. "And your next consulting project?"

"Does this mean I'm fired?" He offered it as a joke, but the answer mattered more than he cared to admit. He couldn't delude himself. He wasn't ready to leave.

She glanced at him, eyes wide. "No, of course not. Just making conversation. Wondering about your future."

"I have files full of ideas. I'm almost considering taking some long-term time off after this project. Recharge the brain." Get over the hellish fallout from having walked away from her for good. "That's when the best inventions happen. Trust me, though, my entire focus is on this project. It's important to me."

She chewed her bottom lip, concern for him so evident in her eyes that it reached into him, drew him closer. And even though he knew touching her couldn't lead anywhere right now, he stroked her face...

And covered her mouth with his.

Seven

Naomi gripped Royce's shoulders, her fingers digging into the hard planes.

To push him away?

Or to bring him closer?

No choice at all. A simple decision. The draw to share this moment with him was too strong.

Her hands slid around his shoulders and up into his hair, then she leaned into him, soaking up the familiar feel of him. Starved for him after so long apart. His strong arms banded around her waist, his palms roving over her back.

She'd missed the focus on *her* as a woman. Need returned with a vengeance. To indulge. To know she was an indulgence to him.

A low growl rumbled through his chest, vibrating against her. She sighed, threading her fingers through his hair.

He stroked her shoulders, then down her arms as he arched away. He cupped the back of her head and guided it to rest against his chest. "Naomi, I shouldn't have done that."

She wasn't sure if she appreciated him stopping or not. But she couldn't deny every second of that kiss had been delicious. Welcome.

"We can't pretend the past doesn't exist." She searched for words to ease the awkwardness—and the pain of lost dreams. Her fingers moved against the crisp cotton of his shirt. "We were drawn to each other for a reason back then. Even going our separate ways doesn't erase that initial pull or what we almost had."

"How about we agree we're not pretending anymore, but we also shelve this discussion for now? It's been a long day."

She pulled away, more stung by his avoiding the discussion than she wanted to admit. He was so very obviously escaping.

Her pride hurt too much, though, to challenge him on that. So she embraced the exhaustion excuse. "Of course. You're right." She backed away from him. "I could use a catnap before the girls wake up. And please don't offer to watch them for me. Go. Take some time for yourself."

He studied her for five heartbeats before nodding slowly. "I'm going to pick up some things from my place and grab supper out. Call me if you need me before the girls settle in for the night."

Snagging his coat from the back of the sofa on his way to the elevator, he walked away without another word. Leaving her alone with the girls and her thoughts.

Her mind churned with memories of that kiss, the

rasp of his fingers on her skin, the taste of him. She'd missed his touch, his kisses.

She'd missed *him*.

Goose bumps prickled as she rubbed her arms. The girls were sleeping, and she was alone. She should be doing something other than wandering around the living room in circles. At the very least, she should shower and sleep, two things in short supply for her these days.

A half hour later, she slid under the covers with a hefty sigh. The babies snoozed on in their nursery and she'd placed the monitor beside her bed, even though her door was open as well as theirs.

As sleep swept over her, her languid thoughts drifted back to Royce's kiss, to so many other kisses. Their attraction had been undeniable from the moment she'd met him, trapped together in an all-glass igloo-style cabin during a blizzard… That chemistry had drawn them into bed so quickly, so very memorably. The desire to leave the heartache behind fell away as the dream drew her under…

Royce's mouth and hands set her body on fire, and as much as part of her shouted that this was happening too fast, she also knew her days for having a no-strings fling were numbered. Casual would take on a different meaning once she gave birth. On a practical level, having a wild, torrid affair with him right now, in this bed made complete sense.

Royce angled back to look into her eyes, stroking her hair with a long sweep of his hands. "Are you sure this is what you want?"

"Are you kidding me? I very much want you."

He eyed her with a gaze that drank her in, launching another wave of excitement through her veins. Antici-

pation swirled through her until her face heated with
a flush. He reached into the bedside table and pulled
out an unopened box of condoms.

Morning sunshine pushed through the snow on the
glass roof, dappling them with light as she tugged at his
shirt and sweatpants. His skin was impossibly warm,
the hard muscles shifting under her touch while she
skimmed away his clothes. The expanse of his muscled
chest sprinkled with hair wasn't that of a sedentary
man. The sinewy planes of him spoke of activity, of a
love of the outdoors.

She wanted to feel him, all of him, against her. Inside
her. She'd never been so hot, so hungry, for any man.
She reveled in the graze of his fingers as he bunched
and swept aside her silk thermal shirt, sliding around
the strap of the simple cotton bra she'd never planned
on anyone else seeing. His avid gaze practically sizzled
the fabric away, her breasts beading to aching points
by the time he freed her. She shivered as he scraped
down the thermal underwear, until at last they were
skin to skin.

The warmth of him, pressing flesh to flesh as he
kissed her, ramped up her need higher, hotter. He
skimmed his mouth to the curve of her neck and she
caught a glimpse of the heat in his eyes as he stroked
her with his gaze, as tangible as his hands caressing
her breasts. Then lower, kissing the inside of her thigh
before moving to the core of her. Circling, plucking.
Teasing a tingling flame higher and hotter until her
own hands clenched into fists.

"You're absolutely...gorgeous. But you have to already know that."

His intuitive touch made her feel carefree. They were

just man and woman, caught up in a feverish attraction. She'd had no idea how powerful that could be.

"You're making me blush."

Royce planted slow, deliberate kisses on her collarbone. "That sounds like an invitation to make you blush all over."

Oh. My.

Breath seemed impossible as he pressed against her. Still, somehow she managed to whisper, "As long as turnabout is fair play."

"Yes, ma'am." His confident chuckle heated her flesh and he angled up to graze his mouth along her ear, her jaw.

"And by the way?"

"Yeah?"

"You're too chatty." She nipped his bottom lip.

His slow, sexy smile gave her an instant's warning before his mouth closed over her breast, one then the other, until the tingles gathered force within her to a tight urgency.

She grabbed for the box of condoms and wrenched it open, fumbling to tear into a packet. He reached for her hand, but she nudged him aside. Wanting. Needing to explore him. She sheathed him and his groan of pleasure brought an answering groan from her.

"Naomi, there are so many more ways I want to touch you, to—"

She pressed a finger to his lips. "And you can. We will. Right now, though..."

She didn't have to finish the thought. He slid inside her, filling her as her legs glided up and around his hips, her ankles locking. In sync, they moved. She didn't know how to explain the strength of sensations already swelling inside her, the way his caresses ignited her, knew her so instinctively. Being with him was insane and somehow so damn right all at the same time...

Pacing in the dark nursery, Royce shushed the fussy baby in his arms, Anchorage's skyline twinkling in the distance. "Your mama's tired, and she's finally not restless. Let's keep it quiet." He kept walking the floor, glad he'd thought to turn off the nursery monitor and close Naomi's bedroom door when he'd returned. "Shall I recite the periodic table to you? I could even sing it."

The tiny face scrunched up, feet pumping.

"Good choice. My voice is nails on a chalkboard. So if you're not into the periodic table, I could shuffle to Newton's Laws of Motion, Hubble's Law of Cosmic Expansion, Universal Law of Gravitation, Archimedes's Buoyancy Principle? Surely I must be boring you to sleep."

Mary blinked again, wide-awake. Yes, Mary. He might not be able to tell one Mikkelson from another, but he could tell the difference between Mary and Anna by the way their eyebrows grew. Even their cries were a little different. The infant shoved a fist into her mouth and sucked, watching him.

He welcomed this time alone to get his thoughts together after that combustible kiss with Naomi. And he couldn't avoid the truth—that he'd wanted to keep on kissing her. Having her in his arms again had been incredible.

Leaving after the gala was going to be tougher than he'd bargained on. Work with the pipeline modifications would ramp up for him, but the evenings would be lonely. Gaining closure and getting her out of his mind wasn't panning out as he'd expected.

Throughout the last few weeks, Royce had attempted to bury the surprise of how naturally and easily he fitted into their routine. But alone with the babies, late at night with nothing but a twinkling city skyline, the reality of how right it felt became undeniable. It was about more than fitting into a routine. It was about the joy of a daily connection.

Mary squawked again and he jostled her lightly, whispering, "If you were older I would let you play with the abacus." His chest went tight, that fear of a future without Naomi creeping back in. "I hope I get to see that one day, kiddo. I can't make any promises, though, because it's up to your mama how that plays out."

He thought of Naomi sleeping just a door away, that glimpse of her burned into his brain. How she sprawled blissfully under the comforter, her hair splayed out on the pillow. Not too many months ago, he would have had the right to turn his face into those silky strands. Their relationship had had a combustible start and an equally explosive ending. He couldn't envision them finding a peaceful friendship. They were an all-or-nothing kind of couple.

Could she have had a point? That he was pursuing her only because he wanted a replacement family? He hated to think that of himself. And damn it, he knew his attraction to Naomi was real. Her intelligence and take-no-prisoners attitude made her irresistible.

But he also knew he wasn't one to deal with emotions. He avoided those memories at all costs. Maybe the babies were bringing the whole of his past out again.

But two things were evident. He couldn't fix what

was wrong between him and Naomi, and he loved the babies, had since before they were born. He was their father in all the ways that mattered, and he was going to bring the fight to them, not let go.

He had a few more weeks to figure this out. Maybe, with time, he and Naomi would find that their connection, their shared interest at work, and yes, raising these two babies together, was more than enough to bind them together.

Or was that just wishful thinking?

The L-shaped loft could not contain Naomi's racing mind. She poked at her eggs with a fork tip, chasing them around the dish—an heirloom from her grandmother—trying to bring her world, heart and mind into balance. Trying to channel the scales of Justice. But rather than needing the scales to sort out a complex legal problem, Naomi needed them to settle the affairs of her heart.

Royce sat across from her in sweats and an MIT T-shirt that stretched across his muscular chest. Sitting here with him was too intimate, with the memory of that kiss and the resulting dream smoking through her mind.

She averted her eyes, which didn't help at all when her gaze landed on the suitcase he'd been living out of since she and the girls got home from the hospital. Now, an empty suitcase. While she'd napped, he'd unpacked everything and stowed his gear in the extra closet and shelves in her bedroom. Just as he had when they'd lived here together, alternating between her place and his until they came up with a more permanent plan. Something that never happened.

"Royce, you have to know it's presumptuous of you to move in here."

He glanced at her, raising one eyebrow, but staying silent.

Damn, but he was arrogant. And hot.

"Tall, dark and brooding isn't going to work on me. We need to set some ground rules if we're going to spend this time together."

And damn it, she realized she'd just conceded he was staying. Apparently tall, dark and brooding did work.

"Royce…"

"Yes?" His voice rumbled in the space between them, luring her.

"Just, um, no more kissing." She started to say more about the presumption of his virtual move-in, but that seemed silly when she was depending on him so much. "I'm taking the girls today and I insist you have the day for yourself."

"What if I say no?"

She bit back the urge to snap, and reached for the decaf coffee. Surely it was the lack of caffeine while still nursing the babies that was making her cranky. "I *will* call you crazy if you turn down the time. Seriously, I'm spending the day with Chuck's wife, Shana. We're putting our heads together for the welcome home party."

He stared at her with narrowed eyes, as if weighing her words for an ulterior motive in sending him off. The downside to having been a couple. He knew her well.

Finally, he turned his attention to spreading berry jam on a thick slice of toast. "She's a good daughter-in-law to do that for Jeannie."

"They all appear to be close. There aren't as many Mikkelsons as there are Steeles, but they're working hard to pull equal hours." She tapped her fingers on the coffee mug.

"You sound…skeptical." Tearing off an edge of toast, he popped it into his mouth, then chewed thoughtfully.

His eyes met hers in that direct way of his that made her feel she had his full and undivided attention. A heady sensation out of bed as well as in. His tousled bed head made her fingers ache to smooth through the strands of hair, to touch him.

She looked at him over her cup of decaf java. "It's hard to trust them after so many years being mortal enemies. I cut my teeth on tales of how Mikkelsons ate kids for dinner."

"I can't envision your dad saying that to his children." Royce bit into the toast, his eyes skating to the nursery.

Her heart tugged at the thought of how much it would hurt him to tell the girls goodbye. But what was she supposed to do? "My brother said so. He seemed wise and ancient then. Sounds silly now, but the foundation for distrust was laid."

Royce set down the last bite of his toast slowly, deliberately. "Do you still question the Mikkelsons' ethics?"

His voice was steady, but genuine concern trickled through.

The very idea made her gut clench, especially with Royce's research on the line…

Could Chuck have an ulterior motive in stating the financials didn't work? But the numbers were the numbers. Unless he'd found a way to turn investors.

She hated having to think this way. But years as a corporate lawyer meant she *had* to.

She drew a breath. "I wouldn't go that far without

proof. More like I question their loyalty, because I know my family will always come first for me. Why wouldn't they feel the same?"

"You seemed to have resolved that before."

"It was easier to try to believe all would be well in the beginning. And then Dad was in the horse riding accident and business affairs were the last thing on our minds. Now, when it's getting to crunch time with the final stages of the merger…it's just tougher." Naomi's nerves churned again. Protecting the family, her family, informed every decision she'd ever made. With two daughters of her own to consider, her resolve doubled.

"What choices do you have?" Royce leaned forward, palms splayed. She could reach out and touch him, like old times. Naomi wanted to feel the strength and warmth of the scientist's fingertips. But that would only make things even more complicated. Blurry as a snowstorm. Perhaps just as dangerous, too.

Instead, she gripped her decaf tighter. "Not many. I'm keeping my eyes open, checking and double-checking documents…"

Royce nodded, his dark eyes registering more and more. "The reason you keep insisting on working."

"Yes." Talking to him was such an easy habit to fall into again. Only three weeks and she was already weakening. "And I'm watching the other side."

"You think Shana may not be as guarded."

It had crossed her mind. God, he read her so well. "Either way, we have to plan the party. We're related by in-law something. It's worth talking to her."

"All right, then." Palms on the table, he stood, pausing, then nodding. "I'll make a plate for myself and gratefully hide out in the study to work. Text if you need me."

He skimmed a hand across her shoulder, the casual touch intimate in its own way. Her breath hitched and she couldn't keep from watching how he moved, loading up with breakfast, his strides to the elevator even, heavy. She wanted to call him back, to share breakfast, to hold his hand and even flirt as if they didn't have a past. As if they'd just met.

The elevator doors slid open, and Royce gestured for Shana to enter the suite before he disappeared from view.

Shana clutched a three-ring binder and a tablet, walking closer. "I can come back later if I was interrupting…"

"No, please," Naomi said, smoothing her loose tunic and leggings. "Royce has work to do. The girls are asleep. The timing is perfect. Join me for some breakfast while we go over the plans?"

Shana half turned, the bell sleeves of her dress swishing. "Sure, if you're absolutely certain you wouldn't just rather relax with—"

Sighing, Naomi rolled her eyes. "Is it that obvious to everyone how…"

"Confused you're feeling?" Shana sat at the table, setting the binder and tablet aside. "Not to everyone. I was a successful detective for a reason." She reached for the orange juice, the morning sun hitting her thick, long hair as she leaned forward.

Shana hadn't needed to scrape her locks into a messy bun this morning.

"I was so sure when I broke things off with him it was the right thing to do." Naomi touched her own top-knot, which was full of tangles from sleeping with her hair wet. Or moving restlessly in the night because of her dreams. "I know I should let him go, but it doesn't feel right anymore. Part of me wants a second chance."

Though she still needed to determine Chuck's and his family's motives businesswise, Naomi found herself at ease with Shana on this subject, at least. Walls and pretenses were evaporating. The woman was becoming more than just a step-in-law. She was becoming a friend.

"That's not a question I can answer for you." Shana eyed her over the glass of juice.

"You're married. You've worked through hard times." Naomi wondered if she'd overstepped, but Shana and Chuck's marital troubles hadn't been a secret.

"I wouldn't say we've worked through them." The leggy blonde swept a lock of hair off her forehead before settling into the chair. "More like we've worked on them."

"I'm sorry. I didn't mean to pry." So much for Naomi's plan to find out more about the Mikkelson family business.

Laughing, Shana waved aside her concern. "We're family now, in a roundabout way. Step-in-laws."

Naomi welcomed the release of a laugh after the tension of the morning with Royce. "I was just thinking the same thing. I look forward to getting to know everyone better."

"Do you trust him?"

Startled at the question, Naomi looked up sharply. Shana couldn't have read her mind about Chuck and the other Mikkelsons, could she?

Oh… Realization dawned. Shana meant did Naomi trust Royce. "Yes, I do."

And damn, but that took the wind right out of her sails. She didn't trust life to be kind to her, or to last. But the people in her world? They hadn't done anything like Shana's father had to her.

Naomi thought back to all Chuck had shared about his wife's past. The pain in Shana's eyes was tangible. Naomi squeezed her hand and an understanding passed between them, a sense that Shana could tell Naomi knew about the woman's father somehow.

Shana squeezed back. "A good, honest man that you can truly trust is worth giving a second chance."

The truth resonated. The stakes were so high with Naomi's children. Royce was digging in deep to make his mark with the company for years to come—although he didn't know about Chuck's numbers.

If he stayed with the company long term and Naomi and he crossed paths, this could make their relationship all the more tense. As if things weren't difficult enough to sift through.

Would Royce blame her for the failed number crunch?

Did *he* trust *her*?

Her heart hammered in her chest, the sound so loud it filled her ears. She still wanted him in spite of their problems and all the unresolved questions.

One way or another, she had to use these next weeks together before the gala to find out how much of a chance she could afford to give him, because she feared another breakup would destroy them both.

Eight

Milla had breached the inner circle.

Well, at least superficially.

She'd been invited to a movie viewing in the plush screening room at the Mikkelson compound. Only a select few employees had been invited. She wasn't sure what had landed her on the list, but here she was.

Sconces on the wall reflected light in the shape of hourglasses. Subdued. Understated. And yet Milla recognized the luxury of the Mikkelsons' home theater.

No amount of low lighting could camouflage or downplay the rows of plush leather reclining seats that had built-in massage options. Never mind the grand hallway she'd walked through to arrive at the media room. The rich scent of mahogany paneling filled the air.

What must it be like to live here? Milla wondered, swirling the pinot noir in her glass.

She took a moment to appreciate her ability to move so seamlessly into this family's world. An infiltration James Bond would be proud of. Her success tonight was as tangible as the heavy plate of hors d'oeuvres she clutched in her due-for-a-manicure fingers.

As she noticed the flaking polish, she clenched her free hand into a fist, hiding her nails. Somehow fearing that the ragged edges of her hard-fought veneer would reveal her intentions to the whole room.

Milla shoved the thought down with a swig of wine. She needed this opportunity to get to know the key players better, in a more informal setting.

Leaning against the maroon wall, she surveyed the media room. Tried to take it all in. Note the family dynamics in this relaxed space. She smiled at two employees from the office who passed her to take seats in the front row.

Chuck and Shana Mikkelson sat side by side without touching. Something like ice seemed to settle in the space between them. The contrast was stark, given how Broderick's arm was around Glenna as his wife leaned her head on his shoulder.

Younger siblings, Aiden Steele and Alayna Mikkelson, whispered and laughed in the corner. Likely teenage stuff such as social media gossip, given their death grips on their devices.

Half a dozen other employees sprinkled throughout were eating gourmet popcorn and sipping cocktails.

And in the back, Delaney Steele and Birch Montoya. Why did everyone else buy their enemies act? Sure, they were on opposite sides of the environmental spectrum, but clearly, they were having a secret affair. The tension between them was so combustible Milla wouldn't have been surprised to see it light up the dark screening room.

They were all so wrapped up in their own worlds, their smaller circles that kept them from seeing outside to the larger picture.

She had to see it all. To absorb every morsel of information she could glean. Because someone here had betrayed her adoptive family in Canada. She owed her family everything—and that included seeing justice served.

Milla stacked her plate on a side table with the others, then moved toward the middle of a row. Settling into a seat there, she lifted her wineglass, hoping to seem as nonchalant as possible as she discreetly tuned into nearby, whispered conversations taking place before *Cyber Ghost* started.

Yet another mark of wealth she could not fully understand. The Mikkelsons were able to debut the film here—an exclusive showing of a feature simultaneously debuting in theaters tomorrow.

Aiden passed to take his seat, his popcorn box right at nose level so she couldn't miss the scent. From the aroma, it seemed a mixture of cheddar and…maple. Yes. Maple syrup.

Images of her adoptive family flooded her. Of warm breakfasts in a tiny, sterile room. Pancakes… The memories threatened to consume her. They might have succeeded, too, if not for the tall presence of Conrad Steele settling into a seat beside her.

Suddenly, she became hyperaware of the here and now.

Conrad was making the rounds in place of his older brother, Jack, who was still on his extended honeymoon.

Conrad smiled, his blue-gray eyes searching hers as if he was trying to understand some essential truth about her in the minutes before the screening began.

He cleared his throat, leaning toward her, his elbows resting on his jeans-clad thighs. In a low voice that made her think of wind blowing through brush, he asked, "How are you liking working for the company? Is everybody treating you well?"

Milla tightened her grip on the stem of her leaded crystal glass. "Everyone's been very welcoming. Thank you for asking."

"It's a time of change," he said, leaning back in the chair, leather creaking, "which makes it all the tougher as a newcomer on staff."

Conrad lazily scratched his head, that smile still playing on his lips, crinkling the skin beside his eyes.

"Others are new, too." And she could get lost in the sea of new faces. Especially if she didn't make waves.

"I can see how that would offer more opportunities for friendships."

"Of course." Was he hitting on her? Sure, he was cute in a middle-aged kind of way. But still. Eww.

"Sage Hammond is about your age. She's good people. Reach out to her if you need anything."

Milla relaxed in the theater seat, relieved that she wouldn't have to rebuff a major Steele player. Yes, Conrad had his own corporate interests, but he was still the younger brother of Jack Steele and a significant stockholder in his own right. He'd even assisted Jack on occasion before the younger Steeles were old enough to help their father in the company.

In spite of his easygoing manner, Conrad Steele was not to be dismissed lightly.

The older man eyed his drained snifter. "Hmm, my drink's empty. Good to talk to you, and again, welcome."

Milla studied him as he walked away, wondering what secrets were hidden in his brain. He played the part so well, being half in, half out of this world. Like he was playing the odds, so he had a stake in a winning side either way.

How deep did his secret agendas go? And was anyone else in his family involved?

As the sun refracted on the fresh snow, Royce inhaled the cold air and awakened his insides with the bracing Alaskan atmosphere. The cool morning breeze raked across his cheeks as he sauntered forward. Everything felt crisper with Naomi around, sending his senses into hyperdrive.

She walked nearby as he pulled the babies in a stroller-style sleigh. Tessie bounded in the snow ahead, kicking up mini flurries.

It should have been a contented, peaceful kind of outing with Naomi. But the frustrated attraction between them sizzled so tangibly he wouldn't be surprised if the icicles started melting off the trees.

Cricking his neck from side to side, he tamped down the passion flaring to life inside him—or at least he tried to. The walk would be over soon. His willpower wouldn't have to be tested too long. Sunshine was brief in the winter. The baby sleigh made clean slices through the drifts as they walked alongside the bay. Having Naomi and the girls with him made the time bittersweet. He wanted to stretch out this outing—having her all to himself—as long as possible.

Restraint be damned.

He turned his head toward her, and her gaze collided with his. Some of his desire must have shown in his face because her pupils widened with awareness. She bit her bottom lip, then released it slowly.

With a brief shake of her head, she backed away. The answering heat in her eyes was disguised with something else.

She'd put a wall between them. A wary one.

Naomi reached down, balling up snow in her gloved palm. Brunette hair fell, long and lovely, on her chest as she turned to him. An overbright smile played on pink lips that matched the pink in her cheeks. God, he wanted to kiss her mouth, stroke her face.

She packed the snowball between her gloved hands. "It's wonderful to be out here. I feel like I've been inside forever. Thank you for suggesting this."

Wind whipped, gusting her turquoise-and-feather earrings across her face. Ethereal and eclectic, Naomi floored him. Always. A life with her could never be boring. Royce swallowed hard.

"Wish I could claim unselfish motives in suggesting the walk. I'm enjoying the solitude." As if that were the only selfish motivation at play. He wanted time alone with her, away from all her relatives. His gaze raked over her again.

"Are we encroaching on your solitude?" She let the snowball fall from her hand. Her cautious question cut through him deeper than the wind. Time to shift away from controversial topics if he wanted a chance at another kiss. Thank goodness the twins were cooperating by sleeping in the sleigh.

"Not at all. This is what I wanted." The walk, the

time with Naomi and the girls, with Tessie bounding through the snow.

"What you wanted for yourself was good for me, too. And the girls. There's nothing selfish about that." She held back a low hanging branch for Royce so he could pass through with the sleigh. A whiff of her perfume carried on the crisp breeze.

The brightness of the sun reflected in her eyes, distracting. Too much so. He nodded with a noncommittal grunt.

"What's that supposed to mean?"

"Nothing." His boots crunched in the snow.

"I know you better than that." She tucked her hand in the crook of his arm, her eyes twinkling knowingly.

The muscles in his arm twitched in response to her touch. "Only trying to figure out how I could think that your love of the outdoors was enough to bind us. Well, that and an off-the-charts sex life."

There it was.

That awkward, weighted silence settled again in the air between them. A silence he felt in his chest and bones. A silence as cool as the northern wind sweeping across them.

He sighed hard, pressing on. Eyes catching on the horizon, where horses and riders gathered. The Mikkelsons and Steeles were making the most of the weekend. So much for solitude. One horse and rider descended in a headlong gallop. Royce couldn't help but watch the way the hooves of the horse seemed to glide across the snow like butter. Naomi let out a pained laugh. "Would you rather be riding? You don't have to stay glued to my side."

"This is where I want to be." He paused for a moment, looking back at the twin girls in their orange snowsuits. Flicking his gaze back to the riders, he played with the lead in his hand before pulling on the sleigh again. There was much about this place to enjoy. "Although it would be nice if the twins were old enough to ride. With their genetics, I'm sure they'll be in the saddle soon."

"Lots of firsts to dream of for them. And individual pursuits, too. I want them to find their own favorites."

Firsts he would miss out on. The hole in his heart felt wider than ever. "You're already a great mom." The wind picked up off the bay. Concerned for the twins, he steered them toward the boathouse.

"I appreciate that, but it's still scarier than I expected."

Royce locked his eyes forward. He wanted to make sure he'd be there for her. Provide support to her by helping with the girls. "You've taken on a lot in a short time."

"I have an incredible amount of support and financial security."

"That doesn't automatically make life simple." As they reached the boathouse, he gestured toward the door and shot her a questioning look.

She nodded, pushing it open, so he could slide the sleigh inside. He did so carefully, without waking the girls. "Well, all the support will help in the future," Naomi said.

"You can always call on me." He glanced around the interior. Slim stripes of light slanted through the vents along the ceiling.

She flicked a switch, electricity humming to life as they continued inside, away from the biting wind. "Is that really fair to you, though?"

"No worries, I can protect myself." He steered her toward a wall-long bench covered in a blue canvas cushion with little white anchors woven into the pattern.

She studied him through narrowed eyes as she sat. He settled beside her. Almost touching. His heart rate picked up with a prickly awareness of how tenuous the line was he was walking as he turned the conversation.

"Are you saying you want to be friends while you're working at the company?"

Friends?

Was that really what she thought he wanted? He was so aware of her—her scent, the way her skin softened under his fingers—that he could *feel* her, and they weren't even touching. He clenched his fingers into a fist to keep from reaching out to her. "I'm not sure anything platonic would work for us. But we didn't take time to become friends before."

"Then you're saying friends with benefits—because of the off-the-charts sex life?"

"Is that such a bad thing?"

He caught her gaze then. The electricity no longer just hummed in the boathouse lights. Instead, sparks danced between them, caught in the way neither of them could seem to look away. He saw conflicted feelings in her dark brown eyes. But also saw the longing. He just needed to be patient.

Naomi blinked, looking down. Breaking the moment between them. "I need to tell you something."

His positive vibes faded. The hesitant tone in her voice didn't bode well.

"You sound ominous."

She bit her bottom lip again. "Chuck has looked at the numbers from the finance department regarding implementing your changes. We're coming up short. We might not be able to fund the overhaul to the pipeline."

A chill settled in his gut. The project he was passionate about—the tweak to the pipeline that would make the Alaska Oil Barons' drilling more environmentally friendly—would go belly-up. All because he'd let himself believe what he'd wanted to believe. That he could work with Naomi, could justify stepping out of his solitary research and still hold on to his world while being a part of hers.

Now all that work was at risk. His time. His research. Everything he'd poured himself into for years.

The reality raked him raw. And it still didn't hurt as much as knowing that—if what she was saying was true—he'd just lost his excuse to stay close to Naomi. That hurt more than anything.

Naomi tried to imagine a moment when this space, her suite, would feel normal and settled again. Or at least as sturdy as the timbers on the ceiling that reminded her of a ship's hull. A ship that could sail into a storm, unflinching.

She could use some of that bravado about now.

Winking sunlight filtered into the enclosed balcony that had been turned into a nursery, golden amber rays dusting the pink embellishments on the crib. Glints of light fractured as they struck the large crystalline bear on the top shelf of the bookcase. The bear had been in her family for as long as anyone could remember. At least something about this moment rang true. Constant. Familiar.

Carefully, Naomi plastered a smile onto her face as

she removed the snow gear from her daughters. Mary was up first. Removing the outer layer, Naomi cooed at her, a new peace falling over her as she watched her baby suck on her fist.

Already, distinct personalities were forming. Mary hated the pacifier, preferring her fists. Anna loved to be held much more than her sister. Mary preferred to take in the world from a distance, content with her surroundings. Anna loved her pacifier, was a little fussier. After Naomi finished pulling the snow gear off Anna, she cradled each baby in an arm for a moment before settling them into the twin bassinet.

A snore interrupted her reverie. Naomi's gaze fell to the big Saint Bernard. Tessie slept in a dog bed by the window. Her brown-and-white fur glistened in the fading light.

Naomi's nerves were ragged after how the magical day had taken such a downward spiral. The walk with Royce had been fraught with tension, that explosive kiss and her dream lingering just below the surface for the whole outing, temptingly so.

Dangerous thoughts, especially when there was no denying he wanted her, too.

Except those feeling had him closing off from her. As the walk had ended, he'd shut down and shut her out. She should be glad for the distance, but her heart stung all the same, reminding her why they'd broken up in the first place…more than once. Moving from her feeling smothered to her worrying that he wanted her and the girls as a replacement for the fiancée and child he'd lost. Her worries that he couldn't thrive in her big, boisterous family.

There were too many ways a relationship between

them didn't work. But that didn't stop her from wanting him more than breath.

Royce's knuckles drained of color as he gripped his key chain, she noticed. His free hand sought the small abacus on the ring, his fingers fidgeting with the device for a moment before he put the baby snowsuits in the laundry room on a hook to dry.

Searching for a way to disperse the awkward silence, she said, "I can take the girls down for dinner if you would prefer to hibernate up here."

"I'm not a bear. I can manage dinner with your family."

He was sure growling like a bear. His slick, all-black clothing hid nothing of his muscled physique. The power of his chest and arms temporarily distracted her.

But then, he had a reason to be grumpy, given the bombshell she'd dropped on him. It was selfish of her, since all the data wasn't in yet from running Chuck's numbers. She'd used the business excuse to create distance, and thereby caused him added worry. "I was just trying to be thoughtful. After all, you've given up your space for me and the girls."

"We could go to my place, if you're concerned about it."

His offer stopped her cold. It was tempting, and totally unworkable.

She gathered her thoughts for three heartbeats before she said, "We wouldn't fit."

Moving to his place would complicate everything even more. No. She needed to stay here. On her turf, her territory. Hold on to a semblance of power before she caved completely to the sensual pull of him. She recognized the push and pull between them, each trying to retain power in the situation, both strong-willed, both battling feelings they'd hoped were just temporary.

"A crib. A couple of car seats. I don't see the problem," he said, with a challenge in his eyes.

Was he trying to push her away? To bail because of what she'd told him? There was a time she would have sworn she could read him. Now, she lived in a constant state of confusion when it came to this man. "You can leave if you're ready. I would understand."

His strong jaw jutted. "I said I was staying until the gala, when your father returns, and I meant it."

The deep timbre of his voice filled the room and Tessie lifted her head from the dog bed with a low whimper.

"You're not obligated to stay." Naomi knelt beside the dog, threading her fingers through the silky soft fur.

"I gave you my word, and where you and the babies are is where I want to be." He walked to the twins' bassinet and gripped the edge.

"Is this situation getting you closure?" The words tumbled from her mouth, the ache in her chest deepening. "Because I'm not feeling it."

He glanced over his shoulder at her. "Naomi—"

"No." She couldn't play this game anymore. Not with the lump growing in her throat, pushing tears to her eyes. She needed to understand what the hell they were doing. "I'm not going to let you steamroll me or charm me or whatever your next plan is. This is so much more confusing than helpful. We're torturing ourselves—"

"Naomi, stop." He straightened from the bassinet. "You and I want each other, there's no denying that. The attraction between us has been the one constant in our relationship and it isn't going away."

"Then put some distance between us. I don't want

my daughters to be hurt because you're using them as surrogates for the child you lost."

"So you've said," he answered tightly. "I care about those girls enough not to do anything to hurt them. Listen when I say I'm not going anywhere—" A squawk from the bassinet had him turning back to the twins.

"Royce." Naomi strode toward him. "They're my daughters. I can handle this."

"Wait," he said, turning back toward her with Mary in his arms.

"What now?" She sighed in exasperation.

His gaze pinned hers. "I think Mary has a fever."

Nine

One step. Two steps. Three. Pivot and begin again.

Royce focused on the motion like a mantra in the examination area of the local emergency room. His fingers slid along his key chain abacus. But the ritual didn't bring much in the way of relief.

Each breath he drew revealed a new layer of pain and anxiety. His throat felt tight. Scenarios unfolded in his mind's eye, each more terrifying than the last.

He barely registered the whispers from the other side of the room as Delaney Steele and Glenna Mikkelson comforted Naomi, taking turns rubbing her back. Delaney's gaze met Royce's, her eyes soft with sympathy and support.

Soon they'd be discharged and could pick up the prescription.

Glancing over at Naomi again, he noticed the way her

shoulders sank as her normally expressive, lithe body seemed to crumple in her oversize fringed cardigan as she cradled a baby in each arm.

Mary had a fever of 102 degrees Fahrenheit. Anna had a low-grade fever, as well. The doctor assured them the illness had nothing to do with the time outdoors. It was just a virus going around. But Royce couldn't help feeling guilty. Had he been so wrapped up in Naomi that he'd missed cues from the twins that they weren't feeling well?

They weren't cranky, though, just sleeping more.

Still, he felt like he'd failed them. Had failed Naomi.

Maybe he wasn't dad material. He'd been pushing his needs onto them, torturing himself and Naomi both because of proximity, temptation and abstaining. Now, it felt as if it was all imploding. With his work at the company in jeopardy anyway, all this—his reason for finding middle ground with Naomi—would be moot.

Their deadline, the gala, was only a little over a week away. After that, his work with the company would begin to pick up speed, provided the contract went through. He would return to his regular hours and wouldn't have this pseudo paternity leave.

A week left to forge some kind of connection that could last into the future. Or say goodbye forever.

Either way, time was running out to get his head together. He drew in a deep breath as he thrust his hands in his pockets to escape the slight chill of the air.

Naomi chewed a bottom lip, obviously rattled. Her hand trembled. Delaney gave her a hug, her reddish-brown hair obscuring her sister for a moment. He wanted to comfort Naomi, too, but she was deep in conversation with Delaney and Glenna.

Naomi's hair framed her slender face, those dark eyes filled with worry for the infants she held so protectively. "I know the doctor says the walk didn't cause this, but I still feel guilty. Why didn't I sense there was something off with them?"

Delaney wrapped her arm around her sister's shoulders. "If you'd stayed inside you would have been blaming yourself for not giving them enough fresh air and sunshine."

Glenna nodded, wisps of her blond hair falling out of her upswept bun. "You're a good mom. You're a careful mom. Babies get sick. It happens." She placed a manicured hand on Naomi's back.

Royce knew in his head that they'd both been careful with the babies. But in his heart? His gut?

A young doctor completing his residency came back into the room carrying a transparent clipboard, stethoscope slung around his neck. Boyish features made him seem impossibly young. As he opened his mouth to deliver an update, something seemed to halt his words.

Royce recognized that look. Calculation and observation became visible in his stare as he looked at Naomi. A longer pause. An assessment. The scientific process in action.

The doctor cleared his throat, his voice commanding much more authority than his young frame suggested. "Let's get a temperature on you."

Royce looked up sharply, understanding the doctor's previous scrutiny. Naomi? Sick, too? How had he not noticed?

"What? I feel fine," she insisted. "Just a little tired, which is normal. I have twins." She twisted her hand in the air, a subtle protest echoed by her rings, as the turquoise-and-silver jewelry clinked together.

"Humor me." The doctor held up the thermometer, waiting.

Naomi sighed, passed Mary and Anna to Delaney, then opened her mouth.

Royce watched the monitor. The numbers climbed… and stopped at 101.2. Ah, hell. He hadn't missed just that the girls were ill. He'd been so wrapped up in having the hots for Naomi, he'd missed the signs that she was suffering, too.

The doctor looked in her mouth and ears quickly, then listened to her heart before nodding. "That virus bug has bit you, as well. Bed rest for all three of you."

Royce knew it was just a routine illness, but his protective impulses fired full force. And a boatload of worry piled on top. These past weeks hadn't brought him any nearer to closure.

The time had only shown him how much of a hold Naomi still had over him.

Naomi had to admit there were times when a big family grated on her, but in moments of crisis, fatigue and trouble, gratitude filled her heart. She'd been so concerned with the twins, she'd failed to take care of her own body and focus on her own health. Thankfully, her younger sister and her sister-in-law were around, ready and willing to give her a much-needed reprieve. A night to practice self-care, sleep, become strong again.

Glenna and Delaney took Anna and Mary, stocked up with bottles of milk Naomi had expressed. Upon arriving at her suite, Naomi had made a beeline for the shower, where warm water caressed her aching muscles.

She'd added an extra layer of indulgence to her routine by changing into winter silk pj's, and sinking into her sofa. She grabbed a burgundy cashmere blanket from a side basket, pulling it over her lap, enjoying the texture as it rubbed sensuously against exposed skin.

Royce had brought her a mug of chamomile tea with lemon before returning to the kitchen to heat up soup Delaney had sent.

And no question, Royce was the sexist "nurse" she'd ever met.

Vivaldi played in the background, and she let her imagination spin with fantasies of waltzing with Royce, his strong arms around her, sweeping her off her feet.

Damn. If she hadn't known better, she would have sworn she was delirious with fever.

She hadn't even realized how bad she felt until the doctor noticed. She'd been so focused on the children. The ER physician had warned her that the viral infection could turn into something bacterial if she wasn't careful. Her immune system had been depleted by childbirth and caring for twins. She'd also been working even when tired.

And there was no denying her tumultuous relationship with Royce had worn her down. He was leaving soon. But saying goodbye and seeing him only occasionally at work wouldn't be any easier than facing him here every day.

She cupped the mug of hot tea in her hands, curling her legs up under the blanket.

Royce glanced over his shoulder. "How are you feeling?"

"Just tired. A little achy. Nothing major." She sipped the tea, the lemon and honey teasing her taste buds, which always seemed to be on hyperdrive around him, like the rest of her senses. "I hate that everyone's making such a fuss. I want to take care of my girls."

He turned toward her, carrying a tray with two bowls of Alaskan king crab chowder and fluffy wheat rolls. "If you run yourself down more, it'll be longer before you're on your feet. They're fine. They're here in the house being pampered to pieces by Glenna and Delaney. If they need you, you're only an elevator ride away."

"I know...it's just hard being away from them."

"Understandable." He set the tray on the coffee table, the creamy soup sending savory steam into the air.

Her heart stuttered with a hint of anxiety over feeling helpless, and the memories that brought up. "Thank you for all you've done."

"It's nothing," he said. "I just heated up what your sister sent."

"All the same, I still have problems with hospitals and being sick. It reminds me of the cancer treatments."

Royce skimmed his hand along her damp, braided hair. "Naomi..."

The images of days spent in hospitals vanished, replaced by other memories. Days with Royce, his touch. The way his mouth felt pressed into hers.

"It's okay. In the past." She leaned into the magic of his touch, which was intense. Too much so... She angled back and attempted to lighten the moment. "Maybe it was a blessing, after all, to have the babies in a car."

They shared a soft laugh, eyes connecting, the bond of that experience echoing between them. Then his dark eyes shifted, serious again. "The thought of what you went through as a teenager..."

"Hey, I'm okay now." She pulled her gaze away from

his in case her eyes might betray the fear that sometimes still gripped her. She reached for a wheat roll and slathered it with butter. "I'm not even sure why I brought it up."

"I didn't mean to shut you down."

She waited for a moment, picking at the yeasty roll while Vivaldi's "Four Seasons" piped softly. Naomi wished she could eat, but having Royce this close to her without the distraction of the babies brought to mind all she'd been missing these last months. "Thank you for being there with me at the ER."

"Of course I was there. I was worried about them, too. Why would you doubt that?"

Of course he was worried about the girls. She felt small for the resentful feeling that thought brought. She shifted to a safer discussion. "Because of the problems at work. With the numbers not coming together for your project." A problem that, if unsolved, could end his connection to her, and she wouldn't have an excuse to see him at all.

Her stomach knotted tighter.

"That's business." He shrugged off her comment. "This is personal."

"But we were working on the personal in order to deal with being in the same work world." A task that was growing harder by the day with all the reminders of why she'd been drawn to him in the first place.

His eyes narrowed thoughtfully. "Are you saying you have a reason to keep my work out of the company?"

"No!" she exclaimed without hesitation. "God, no. I want your safety improvements on the pipeline to be implemented. I haven't given up. It's just going to be tougher than we first anticipated."

"Hey, it's okay, don't get wrought up. You should be taking it easy." He moved aside the dishes and adjusted the blanket on her lap, his hand lingering to palm her hip. "How about we put a pin in that conversation until we've both had a good night's sleep?"

She swallowed hard before continuing, "It's tough to think about anything other than the babies right now."

"Understandable. But they will be okay."

"I keep thinking if I hadn't taken them outside…"

"The doctor assured you their illness has nothing to do with our walk." He squeezed her hip lightly. "A virus just…happens. I'm more surprised that they both caught it at the same time."

She shifted back, tugging at the blanket until he got the message and pulled his hand away.

With an arrogant smile on his face.

She sat up straighter. "About Mary and Anna… I've learned not to question the twin connection. Brea and I even had our own twin language until we went to elementary school."

"And no one could understand what you were saying?"

She laughed softly. "Not a clue."

"The science of that is mind-boggling. The creation of a new language." His voice rumbled in the quiet room. "Watching them grow will be an adventure."

One he wouldn't be a part of. Her eyes stung. She blinked fast before looking up at him. "I'm sorry I didn't get things right when we were first together. I should have known it wasn't fair to let things move so fast, especially with kids involved. I never wanted to hurt you."

"We hurt each other." He stroked her face, then let his fingers continue down her throat to her collarbone. "Let's declare a truce for tonight."

She was tempted. So very tempted to take him up on that offer. Words dried up for a moment.

He tucked a knuckle under her chin and tipped her face to his until only a whisper of space separated them. If she swayed toward him even a hint…

Then she would be right back in the middle of a sea of desire that would lead to heartache, lead to losing herself in the kind of kiss between lovers who knew each other well and connected even when sex was out of the question.

The most dangerous kind of temptation of all.

For Naomi, the last two weeks were filled with forward motion. And yet she felt her emotional state slide back. Go to the past. To dangerous thoughts of Royce. Unarticulated futures. She was going through the motions, all right, and not making a damn bit of progress.

And yeah, the twins were fine. They'd made full recoveries. Their personalities continued to deepen and blossom.

But Naomi couldn't deny the pressure in the air between her and Royce. Knowing her struggle—and apparently determined to play meddling matchmaker—Delaney had encouraged Royce and Naomi to head out. Together. Alone. Under the guise of shopping for the girls, even though the very next day there'd be a baby shower at the Steele headquarters. Naomi had noticed that mischievous gleam in Delaney's dark brown eyes. Understood her sister's silent encouragement.

Yet here she was, enjoying an afternoon outing with him and the girls in a stroller at the Anchorage Museum. Playing with fire. Her chest tight with residual awareness and undeniable chemistry that she didn't know what to do with.

Right now, she and Royce were at a wary détente that only served to make willpower all the more difficult. Every day the desire to indulge in the mind-blowing attraction was damn near irresistible. Even a simple museum tour had her tied up in knots.

She couldn't stop herself from taking in the strong line of his jaw, the stubble as they moved through the Anchorage Museum.

A cluster of children holding museum maps sauntered by, being corralled by an overwhelmed looking young mother. She placed a hand on her hip, calling out to her group, attempting to draw the triplets' attention to the rotating cultural history exhibit. Naomi glanced at her babies sleeping in the stroller. She couldn't help but think of one day guiding her girls through here when they were older, seeing the wonder in their eyes as they took it all in.

"But, Mo-o-om, I want to go to the Earth and life science exhibit." One girl's bottom lip jutted out as she held up her hands in a state of total exasperation.

"We will, I promise. After this part," the mother cooed, steering her daughter toward the exhibit's entrance.

Naomi watched the scene, her smile deepening. She leaned against Royce, felt the slight heat radiating from his body as she whispered, "I can envision you as a kid with one of those little science kits, mixing chemicals and making an overflowing volcano."

"Actually, I wanted to be a football star."

His deadpan delivery caught her off guard. Lowered her defenses. She couldn't stop herself from drinking in the sight of him in well-worn jeans and a cable knit sweater. He wore his wealth so casually, a man comfortable in his skin with no need to flaunt his success.

She pulled her attention back to the conversation. "A football player? Really?" she asked, surprised that Royce would have ever considered such a career path.

"Hell, no. Too many people."

Laughing, she pulled him toward the rotating art exhibit, passing by the windowpanes that showcased glimpses of the city. Of her fair state. "So you built volcanoes, after all."

"Actually, I wanted to be either an astronaut or a zookeeper."

"Wow, that's a surprise. A fun one, though. I can see it, and it's endearing."

Royce grimaced. "Endearing? That's not what I was going for."

"You do just fine giving off the brooding vibe. It's okay to let people have a peek inside every now and again."

"I don't want to argue with you." He took her hand in his.

"Okay then." She linked their fingers. "I want to hear more about Royce the Zookeeper. What derailed you from your path?"

"I realized I couldn't take them all with me out into the woods."

"Valid point. And the astronaut dream?"

He quirked an eyebrow at her. "I might not have come back?"

She squeezed his hand while staring into his eyes, the crowd around them fading so that all she saw was this man. "How did we never talk about this before?"

"We didn't do a lot of talking back then. Remember?"

Heat washed over her at the shared memory. Especially knowing he was thinking about the same things she was. Tearing off each other's clothes. Tasting and touching. Feasting.

She swallowed hard. Maybe she looked as breathless as she felt, because Royce smiled with just a hint of male satisfaction before he guided her to sit on a bench by a display of Inuit art that made Naomi think of her grandmother. Nights spent by a fire as a child enthralled by the oral history of half her soul.

"And what about you, Madame Lawyer?" Royce asked. "Childhood career dreams?"

She was grateful for the redirection. They didn't need to wander down those old paths again, as tempting as it might be to simply lose herself in his touch. Drawing a deep breath, she reached back in her memories.

"I wanted to start a glacier wedding business, complete with all the plane rides out to the remote location to say their vows."

"For real?" He leaned back on the bench, his arms spread wide so that one lay close to her back. Almost touching.

With an effort, she forced her thoughts back to the conversation.

"Absolutely. Uncle Conrad got married in a glacier wedding when I was in elementary school. I thought it was the most romantic thing ever." She could picture the perfect crispness even now. Feel the icy wind on her cheek. Remembered the way the Milky Way had provided a backdrop even princesses in a fairy tale would envy.

"What stopped you?"

"He got divorced and I decided glacier weddings were like a *Titanic* jinx."

Royce winced. "Ouch."

"I had a lot of fun with the idea for a while, though. I dressed up my siblings for the occasion."

Hoisting herself up from the bench, Naomi pushed the stroller as she circled around one of the installations, taking in the details of the painting of a fishing village. Remembering the way her grandmother had supplied all sorts of clothes for her business.

"My grandmother was on board. Anything to make me happy. She had a chest full of clothes I was allowed to use. Delaney always enjoyed playing dress-up and performing the ceremonies. Broderick says he hated it, but to be honest, that's not how I remember it. I'd make us all walk into the wood's edge for the ceremony. Dad never liked us being by the water. Always afraid something would happen to us."

A lump filled her throat. The memory of her sister ached in her bones. Even now, placing Breanna in memories felt like a private act. Something that would recede if Naomi shared too much. Selfishly, she kept her deceased sibling's role to herself.

"That's quite a memory," he said.

"There are photos. I've used them to shut up a big-mouth sibling on more than one occasion."

"And then you turned your back on romance."

"Not romance. Just weddings." Suddenly she became very aware of her pulse. The touch of his fingertips to hers. And the silence. "I even did some freelance work last year helping people edit their online dating profiles."

"The romance dream lives on. Perhaps your glacier wedding dream can come back to life, too."

The wry tone in his voice gave her pause. Was it just a dream that they were rediscovering something between them here? Something romantic? Something more than explosive chemistry and opposing views of the world? He had losses and deep feelings, and so did she. She'd grieved for her sister and her mother. She'd blamed Royce for not moving on, but maybe she'd had a hard time moving on and trusting, too.

Could they forge a true connection? One that would allow them to grieve for their pasts together? One that would last?

Outside the Steele boardroom, Royce braced himself for a killer confrontation.

Hordes of family and friends were throwing a baby shower.

He took a deep breath, steadying himself. Thankfully, the great windowpanes bathed the room in natural light. Made the space feel more open and encompassing.

He stood next to the tall, suave Birch Montoya. The man reminded him of old Hollywood films, bourbon and cigars. They stood in the reception area near the glass wall that separated the entry from the boardroom. Muffled noises ensued, punctuated by shrieks of women's laughter.

Apparently, the party was already under way.

Beer in hand, he stayed by Chuck, Broderick and Birch. Half paying attention to the conversation, half taking in the scene.

The men flocked around the small table covered with

food. Chuck tossed shrimp onto his plate. With a Viking-like build and complexion, he exuded a sense of power.

Royce leaned back, peering through the doorway to where the women were gathered. The blue chairs that normally flanked the table had been rearranged into scattered semicircles. Perfect for small group chats.

There was no denying the elegance of this event. Pink and white balloons were clustered here and there. And although it was winter, spring seemed to have exploded in the room. So many flowers. He recognized roses and lilies, but not the other blooms poking through the central arrangement.

A time capsule in the shape of a baby bottle had been placed at the entrance for attendees to write to the twins. They'd crack that sucker open on their eighteenth birthday. A nice idea, really.

Would he be a distant memory to them then? Even a memory at all?

He couldn't help the way his eyes trailed after Naomi. Taking in her curves in that short pink dress with brown tights. The way her fringed boots seemed to deepen her mystique, accentuating her knack for bringing eclectic textures and threads together.

He watched the way she straightened the ceiling-high stack of presents. Careful, he realized, to keep them from falling on the elaborate cake. And what a cake it was—an icing creation of twin polar bear cubs in mittens and hats. Extravagant.

He was thankful she felt well enough to celebrate. Even knowing she was healthy now, he couldn't help but think about time closing in on them to end this togetherness experiment. He needed to accept that she knew her limits. Naomi had always been a workaholic. Her

dynamo personality was only one of the many things
that drew him to her. He'd been so determined to find
closure, and somehow this time with her and the girls
had only made the prospect of losing her all the worse.

Breaking his stare, he placed a chicken salad crois-
sant on his plate. Passed over the chocolate fondue fountain, nuts and shish kebab fruit.

Jack stood at the wet bar, his still jet-black mustache
making his white teeth seem even brighter. Wiggling
his fingers, Jack paused indecisively, hand oscillating
over a mimosa and a beer, avoiding the sparkling water
altogether. "Great shindig to celebrate the twins."

"A nice way to celebrate everyone getting over that
virus." Royce took a swig of his beer—the Steele-
Mikkelson brand, Icecap Brews—letting the hoppy
flavor linger on his tongue. If only the merger of the
two oil businesses could be as easy as the new joint
ownership of their two merged small breweries. "It's
good to have you back."

The timing of the shower had been scheduled to accommodate Jack and Jeannie's return.

Jack nodded, his eyebrows expressive. He crossed
his hands over his chest, compressing the flannel fabric as he continued, "Good to see those babies again.
FaceTime didn't do them justice."

"And your honeymoon?"

Jack paused once more, looking up at the material
that covered the ceiling. For a moment, Royce wondered
what it was. Chiffon? Tulle? Was there a difference?

"Well…" Naomi's dad scooped up some peanuts and
shifted them in his fist. "Jeannie and I are family people. That's part of what drew us to each other. But the

time away was good for us. No work. A rarity for me, but I'm a convert."

"You're really going to retire?"

"Semiretire. Jeannie and I will both be on the Alaska Oil Barons board through the transition. After that, we'll see." The older man pinned Royce with a contemplative stare. "How are you and Naomi?"

He wanted to stay present. Not think about their budding connection that went beyond the physical, or how much he would give for one last time with her in his bed, or how nothing had really changed.

Or worst of all, their looming goodbye.

But still, Naomi kept crossing his mind. His eyes kept searching for her.

Angling more to the left, Royce kept her in his line of vision. Naomi stood with some of the employees. The new assistant, Milla, laughed as baby songs were played and excited participants shouted out the name of the mystery tune.

All the men watched the commotion from afar. These baby songs were not nearly as inventive or creative as Royce's periodic table lullaby. But whatever. Time to focus again.

And stop avoiding Jack's question about Royce's relationship with Naomi. "We're taking care of the girls."

Not untrue. The answer betrayed nothing of his feelings. Or her feelings, the ones he couldn't read.

Jack narrowed his gaze. "You've gotta admit it's unusual for exes to spend this much time together."

"Like I said, we're here for the girls."

"I understand how deep the love can be for kids. It's about more than a biological bond… But is that all this is? For both of you? Because if one of you is hoping for more, this is going to go bad fast."

"I understand you care about your daughter. But this is between Naomi and me." Royce set his plate down on a nearby table. Sometimes his quiet nature, his calling as a researcher, gave off the wrong impression. He had a helluva backbone and he knew how to use his voice. "How about we discuss work. I hear my project is at risk due to financing."

Chuck and Birch sidled closer, as if sensing the tension. Their posturing was somehow softened by the presence of Mary and Anna's pictures on a makeshift clothesline in the foreground.

Seeing Chuck reminded Royce about the whole numbers-crunch mess. He hadn't planned on bringing that up here. Now. But it beat the hell out of talking about his relationship with Naomi. And bottom line, if he wanted time to figure out the answers, to decide if they even had a future, he needed to keep his "in" with Alaska Oil Barons, Inc. "Any progress on retooling the numbers for the pipeline upgrades?"

Chuck's eyebrows shot up. "I guess I shouldn't be surprised Naomi read you in on that," he said with a tight jaw. "Business loyalty has always been iffy around here."

Royce bristled and Broderick didn't look much happier. Jack stepped between them. "This isn't the time. We're not going to ruin Naomi's baby shower." He turned to his son. "You and Glenna are the CFOs. Set a meeting." It was an order. No mistaking it.

So much for the older man backing off and letting the next generation take over. Things were coming to a head. Fast.

Getting Royce's designs into actual production on this project could have ripple effects worldwide. An affordable solution to prevent disasters—like oil spills—was groundbreaking. And yeah, for a scientist like him to be remembered for that kind of contribution was a definite plus.

This deal falling through meant the end of those particular aspirations. It would mean the loss of more than a year of work. But when he thought about leaving, it wasn't losing the work that made Royce's chest feel like he'd just taken a sucker punch. It was losing Naomi and the girls.

And Royce had less than a week until the gala to lock this down, one way or another.

Ten

Time was running out.

Sitting on the floor by Tessie's dog bed, moonlight bathing the babies in a hazy glow, Naomi thumbed through photos on her phone, scrolling back from the day the twins were born to her baby shower. Six weeks had passed in the blink of an eye since the snowstorm delivery. The date for the gala for her father and Jeannie was just around the corner.

And her time with Royce as the girls' "nanny" was drawing to a close.

She threaded her fingers through Tessie's silky fur with one hand, phone clutched in the other as she scrolled past another photo. The babies were asleep. Royce had gone for a trek in the woods to clear his head after a large family supper.

So quickly, her device storage had transitioned from a repository of memes and Alaskan scenery to images of Anna and Mary. A chronicle of their first few weeks of life. An amazing technological advancement, really.

She stopped for a moment to look at a picture of Anna and Mary bundled up in the sleigh, Royce standing protectively in the background, legs braced against the wind. Her heart panged. All her stories, all her memories of feeling like a mother, placed him in proximity. Royce wasn't someone she could easily rend from her life. From the way she understood herself.

It wasn't just the photos. No. His impact was so much more than that. Everywhere she looked there were visible, material traces of their cohabitation, round two. His globe found residence on the bookcase next to her grandmother's map of Alaska. His gloves were lying near the twins' snowsuits and hats. Everywhere, reminders. Everywhere, places she'd notice an absence if he left.

When he left.

Leaning forward, she reached for his MIT pullover hanging from the doorknob. She brought the fleece to her face and inhaled the scent of him. As if she could ever forget. Every facet of him was imprinted in her mind.

Saying goodbye would be tough. Breaking things off, but still seeing him, felt equally as painful. These weeks together had made her decision only more difficult as she felt the joy of being around him, felt his love for her daughters and saw his tension ratchet up at the large family gatherings. No matter which way she turned, there was heartbreak.

Was it wrong of her to want to hold tight to these last days together?

Hell, where was her spine, her grit, her take-charge spirit?

She brought his pullover to her face again, breathed in the scent of him and let it swirl around inside her, arousing and intoxicating. Her body came to life, waking from the recovery slumber of the past six weeks. Her need for him flamed back to life as her body reclaimed her sensuality.

More specifically, her sensual need for *this* man.

She might not be able to have everything she wanted—a future—with Royce. They were both too wounded from their past losses. They both just had too much baggage between them. But she could make the most of her week left with him to say goodbye before she moved on with her life.

Royce had expected to work like hell to get closer to Naomi during their last week together before the party.

Staring at the trail of rose petals leading through the living room toward the master bath, he had a feeling she was ahead of him on this.

He had no idea what had changed her mind about sleeping together again. She hadn't mentioned anything about being together again long term and he couldn't deny there would be emotional fallout from any sexual encounter.

And still he didn't intend to argue with her.

This was what he'd wanted. To be in her bed—or shower—again. To be with her.

Anticipation ramped higher. Hotter. He shrugged out of his parka and boots, following the petals. His steps crushed the blooms and launched microbursts of perfume into the air. He considered ditching all his clothes, but he needed to hear the words from her lips first. Her plans. Her wants.

He rapped his knuckles against the door. It creaked open, as if left ajar just for him. He stepped inside, the sound of the shower greeting him, along with soft jazz music.

She'd once told him the luxury bathroom was her haven, from the spa tub to the oversize Swedish shower with water jets along the sides as well as overhead.

However, those didn't draw his attention nearly as much as the woman.

Steam filled the shower stall, her body a sexy silhouette. The small stone fireplace nearby glowed with flames, a decorative pot of potpourri simmering over the blaze.

"Care to join me?" Her voice rode the steam, sending a bolt of desire straight through him.

Hell, yes.

"Where are the babies?" He should have thought to check before following the rose trail.

Naomi skimmed her fingers down the glass, streaking away steam, before pushing the door open. "Delaney is watching them for a few hours."

Was she already shifting from his help to her family's? A quick thought, an unsettling possibility, but one he brushed aside as swiftly as his clothes.

Eyes locked on her face, her curves, he closed the space between them. His feet soaked up the warmth of the heated floor. Then he had her in his arms again, her body flush against his. No words were necessary. He knew her. She knew him. His mouth found hers, familiar and new all at once.

It had been too long. Water sluiced over them as his tongue swept hers, touching and tasting. Desire pulsed

through him, so intense his hands shook. He needed to
stay in control. To go carefully with her.

He cupped her face, his forehead resting on hers.
Maybe some words were needed, after all. "Did the
doctor give you any restrictions I should know about?"

Naomi scored her nails lightly down his back, then
sank them into his hips. "She said I'm cleared for all
activities, only no trapeze." Naomi paused, arching
against him. "I'm just supposed to listen to my body."

The teasing look in her eyes made his breath catch.
Hold. His hands skimmed her slick skin, settling at the
indentation of her waist.

"And what is your body telling you?" He'd missed
this playfulness they'd once shared so easily.

"That I want your touch." She kissed his mouth, his
jaw, nipped his collarbone. "That I need you. I need
this—and I think you do, too."

Desire roared hotter than the steam heat of the
shower.

"Damn, but you are gorgeous." His words were a
husky growl.

She pressed closer, her hips arching toward his before she looked up at him through eyelashes holding
droplets of water. "And you sure know how to make a
new mom feel good about herself."

Seeing her this way, being with her again, was a gift
he would not waste. A gift beyond measure.

"You've always been beautiful." He cradled the
weight of her breasts in his hands, his thumbs circling
her hardening nipples. "But now you are even more incredible. You're turning me inside out."

He tracked the way her pupils dilated. The way her
head rolled back with pleasure at this touch.

"Glad to know." Her words were a breathless rush, her lashes fluttering. "The feeling's so very mutual. It's been far too long."

Damn straight. Hunger for her all but overwhelmed him. "Give me a minute to get to my shaving kit for—"

"A condom?" She pulled the packet from behind the shampoo, one step ahead of him on this, too. "I saw them there. A clue that you were hoping, too."

"Always." Sliding aside the damp length of her hair, he trailed kisses down her throat. Tasted her skin scented with lavender soap.

She tore open the packet and sheathed the hot, pulsing length of him. Taking her time. Teasing a response from him. But after so long without her, without this, her touch threatened to send him over the edge. He took her hands in his and lifted them over her head, to the tile wall, the warm spray showering them from all directions.

He slid into her slowly, carefully, his eyes on her every moment, watching. Willing her to feel his caring, the restraint.

She rolled her hips, drawing him deeper. "I'm okay. More than okay. Being with you…" Her breath hitched. "It's everything."

Passion, the physical connection, had never been in question. Their bodies were in sync. Even more so having been lovers who knew exactly what made the other melt with need.

He'd been drawn to her from the moment he first saw her. Unwillingly drawn, but unmistakable. This connection between them didn't make sense, but it was undeniable. The clamp of her around him, the slick glide as her body welcomed his in a way that made him never want to leave.

She swayed, then looped her arms more securely around his neck. In seamless response, he anchored her against the tile wall, whispering his desire in her ear, his breath hot against her neck.

Steam filled the oversize stall, blotting out the rest of the room…the rest of the world. Moisture in the air carrying the scent of lavender and their mingled perspiration.

A heady perfume.

Desire simmered hotter and hotter, the flames building, stoked by the feel of her breasts in his hands, her hands on him. Until he was close. So close to the edge. He tucked his hand between them, helping ease her toward her release.

Remembering. Wanting more of her.

Her breath caught just before her neck arched, a moan sliding between her lips. He caught the sound with his mouth as he thrust to his own release, the power rocking through him with an intensity even beyond his dreams. And his dreams had been mighty damn intense.

He held her against him, bracing her as the aftershocks of her release rippled through her. Then in a fluid move, he slid his hands under her bottom and lifted her against him as he turned to sit on the shower bench. He settled her across his lap, holding her, her head resting on his chest.

He'd missed her, missed this, missed so much about being with her in the months apart after their breakup.

How could she have changed his life so monumentally in less than a year?

Something found so fast could be taken away just as quickly.

As he drew in gasps of humid air, he couldn't stop his

mind from traveling back. To how when she'd needed him most, he'd let her down. She'd been put on bed rest for her blood pressure and he'd overreacted. Gone into overprotective mode. Damn near smothered her, when her free spirit was one of the things he admired most about her. He of all people should understand her need for space.

Why the hell couldn't they get this right?

He didn't know the answer to that. But one thing shone through.

He wasn't giving up searching just because of some artificial deadline at a party.

Even the smallest movements felt alive with a new, visceral energy.

And yes, it had everything to do with the rekindled romance between her and Royce. Naomi pushed aside her doubts, resolving to enjoy this last week together and not think about goodbyes.

Leaning against the kitchen countertop just before midnight, she hungrily took him in as a growl erupted from her stomach. Many kinds of feasts were present here.

Royce's jeans hung low on his hips, his chest bare and calling to her fingers to explore. Her skin tingled under her winter silk pajamas. She hadn't doubted her decision to make love in the shower, but she had been nervous about showing her post-delivery body.

A concern he'd dispelled.

And she'd also been a hint apprehensive there might be discomfort, in spite of the doctor's assurance that she'd healed.

A concern Royce had also ousted with his tender,

patient lovemaking that added an extra layer of steam to the shower.

The girls were settled in their bassinet and she should go to sleep soon or it would be a long, bleary-eyed day tomorrow. But she planned to make one more memory tonight to tuck away.

Perhaps she played with fire here.

Part of that statement felt literal as they assembled the chocolate fondue and fruit spread. Sweets and junk food were Royce's guilty pleasure and she'd made sure to order his favorite indulgences. Strawberries, blueberries and apple slices filled the trough around the chocolate fountain.

Bluegrass music provided a tempo to their movements as they prepared the meal. Notes that occasionally inspired Royce to grip her tightly, making her heart flutter.

Tessie watched thoughtfully, careful as she swept across the floor. Naomi tossed the Saint Bernard a soup bone. The dog graciously accepted the treat, circling before sprawling out.

Naomi rinsed her hands. "It's strange how many things I didn't notice while we were together."

"Such as?"

"I can't seem to recall you having a hobby for your free time."

Shrugging, Royce picked up the bowl of strawberries. "I like my work. Besides, you're one to talk. You live for your work, too." He ran water over the strawberries, then patted them dry.

She stared at him, waiting for the answer.

"I hike, I ride, I camp—any number of things out in the wilds."

She grinned. "Where it's quiet, with little risk of other people showing up?"

"I'm not a total hermit. I just prefer to avoid large crowds." He tossed the hand towel over his shoulder again.

"I like the outdoors, too, and experiencing that with others." She stirred the melting chocolate, until the lumps smoothed into a creamy blend. "When the girls are old enough, I'll show them all the places I went with my family."

"And camp there, too?" He popped a strawberry in his mouth, his gaze dropping to hers.

How was it a movement so simple could make her heart beat faster?

"Maybe. If they want to." She parted her lips as he brought a chocolate berry to her mouth.

His thumb stroked briefly, the slightest of touches, and still the connection flared hot between them before his hand slid away.

"Why the hesitation?"

She chewed, the taste exploding in her mouth. Everything about this man made her moan. "I can't recreate the past, and they deserve to make their own memories."

"Is that another dig at you thinking I don't have my past resolved?"

"It would only feel like a dig if it were true. You would know that better than me," she blurted. Damn. She closed her eyes for a moment before continuing, "Why are you still so good to me?"

"You deserve it."

"A lot of people deserve it." She stirred an apple wedge in the chocolate, leaning one hip against the cool granite counter. "My head's spinning here."

He clasped her waist, stilling her fidgeting. "You think I'm not over my ex and losing the baby."

"Never mind. Forget I brought it up. I'm wrecking a wonderful evening." She brought the fudge-covered apple slice to his mouth.

He took the fruit, licking the last drop from her fingertip. Shivers of awareness skittered down her spine.

Warmed chocolate and fruit.

Juices from the strawberry stained her hands. She licked her fingers, watching his eyes dilate with desire. Then Royce brushed against her, the muscles of his back rippling as he dipped fruit into the chocolate fountain.

He pushed aside the neckline of her shirt and drew the tip of the berry along her shoulder, leaving a barely there trail of warm chocolate. He ducked his head and kissed the sweetness from her skin.

She melted more than the chocolate, losing herself in the flick of his tongue against her skin. Memories of their lovemaking racked her again, rekindling her desire. She wanted more from this man, here and now. She ran her fingers over his chest, savoring the flex of his muscles, his awareness of her touch.

Her hand slid down, along the waistband of his jeans, finding the hard length of him, curving to fit and stroke. His low growl of approval reverberated in the space between them. Naomi parted her legs, inviting him to step closer, an invitation he quickly accepted. She thrummed with passion, her body crying out for him so tangibly she could swear her ears rang with it. Louder, until she realized—

The fire alarm was wailing.

The blare hammered through the tender moment. Followed by the cries of the babies waking.

Panic surged. Thankfully, Naomi's feet moved faster. She raced to pull clothes on. Her protective mothering instincts notched into overdrive. A quick pivot on her heel, and she took off for the nursery, Royce right behind her.

Tessie whined and barked, urging them to move faster. Faster. Hands fumbled to secure her daughters in warm clothes. Not knowing how much time they had, Royce brought thick blankets.

They moved together as if the plan to see Anna and Mary to safety silently sounded between them. Anna cried in Naomi's arms as they made their way to the staircase, past the fireplace.

Another sharp bark came from Tessie as they descended the stairs. As they reached the bottom floor, a wafting hint of smoke sent her fear higher. This wasn't a false alarm.

Chaos filled the house. Naomi barely registered the other members of her family rushing outdoors. Thank God Royce had been with her. She couldn't miss how quick he was in a crisis. How steady and secure.

Naomi couldn't say the biting cold of the Alaskan night burned against her cheeks, sending a shock to her system.

No. That wasn't it.

It was the sight of her younger sister, whose rich brown hair contrasted against the paleness of her mostly bare skin. Delaney wrapped in a cream-colored quilt really woke her up.

Mostly, it was who *else* shared that quilt. Birch Montoya.

Naomi couldn't decide what to make of that sight. And even more confusing?

Her sister and Birch were so different, so opposi-
tional, that friction happened just from them being in
the same room. So why were they huddled under the
quilt together, a smirk on Birch's face, a satisfied secret
smile on Delaney's?

Was it the same with Naomi and Royce?

She'd been so convinced they were wrong for each
other and that all she felt was just lust or infatuation.
So why was he the first person she turned to in a crisis?

And why was she so reluctant to let him go?

Eleven

Royce cradled the infant to his chest, his heart still jack hammering.

When the fire alarm went off, his first thought had been of Naomi and the girls. A gut-wrenching flash of what his life would be like if something happened to them.

And the pain damn nearly tore him in half.

Smoke tightened the knot of dread, triggering memories of that fatal accident years ago.

Just as fast, he'd pushed those distracting thoughts aside and focused on getting them all out of the house. Only to find it was a false alarm.

The aftermath of the adrenaline surge still scoured his veins. He forced even breaths in and out of his mouth, holding Mary while Naomi cradled Anna.

His breaths puffed in the night air as they waited for the house to clear. His mind spun with what-ifs that still haunted him. What if they hadn't pushed that first traffic light? Instead of gunning through on the yellow, he could have slowed. Been steady. Been more reactive and reflexive.

Had his inability to stop at the warning yellow light indicated a default in his ability to take care of the ones he cared for? Was that really why his former fiancée had left after the miscarriage and accident?

More important…was he now a ticking time bomb?

And could he forgive himself if lightning struck his life again?

Damn, but the past was a dogged beast. He drew in another icy breath and looked around, grounding himself in the present. He wasn't surprised to see the family in nightclothes. He was, however, stunned to see Birch Montoya with Delaney, both disheveled.

Even in the dim light of the stars and moon, Delaney's blushed cheeks were visible. Likely a combo of embarrassment and the chill. "Sorry, everyone. The fireplace flue got stuck and we couldn't put out the flames before the smoke set off the detectors," she said.

The throng of family fanned smoke through the open doors as Naomi and Royce stayed back with the twins, keeping them away from the noxious air.

"Um, Delaney…" Naomi kept her voice low. "You and Birch Montoya? An item? Did I just step into the set for *Sleeping with the Enemy*?"

Royce wondered the same thing, but at least the attention was on someone else, giving him and Naomi a break from questions about their plans.

But even as the sisters exchanged glances, Royce's mind slid to his next dilemma, rocking Mary in his arms. She gurgled a little, a smile on that rosebud mouth. What if that fire alarm had been real? If there'd been a legitimate crisis? If the babies and Naomi had been alone and asleep with a real fire raging through the house?

The possibility struck too close to his past.

He felt his heart tightening again at all that he'd lost. His unborn child and fiancée. The ache was so intense he forced himself to shut it down and focus on the present.

Delaney quirked an eyebrow at her sister. "I thought you liked Birch."

"I do," Naomi answered, her fingertip grazing Royce's arm. Sending him not into the normal wave of passion, but back to the moment of the accident. To the moment he'd lost it all. "You're the one who paints his business practices as evil incarnate. Although this—" she gestured toward Birch "—whatever it is, it definitely isn't business."

"We've been on again, off again for a while now," Delaney admitted. "We're just not so sure we won't get egged on by our friends if we go out in public together."

Naomi's laughter grabbed his attention again.

"Since when did our parents bring us up to bow to peer pressure?"

"My friends share my values."

Naomi angled in to say softly, "But you're totally hot for him."

"You're one to talk about having conflicted feelings for the guy you're sleeping with." She nodded toward Royce.

Royce winced. But then the truth was unavoidable. He nudged Naomi. "We should get the babies back up to the room and away from the smoke."

"Of course." Naomi pointed to her sister. "But we'll talk later."

"Uh-huh. Sure," Delaney said with a dismissive shake of her head, before she rejoined the smoke-waving effort.

Maneuvering away from the family, Royce felt another weight slam through him. This time not from the past, though, but rather from the present—Birch Montoya. Sending a quick glance over his shoulder, he picked out Birch's silhouette, a thought tugging at him, persisting even when the rest of Naomi's family faded from sight.

"Is something wrong?" Naomi asked, as they took the elevator back to her suite.

"The numbers," Royce answered, still chasing the notion through his mind. If he was right, at least there'd still be time to intervene.

"What do you mean?"

He leaned back in the elevator as the doors slid closed. "For the upgrades to the pipeline. Montoya is made of money and yet his bid for something he says he wants to help promote comes in just short."

Naomi gasped. "You think he's gaming the system? Using my sister for insider tips?"

The pain in her voice for her sibling couldn't be missed. All the more reason to figure out the truth sooner rather than later.

"I like the guy, so it bugs the hell out of me even considering this." Royce wasn't one to make friends lightly. "It also bothers me that my gut instinct may have been wrong. But something's off and he doesn't exactly have a reputation for bending over backward to save the planet."

"True... I'll talk to Glenna and Broderick about looking more closely at how the data was disseminated." She
frowned as the doors slid open. "But God, I hope it's not
true, for Delaney's sake. Not that I think he's right for
her, given how different they are. But to be betrayed that
way..." She shook her head. "I just hope it's not true."

Her flat assessment that Montoya and Delaney
weren't right for each other caught Royce right in the
midsection. He couldn't avoid the natural conclusion.
The parallel.

If Naomi believed Birch and Delaney's differences
should keep them apart, then in spite of what Royce and
Naomi had shared earlier tonight, they were finished.

Milla watched the Steele family from the icy woods
as they went back into the mansion. Although she remained hidden, huddling in the pine branches, she still
held her breath. As if a loud exhalation might give away
her position. Compromise the whole operation.

A silly thought, maybe. But still one she couldn't
shake. Not when Milla's future mingled in with the success of her mission. Which meant remaining hidden in
the trees until the mansion settled back down.

She'd taken a risk tonight coming to the sprawling
waterside home. It had been a silly, frivolous indulgence. Like the night she'd sneaked into the hospital
under the guise of delivering flowers. But coming to
Anchorage at all had been a risk. A risk she was willing to take—if it paid off.

Maybe she'd gotten overly confident these past
weeks with her success at leaking data to the Florida
investor. The stock shares had adjusted as she'd hoped.
The pipeline innovations were all but a no-deal, which

would be a huge blow to the Steele-Mikkelson merger into Alaska Oil Barons, Inc.

Wind whipped and trees moaned in response, the scent of smoke heavy on the breeze. She pulled her ponytail tighter, letting out a deep, satisfied breath as the door of the mansion finally shut. Remaining crouched, she felt a smirk tug at her mouth.

Through the thin gloves, Milla could feel the texture of the bark as she counted her successes. Her almost-compromised successes.

But she'd made the mistake of being greedy for a bigger win. For revenge. She'd used the excuse of dropping off papers to stop by the house, telling Broderick she would show herself out.

She'd sneaked into the study to see if the family portrait was still in place, the one of the entire clan before the airplane crash—easy enough to do, since she knew the layout of the house. Except Delaney and Birch had come into the room for their sneaky affair. She'd barely had time to hide in the nook behind the grandfather clock.

A favorite hiding place from Steele childhood days.

Yes, the Mikkelsons had to pay for all they'd taken.

Clutching the nursery monitor, Naomi padded back into the living area, where Royce was putting away the chopped fruit.

The man worked with such precision an automaton would be jealous. And while restoring order had its charm, she realized by his restricted movements and the tightness hinging in his lower jaw that Royce had yet to settle. He seemed to crackle, he was so visibly upset. As he had been ever since the fire alarm went off. She just wasn't sure if the cause was the pipeline discussion or the safety scare with the smoke.

Either way, their romantic evening was officially wrecked.

Logic told her the best approach would be to go to sleep, then discuss their concerns with a clear head in the morning. But the restlessness inside her, the raw emotions from their lovemaking earlier, pushed her impulsive nature to the fore. The silence weighed between them, cut only by the hum of the baby monitor and the dog's light snore.

Tension inched higher, along with the ache for things to be different between them. Easier. For Royce to walk over to her, sling an arm around her shoulders as they went to bed together. But still he kept his broad back to her.

Hadn't they flirted with that version of their lives just a few short hours ago?

As much as she wanted to be with him again before their time together ended, she'd been through the pain of losing him before. Soon, her daughters would grow closer to him and feel that pain, too. And the more she delayed it, the worse it would be. He'd helped her—for whatever reasons of his own—and the time had come for her to stand on her own.

She joined him in the kitchen, leaning against the granite countertop, just like earlier. Though everything felt different now. "No one is making you stay."

Placing the fruit in the refrigerator, he glanced sideways at her, his handsome face inscrutable. "For someone who's such a fighter, you sure do quit easily."

"I just think we're delaying the inevitable." Even as she said it, she couldn't help hoping he had a magic reason ready for why this time would be different. A too-familiar lump formed in her throat.

She'd picked a helluva time for this discussion.

"Just like that, you're through?" he asked, his gaze unflinching, unreadable.

"The whole reason for this nanny experiment was to gain closure, since we would be working together. That's unlikely now." She clenched her hands in front of her, resisting the urge to shout at him to fight for her. "The money isn't there for your work to be implemented with our company."

"You want me to take the research elsewhere?" Still, he didn't touch her. Didn't deny what she'd said about *them*.

He took a step closer, as if he might reach for her. Her heart fluttered.

Yes. Perhaps now. Was this the start of the fight for her? He didn't draw any nearer; his arms dangled at his sides.

"Of course I don't." She bit her lip, tears welling. Not that she would let them fall. If she cried, he would try to comfort her and that would only make this tougher. "But it's your life's work. Business is business. Delaney will probably join you, anyway."

A flash of pain shot through his eyes, the first sign this was hurting him, too. "We are more than the sum of our work." He rested his hands on her shoulders, that touch she'd craved. His fingertips felt at once foreign and familiar. "This isn't about business. This is about you and me and the kids being a family."

"A family." Her breath hitched on the word, her emotions churning as he offered that morsel of hope. Still, she couldn't ignore the gut-deep fear that he was using her and her daughters as substitutes for what he'd lost before. There'd been no evidence to the contrary. Naomi could not divorce her lawyer sensibilities in this manner. "You say this is about being a family. Where does being a couple fit in?"

"You and the girls are a package deal."

True, but she wanted more from him. Needed more from him. "I should be grateful you aren't running screaming in the opposite direction from a single mom with newborn twins." Her voice rose with each word. She flattened her palms on his chest. Feeling so emotionally vulnerable after making love to him, she had to fight against putting up a wall, and his prickliness was enough to send her into Fort Knox mode. "Silly me, wanting to hear I'm someone's soul mate."

"Is that what you want from me?" he asked—rather than reassuring her.

"I want you to want it," she said, defeat already weighing her down. Knowing the path from here would be harder, more painful than what they'd tread before. She was not a replacement. Not a transferable part in a design.

And yes, he wanted to be there for the girls. But did he love *her*?

The fact that he'd referred to them as a package deal dealt a blow to her heart. It'd been run through by a broadsword. Confirming her fears that she, Mary and Anna were stand-ins for a life he would never recover.

Naomi couldn't make him understand how she felt. She couldn't make him want the *here*, the *now*, and not just another round at the back *then*.

"I want us to help each other thrive as a team." She choked on the words as she pushed them past what felt like lead in her throat. "And all I see is the ways I hold you back from being who you're meant to be."

His hands fell away from her and he stepped back. Lips thinned into a line, and his deep brown eyes full of anger and sparks. "And I see you're no different than when we first met. Too afraid to risk your heart." He grabbed his parka and snapped for his dog. Tessie obediently leaped to her feet, already moving with speed toward the staircase. "Don't bother trying to drag out this argument any longer. I'll save you the trouble."

Without another word, he left her. No arguing. No fighting for her. Not even attempting to say what she wanted—needed—to hear. He'd initially said he wanted closure. And they'd gotten it.

She'd just been hiding from the truth. That the only closure she wanted was a fresh start to be with the man she loved.

And judging by the set of Royce's rigid shoulders as he walked away, that was never going to happen.

Twelve

Naomi had never felt less like going to work than today.

Reading over notes before her meeting with Glenna and Royce, she struggled for focus. Thank goodness her father and Jeannie were able to watch the twins for her. They were even going out of their way to bring them to her this afternoon, so she could nurse the babies then take them to their wellness checkup at the pediatrician's office.

Words on the printouts blurred. Her heart was in tatters from just a week away from Royce. They hadn't spoken since he'd left, and even if he'd called, she wouldn't have known what to say. Of course, she hadn't called him, either. The grief of this breakup overshadowed their other, the depth of what she'd lost so much more tangible.

But one foot in front of the other… She had to be

here today for this meeting about the pipeline financing. Her children were in good hands. She'd hired a day nanny, who was basically watching Jack and Jeannie fawn over the twins. Still, Naomi couldn't help but recall the synergy of working with Royce to have the girls here at the office...

Her chest tightened at just the thought of their time as an almost-family. She blinked back tears and strode into the boardroom.

Game face carefully in place, she adjusted her weight on her heeled boots, entering the room for her meeting with all the bravado she could muster.

Business had to be done. The matter pressed into her chest, wearing another ache into her heart.

As she made eye contact with Glenna, Naomi registered pain and fear in her gaze.

Cocking her head to the side, Naomi opened her mouth to express confusion as Broderick placed a hand on Glenna's back. Concern lined his face, too.

Something terrible had happened. That much she understood. She could practically taste the unease lingering in the air of the well-lit boardroom. Worry racked Naomi, that chest-tightening feeling an all too familiar response these days.

Glenna's eyes grew shuttered and her expression became determined. "An emergency came up with Shana," she said, her voice shaky. "They hadn't told anyone yet, but she was expecting. She miscarried last night."

Naomi pressed a hand to her mouth. "Oh, no, I'm so sorry to hear that."

Her mind wandered to Mary and Anna, to an impossible what-if. She sent up a silent prayer of thanks for the health of her baby girls, and a second prayer of comfort for the obviously grief-stricken couple.

"This isn't their first loss." Glenna's low voice was raspy, no doubt from recently shed tears. "They've stopped sharing any news right away."

Naomi nodded, setting her binder on the table as she slipped into the chair at the head. "That's totally understandable."

She'd felt the same in telling people about her pregnancy, although the news had gotten out in spite of her efforts to keep it to herself. She'd been so upset with Royce for blurting out the news when she'd fainted. He'd been concerned, though. He was a good man, which made walking away from him all the tougher.

Broderick opened his briefcase on the conference table. "Glenna and I dug deeper into the numbers and we want to go over our thoughts with you before talking to Dad and Jeannie this afternoon. We noticed a trend in stock buy-ups and sell-offs that are affecting our bottom line."

"That's why we're short?" Naomi blinked fast, wondering how it could be that simple. And then, at the same moment, she remembered how Royce had been close to arriving at a similar conclusion. The numbers had been off. "Bad luck?"

Broderick shook his head, withdrawing a stack of bound printouts. "The timing is too suspicious for it to be coincidental. It would take a million-and-one odds for things to roll this way." He leaned back in the leather chair. "My gut—a very seasoned gut—tells me there's insider information being leaked. Someone who doesn't want this merger to happen."

Her stomach sank. "Who?" Naomi sat up straighter.

All those fears about the merger. That the families couldn't trust one another. What if they'd made a grave mistake?

"The person I'm thinking about doesn't make sense." Broderick's eyes slid to his wife.

"Who?" Naomi pressed, needing answers. Whoever it was had not only sabotaged the merger, but had torpedoed Royce's research, his life's work.

And in spite of everything, that sent a surge of defensiveness through her for him. He didn't deserve this.

Broderick drummed his fingers on the stack of papers. "Glenna's new personal assistant. Milla Jones."

Milla?

That was the last person Naomi would have expected. Sure, she'd had the occasional sense that something was "off" when the woman was around. But insider trading?

Naomi was grateful that Broderick didn't suspect anyone in the family. "She's new to the company. Very low level." She turned to Glenna. "What do you think?"

Her sister-in-law thumbed the corner of her copy of the printouts. "No company is safe from someone who is computer savvy."

Having a face to put with these problems was a step toward being able to fix them. If they could, that would mean Royce would be back at the company on a regular basis. Naomi should be glad for him. And she was. Only now… Their paths would cross regularly. How would she handle that without losing her mind—and her heart?

She swallowed down the lump of emotion in her throat and focused on what she had to do, or what was right—making Royce's innovations a part of the company. "What do you think is the best approach?"

"I say we ask her to take a lie detector test," Glenna

said. "We're within our rights to do that, aren't we, Naomi?"

"With the contract she signed, we could…" She visualized the document, certain of the legal precedent, but wanting more information first.

Broderick leaned forward, hands pressing on the oak table. "That would also risk tipping off whoever she's working for."

Royce's career was riding on this. Naomi had drawn him into the company, and even if he didn't love her, she could still give him this one thing—his work. His dream.

"Quite frankly," she said, "I don't think we have time to set a trap. We need to plug this leak now if we want there to be any chance of incorporating Royce Miller's work into the next phase of our construction."

"No use waiting. Let's get this settled." Glenna clapped her hands together. "Perhaps you should handle the questions, use those lawyerly skills of yours."

Nodding, Naomi tapped the pager, ready for the battle, a fight she would relish tackling.

"Ms. Jones, please come in." While waiting, she glanced out the window at the stunning Alaska mountain range They had to succeed in getting Royce's designs online. The beauty of this wild land counted on research like his to thrive.

With a deep breath, Naomi focused on the task at hand, sitting straighter in her ruffled work dress as the door swung open.

"Yes? What can I do for you?" Milla asked.

"You can sit and have a chat with us," Glenna said, gesturing to a chair at the boardroom table.

Glenna's assistant raised her brows, surprise coloring her features. And then there it was. The strangeness Naomi couldn't articulate. The way the young woman held their gazes felt…well, that was what she couldn't name.

Smoothing her blue, A-line dress, Milla sat.

Naomi fixed her with a pointed stare. "What brought you to Alaska Oil Barons, Inc. to work? You're far away from home."

"I read about the position on an online job board." Milla moved her hands from the table to knot in her lap. "It sounded like an adventure."

"We've had an incident," Naomi said, watching for a reaction in the woman's eyes—which quickly became guarded, blank almost. More telling than an overt twitch.

Milla Jones was hiding something.

Even if they didn't plan to use a lie detector test at this juncture, it would be interesting to see how the woman reacted to the possibility. "We've discussed having you take a polygraph."

"No need," Milla said.

Broderick leaned forward, elbows on the table. "You're refusing?"

"Not at all." Milla crossed her arms over her chest. "I'm offering to tell you what you want to know now."

Naomi regarded her warily. "And what would that be?"

Flattening her palms on the conference table, Milla stated baldly, "I know who's responsible for your stock flow problem."

Glenna gasped. Broderick's eyes narrowed.

Naomi held herself immobile, surprised but wary. She hadn't expected the woman to offer up information so easily. "So you're admitting to being a party to insider trading?"

"I'm giving you what you want, since you've already figured out the worst parts yourself." Milla's face became set in hard, bitter lines. With her voice defiant, she looked and sounded nothing like the smooth, accommodating professional of the past weeks. She was a damn good actress.

Naomi didn't appreciate the woman's flippancy—at all. Time for Milla to feel the weight of what she'd done. "Pardon me if I don't find this a joking matter, and perhaps you shouldn't, either. You're admitting to committing corporate espionage."

"I have information. You need it. And trust me—" she smiled darkly "—you'll never think of the right questions to ask on your own."

Broderick swept the air with both hands. "Then by all means, say your piece."

Milla's gaze flicked to each of them before she spoke. "You're a family of power. Power doesn't always treat others fairly."

"You'll have to do better than that," Broderick barked, launching a stare-down.

Finally, Milla looked away. "I don't know who the mole is. But I do know who, um, *he* or *she* reports to."

"Who would that be?"

"The same people responsible for the plane crash that killed your mother, Mary Steele." The words felt like bombs shaking Naomi's foundation.

Shock knocked the air out of Naomi's lungs over the unexpected words, bringing a fresh wash of pain.

Reeling from the information, she reached for her

brother's hand and squeezed tightly for comfort, until her fingers numbed.

A desperate need for the truth clawed at her. "And our sister Breanna."

"Are you absolutely certain she died?"

Naomi couldn't have heard what she thought she had. No way would this woman be so cruel. How dare she? There had been proof. But before she could rip into the woman for her heartless gall, a gasp sounded from behind her, one that hitched with a groan of pain.

She turned to see her father in the doorway, holding Anna, while Jeannie stood behind him, cradling the other twin.

Naomi wanted to go to her dad and comfort him, but she couldn't move, stunned still, processing all this through a haze of shock. That someone could toss out such a false hope tore her apart.

Jack Steele's face was twisted with grief, pain, then anger. Glenna leaped to her feet and took both infants in her arms, leaving quickly. Jeannie stepped up to place a comforting—or restraining?—hand on Jack's arm.

Whoever this Milla Jones woman was, she was sick. Twisted. Naomi wanted to scream until her throat was raw. To throw things until she battered holes in the wall. Anything to get out the pain that woman had brought on by suggesting Breanna might not have died. Her family had worked so damn hard for closure.

She had grieved so hard in search of closure.

Having that ripped away with a simple sentence was beyond imaginable.

Because there was no way Breanna could be alive. There had been DNA tests run on remains.

Hadn't there?

Her sister was dead. It was cruel of this woman to dangle the hope that Breanna could be out there somewhere, to offer them a hope that couldn't be, a hope that would deny them closure forever.

Naomi's hands shook. More than air, she wished she had Royce at her side, the way her father had Jeannie.

But no matter how much it hurt, Naomi was done leaning on Royce's strong shoulders. It wasn't fair to him, to either of them, when he would never love her.

Royce couldn't remember when he'd last needed time in the saddle like this.

The past week without Naomi had been hell.

So he did what he did best. He pulled away.

He sequestered himself and tacked up, taking solace in the ritual of tightening the girth, slipping the bit into the bay horse's mouth.

In the freedom afforded by the open trail, the tufts of falling snow.

Sinking into the saddle, he took off on horseback, in a gallop that allowed him to examine these last few weeks.

Heading up the mountainside, he held the reins loosely. Remembered how sensitive this gelding was to the slightest touch. He needed to be gentle and open, give the horse his head. When he'd heard about Milla Jones's stunt from Broderick, Royce had wanted to run to Naomi's side, to be there for her.

Even if the woman's claims were false, she'd stirred a wealth of turmoil in both families, resurrecting grief. But strangely, she'd also unified their bonds, since they were all working together now. Chuck's wife, Shana, had notified private eye connections to investigate the issue. Milla had taken off and no one could find her.

Turning a corner in the trail, Royce guided the bay on up the mountainside, slowing to a trot as he navigated the thicker parts of the forest, finding more clarity the higher they went. Feeling alive and connected.

The way the Steeles and Mikkelsons came together in spite of something that should have sent them all into a tailspin…it blew him away. And yes, it surprised him, too.

So often, he'd viewed the two large families as a distraction from his work. From Naomi. But seeing the way they leveled one another out now, the way they functioned as a unit despite their differences, gave him a balanced perspective. For the first time, Royce realized that he wished he could have been a part of the effort.

The balance.

It was a scientific principle. A law of the universe. And one Royce couldn't seem to master in his personal life.

He slowed the gelding to a walk, keeping his weight centered, a light hand on the saddle horn. The bay shook his black mane with a snort.

As he looked at the deserted woods all around him, Royce realized it was damn difficult to help when he was living in solitude. Naomi and her family were there for each other, and yes, sometimes that came with crowds and static. But it also came with a wealth of support. Of common resolve. Dynamic energy.

He'd always been a man of science. How had he missed seeing the balance that he and Naomi could bring to each other's lives?

Her big family showed him a world of extended strength. And yes, maybe he'd been holding back from commitment because all this was too much to lose.

Naomi was too special to lose. She wasn't a substitution or replacement for anyone. She was a once-in-a-lifetime love.

But then hadn't he lost her already by walking away?

He loved her.

He had never stopped, really. He'd only deluded himself.

She was a part of him and there was no escaping that. If he could only convince her how he felt.

And he didn't intend to wait another day to tell her.

He hadn't planned on going to the gala celebrating Jack and Jeannie. But he realized now that he had to be there for Naomi. A swift, light tug to the right and the bay turned around. Responsive. As if he, too, could feel the building need. The urgency swelling in Royce's heart.

Light pressure from his calves sent the horse into a working trot as they wound through the trees. Then they were at the edge of the woods, with open land in front of them. Open for all his possibilities. More pressure to the horse's sides sent the bay into a headlong gallop.

The racing horse matched his racing realization. There was nowhere else Royce would rather be than by Naomi's side.

For the rest of his life.

Naomi adjusted the black velvet cape over her red satin gown, scrambling to gather up her ragged nerves and courage before stepping out of the limo and into the masquerade-themed gala.

Into the chaos.

It'd been a helluva week.

Shana was recovering, Chuck by her side. Milla had

been fired, and so far the investigator hadn't found anything out of the ordinary about her or her family in Canada, where she'd returned. Having her out of reach worried Naomi. What if she tipped off someone else? Bottom line, they didn't have enough cause to call the cops, but Milla had left a boatload of questions behind.

And Naomi wrestled with a niggling twinge that maybe, just maybe, there was truth to her insinuation that Breanna was alive.

Cutting the thought short, she popped open a compact, investigating the subtle smoky eye makeup Delaney had promised would make her feel fierce. But the mirror only served to remind Naomi of her nightmare.

She had been dreaming about Breanna, envisioning what she would look like. Seeing her in a mirror, unable to tell if it was her own face or her sister's reflected back.

Snapping her compact shut, Naomi closed down the thoughts that would have her crying her smoky eyes into a mess. She took a moment to center herself before stepping out into the cool winter air, tugging her velvet cape tighter to shield her back-baring dress from the elements. Her jeweled velvet shoes were safe from the snow on the red carpet arranged by the event organizers.

Placing one high heel in front of the other, she took in the sight. Twinkling string lights led up to the Steele office building. Snow gathered on the ground bathed the whole scene in an idyllic winter wonderland.

In her peripheral vision, Naomi saw a familiar silhouette.

Her heart hammered and her chest convulsed as the tall, dark man approached, impeccably turned out in a sleek black tuxedo.

Royce.

Had she been holding her breath for long? She certainly felt light-headed.

He fell into step with her as she traversed the red carpet, passing the smaller trees adorned with twinkling white lights. The way the lights were arranged made them appear like up-close constellations. Perfect for wishing.

Which she did as she passed by. Needing her night to go well. Wishing for some sort of stability as her whole world felt uprooted.

The doorman smiled, opening the Steele office to her and Royce.

Ruggedly handsome as ever, Royce picked up two masks from the table full of beaded and feathered creations. "You look absolutely beautiful."

"Thank you… Why are you here?" Her voice came out whispery as she took the mask he handed her, an ornate Venetian recreation adorned with golden accents and decadent feathers. She fastened it to her face, looking at him.

"I'm here for you."

"That simple?"

"Let's just say I've reacquainted myself with the universal laws of balance and realized I need to be with my equal and opposite tonight. Unless you have another date." His burgundy-and-gold mask somehow intensified the amber flecks in his brown eyes.

"You know I don't." She swallowed, thankful that her mask obscured her cheeks.

"Good. Then we won't be late, since I won't have to remove the guy." He offered her his arm.

A whisper of apprehension spiraled through her. She

knew now how much it hurt to get close to him when he couldn't open his heart to her, but something prodded her to take what he offered this evening, this one last time.

The live jazz band was already playing in full force, a trumpet cutting into the greeting area. A beacon. A call to dance and to mingle.

How hard it was to focus on the party with her heart pounding from Royce's nearness. The old pull of desire was as sharp as ever. Sharper, even, since she knew she couldn't heed that wild call to lose herself in his touch.

They moved on in beneath the gold and white tulle that hugged the ceiling. Guests in masks filtered through, posing for pictures with each other in front of the Renaissance-inspired art installation that tied the masquerade's theme together.

Glimmering gowns pressed to dark tuxedos kept catching her eye, making her aware of the way romance seemed to hang in the air. But more than romance, she realized. People embraced each other. Steele and Mikkelson families hugged and toasted.

Tonight, there were no sides, no enemies.

Just love. In all its forms.

Jack and Jeannie greeted the guests as they arrived, so many people in their circle of family and close friends. Only the immediate family knew about what Milla Jones had claimed, and looking at Jack, no one would have guessed. However, Naomi saw the way Jeannie carried more of the conversation for him. She stroked his wrist lightly, which looked like simple affection, but to the finer tuned eye was a comforting gesture.

Perhaps for the first time since her family was put on a collision course with the Mikkelson clan, Naomi saw her father and Jeannie. Really saw them and noticed the way they continuously offered each other support. She could see it as they stood together, unified.

They truly loved each other.

There *were* second chances at love.

It sounded so simplistic. And perhaps it could be. Royce hadn't bolted, no matter how many times she pushed him away. He stayed if not by her side, at least close enough to reach. Seeing him here tonight blew her away as he powered on, even though not at all in his favorite venue, but still checking the boxes.

And looking damn fine in the process.

He'd found balance. She was the one tipping the scales too far in one direction.

Had she been wrong to push him away again?

A crescendo swelled from the stage, signaling the end of the song, followed by a drumroll. A spotlight shot down to the side stage.

Revealing Royce?

"I'm honored to join in the festivities celebrating Jack and Jeannie's marriage. They are an inspiration in both their personal and business worlds." Royce lifted his champagne glass, the cut crystal refracting the spotlight, sending prisms through the room like northern lights, bathing everyone in fire. "I know they've requested no gifts, but I have an offer I feel certain they won't be able to refuse, and I challenge others here to join in. I'm contributing personally to their oil pipeline safety initiative. All profits from my patent on the new equipment will go directly toward seeing the project come to life."

In the crowd, Birch Montoya lifted his glass, as well. "Count me in for an extra million."

Gasps went through the packed room, before a round

of applause swelled and other voices shouted their intent to join in. As it faded, Royce lifted his glass again. "To Jack and Jeannie. To Alaska Oil Barons, Inc."

Naomi soaked in the vision of Royce onstage, unable to deny the rush of excitement that he wouldn't be fading away. He'd done this for her and her family. And he'd done it in such a public way. He'd embraced this crowd. Stood strong in the harsh spotlight with a new ease. For her.

The applause faded and he made his way toward her, grinning.

"I don't know what to say. Thank you doesn't come close to being enough." Her hands shook so, she had to place her champagne flute on a passing waiter's tray. "You're still going to work with the company, aren't you?"

"Of course," he said. "Let's step aside and talk. Or rather, I have something I need to say."

Her stomach did a flip—half hope and half fear of hoping.

His callused fingertips grazed her hand, their palms joining together as he wound through the crowd. Champagne glasses clinked as they passed by. But he never let her go.

After pushing down on a brass door handle, he brought her out on a balcony where heat lamps had been placed to chase away the winter chill.

Dropping her hand, he led her to the edge to view the bay. "The party came together well. A solid launch of the two families merging."

"It seems surreal, given all the turmoil with the possibility that Breanna…" Naomi's throat closed and she couldn't continue.

He pulled her to his chest, her mask crinkling. She drew in the comfort and spark of being close to him. She'd missed him. She needed him. She closed her eyes and breathed in the familiar scent of his aftershave.

But why was he here?

She licked her lips, swallowing to moisten her dry mouth. "But there's nothing I can do about that tonight." She angled back. "This is an evening for celebration. For Dad and Jeannie."

"For us, too, I'm hoping."

Her heart leaped to her throat and she bit her lip to keep from blurting out right here and now how much she loved him. She needed to listen, hear him out.

He gestured toward the bay just as fireworks lit up the sky. The blue light was reflected in the water. Another firework erupted. And another. A vibrant display shimmered through the night dome.

"Oh, how gorgeous. Dad must have ordered them from the event planners. I wish I had thought of it…"

Royce took her hand in his again. "I arranged it. Timed it even."

Surprise stunned her into silence for a moment, and she lifted her mask to see him more clearly. He hadn't put his on again after his moment in the spotlight inside.

"That was thoughtful of you to do for them," she observed carefully, telling herself not to read too much into the gesture.

"They're for you," he said. "As I said, timed. For right now."

The romance of that twined around her heart. Her breath hitched in her throat, hope gaining ground fast. "They're stunning."

"*You* are stunning."

She smoothed a hand down the lapel of his custom tailored tux. "You clean up quite nice yourself. Although I do have a partiality to your MIT sweatshirt." She looked up at him. "Your announcement about the donation was…astounding. I'm almost afraid to hope…"

"It's okay to hope." He traced her jaw with his thumb, his touch unleashing feelings she'd been trying madly to hold back.

"That seems rather intangible coming from a scientist."

"The more I learn, the more I realize there are things in life that defy logic. You, us, what we have together—one of a kind—is worth fighting for."

One of a kind. Not a replacement. But their own unique, beautiful bond.

From the light in his eyes, she could see he, too, was hopeful.

"One of a kind." Naomi added, "I agree." Ready. She was so very ready to have him in her life. No more reservations.

A smile spread across his face as he hooked an arm around her shoulders. "You must know I love you. Even when I tried to tell myself otherwise, I couldn't stop."

"I do understand. It's scary, but so very exciting. I love you, too, Royce Miller."

"Thank God," he said, with a sigh of relief before he pulled her into his arms and sealed her words with a kiss that sizzled even more than those fireworks.

They had loved each other even before that first breakup. They just hadn't learned how hard they had to work to make that love last. To protect it. Cherish it. Put it first. The connection was deeper now. Stronger. Unbreakable.

He might not have used the words *soul mate* when she wanted, but he was constantly showing her with the things he did. He wasn't just there for the twins, he was there for her, too, making sure she had everything she needed, somehow knowing that if the babies were safe and happy, she would feel safe and happy, as well. Yes, he loved the girls, but he loved her, too. Just as she loved him.

Royce rested his forehead against hers. "Naomi, you are my love, my life, and yes, my soul mate."

She could hear the emotion in his words, felt the truth in the hitch in his voice. She'd known he loved her daughters, and that meant the world to her for them. But now she knew he also wanted—and was in love with—her, as deeply as she wanted and loved him.

Smiling, she angled back. "I think we have some celebrating of our own to do."

He grinned at her. "Lead the way."

"How about side by side?" She looped her arms around his neck. "Right after you kiss me again."

"Yes, ma'am," he said, with a smile and a promise.

A promise he fulfilled.

Epilogue

One Month Later

Some women dreamed of getting married in a church, husband holding her hands.

Some visualized saying their vows at home, man of her dreams gazing adoringly into her eyes.

But Naomi couldn't think of anywhere better to begin her wedded life than on a glacier. Officially marrying her forever love, the father of her twins.

Now, standing in the receiving line to greet their family, who'd flown in on seaplanes, Naomi was dancing on air with how their ceremony had been everything she'd hoped for and more. Her in a long-sleeved wedding gown and formfitting white satin jacket with white fur around the hood. Him in a tuxedo and Texas cowboy hat and boots.

Violins and a small harp had played modernized

versions of old Inuit tunes, the songs her grandmother had loved best. A way to honor someone special to her, and feel like her grandmother's spirit was there, smiling down on them. Naomi stood beneath a large Inuit tapestry serving as a canopy for the reception food table, the simple decor just right for their remote glacier venue.

And the backdrop for it all? Her magnificent Alaska homeland, mountains capped with snow. Stretches of crystal water dotted with other, smaller pieces of ice.

The world glittered, humming with life and joy, no other adornment needed. The Alaskan outdoors was a place where Naomi and Royce had always been in harmony, a place they both hoped to spend more time together. The hubbub of her loved ones around her, the hum of family, were a welcome part of her life.

She and Royce had spent the past month making plans for this celebration and how to blend their lives. She was ready to branch out of the Steele compound and claim some dedicated space for their family. They'd kept the glass igloo retreat for camping vacations with the twins, but realized they needed more room, not just the occasional getaway cabin. A larger place to accommodate their own family that would also give Royce the square footage needed for cave time. They'd bought a sprawling home on the outskirts of Anchorage, complete with a barn that sported a loft office being custom renovated for Royce.

And they'd definitely need the extra space once Anna and Mary would be crawling to get the brightly colored abacuses Royce had bought them.

Shana and Chuck stopped in front of them now, shoulder to shoulder without touching, their relationship seeming as strained as always. Shana had been digging deep into Milla Jones's past and following leads about the woman's disappearance into the Canadian landscape. Naomi felt confident that if there were answers to be found, Shana would unearth them.

Clutching Naomi's hands, Shana leaned in to whisper, "Don't you worry, if your sister is out there, we will find her."

Naomi squeezed her fingers. "I know you will. Thank you." She hugged her hard, then said, "Thank you, too, for watching Anna while we're away."

"My joy," Shana said, a hint of yearning in her eyes that spoke of longing for a baby of her own. "It's worked out well that Delaney and Birch can take Mary."

Naomi's eyes went to her sister, who swayed from side to side holding the baby, Birch staring over her shoulder. Just beyond them, Jack and Jeannie shared a private moment at the side of the gathering. Jeannie twirled under Jack's arm for a kiss.

Royce chuckled. "Hopefully, both girls will get some sleep when they're not waking each other up all night to play."

Naomi rolled her eyes, laughing along with him. "Um, more like you waking them up to rock them."

She loved how he adored her daughters as his own. How could she have ever worried? Royce's heart was big enough to love them all.

They were going to spend their honeymoon at the igloo cabin where they'd met, hiking and exploring, for a couple days before the twins would join them at their large new home on the water, the main renovations complete. Their latest remodeling idea included a sauna with a glass roof, perfect for romantic moments

spent watching the northern lights. Now that they'd unlocked the secret to balance in their lives, she'd taken so
much joy from finding ways to nurture their needs as a
couple, and as strong-willed individuals, too.

She hooked her arm in his, leaning in to whisper,
"It's everything I ever dreamed of."

"Me, too," he answered, his eyes full of love and
commitment as he bent to kiss her.

They'd worked hard for their happily ever after, but
were the stronger for it. Their bond now was solid. Unbreakable. She would count on Royce forever, and she
couldn't wait to be the woman he turned to day after
day for the rest of their lives.

The feel of his lips on hers stoked the fire in her
veins for him. Her husband. Every kiss even more exciting than the last.

She angled back, his eyes warm on hers with an answering fire as the music from the quartet crescendoed.
"Can I have this dance?"

He tipped his Stetson with a roguish glint in his gaze.
"This one and every one thereafter. Consider your dance
card full, my love."

* * * * *

LET'S TALK
Romance

For exclusive extracts, competitions
and special offers, find us online:

f facebook.com/millsandboon

⊙ @millsandboonuk

𝕏 @millsandboon

Or get in touch on 0844 844 1351*

For all the latest titles coming soon, visit
millsandboon.co.uk/nextmonth